PLAGUE OF DEATH

ANCHORESS SERIES BOOK TWO

D. L. ARMILLEI

First edition, February 2019

ISBN 978-0-9986720-4-5 [Mobi]
ISBN 978-0-9986720-7-6 [ePub]
ISBN 978-0-9986720-5-2 [Softcover]
ISBN 978-0-9986720-6-9 [Hardcover]
Library of Congress Control Number: 2019900996

Diamond Cove Publishing, LLC,
P.O. Box 2292, Palm Harbor, FL 34682-2292
DLA@DiamondCovePublishing.com

In loving memory of my brother
Dean R. Armillei.
You live on in my heart.

Plague of Death

I Ching #29 - The Abysmal

Remaining emotionally numb in reaction to past events blocks the Creator from resolving present difficulties in your favor. You must accept the situation by flowing with it like water. If you persist in improper behavior, then you will become hopelessly entangled in troubles. Eventually you will fall into an abysmal pit. By following the good you can save yourself and return to the light.

— The I Ching or Book of Changes

CHAPTER 1

To Vanessa Cross's benefit, her sixteen-year-old heart had hardened over the past year, which made it easy for Van to shoo Wiglaf off of her bed.

"Beat it," she said to the furry, white bunfy curled up, sleeping beside her.

As Van wriggled upright, the critter raised his head, followed by his long ears.

"Urrrp. Eeep," he said in mild protest. He shifted his tiny body, stood on all fours, and blinked his warm-blue, round eyes at Van, looking sleepy.

His adorable whiskered face triggered a comforting swirl in the center of Van's chest. She tensed and brushed the feeling aside.

"Move it, pal." Van used her thumb to motion for him to get off the bed. "Time's a ticking. Don't want to waste the day."

She threw aside her orange and gold-laced curtains. The muted brightness of the clear June sky told her it was slightly past dawn. Her eyes moved down the expansive lawn to the edge of the forest surrounding Mt. Hope Manor. The brilliant green leaves barely fluttered in the mild breeze.

"It's a glorious morning for surfing," Van declared as she admired the majestic beauty of the oak, pine, and beech trees that blanketed a good portion of the small, hour-glass shaped island off the coast of Massachusetts.

The bunfy stretched his front legs and arched his back in a cute way that raised his butt and coiled tail.

Van watched as Wiglaf took his sweet time kneading the mattress.

"This proves you aren't a hundred percent bunny." She restrained herself from scooping him up in her arms and giving him a loving hug. It wouldn't do for a Giorgi warrior, albeit even a junior one, to show affection. Emotions equated to weakness.

Van patiently watched as Wiglaf finished his morning stretch.

"Definitely the Living World's version of a rabbit." She caught herself smiling at the critter. "Or maybe a cat."

The parallel world, separated from Van's Earth World by an invisible membrane-like veil, contained a variety of unusual animals. Van, unfortunately, discovered this last year after the Elders had sent her on a mission to retrieve a magical relic called the Coin of Creation. Some creatures she'd encountered on that journey were harmless like Wiglaf. Others were terrifying like…

Van's smile turned into a scowl. Her skin prickled as she unwittingly clenched her fists.

"Hey!" Paley threw open the door and strutted into Van's third-floor bedroom. "Get up."

Van leaped out of bed, poised and ready for battle.

Wiglaf disappeared in a snap, back to his magical realm.

"Paley!" Van calmed after recognizing the intruder as her best friend since kindergarten.

"Whoa. Take it easy, warrior queen." Paley held up her palms, expressing wide-eyed faux fear. "It's time for our morning surf. Get moving."

Van leaned in and squinted at Paley's eyes. "Are those lightning bolts?"

"So?" Paley flipped her wavy, dyed-blond hair over her shoulder, a nervous tic she had picked up since suffering trauma during their journey to the Living World last summer. "They look amazing, right?"

Paley's habit of wearing crazy colored contact lenses never grew old. Today her irises were deep green, with streaks of yellow lightning bolts shooting from the pupils.

"Yeah. Great," Van said with as much enthusiasm as she could muster. She thought they made Paley look like a crazy person, but didn't want to diminish her friend's fragile self-confidence.

Excited by the prospect of catching the ever elusive perfect wave, the girls hurried down the stairs and out of the manor before Van's step-mother, Genie, woke and started interrogating them with annoying questions like, "What're you girls up to today?" or "How's your summer training going?"

The girls scurried down Sandy Cove Lane in the direction of the crossroads, an intersection of Providence Island's seven main roads.

"Blackrock?" Van shifted her eyes toward Paley.

"Blackrock? Since when?"

"Whitecap Beach is for wimps." Van raised her chin and ran her hand over her silky white-blond hair, smoothing it behind her ear.

"Blackrock is off-limits," Paley said. "Jagged rocks, dangerous surf—"

"Surfing helps strengthen our core. Makes us better warriors. We need more of a challenge."

"Dangerous… off-limits… I'm in!" Paley's eyes sparkled.

Van used to fear her own shadow, unwilling to walk on the wild side. Once she recovered the Coin of Creation, a door opened she couldn't close. Being able to retrieve the Coin proved Van had inherited the magical Anchoress bloodline from her Lodian mother, Aelia. She also inherited a sense of duty from her Balish father, Michael. Over the past year, Van had absorbed the magnitude of her responsibilities as the Anchoress heir. The designated savior of the worlds. She developed an intense, almost obsessive, desire to protect her people, the Lodians.

Being the Anchoress also meant Van had the highest concentration of Elemental blood of any person alive. That, along with an innate ability to channel the energy of the moon, allowed her to access powerful warrior magic. So far, she could only get this power while in the Living World.

As long as she remained trapped on Providence Island in the Earth World, she could do nothing but train and wait for the Alignment. Or Luxta, as the ancients called it. The annual thirty-day window when Van could safely travel to the Living World.

"I need the challenge of Blackrock." Van wanted to stay in peak physical condition. Keep her reflexes and mind alert, ready for threats.

She trained every day, usually twice a day. Sometimes formally in her classes, other times she would offer to lead a session outside regular classroom hours. She only invited her peers in the special classes called the reservation program. They, like Van, were the students selected to become Grigori warriors. But, mostly, Van liked to train alone.

"You're taking this whole thing too far," Paley said.

"You're a warrior, or you're not," Van snapped. "You want to go to the Living World with me or not? Make up your mind. The Alignment begins tomorrow." She stormed ahead onto a path in the woods.

"We have to talk about this situation between you and Brux," Paley shouted to Van's hastily departing form.

Van rolled her eyes. Of course boy-obsessed Paley would mention Van's ex-boyfriend. Brux had anguished because of Van. His sister Daisy was lost in the Living World, kidnapped by the Balish Prince Merloc, the Merciless, probably being tortured daily, if not already dead.

After completing their mission last summer, the Elders forced Brux and his father to leave their home in Salus Valde, the Lodian region of the Living World, so that Brux could fulfill his duties as Van's assigned protector. Until Van came into her full power, the allusive demigods, the Elementals, appointed a specific warrior to look after her.

Usually, Van would be delighted for the guy she wanted as her boyfriend to be re-assigned to Providence Island. However, the Elementals didn't allow the Anchoress and her assigned protector to become romantically involved. Their reasoning: the protector cannot protect if he's distracted by love.

Van's blood duty required her to follow the ancient traditions, put in place to protect the Anchoress and the Lodian people. She was required to marry a pure-blooded Lodian and have a child to pass down the Anchoress bloodline. Brux would've been a perfect choice.

She shook her head. *I'm much too young to be thinking about such things.*

Besides, Brux remained angry at Van for causing him and his father to move to the island. The assigned protector stipulations forced Brux to stay there to "protect" Van rather than run off to the Living World to rescue his beloved sister. Professor Lake, Brux's father, was an adult, making it illegal for him to go outside the boundary of Salus Valde. So neither could search for Daisy, causing frustration in them both.

"V-Van," Paley said huffing, out-of-breath from her quick jog to catch up with her friend. "You haven't opened up at all about last summer. You can talk to me."

"You and me." Van kept her attention on the path ahead. "We're different."

"It's okay to feel sad about losing your dad," Paley said.

Van stopped short and glared at Paley.

"My dad?" Van's cheeks flared. "How about my mother? How about Jorie, Trey, Elmot?" The latter three had been on Van's team to retrieve the Coin. Van wanted to include another person who had died because of her, but she couldn't bring herself to push the name through her pursed lips.

"Solana," Paley said softly. "You avoided mentioning Solana. Again."

Hearing her name made Van's stomach clench.

Van straightened her spine as she continued walking, and said, "Strong warriors have to sacrifice for the greater good of their people." With renewed determination, she pressed on through the woods.

The path ended, dropping Van and Paley onto Whitecap Beach. They ignored the ongoing beach volleyball game, or at least Van did.

"Brux isn't there, but I see Ken," Paley whispered. "And Pernilla."

Van glanced at the players, then scowled for doing so.

"I don't care where my ex-boyfriends are." She headed straight to her family's beach hut. "Or who they're with." If she couldn't have Brux, the love of her life, then she didn't want anyone. Dating and boys. They were both *out*.

In the Cross family's beach hut, Van and Paley wriggled into their wetsuits.

"Ugh." Lately, Van had trouble fitting into hers.

"Maybe it shrunk," Paley offered.

Van glared at the suggestion.

"I have an extra one in the bin if you need a size bigger." Paley zipped her suit.

"No, it's just," Van struggled with all her might to stretch the rubber suit, "I've packed on extra muscle from all my training." Though she had a sinking feeling, there might be something to her step-mother's criticism. Van's compulsive overeating had caused her to gain weight. She sucked in her stomach, and with some effort, zipped it. "I'm good."

Once sealed into their wetsuits, the girls flung beach towels over their shoulders, grabbed surfing boots and surfboards, and headed away from the beach hut.

There was no direct route to Blackrock, other than an access road used by island security, so they slipped back into the woods and followed the winding, sandy path to the off-limits beach.

Blackrock was deserted, as expected. The beach's sharp rocks and wild currents petrified Van. Over the past year, she had made great strides to confront and overcome her fears. Paley had no fear, though, when it came to showing off for the island boys. Too bad none were around.

Paley dipped her toe in the water, knowing it wouldn't be a comfortable temperature this early in the summer. "Yikes!" She yanked back her foot. "Need these." She sat down on the sand and slipped on her surfing boots.

Van frowned. She chucked her boots onto the sand. "There's nothing like the feel of the board under bare feet."

Van splashed into the water and then stretched out on top of her board.

Paley scrambled to follow.

They paddled until reaching a suitable distance, stopped and sat upright, straddling their boards. They idly soaked in the early summer sun while waiting to catch a swell back to shore.

Paley grinned, at home bobbing up and down in rhythm with the waves. "Look!" She pointed to the horizon at a rise Van would call a tidal wave. "Here comes a good one!"

Van gathered her nerve. "Let's go!" She laid on top of her board and paddled like crazy, catching the rise.

Her body and board rose along with the wave. At the crucial moment, Van placed her hands on the board, elbows up, arched her back, and moved her feet into position. She crouched, arms wide, weight on her back foot, heart pounding. Her leg muscles cried under the familiar strain as she found her balance and stood. *I got this!*

The adrenaline high achieved from being in sync with the perfect wave hummed through Van's being. Her body, the board, the water—all came together and worked in harmony.

"Woo-hoo!" Van controlled the wave. It didn't control her. Over-confident, Van made the mistake of glancing back to see if Paley had also caught the wave.

The slight movement threw Van off balance. She wobbled. Every muscle in her core tightened as she struggled to regain command of the board.

Van's mind whirled in a panic. Her arms flailed. Instead of focusing on controlling her breath and concentrating on getting back her balance, she focused on how dangerous the undercurrents were at Blackrock and the jagged rocks that would rip her apart if she were to fall.

The dark, depthless water snapped at her like the jaws of a giant monster.

Van's feet, legs, and arms wouldn't cooperate, and she crashed into the deadly sea.

CHAPTER 2

Chilling blackness engulfed Van.

The undercurrent shoved her deeper, like a murderous villain. She tried to orient herself by looking for the surface and couldn't find any light. Her ears rang. Her face, feet, and hands stung from the cold.

Something bit her fingers.

Her blood colored the water around the jagged tooth of a sharp rock. Van protected her head from the rocks with her arms, but the monstrous undercurrent had complete control. The violent water twisted Van as if she were nothing more than clothes spinning in a washing machine.

Her body slammed hard against the rocks, again and again. Van's lower spine erupted with pain. Her lungs felt as though they were about to burst as the icy darkness suffocated her.

Forget about being the best warrior, protecting my people from demons. I'm done, thought Van as she jerked at the water's will. *None of that matters now.*

Her desire to breathe increased in intensity until she couldn't hold it in any longer. Icy-cold liquid filled her lungs.

Death had come for her.

Terrified, her mind searched for a way to survive. She didn't want to die, to be absorbed into the blackness. To become nothing.

But there was no way out. Her life journey had come to an end.

Fight! A voice came to her. It was her spirit guide, Jacynthia. *The beast is coming. You must protect your people.*

The beast? Van's attention moved to her surroundings. A roar filled her ears. The beast was here. It had disguised its jaws as the undercurrent. Slimy seaweed, its saliva. Rocks, the beast's teeth.

The Quasher! The supernatural shadow-wolf never stopped hunting the Anchoress, hunting Van. It had broken free from its bindings and swam through the ocean to snuff out her light. To kill her.

Van trembled. She wasn't equipped to face such a deadly enemy, one she could never beat.

And she was out of air.

As the Anchoress, Van's bloodline belonged to her people. She had a responsibility to never surrender her light to the darkness.

"Fight!" Van said to herself at the same time as Jacynthia.

Van twisted and punched in the water, but the current slowed her movements. The dark beast gripped her and pulled her deeper into its mouth.

Her head and shoulders jolted against something sharp. *The beast's teeth?*

Her body became weighted with pressure.

The Quasher's tongue?

She closed her eyes tight, as if doing so would block out the certainty of her death.

The beast's tongue rolled her body, causing her to face upward.

Her chest ached. Pressure from the Quasher's teeth crushed her as it chewed her torso.

Light filtered through her eyelids. So dazzling she partly opened them.

A shadowy figure eclipsed the brightness. Van assumed the Creator had come to claim her soul. To snuff her out of existence.

A swoosh of heated air drifted over her face, and then warmth covered her lips.

What the—?

Her stomach lurched as a wave of nausea consumed her. She didn't want to puke, but up came seawater and bile, splashing over her chin and neck. Some trickled into her nostrils.

Van coughed hard, as if trying to expel her lungs to get enough oxygen. Finally, the coughing seizures stopped and her head cleared. She fully opened her eyes and saw a boy's blurry face hovering in front of her.

"Van?" She heard Paley's worried voice off to the side.

"She's breathing," the blurry boy said.

The sound of his voice filled Van with a sense of cozy safeness.

She gasped in a breath of salty air and hacked again. She threw up a bit more.

"She's fine," Brux said dismissively. He had been the boy doing CPR on her.

Van rolled onto her side and used the back of her wrist to wipe the salty vomit off her mouth.

Brux helped her sit upright.

"Besides a few scrapes here and there, you seem okay," he said.

"W-w-wipeout!" Paley sang and swirled her hips in a dance, trying to cheer Van. Or at least take away some of Van's embarrassment, especially after Brux had dragged Van out of the ocean and saved her life.

"Did your imaginary friend keep you from drowning?" Paley gave her a cute smirk.

"Her name's Jacynthia," Van croaked. "And she's *not* imaginary."

"Still haven't seen her, but after last summer, I won't take anything for granted." Paley chuckled.

"Not funny." Brux scowled. "Van, you almost drowned. What's wrong with you? Risking your life. A life that's not yours to lose."

"I was practicing." Van's words triggered another coughing fit.

"Practicing what? How to die?" He stood, scowling.

Brux irritated the snot out of Van. He never gave her room to breathe. He treated her like a child, always telling her how she should act and what she should think, based on his own opinions rather than letting Van figure things out on her own. She preferred to use her own mind so she could grow in a way that suited her, not him.

"It's an uphill battle with you." Brux rested curled fists on his hips and glared down at her. "You're not fully trained, *and* you're fighting the curse your ancestor Amaryl put on the Anchoress bloodline. Do you want to throw your life away? Your powers? That would be a pretty rotten thing to do to us—your people."

"I'm in training to protect your ass from demons, or did that slip your mind?"

"*My* ass?" Brux's eyes widened in offense. "You're sick. You know why? Because it seems like I just saved *your* ass from drowning!" He shook his head as he stormed away. "Bad luck follows you, Van."

"You're my assigned protector," Van yelled after him. "What? You want a medal for doing your job?" She raised herself from the ground with tired, shaking legs.

"I'm well aware of why I'm stuck on this island." Brux's voice trailed off as he stomped away, leaving deep footprints in the soft sand.

Van glowered at his departing form.

Paley placed a gentle hand on Van's back. "He'll be okay."

Done with surfing for the day, the girls retrieved Van's board that had drifted down the shore and then headed back to the Cross family's beach hut at Whitecap Beach.

Van spoke little. She mostly listened as Paley rambled on about who was wearing what to where and who her friend suspected had a crush on whom. Van used Paley's chattering like white noise, allowing her to process the encounter she'd just had with Brux.

He knew how to pry open Van's wall of indifference, second only to her step-mother, Genie. Van's greatest fear, even more so than facing the Quasher, was falling into the gaping emotional abyss inside her. She hated the idea of breaking down her wall and exploring her feelings. Especially about last summer.

Her stomach knotted every time she tried to reconcile her confrontation with Solana. The Balish princess possessed wealth, privilege, and power, yet still succumbed to the lure of evil… to her

Dark Master. A master demon so powerful it seduced an heir to the Balish kingdom.

In self-defense, Van had used the Coin of Creation as a weapon against Solana, murdering the Balish princess. However, Solana's death wasn't the most upsetting part. Van had used her Anchoress powers to kill a person.

As a Grigori in training, her career would involve hunting and slaying demons in the Earth World. The unwitting terrigens' anger, violence, and misery generated demons over time. Once formed, they lurked, existing at a low vibration like that of the Earth World, gaining strength from negativity. This allowed them to continue searching for ways to break through the veil between the worlds. Seeking the higher vibration of light, something abundant in the Living World, so they could destroy it.

Ancient writings had warned Van to use her powers to fight true evil, such as demons, not to use it against other people. By using the power of the Coin to defeat Solana, Van had attached to the dark part of her Self and therefore paid a heavy spiritual price, damage to her soul.

Though Solana was evil in human form, Van had used abilities that gave her an unfair advantage in her fight against the Balish princess. Did that make Van evil, too?

Pondering this question made her queasy.

Ever since Solana's death, the restless pull of darkness writhed inside Van. A constant tug-of-war between the good and evil parts of her soul. She feared looking too closely inside her Self, terrified she would end up like Solana, drawn to a life of evil.

Van's throbbing hand drew her attention. The cut from her encounter with the rocks remained bloody and painful. Her body ached in at least three places from the thrashing of the undercurrent. *Good*. Fighting physical pain kept her on track. Helped her to hone her toughness and maintain the inner strength of a warrior.

By the time Van and Paley entered the small, wooden beach hut at Whitecap, Van had begun hyperventilating.

"What's wrong?" Paley clasped Van's arms to steady her.

"I just... need to sit for a bit." Van collapsed into a cushioned wooden chair.

"Are you injured?"

"Shh." Van covered her eyes with her palms and hunched over. Her head pounded so hard it hurt her eardrums.

I'm weak. Evil lurks inside me. The Elders should lock me away for the safety of my people.

She deserved to suffer the same fate as Solana. Maybe Brux should murder her. No, even better, Ferox, Solana's younger brother, the current heir to the Balish kingdom. Or Van could ask Jacynthia to extinguish her Anchoress light, or give it to someone else.

Unfortunately, only Van had the power to transfer the magic of the Anchoress bloodline, and only to her first-born daughter. Without an Anchoress, Van's people, the Lodians, were at risk of being taken over by the Balish and vulnerable to losing Dishora, a Lodian prophecy about an inevitable war between good and evil. A time when darkness rises, seeking to destroy all light.

That wouldn't do at all.

Van leaned back in the chair and took in deep breaths. She allowed her hectic thoughts to be overridden by the distant splashing of the waves... the lull of the seagull's cry... and the distant voices of her classmates playing volleyball. Paley remained mercifully silent.

Using this controlled breathing technique quieted Van's anxiety.

An amaranthine glow entered her mind's eye.

Van's lips curled into a smile. As expected, the luminescence came into focus.

An elderly woman appeared before her with white-gray, waist-length hair that flowed in an ethereal breeze. Her light-blue eyes twinkled with the energy of youth.

Jacynthia! Van's spirit guide appeared in times of emotional crisis, to offer Van guidance.

Van's delight over a visit from her friend faded as she noticed Jacynthia wasn't smiling. She braced, ready to get another scolding for surfing at Blackrock. In her mind's eye, Van looked questioningly at her spirit guide.

Jacynthia said in her monotone voice, "All losses have a purpose. It aids in our understanding that true reality is something greater than ourselves. We should not seek reality in form but in the infinite."

Like so often, Van didn't understand the meaning behind Jacynthia's words. Van's aching body entered her consciousness. Her connection to her spirit guide faltered, and Jacynthia flickered.

Van breathed to calm herself again and refocused her attention on Jacynthia.

She was about to ask for clarity, but Jacynthia continued as if to answer Van's unspoken question.

"You must heal the soul before the physical body is healed. Although emotions are painful, we cannot escape them. Do not attempt to avoid them or it will lead you into darkness."

Van scrunched her brow. Jacynthia's words made her feel so... *alone*. She wished the Elementals would just let her date Brux.

"Life is not always going to give us what we want," Jacynthia said. "Negative emotions like bitterness and disillusionment will feed the dark part of the Self. An important step on the path to spiritual maturity is to learn how to relate to these realities. Remember, you are never alone. You are never separate from the Creator."

"Van!"

Her shoulders shook from Paley's grip, breaking her connection with Jacynthia.

Van's eyes snapped open, and she glared at Paley. "Why would you do that?"

"I didn't know if you slipped into a coma or something." Paley looked pale. "You scared me."

"I'm fine." Van raised herself from the chair. "Let's get going."

The girls changed and headed back home. Along the way, Van updated Paley about her latest visit from Jacynthia.

"I don't get it." Paley shook her head. "Why can't she tell you what you need to know straight out? Why be so cryptic?"

Van shrugged.

They reached the crossroads, an intersection of the island's seven main roads.

"You coming over for breakfast before we hit training?" Van asked.

"I can't today. Head Mistress Griselda is going through a phase where she wants all of us orphans to eat breakfast together, to make us feel like a family."

Even as Paley gave Van an eye roll, Van could see joy shining in them.

"Make sure you take care of that hand." Paley continued walking forward as she turned to give Van her parting words of concern, paying no attention to where she was headed.

"Watch it," Van cried.

Paley swerved, almost taking down a slim tree with a bird's nest tucked between its branches. It wouldn't have hurt Paley to walk into the sapling, but Van could hear the chirping of hatchlings, and Paley plowing into the tree would've upset the nest.

The thought of it caused an ache in Van's chest. Confused, she rubbed her fingers over the area of her heart, hoping to make the sensation stop.

"Be on time for training," Van said, disappointed over the obliviousness of her friend. Being a warrior meant having an awareness of your surroundings.

"Natch." Paley smiled.

Van grimaced as she watched Paley disappear down Reservation Road toward the Gables Orphanage. Her friend had no ichor in her blood, meaning she was a terrigen, a person who belonged in the Earth World. A terrigen couldn't become a Grigori. The Elders would never allow it.

Van made her way down Sandy Cove Lane toward Mt. Hope Manor, worried about her concern for the baby birds. Emotions taking control was a detrimental episode for a warrior. She resolved to train harder to make up for it.

When she reached her yard, Van stopped to scrutinize a lone, amber-colored flower growing out of a crack in the driveway. The beautiful flower had risen despite the adversity of the concrete. It had grown from a small glimmer of sunlight filtering into the dark opening, giving hope to passersby that they, too, can break free of their own difficulties.

Van huffed, disgusted with herself for wasting time over an emotional distraction. She redoubled her goal of building her inner strength so she could fulfill her destiny as a legendary warrior.

Van strode toward the manor's front door, crushing the flower with her step.

CHAPTER 3

Van swept through the back door of Mt. Hope Manor, expecting to see Genie prepping breakfast. But a deserted kitchen echoed back at her.

Genie had reduced their housekeeper's hours after Van's father had died. Luma used to cook all their meals. Now, she only cleaned the house, and grocery shopped for Genie. At first, Van dreaded the thought of Genie taking over the household cooking. Van quickly realized Genie excelled at everything she put to task.

Another behavior change in Genie included her rarely leaving the manor. Her step-mother still traveled by portal to the Living World for her shopping trips in Lodestar Village. But that was about it.

Van never cared much for her hypercritical step-mother. This past year, her disrespect grew as she watched Genie ramble around the manor like a lonely old lady.

She glanced at the ticking wall clock. It was a few minutes before eight a.m.

"Humph." Van leaned back against the wall by the open window and crossed her arms. If she couldn't be eating or training, then she didn't want to be doing anything. She wondered when Genie would decide to get her butt out of bed. In the meantime, Van had time to do something, but what?

"Eep errp."

A fluffy white puff nestled on the rich, green lawn looked up at Van through the open window.

"Hi, you funny little thing," Van answered, grinning.

Wiglaf chirruped and fully raised his long ears.

She hastened out the door, to side of the house, and met her bunfy on the grass. They meandered through the manor's hedge maze. Van's footsteps crunched under the river rocks as she walked down the path. Wiglaf hop-scurried beside her, not making a sound. He happily accompanied Van on the way to her favorite spot on the property, a hilltop overlooking the Atlantic Ocean.

Van stood at the peak and stretched her arms above her head.

She blinked.

"Did I just see a speedboat?"

Wiglaf turned his whiskery nose toward the sea. Then he quizzically looked up at Van.

"I saw something bobbing in the water." She furrowed her brow. "I think."

Strange. The authorized docking areas were in Buzzard's Bay, on the opposite side of the island. She blinked again to gain focus and saw nothing but empty ocean.

She shrugged, kicked off her sneakers, and placed her feet with big toes touching and heels slightly apart. She raised her arms toward the sky and settled into the mountain pose. Then, began the Sun Salutation yoga sequence.

Wiglaf curled into a ball on the perfectly landscaped grass for a snooze.

Doing yoga made good use of Van's idle time. The practice increased muscle strength, tone, and flexibility, enhancing her ability to excel athletically.

She bent forward. Her injured hand throbbed, her back and ribs ached, but she pushed through the pain. Warriors didn't feel pain. *She* didn't feel pain.

Van moved into her favorite pose. Virabhadrasana, the warrior.

She had learned to do the Sun Salutation in her gym class as a continuous sequence, with no stopping between poses. But Van held the warrior pose to push her body.

She breathed deeply, filling her lungs with salty sea air. She took in the horizon's beauty… the gorgeous blues in the sky, the blue-greens of the ocean, and the varying shades of greens in the trees below her and in the surrounding fields.

Even as her muscles strained to maintain her pose, Van fully appreciated the marvelous day. She treasured the scents of pine, the freshly cut grass, and salty air. Positivity vibrated from the brilliant colors of the landscape. Thankfulness washed over her, for having the fortitude and physical ability to do her yoga sequence.

From this, a stirring of love and peace encroached on her heart. Van took this sensation, rolled it in a ball in her mind, and disconnected from it. Separating herself from the pleasantness until she felt… nothing.

Perfect.

Wiglaf stirred from his nap. He raised his tiny head and blinked at Van.

This spurred Van into releasing her pose. She bent at the waist, placed her palms on the ground, and moved into the downward facing dog. Then seamlessly moved into the most challenging position. The plank.

Her muscles ached from the beating her body took earlier during her surfing wipeout and intensified from the strain of the pose. *Excellent.* She breathed through the pain.

Van challenged her mind and body by holding the plank for an unnecessarily long time. Pain made her weak. She wanted to be strong. *Stronger.*

Van shifted postures and flowed into the upward facing dog. Transitioned again into the downward facing dog. Then ended her routine in the mountain pose.

In class, her teachers had concluded yoga sessions with śavāsana—the corpse pose—for at least twenty minutes.

Although not wanting to, Van followed the rules and laid face-up on the grass. She relaxed into the sleep-like position.

Van fidgeted. She forced herself to hold still. Then squirmed again.

She popped to her feet. "I've no patience for this."

The bunfy hopped up, ready to trot back to the house with Van.

By the time Van and Wiglaf returned to the manor, Genie hovered at the large butcher block table in the kitchen, busy fussing with breakfast. Her step-mother turned her delicate blue eyes in Van's direction. Her long, silky, white-blond hair sparkled as it caught beams from the morning sun.

"Oh! Van." Genie stopped cutting a stalk of celery as her eyes darted toward Van.

"You sound surprised." Van took a seat at the kitchen table.

"Nonsense." Genie's pink, pouty lips curved into a smile.

Wiglaf leaped onto Van's lap and then hopped on the table. He peered intently, nose-to-celery stalk, fascinated with Genie's project.

Her step-mother ignored the bunfy and carried on with her prep.

"I thought you would already be off doing your training." Genie dropped a celery stalk into each of two tall, icy glasses filled with tomato-colored liquid.

"You *want* me to go to training?" Van's curiosity piqued. What was her dingbat step-mother up to now?

Genie fussed with the celery stalks making them just-so.

Van reached for one of the glasses.

Genie slapped her hand. "Not for you!"

Van winced. It was the hand she had scraped against the rocks earlier.

"This is my special morning drink. Not for children."

Genie noticed Van cradling her injured hand.

"What happened?"

"Who's the other drink for?" Van changed the subject, hoping to avoid talking about her personal life with her step-mother.

"Purely medicinal!" boomed a male voice. The man chuckled as he barreled through the archway into the kitchen.

"Oh, uh, um. Van—" Genie stammered, flustered.

"Who are you?" Van bounded from her chair, alert and ready to protect her step-mother and their home from this intruder.

The loud man either scared Wiglaf or annoyed him because, in a flash, her bunfy disappeared back into his magical animal realm.

"Call me Uncle Rummie," thundered the jovial man. He extended his meaty hand to Van.

Instead of taking it, Van stared at her step-mother dumbfounded. "You have a *boyfriend?*"

"Secret's out." Uncle Rummie guffawed, causing his protruding belly to bounce in and out.

Genie giggled.

Van's jaw slackened. She had never seen Genie giggle. Her step-mother's rules of etiquette stated that giggling was "unladylike and simply not done." A rule Genie had drilled into Van's head since birth had just been flushed down the toilet.

Genie placed a gentle hand on Rummie's shoulder and gazed at him with doe eyes.

Van squinted to get a closer look at Genie. Her stomach soured seeing her step-mother emanate the glow of a woman in love.

Van slid back into her chair at the kitchen table.

"Honey," Genie said to Van. "I wanted to introduce you, but we were trying to keep our relationship—"

"Love affair," Rummie winked at Genie.

"—private. Now that you've met, I'm glad." Genie paused and tentatively asked, "Are you glad, Van?"

Van floundered, opening and closing her mouth like a fish out of water. She didn't know where to begin.

"You might think it's too soon after..." Rummie paused to find the right words. "The departure of your dear, sweet father. That our relationship looks bad for the family. But—"

"The vicious gossips on the island certainly will," Genie added.

"I can assure you, I'm taking the utmost best care of your mother." He grinned at Genie in a way that reminded Van of a stray dog eyeing a juicy steak.

"Step-mother." Van corrected him.

"We know this is upsetting for you." Genie placed her hands on the table as if to add sincerity. "I mean, you... with no boyfriend, and here I am, moving forward with my life." She placed a hand on Rummie's shoulder and smiled at him.

Genie's loosely tied belt barely held her lacy bathrobe closed, as if the forces of nature thought it blasphemous to hide her staggeringly perfect figure.

"Don't tell me how I feel," Van snapped. Then, she suddenly realized she was an unwanted third person in the room. Her shoulder twitched from irritation.

"See. She's upset. I told you so," Genie said to Rummie as she glared at Van. "This is why I didn't want to tell you," she said to Van. "Now you're going to go around spouting your mouth to all your little friends about my private life." Genie's cheeks flushed pink.

Even furious and spitting out insulting comments, Genie remained exquisitely beautiful, which further irked Van. She used sheer willpower to neutralize the feeling. Genie's life had nothing to do with her, or her training to fight demons, or her duty to protect her people. Genie meant nothing. Her stupid boyfriend meant nothing.

"I don't care." Van shrugged. "Good for you."

Van relished the look on Genie's face. Relief mixed with disbelief.

"By jingo, that's wonderful!" Rummie reached over and clapped Van on the shoulder, practically knocking her face into the surface of the butcher block table. "Could you do us a favor? Keep our little tryst a secret?"

"Especially from your nosy teacher, Uxa," Genie added.

When Van didn't respond, Rummie grew serious and asked, "Can we count on you, girl?"

Genie caressed Rummie's back as if it were impossible for her not to touch him.

Van pitied her step-mother. Genie believed she was less of a woman without a man in her life, which revealed her step-mother's only noticeable flaw. Desperation. In Van's opinion, that made her pathetic. Genie wanted someone to love—*anyone* to love—solely for the sake of being loved in return.

"I couldn't care less about you two and your love life." Van shrugged again. "Do what you want. I won't tell anyone. Warriors don't have time for island gossip."

"Beautiful," Genie cooed with a smile, showing perfect white teeth. She detached herself from Rummie and twirled to reach the refrigerator. "Let me get you some fresh fruit."

"I want grains. Warrior food. Barley, oatmeal—"

Genie's eyes roamed up and down Van. "With the weight you've gained lately? I think not."

"Since when do you care what I eat?" Van asked, provoked. "Stop trying to put on a show for your *boyfriend*."

"Girls, girls—" Rummie interjected.

"Shut up," Van snapped at him.

"Vanessa." Genie turned to face her step-daughter. "Apologize this instant!" The swift movement opened her loosely tied bathrobe.

Van glimpsed a tattoo below Genie's belly button of a red snake entwined with a gold snake. The larger red snake rose upward, giving the overall impression the tattoo was of one massive serpent.

Van stammered, "I—I apologize." The tattoo contrasted with the prim, proper step-mother Van knew. The discovery completely threw her off balance. *Who is this woman?* Van waved her index finger at Genie's pelvic area. "Is that new?" *Did Genie get the tattoo to please her new boyfriend?*

"Of course not." Genie hastily pulled her robe closed. "You'll like Uncle Rummie once you give him a chance," she said, changing the subject. "I'd like the two of you to get along. It would mean a lot to me."

"Me too," Rummie said. "All that stuff about your weight is pure hooey. Come on. Let's eat." He tried to whisper that last part in a conspiratorial tone, an impossible feat for the boisterous man. He gave Van a sloppy wink.

"How'd you get your nickname?" Van asked, warming up to him.

"Because he likes to drink rum," Genie answered, smiling. She placed a bowl of oatmeal on the table.

"Oh, I thought it was because I like to play gin rummie." He sniggered.

Genie giggled. "Oh, you're such a card." She poured hot water on the oats and then dropped in some cut fruit. She pushed the bowl toward Van.

Puke rose in the back of Van's throat at their banter. If she weren't so hungry, she would've left.

"A real joker." Rummie chuckled, continuing the joke. He grabbed Genie by the waist and pulled her in for a hug, exposing the gaudy gold chain of a necklace.

Genie gleefully hugged him back, still giggling.

Rummie's chain reminded Van of the necklace her father handed to Genie the night he died, with instructions to pass it on to Van. But Genie never gave the necklace to Van.

When Van had asked about it, Genie claimed she hid it in the hollow of a tree for safekeeping when the Grigori stormed the manor last summer searching for clues about Van's missing father, who was wanted for treason at the time. When Genie returned to the tree to retrieve it, she claimed the necklace had disappeared.

Van made it her personal mission to find that necklace. Not only because it belonged to her birth mother, but her father had risked everything to deliver that necklace to Genie. Van scolded herself for being unable to locate it. She'd traveled to the Living World, suffered a grueling journey to find and retrieve the Coin of Creation, yet she couldn't find a simple necklace lost somewhere on Providence Island?

"Now, now." Rummie released Genie from his hug. "We're making the girl uncomfortable."

"What plans do you have for the summer?" Genie asked Van. "Are Uxa and the Elders assigning you to another summer project?"

Genie used the word "project" and not "mission" leading Van to believe Rummie hadn't been told Van carried the magical warrior bloodline of the Anchoress. Van hadn't seen Rummie around the island, which meant Genie picked him up somewhere in Salus Valde, in the Living World, probably during one of her shopping trips.

Rummie must've traveled to Providence Island through the portal in the House of Lacus, otherwise known as the transportation building, on the reservation. The off-limits side of the island to all except Grigori, Elders, and a select few, like Genie, and the children in the special classes, like Van.

Yet, he apparently didn't have a high enough clearance to be told about Van's true identity or her importance to the Lodian people. Rummie probably thought Van was another teenage "Grigori groupie." Van appreciated him not disparaging her interest in warrior training.

"Summer projects are great," Rummie said. "Builds character."

"Embrace your destiny," Genie said with a wink.

Van scooped the last of her fruit-topped oatmeal into her mouth. "I'm late for training." She scraped back the chair.

"Training on a Saturday?" Rummie asked. "Good for you."

Van lied. Training was in an hour, but she got sick of being around the two of them and hurried out of the manor.

She arrived at the park early, and with nothing else to do but wait for the others, she decided to finish her earlier yoga routine.

Van laid down on the thick grass and entered the corpse pose.

CHAPTER 4

Van rested on her back, eyes closed, palms up, heels shoulder length apart. She fidgeted, unable to get comfortable.

I'm sick of training. The thought pinged inside Van's mind. *It's time for me to kill demons, side by side with the adults, like a full-fledged Grigori.*

Final exams at Canterbury Bells Charter School were over. The grueling series of tests included standard academic testing done inside the classroom, and then the kids in high school were also required to compete in sporting events called the Jaychund games. All the exams challenged the students' wits, physical skills, and ability for teamwork.

After the final exams concluded, the Elders assigned the undergraduates to a career track, and the seniors were awarded their permanent career placements. The seniors had to accept the career chosen for them. Otherwise, the Elders would excommunicate them from the island. "Elders' rules or take a cruise" was a common saying to those who were unhappy with their placements.

Pfft. Van's classmates didn't know the half of it.

None of her peers, except Paley and Brux, knew the reservation was off limits to the island's townies because it housed the portal to the Living World. Few people on the townie side of the island, including her classmates, were aware the other world existed.

This was neither here nor there. Van had come into her Anchoress powers so she could protect the townies and all the other oblivious terrigens from the demons running amok in their world. Controlling the demon population in the Earth World would prevent the evil creatures from accumulating enough strength to reach the Living World.

Last year, Van had no desire to leave Providence Island, but Uxa had coerced her into going through the portal to the Living World. Uxa used Van's missing father and words like "family duty" to pressure Van into accepting what Uxa called a "summer project," allowing Van the chance to earn placement as a junior Grigori.

The mission proved successful. Van found out why her father had disappeared and much more. Then, she discovered she was the only person in both worlds who could stop the Balish from invading Salus Valde by retrieving the Coin of Creation, an ancient relic that proved she, the Anchoress, existed.

Van couldn't wait to get back to the Living Word during this year's Alignment. She wanted to check on the Moors, the ruling monarchy, to make sure none of them were conspiring with demons like Princess Solana had done. Van had a particular interest in meeting the newest heir, Solana's younger brother, Prince Ferox, to make sure he didn't carry the same dark thread as his sister. Van also hoped to get an in-person update from the team Uxa had sent to find Brux's sister, Daisy.

But Van wanted to stay in the Earth World, too. She needed to intern with the adult Grigori on the mainland, also known as being "in the field."

Van's desire to do both pulled her in two directions.

Lying in the corpse pose—*waiting*—bored Van. Her restlessness made her unable to concentrate, so she couldn't call on Jacynthia for guidance. But her spirit guide had given Van advice in the past about dealing with boredom. What had Jacynthia told her? *Oh yeah—*

"In life, there is a time when everything becomes boring, even beautiful

sunsets. Excess of all things becomes boring in the end if we do not understand the essence of our enjoyment of them comes from within. One's senses may tire, but one's soul never does."

Van huffed. Paley was right. Why couldn't Jacynthia just tell her what to do? Why be so obtuse? How could enjoyment come from *within*?

Her stomach gurgled. Hunger invaded her musings, although she had already eaten breakfast.

Van got great enjoyment from food. She envisioned eating a bag of cheese doodles and licking the orange, flaky coating off each of her fingers.

Hey Jacynthia, Van said in her mind. *I could get enjoyment from within by eating these, right?*

"If you continue to indulge in a bad habit, no matter how small, it will eventually lead to misfortune," Jacynthia warned.

Van's mysterious spirit guide had returned. She had called out to Jacynthia in jest, and the woman had appeared in her mind's eye. This made Van aware of two things: she must be nearly asleep, and Jacynthia's visits into Van's consciousness were increasing in frequency.

Nice to see you too. Van used non-verbal words only heard by Jacynthia.

Her spirit guide continued, "Leave behind your incorrectness now and follow your heart. It knows what is correct. If you persist in improper behavior, you will become hopelessly entangled in troubles. Act with sincerity and the Creator will deliver you from danger. By opening your heart, you can save yourself and return to the light."

Before Van could respond, she heard a twig snap. Her eyes shot open, disconnecting her from Jacynthia.

Someone crept nearby, trying to sneak up on her.

Van cautiously raised herself from the ground. Her eye caught the flicker of a shadow dashing behind the unmarked statue of Zurial, one of the four honored warriors from the Dark War.

To Van's understanding, the shadow couldn't be a demon. Demon's vibrations were too low for them to reach Providence Island from the mainland. The island was a Grigori outpost in the Earth World. Their presence made the island's vibration too high to sustain the existence of demons.

Van held her position, waiting for the intruder to make a move.

It couldn't be the Quasher, either. The wolf-like shadow beast only appeared in the Living World. The Elementals had magically bound the Quasher from being able to enter Salus Valde, which included the portal to Providence Island. And if it were the Quasher, the shadow beast wouldn't hide. It'd attack. Unstoppable in its quest to destroy Van's light.

But it could be something else. Some new creature.

A figure wearing a black cloak peered out from behind the statue.

Van glimpsed a skeletal face under its hood. Hollowed out eyes, severe cheekbones, and stitches crisscrossing its mouth.

It glided toward Van. Its abnormally long phalanges clamped tightly around a scythe.

She gasped, terrified. Death-personified had come for her. Van's warrior training kicked in. She raised her fists, bracing for a fight.

A rustling noise emanated from the trees behind her.

Death's gaze shifted, landing on Paley, who had sauntered into the park. It pivoted and dashed straight for her.

"Paley!" Van screamed. She charged at the cloaked figure.

Paley froze. Her eyes widened with fright.

Van tore across the field so hard, her sneakers ripped into the grass, leaving divots.

"Paley, stay back!" Van leaped and landed directly in Death's path.

It stopped short.

"You'll have to get through me first." Van crouched into a combat stance and raised her trembling fists.

The figure used its bony fingers to twirl the scythe in figure eights, passing the weapon from hand to hand.

Wait a minute. Van recognized that routine.

It got sloppy, and the scythe wobbled. The figure convulsed—no, wait—it was *laughing*!

The cloaked figure dropped the scythe.

"This is too hard to do wearing these finger-boned gloves." The figure yanked off its hands and removed its skeleton mask. "Too funny. You should've seen your face." Pernilla burst out laughing.

"You—that wasn't funny."

"Oh, it's funny." Pernilla used her knuckles to wipe tears of laughter from her eyes.

"We all think you're taking this training thing too far." Brux came out from behind another statue.

"You were in on it?" Van couldn't stand the butterflies fluttering in her stomach whenever Brux entered her line of sight.

"You were never in danger," Brux said.

Thankfully, after he opened his mouth, the butterflies always flew away. "No, but Pernilla was." Van glared at her nemesis.

"We wanted to show you how ridiculous you're being." Pernilla slipped out of her cloak. "You call for a training session every Saturday morning. The school year is over. Time to take it down a notch."

Van couldn't understand why her classmates weren't interested in pushing their limits. To be the best version of themselves, which meant training hard. Maybe if her peers knew her true identity, they would. As it stood, Paley and Brux were her only classmates aware of Van's Anchoress status.

"We need to train harder. Be faster. Be better. Be *ready*. In case Uxa assigns us to a miss—summer project," Van said.

Pernilla didn't have a high enough clearance to be given information about their previous mission. No one did, except Uxa, the other Elders, Uxa's first assistant, Tussel Fynn, and any member of the teams that went on the mission and survived—Brux, Paley, herself, and, perhaps, Daisy.

Pernilla's light-blue eyes dazzled against her naturally tanned skin, inherited from her partly Native American ancestry. "If you paid attention at the Placement Ceremony, you'd know my permanent placement. I'm entering Advanced Studies Grigori. Accelerated. Instead of starting classes in the fall, I'm starting tomorrow. Uxa assigned me to intern with her on a summer project."

Van managed a deadpan expression. "When do you turn eighteen?"

"None of your business." Pernilla tossed her thick, light-brown hair over her shoulder.

"September first," Brux answered, catching on.

"Dammit," Van muttered.

"Makes sense that Uxa's already formed the team," Brux said.

Paley's eyes widened. "I better be on it."

Uxa needed teens to do her bidding in the Living World because of Manik's law. A millennium ago, the Elementals worked with the Balish King Manik to place a magical boundary around Salus Valde. The law forbade Lodian adults to cross this line, to leave Salus Valde. To this day, the Balish occupied and controlled almost all other regions in the Living World. However, the Elementals refused to use their magic to bind the law unless the restriction didn't include children or the Anchoress.

"You don't have to be so secretive anymore." Pernilla raised her chin. "Uxa told me everything yesterday. I know all about the terrigen-generated demons in the Earth World. I assume that was your 'summer project' last year. Well, this year I'm going, too. I'm on your team."

"Oh hell, no." Paley's eyes shifted toward Van for confirmation.

"You two need to get over it," Pernilla said. "Ken dumped you a year ago, Van—for *me*. Grow up."

"I don't care about your infatuation with Ken." Van's concern had nothing to do with their personal history. Although Pernilla excelled as an athlete, including winning the Jaychund games this year and last, her abrasive personality made her a poor fit for teamwork. She was the type who always made waves.

Paley's face slackened in surprise over Van's calm response. She gazed dubiously at her friend.

Van said to Pernilla, "Being part of my team means you need to get over yourself and train harder."

Paley nodded in solidarity, satisfied with Van's latest response.

Pernilla's nostrils flared. "Everyone thinks you're such a good little girl. But I know the real you. Deep down you're a rotten little—"

Van raised her palm to stop her. "I've no time for drama. All I care about is protecting my people, protecting terrigens, and defending Salus—Providence Island."

Pernilla hadn't mentioned the Living World yet, and therefore, most likely assumed the summer project would take place in the field, in the Earth World.

"If you want to train with a rotten teacher, you're welcome to stay." Van glanced at the handful of her classmates meandering onto the field. She didn't want them to overhear their conversation, so she stopped talking.

Brooke, Davy, Wade, Adrian, and Deacon were all in the reservation program with Van. She expected a good number of her RP classmates to show up for her extra-help training class.

Maren, Pernilla's best friend, arrived last.

With reinforcements, Pernilla gained resolve. "I'll stay," she said, nose in the air. "I could use some additional training—despite having an incompetent teacher."

Maren wasn't even in the reservation program. As a graduated senior, the Elders had assigned Maren her permanent placement in retail, as an assistant manager at the downtown clothing store called Ropa Moda. Since Maren was a terrigen, as long as the Grigori secretly continued to patrol the Earth World, she'd never need this type of training. But, for the sake of beginning the class, Van didn't throw a fit and ask her to leave.

"Looks like no one else is coming today. Let's get started." Van began the sequence of koga-clava. A form of combat training that integrated rhythmic gymnastic techniques with weapon-based martial arts.

Van began with the standard warmup she had learned in class. She liked how similar the movements were to yoga. Like doing yoga in motion or Tai Chi—soft, fluid.

She turned to the side, bending her knees as she stretched her arms forward. The class followed.

Although these movements seemed gentle, slow-paced, and non-competitive, the practice offered spiritual and health benefits. Like enhancing the mind-body connection and helping to clear stuck, problematic emotions. Van considered these weak advantages. Her interest in the routine was about how it increased strength, flexibility, body awareness, and mental concentration.

Although she considered these "easy" moves, beads of sweat glistened on her students' foreheads.

The routine came effortlessly to Van, ingrained into her being. This allowed her mind to wander. She wondered who else Uxa would place on their team and what the team's assignment would be this summer.

Her attention shifted to Brux. His mental well-being concerned her. Not knowing if his sister was dead or alive must tear him apart. Van's eyes swept over his body. Confidence radiated in his moves, which were near perfect.

Brux effortlessly followed Van's lead, flexing the muscles in his legs and arms. She noticed the tight stretch of his cotton t-shirt across his chest, the pull of his pants over his thighs as he infused the cat foot pose and the dual arm rotation. His soft blond hair rustled in the light breeze...

Dammit. That annoying warm feeling swirled in Van's chest again. She pushed it away and refocused on teaching the class.

"There is only right and wrong," Van said in a confident voice as she continued the motions of koga-clava. "Good and bad. Light and dark. Anything in between is a distraction."

Van's number one rule of being a warrior—*don't* fall in love.

CHAPTER 5

They didn't have any practice weapons like knives, staffs, or swords outside their classroom. So Van decided her session today would focus on grappling techniques.

"Martial arts aren't all about kicking and punching." Van laid down; the cool grass chilled her back. "Grappling techniques can control or defeat your opponent."

She began with the shrimp move. As she rolled from side to side, using her feet to push her body while rocking her arms, her muscles strained. Her movements scraped the skin on her back, even through her clothes, causing pain. She pushed through it.

"Side shrimp," Van barked. "It's tough, but great for building the core and abdominal muscles."

Wet spots from exertion formed in her students' armpits. Something Van liked to see. It meant she was doing her job.

She led the class into the forward roll. Then the backward roll. Next, the crab walk. She finished with the fallback and stand technique.

Van stood, brushing the grass and dirt off her backside, breathing heavily from the workout. She placed her feet together, spine straight, eyes forward. Then placed her hands in prayer position.

Her class did the same.

"We are part of the same team. We are one." Van bowed.

Her students returned her bow, all of them sweat-stained and panting. "We are one," they chanted.

"We'll be pairing up and practicing hand-to-hand combat and submission techniques." Van loved the feeling of sweat dripping down her back. "Clinch holds and ground fighting. First, let's take a short break."

"Break?" Pernilla stomped toward Van. "I'm not even sweating yet." She brushed past Van, slamming shoulders. "Weakling," she muttered.

The others relaxed and grabbed their water bottles. A couple of them said, "Great class, Van."

"She's such a jerk." Paley glared at Pernilla. "You're an awesome teacher. Your moves are perfect, like everything you do." She used the back of her hand to wipe her sweaty forehead.

"I'm far from perfect." Van kept her eyes on Pernilla, who was doing cool down stretches with Maren. "I need to talk to her."

Paley scrunched her face. "Ew. Why?"

"I'm not looking to be her friend or anything," Van quickly added. "It's just…"

Pernilla would always be a turd, but Van had a responsibility to protect her people. This made gathering intel a priority. Informed warriors made good leaders. Since Pernilla attended most of Van's non-mandatory, ad hoc training classes, she might talk to Van out of a sense of reciprocity.

Encouraged by this hope, Van cautiously approached her nemesis. "Hey, Pernilla."

Pernilla and Maren stopped chatting but continued doing stretches.

"I was, uh, just wondering what made you… uh, what made your parents and Uxa decide to place you in the reservation program this year? You know, your senior year."

Pernilla's intense stare made Van wary. She didn't know what to prep for—a long story or a punch in the face.

"Still stupid, I see." Pernilla sneered.

Punch in the face, it is.

Pernilla grabbed her opposing elbow, doing a triceps stretch. "I got placed in the RP because I'm a superior athlete and can kick your ass all day long." Pernilla switched arms, carrying on with her routine.

"I guess Uxa wanted someone smart in the class," Maren said, holding a runner's stretch.

"That explains why you're not there." Van winced. She'd let her emotions take over. Failing to get information from Pernilla meant failing as a warrior. Unacceptable. "Sorry."

"*Sorry! Sorry!*" Maren and Pernilla cruelly mimicked Van. They burst out laughing and walked away.

"Wow." Paley appeared next to Van, chewing her cuticles. "That idea really tanked."

Van shrugged.

Brux joined them. Having overheard Van's attempt at a civil conversation with Pernilla, he said, "Pernilla got the *call.* That's why she got placed in the reservation program."

The call! That was what Van wanted to know. "Tell me more."

"It's when a terrigen gets a sudden, intense awareness of the Living World," Brux continued. "A feeling they're in the wrong place, and it gets stronger. It's an inner 'calling' that they're meant for a different life, a better life. This realization comes from the development of ichor in their blood."

"The magical ingredient giving you a higher vibrational signature than terrigens like me." Paley cast her eyes downward.

Brux nodded sadly at Paley. "It raises the terrigens' vibration to the same frequencies as vichors. They become vichors once they recharge in the Living World. Or, I guess, the first time would be called 'charged.' If they don't charge, then they'll get sicker and sicker until they die."

Van already knew about ichor first hand. She had been sick as a child and labeled as a "slow learner." But her issues came from having ichor in her blood, making her a vichor, or someone who belongs in the Living World. Vichors had difficultly living in the low vibration of the Earth World, even Providence Island. Ichor had made Van exhausted, unable to concentrate, and caused trouble with her breathing, which caused problems with her learning and completing schoolwork.

She, and all the other vichors on the island, needed to travel to the higher vibration of the Living World to restore their health by recharging. "Slow" kids were placed in the special program because the additional courses were held on the reservation. Unbeknown to the kids, the elevator they entered to get to their special classes took them through the portal and opened onto the third floor in Lodestar Station, the building that housed the Transportation Center and Grigori headquarters in Salus Valde.

"That's why Pernilla was sick last year!" Paley said.

Brux turned to Van. "Pernilla's a vichor now. She belongs in Salus Valde, like you and me."

"And the rest of the kids in the RP." Paley's stared at her feet, to help her cope with the sting of being left out.

"How come I never got the call?" Van asked.

"You were born with ichor," Brux said. "Pernilla developed it."

"It seems pretty unusual at her age." Van squinted at Pernilla.

She knew the Elders secretly monitored all the kids through their class assignments at Canterbury Bells—grades pre-school through high school—to see if they developed ichor. All newborns were tested but, unfortunately, the Elders waited for kids to become sick before re-testing their blood.

The Elders' career track placements for the students weren't only about filling needed-island-skills, they were about identifying potential recruits to become demon fighting Grigori. The Jaychund games were actually secret Grigori tryouts designed by Uxa and the Elders.

"We either develop ichor before the age of eighteen or not at all," Brux said.

"I haven't been feeling well," Paley said, looking fine. "Maybe I have the call?"

"You're only sixteen." Brux broke into a huge smile. "There's still time."

Van scrunched her brow. "Why aren't bunches of mainlanders pulled to the island by the call?"

"They have a different experience," Brux said. "Once the terrigen adapts to their higher vibrational frequencies, a doorway to the Living World opens for that one person, called a random doorway. They're drawn to the door like a magnet, and it allows them a one-way transport into the Living World. After they walk through, it immediately closes and never re-opens. It can drop them anywhere, not only Salus Valde."

"Like where?" Paley asked. "How does it know where they belong?"

Brux shrugged. "The doorway knows to exit the person in their correct place. Once they're in the Living World, they're picked up by the local tribe and integrated into their culture."

Van narrowed her eyes. "Doesn't anyone on the mainland search for these missing people?"

"They're accounted for as missing persons, lost children, old childhood friends you never hear from again. Some terrigens fight the feeling and deny the call by not walking through the door. If this refusal continues into adulthood, their energy becomes depleted, and they die at an early age."

"So Pernilla went through a random doorway to Salus Valde?" Van asked.

Brux shook his head. "Pernilla lives on Providence Island, so her call intuitively pulled her toward the closest doorway to the Living World, the portal. Our island is a quasi-world—partly in the Earth World, partly in Living World. The rules here are different." Brux ran his fingers through his hair.

If he was trying to fix it, he didn't need to. Van thought he looked perfect.

"Here, the kids who're born with, or develop ichor, go to the special classes. They're considered slow... well, you know."

Paley nudged Van, breaking her attention.

Van saw her ex-boyfriend, Ken, wandering onto the field from the woods.

Pernilla rushed over to greet him, so excited she hop-skipped like a child.

Ken had grass and dirt stains on his loose gray pants and looked both refreshed and tired after finishing lacrosse practice. He called over to Van. "Okay if I stay? I'll just watch."

Van nodded. He apparently came to support Pernilla's training.

Pernilla ran her fingers through Ken's sweat-matted hair and then rested both arms over his shoulders, paying no mind to the damp spots on his tight-fitting, gray t-shirt.

"How cute." Paley rolled her eyes.

"The Alignment starts tomorrow," Brux said in a low voice to Van and Paley. "Why hasn't Uxa mentioned anything?"

"Uxa's been putting me off for a year. I'm scheduled to meet with her later tonight, but I'm going to her office after training. I can't wait any longer."

"I haven't been able to get anything out of her either." Brux frowned. "I'm going with you."

"Me too," Paley said. "We need answers."

Van nodded in agreement as she watched Ken embrace Pernilla.

He caressed his hands up and down her back. They chatted and smiled, exchanging light kisses as if they were alone in the world.

"Get a room," Paley muttered.

"Let them be." Van pulled her attention away from the lovers and redirected it back to Paley and Brux. "Pernilla's in for a rude awakening. Once she finds out the adult Grigori take an oath to put the job first, Ken will be history."

So why bother dating anyone? Van wanted to add, but she wasn't in the mood to hear a rebuttal from Paley, or Brux.

"Break's over," Van shouted. "Next up, hand-to-hand combat. Pick a partner."

Paley zipped over to Brux.

"Partners?" Paley gave him a big smile.

"Sure." Brux smiled back.

Between watching Ken and Pernilla being lovey-dovey and Brux and Paley flirting, Van felt an ensuing wave of grouchiness coming on.

She couldn't care less about Ken. But Brux's constant presence annoyed her.

She internally struggled with the difficulties caused by Brux living on the island and sitting near her in class. It's not like she wanted a boyfriend, or anything. She had no time to fool around. But watching Brux and Paley had made her acutely aware of something. If Brux couldn't be *her* boyfriend, then she didn't want him to be *anyone's* boyfriend.

She sighed, trying to grasp the reasoning why the Elementals chose Brux as her assigned protector. Brux took his position seriously. That meant Van had no chance of having a relationship with him. She had to trust the Elementals knew what they were doing.

But… why did it feel so… *wrong?*

Pernilla unglued herself from Ken and, like magnets, Maren and Pernilla partnered with each other.

"No, no, no." Van marched toward the duo, flapping her hands. "You two together? No. You won't learn anything. You'll just goof off." Van eyed the others in the class. "Pernilla, you pair with Deacon."

"That leaves me without a partner," Maren huffed.

"You'll pair with me," Van said.

Pernilla snickered. "Good luck with that, Maren."

Van ignored her and barked, "Get into position!"

The couples snapped into fighting stances, except Maren, who had no clue what to do.

"Begin," Van said to the class.

As the other students sparred, Maren copied their postures and faced Van. "I know you're trying to leave me out." She fumed.

Van responded by moving into fighting position. Knees bent, hands raised.

"You think I should sit on the sidelines with Ken," Maren said, as she and Van circled each other. "You and all your crap about who's a *real* warrior and who's not."

Van snorted. Last year Pernilla and Maren had made fun of Van for being in the reservation program, calling it classes for stupid kids. But once Pernilla got sick and added into the special classes—and experienced how recharging in the Living World helped ease her illness—she never stopped bragging about being an RP student. All year, Maren wanted in, too.

Maren lurched forward and took a swipe at Van.

Van easily dodged out of the way. "Your swing is too wide. Try again."

Poor Maren. Van could tell she feared being left behind by her best friend who had earned a coveted permanent placement on the reservation side of the island, working with the Grigori and the Elders. Maren and Pernilla were headed down two different life tracks. Maren's awareness of the inevitable end of her friendship with Pernilla caused her anger, not Van.

Maren flew at Van, waggling both of her fists.

In one swoop, Van stepped aside, grabbed one of Maren's arms, straightened her leg, and used Maren's momentum to toss her opponent to the ground. "Watch your form."

Pernilla risked glancing over and yelled, "Maren! Get up. Try again—oof." She took a hit to the chest as Deacon used her divided attention to his advantage.

Pernilla scowled at Deacon's cheap shot and fought back in a fury.

"You go, girl." Ken's proud smile beamed from the sidelines.

Maren snorted and glared at Van. She rose. Cheeks flushed, jaw clenched.

"Control your moves," Van instructed.

Maren's nostrils flared as she curled her fists into balls.

"Take it easy. This is training. Don't knock yourself out—or let me do it." Van snickered. She couldn't help herself.

Maren flushed a deep red to the tips of her ears, sweat beaded on her forehead. Using no form, she charged at Van in a feral rage.

Van dodged. "Calm yourself," she said, unable to hide her growing frustration with Maren.

"Argh!" Maren charged again.

Van stepped aside and, again, tripped Maren.

She crashed onto the grass. Then immediately jumped to her feet and lunged at Van.

"Enough." Brux caught Maren around her waist.

Maren squirmed against Brux's grip. He placed her feet on the ground but held firm.

The others stopped training to watch the spectacle.

Brux raised his brow. "You're burning up."

Maren stopped struggling. "I don't feel so good."

Van placed the back of her hand on Maren's forehead. "You feel hot."

"She has a fever?" Pernilla furrowed her brow in concern.

Maren turned pale. Her eyes rolled into her head. She slumped into Brux's arms.

CHAPTER 6

Maren remained semi-conscious and burning with a fever the entire time the group carried her to Providence Island General Hospital.

As soon as they arrived, the triage nurse admitted Maren and the hospital staff whisked her away to a room. Pernilla took the responsibility of calling Maren's parents using the hospital's Inter-Island Connect landline. Shortly afterward, a doctor strolled into the waiting area and told them Maren had appendicitis.

"She'll be fine," he said. "Go home and get some rest."

Pernilla and Ken wanted to stay at the hospital and wait for Maren's parents. Brooke, Davy, Wade, Adrian, and Deacon bid their goodbyes and well-wishes and went home. Van, Paley, and Brux's presence was no longer needed or wanted, so they left the hospital, too.

The hospital was close to a place the islanders called "downtown," a main commerce area that had banks, hardware stores, Big Wheels Buggy Rentals, a couple of beauty salons, a mechanic, and places to eat.

The trio walked along Rudder Road, a side street leading to the downtown.

"We need to go see Uxa, find out what we're doing tomorrow," Van reminded them.

Brux stopped walking. "We can head there right now, if you want."

"Uxa will wait until the last second to tell us anything." Paley playfully grabbed Brux's arm and tugged. "Let's go downtown for a bit."

"True." Van continued walking. "And I've been really pestering her about our next visit to—well, you know." Although no one else was around, she still didn't think it wise to say "Living World" out loud.

"Uxa has her reasons for keeping quiet," Brux said.

As they got closer to the main road, Paley chatted about the Jaychund sales. "I definitely want to stop at the Nifty Nook. Everything is thirty percent off."

Brux glanced at Van. "You're awfully quiet."

"Appendicitis?" Van asked, skeptically.

Paley nudged Van with her elbow. "Can't you ever go with the flow?"

"Appendicitis gives you pain on the right side." Van pushed her lower abdomen. "She didn't have pain there."

"Well, she was really sick," Paley said. "Whatever she has, I hope she'll be okay."

Van shrugged. "It's probably just a bug."

"Why are you so sure it's not appendicitis?" Brux asked, taking Van's concern seriously.

"I'm not." Van glanced at the sky. "I'm sure she'll be shipshape in no time." Thick gray clouds cloaked the sun, casting a shadow over the road like a funeral shroud.

"She's in good hands." Brux curiously followed Van's glance toward the cloudy sky. Not seeing anything unusual, he continued. "We have our summer project to focus on."

Paley twisted her hair. "You don't think she's contagious, do you?"

"If she is, we all have it," Van said, as they strolled onto the main road, Oceanview Avenue. "There's nothing we can do about it now."

Brux wrapped a comforting arm around Paley. "We'll be fine."

Delighted, Paley grinned.

"Yeah, we have a different invasion to worry about." Van grimaced at the mob of people roaming the sidewalk. Mainlanders packed the restaurants and shops, infiltrating their downtown like a virus spreading across their small island.

The quaint downtown comprised one main road with many side streets and hadn't changed in appearance since, well, ever. Built to support the island's inhabitants, not the flood of visitors who came for the annual three-day Jaychund festival.

Not anyone could set foot on the island. The Elders controlled all boats to and from the docks. The Grigori screened and pre-approved visitors all year round, not only during Jaychund.

Occasionally throughout the year, Van glimpsed black-suit types wandering down the streets. Visitors from the government made sense since the Grigori were a division of Homeland Security. Being allowed on the island meant they had high-level national security clearance. But for this year's festival, Van noticed an influx of black-suits, more so than in previous years.

Even fifty extra visitors took up a lot of space in their downtown, never mind a hundred. The Elders limited vehicle usage, so most people walked everywhere, causing cluttered streets and sidewalks.

Boys' loud, taunting voices caught the trio's ears, coming from down a side road.

"Someone's up to no good," Brux grumbled. He dashed toward the ruckus. Van and Paley followed.

They came upon a handful of elementary school boys, all clutching water balloons. The boys stood circled around an adult Van immediately recognized. She didn't know his real name. The islanders called him Bicycle Bob.

Bob had a learning disability, and not the kind fixed by a rejuvenating trip to the Living World. For as long as Van could remember, Bicycle Bob riding his old red bike along the roads had been a cherished fixture in their community. As a ward of the island, he remained under the Elder's care. But, because of the overflow of visitors from the holiday weekend, the Elders, along with island security, were overworked and stretched thin. A lapse noticed by the trouble-seeking boys.

Brux marched over, Van and Paley right behind him.

"M-my b-bike! My b-bike!" Bob cried. He held his arms over his head as the boys whipped water balloons at him.

Bob's beloved red bike lay next to him on the sidewalk. He curled his body, bending over it to protect it from the barrage of water balloons, while still protecting his head.

One boy hovered his foot over the bike. "What? This?" He kicked it across the street.

Another boy mocked, *"Oh! My bike! My bike!"* He sniggered.

"Loser!" a third boy said as he grabbed another water balloon from his backpack.

All five had backpacks stuffed with water balloons. Causing trouble had apparently been on their agenda.

"Retard!" one boy said, as he chucked a water balloon at Bob's head.

The boys guffawed, having the time of their lives at Bob's peril.

"Stop it!" Van screamed at the boys, as Brux stormed toward them.

Paley's index finger zipped to her mouth. She chewed on her cuticle.

Brux grabbed the closest two boys by the back of their collars. "You think you're funny?" He crashed their skulls together, causing a loud crack. "How's that for funny?" He shoved them to the ground.

Van dashed over to Bob and helped him back to his feet. She glared at the boys. "You're a bunch of jerks!"

"Who's next?" Brux roared. He towered over the boys. His eyes met one of them. "You?" He took a step toward the boy and the entire group scattered. Even the two boys dazed from their skull-bashing scrambled to their feet and ran.

Paley rubbed Bob's back. "Are you all right?"

Van brushed his wet bangs from his eyes.

"Th-tha-th—" Bob's trembling made his stutter worse. "Th-thank you."

"Let's get you home," Van said. All the islanders knew the basics about each other, including where Bob lived, a studio apartment in

Hide-a-way. She rubbed his drenched arms, trying to get him warm, but he continued to shiver from the trauma.

"You're safe now," Brux said.

This triggered something in Bob. He tensed, and his face grew pink as he strained to find his words. "N-not n-not." His stutter got worse which made him more distressed. "N-not n-not." He grasped Van's arms and locked his doleful, hazel eyes with her blue ones. "Not safe! N-not safe!"

"What do you mean?" Van grew more concerned. "Are you telling me you're not safe?"

This upset him even more. Spittle flew from his mouth as he struggled to get his point across. "Y-you. P-Paley. N-not safe. Stay s-stay a-away from th-the T-twin G-gemstones! Th-they m-make you g-go. S-stay a-away fr-rom—"

Bob's eyes moved beyond Van, to the main street. He twitched. "O-okay. O-okay." He picked up his bike while bobbing his head. "O-okay."

Van twisted to see what had spooked Bob. She glimpsed a man in a dark suit standing at the entryway to the side road. At first, Van thought he had also heard the commotion and stopped to see if they needed help. But as soon as Van caught his eye, the man turned away and disappeared into the bustling visitors on the main street.

She looked back at Bob, who had mounted his bike. "Who was that guy?"

He hastily peddled away without another word.

"Wait!" Van cried.

"Poor guy." Brux shook his head. "What a horrible life."

"How does he know about the Twin Gemstones?" Van asked.

"He's really messed up. There's no way we can ask him," Brux said.

"We should check on him later," Van said. "Or at least let Uxa know what happened."

Paley stopped chewing her cuticles and smiled at Van. "So you do have feelings."

"Doing what's right has nothing to do with feelings." Van scowled.

"Taking action based on good decisions without an emotional handicap must be done to be an outstanding warrior."

"What book did you read that in?" Paley flipped her hair.

"It's never good to suppress your feelings," Brux said. "Feelings connect us to nature, to the continuity of life."

Van threw him an eye roll. Brux ignored it and continued to drive his point. Into her brain. Like a spike.

"Your connection to nature gives you power as a warrior. You'll feel less lonely and isolated if you open up."

Van wanted to scream at his offensive "helpful" advice. Instead, she held a poker face. No way would she allow him to see the turmoil raging inside her caused by his words. Brux, the *love of her life*—who she could *never* be with—had counseled her on *how not to be lonely*. It was tough to take.

She stomped down the side road, back to the main street.

"Know the difference between what you want and what you choose," he cried. "The best advice is worthless if you don't take it."

Van heard Paley say to Brux, "Makes sense to me."

Van tsked, disgusted by the whole thing. She weaved into the crowd so she could ditch her friend and her "protector." Paley and Brux could have each other. She just wanted to be left alone.

Friends were nothing but distractions. They ate away at time better focused on warrior training. She'd be better off not hanging out with them anymore. Except they were most likely part of her team to the Living World, which reminded Van to get her butt over to Uxa's office on the reservation.

She hustled through the throng of people on the main street. Despite the multitude of dark suits milling about, she caught sight of the man who scared away Bicycle Bob. Although eager to see Uxa, she made a detour and followed him into the Dock Side Cafe, a small coffee shop crammed with people.

Van strained to find the man and saw him in line. She maneuvered herself next to a group of "suits," eager to eavesdrop on their conversation while she waited.

"—excited because we found traces of terbium, holmium, and erbium."

"You're the physicist. What are the developmental implications of the find?"

"You'll need to speak to Chuck. He's the finance guy. Or maybe marketing—"

The man got his coffee. He jostled through the crowd and left the shop.

Van hastily weaved her way through the horde, trailing him. She stepped out of the cafe onto the sidewalk, looked up and down the street, and couldn't find him among the visitors.

"Dammit." She was about to move on when she glimpsed him dash down the alley between the Sea Escape clothing store and the Beach Wok restaurant. She dashed after him.

The stench from the dumpsters permeated her nostrils. Seagulls picked on open garbage loosely tossed in bins by the restaurant's hurried employees. Van's sudden presence startled the gulls; they cawed and flew away.

A fresh Dock Side Cafe coffee cup lay spilled on the ground nearby, causing the hair on the back of her neck to prickle.

A man grasped her from behind and cupped her mouth.

The intimacy of his body pressed against hers, along with his hot breath on her ear, terrified her. She wanted to scream for help. But with his hand covering her mouth, she couldn't yell.

She could barely breathe.

CHAPTER 7

Van's hair caught in the man's lips as he growled into her ear.

"What they did to her, they'll do to me. If you don't stop following me." He released his sweaty grip.

Van gasped for breath and wiped her mouth with the back of her hand. She turned to face her assailant.

"Stop following me," he growled over his shoulder as he hurried away, deeper into the alley.

"Wait!" Van rushed after him. "What are you talking about?"

He stopped and turned around; Van halted, startled.

The man stomped toward Van and spoke close to her face. "You and your little friend already got me into enough trouble!"

"How?" Van asked. "What friend?"

He pointed his thumb at this chest. "I was head of transport last year when you illegally brought your pal through the portal. I got fired because of you two."

Van's jaw dropped. The Elders assigned Grigori to deal with the traffic of vichors traveling back-and-forth from Salus Valde and Providence Island. She never thought about the Grigori responsible for monitoring the portal the day she smuggled Paley through, using the Twin Gemstones they had stolen.

"Sorry." The word escaped Van's lips because it was the right thing to say. But Van believed if two teens with no clue managed a travel-through on his watch, perhaps his being fired was a good thing. "You're here now. In a suit. The Elders must've re-hired you for something."

He snorted. "Yeah, crowd control. I'm here to help during Jaychund weekend. I'm headed back to Salus Valde tomorrow. To sit at a desk, doing paperwork for the rest of my life."

"What did you mean by 'what they did to her'? Who?"

"Don't play innocent with me."

Van stared blankly.

"Miss Nutting," he said.

Van saw the look of enlightenment spread across his face as he correctly figured out no one would fill in a sixteen-year-old on important secrets, even if she was the Anchoress. Although Van was pretty sure he didn't know this last part.

"The Elders excommunicated her as a punishment for telling you about the Twin Gemstones and how to use them to transport a terrigen through the portal."

His words hit Van hard. She and Paley had both choked under the pressure of Uxa's interrogation last year, and they confessed Miss Nutting had helped them.

"Miss Nutting sold her beauty salon. She went to the mainland for an extended vacation." Even as Van said it, she knew it didn't sound right. *Why was I so ready to believe it before?* Miss Nutting would never again set foot on the island. Van's stomach sickened over it.

"I was lucky in comparison." He seemed to warm up to Van. "The desk job is really more of a demotion. Once a Grigori, always a Grigori. I still maintain the status of wearing a suit." He straightened his right hand and made a sideways figure eight motion in front of his chest. "Thank-the-light-and-all-that-is-good."

A gesture Van recognized as one performed by orthodox Lodians.

Keen on getting more information, she asked, "Can you tell me about the—"

"Gotta go." His eyes darted beyond Van. His friendly tone came to an abrupt stop. "Take care of yourself." He took off in the opposite direction of the main street.

Van twisted around to glimpse two men in black suits disappearing into the busy road.

"Damn suits again."

All these government-types weren't on the island for Jaychund. Something was brewing under the surface. She wondered if it involved her next mission.

This time she wouldn't make any stops no matter what, and again, headed to Uxa's office. The long walk to the reservation didn't bother Van. Top-level Grigori knew she carried the Anchoress bloodline and now allowed her onto the reservation without restriction. Last year, she had to sneak through the woods behind her house to get there. She passed through the security checkpoint with no problems.

Van reached the familiar cluster of three interconnected buildings known as the complex that housed the island's government. Van knew little about the flat, rectangular structure called Providence Island Research Facility.

The domed building, or the House of Lacus, she knew well. It held the portal and the elevator she took to her special classes. The tallest building, called Marble Hall, was filled with offices, including Uxa's.

Van rushed into the waiting room on the third floor.

Uxa's secretary popped up from her seat.

"Hi Creenelia," Van said without stopping. "Uxa in?"

"Uh-ah. She's, uh," Creenelia sputtered. "You're early. Your appointment isn't until later this evening."

She always got flustered around Van. Probably intimidated by Van's high-status and special privileges with Uxa. She had probably guessed Van carried the Anchoress bloodline.

"Let me check." Creenelia picked up the phone basically for show, knowing Van had no intention of stopping to wait.

Van burst into Uxa's office and stopped short, startled by the suit, who sat in a chair across from Uxa. He twisted around at Van's brash entrance.

She gathered her wits and marched over to the man. "Who are you? Why are you here?"

He grinned, but said nothing.

Uxa rose from her desk chair and said with a composed demeanor, as usual, "Vanessa, may I introduce you to the terrigen ambassador to the Living World? Ladd Kasey."

Van narrowed her eyes at the man. "Vanessa Cross." Her ingrained etiquette took over and Van extended her hand for the terrigen custom of shaking, rather than the Living World's custom of clasping of wrists.

"Oh, I know who you are." Ladd rose and eagerly pumped Van's hand.

"What brings you to our island, Ladd?"

"Ambassador Kasey," Uxa corrected.

"No, no. No fuss. Ladd is fine." He continued grinning and staring at Van.

Van's eyes darted to Uxa. "This is a security breach." Being HG, or Head of the Grigori, Uxa knew the Grigori's job involved keeping the portal a secret from terrigens.

"Come," Uxa said. "Let us take a walk."

Uxa wore her standard issue reservation Elder uniform, a tunic-styled sky blue ensemble with silver edgings and exaggerated shoulders, with a matching cape that fluttered as she moved. It always impressed Van how the blue color enhanced Uxa's black skin and dark blond hair, always worn scraped back into a long braid.

The trio walked in silence down a hall dotted with closed doors. Van had a bunch of questions and Ladd held in so many he looked like a damn about to burst. Taking a cue from Uxa's warning glances, they both kept quiet.

Van had never ventured this deep into the complex. They came to a metal door. Uxa placed her palm onto a scanner and then allowed a red laser to scan her eyes. The door clicked, and they entered the research facility.

Van's curiosity bubbled. With the terrigen ambassador there, she had deduced the men in suits were connected to the research facility.

A different vibe flowed in this building than in Marble Hall and the House of Lacus. The latter two structures were gorgeous, efficient, and designed to please visitors. This room had dull yellow painted concrete brick walls, lay-in ceilings hanging gloomily overhead, and worn metal cabinets lining two walls.

A sea of depressing-looking cubicles confined workers like human-sized lobster traps and occupied most of the open floor plan. Dreary illumination coming from the rectangular, flush mount ceiling lights didn't help matters. This clunky, inefficient, utilitarian building was no doubt designed by terrigens, for terrigens.

Uxa allowed Van to soak up the inner workings of the facility for a moment before saying, "Ambassador Kasey is a member of the Brotherhood of the Magic Circle."

Van glanced at her questioningly.

"They're a secret group of powerful men who operate outside the terrigens' government."

"We know about the portal, the demon problem in the Earth World," Ambassador Kasey interjected, "and about the Grigori's work."

"The Brotherhood controls and influences every aspect of the terrigens' society," Uxa said.

"The Elders of the mainland," Van quipped.

"More than the mainland." Ambassador Kasey snickered. "The entire Earth World."

Van's interest piqued. "Does the President of the United States know about us? The island?"

"We've informed some high-level members of the US government about demons and the Living World." Ambassador Kasey bobbed his head.

The cubicle workers paid no attention to the trio as they moved through the drab room.

The ambassador continued, "Most of our top government officials already know because they're members of the Brotherhood."

Van's eyes widened. "You fix the elections?"

Ambassador Kasey shifted his body, looking uncomfortable. "Er... mostly, we place our own people in the seats. Yes."

Van remained dumbfounded as she entered an expansive room. Several semi-circle rows of desks faced a curved wall covered with video monitors. A good portion of them broadcasted TV news channels from all over the world, some monitored the island. Others displayed screens filled with changing numbers and line charts, reminding Van of securities exchanges.

People dressed in suits, mostly men of varying ethnicities, sat at the desks busily typing on their keyboards while staring at their desktop computer screens, or glancing at the wall monitors. They chatted on headsets with intensity and concentration as if their work meant life or death.

Van gritted her teeth in annoyance. Not because of the surveillance, but because they got *mainland TV*! Access to all the channels!

Van's family could afford to buy a hundred times the equipment in this room, yet the TV in Mt. Hope Manor only broadcast three Elder-approved channels that went in and out depending on the weather. The entire island experienced the same thing. Nobody complained, though, besides the kids and teens. Most adults rarely watched TV, and many families didn't have televisions by choice, claiming reduced dependence on technology was part of the charm of living on the island.

"How are you getting this great reception?" Van asked.

One suit near Van twisted around in his chair, removed his headset, and responded. "The residents and businesses on the townie side of the island get bad reception because this is a place mostly in-between both worlds."

The suit realized he answered a teenager and furrowed his brow. He glanced at the ambassador.

Ambassador Kasey nodded, giving the suit the go-ahead.

"The island is part-magical, part-structural," the suit continued in his monotone voice. "The magic used to hide the island while in the

Earth World creates interference, even when we're in the Living World."

Van's mouth formed an "O" from this staggering bit of news. "That's why excommunicated islanders can never find their way back. The island hides by changing locations between the worlds, kind of like a cloak."

The suit nodded. "The protective magic also makes the island unable to be navigated. Unless our Grigori give the captain coordinates."

"And it's not on any maps," the ambassador added. "The Brotherhood saw to that."

"You get so many channels." Van gaped at the TVs in awe. "We never get that many, even when the reception is good."

"The island's TV network runs on a loop." The ambassador snickered. "It's programmed to rerun shows and movies approved by the Elders as if it's broadcasting."

Van glared at Uxa. "You control what we watch?"

"For the good of the cause," Ambassador Kasey said, answering for Uxa. "You're lucky she lets you watch TV at all. If it were up to the Brotherhood, the townies would get nothing."

"Why is the reception in this room so good?" Van asked the suit. "This is part of the island, too."

"In the complex, we get our power from the Universal Energy Grid. A magic-based connection to the Living World that controls our frequencies. It holds the island's vibrational frequency steady when it moves back and forth between worlds. Otherwise, all us terrigens would be dead from the increased frequency."

"By power, you mean electricity?" Van asked. "Because our lights flicker on and off all the time."

"We don't use electricity from the mainland," the suit said. "The power in the complex comes from the grid. Anything that runs on electricity on most of the island is sort of battery operated."

"*Sort-of* battery operated?" Van raised her brow.

"Your lights flicker because your electrical power comes from a type of crystal gemstone that acts like a battery. Each device must be reconfigured to work with the gemstone to create an electricity-like effect."

"Is that why our internet is so bad?"

"There's no internet on the island," the ambassador said.

Van put her hands on her hips. "We have internet."

Though, now that Van thought about it, she had learned how to use the internet in the computer lab at Canterbury Bells. None of her friends, or anyone she knew, had a home computer, a laptop, a smartphone, or any other device found in homes on the mainland.

"What you're accessing is an *intra*net disguised as an internet." The ambassador grinned, as if proud of this little trick.

Stunned, Van looked at Uxa for confirmation.

Uxa nodded. "No one is allowed to contact anyone off island unless it is authorized by a Grigori or an Elder."

"Or the Brotherhood," the ambassador interjected.

"So you can control the narrative, like with the TV shows." As Van processed all this new information, more things made sense. "That's why the Elders discourage use of electronics and tell us to live more dependently on nature."

"One reason," Uxa said.

A nearby landline phone rang.

The suit swiveled back to face his desk and snatched the handset.

"Is his phone connected to the mainland?" Van hadn't even noticed the landline phones on the suits' desks before one rang.

The islanders used phones that looked like landline telephones, but the Inter-Island Connect only operated between the residents and businesses on the island. They couldn't dial any off island phone numbers.

"The Grigori monitor all the Earth World Security agents' work," Uxa said. "They are given access to lines connected to top officials in the United States and to other countries' leaders, and to Lodestar Station."

"Here, smartphones aren't smart." The ambassador snickered. "They're dumb. Don't work. There's too much interference from the magic. That's why we need to use landlines. But the Grigori have an acceptable replacement for smartphones. They're called multi-tracks."

"We do not allow members of the Brotherhood or the EWS agents to touch MTs," Uxa hastily added. "They are only used by Grigori."

"So this building, the research facility, is where the EWS agents do what? Spy on us? Spy on the mainland? What?" Van asked.

"It is where the agents and Grigori congregate and work together to keep the Earth World safe from demons," Uxa said.

"The Grigori take orders from the Brotherhood?" Van's mouth gaped in disbelief.

"While we are operating in the Earth World, yes. We are considered EWS agents to their government." Uxa seemed miffed to admit this.

Van could see why. These people had none of the finesse, physical strength, or elegance of the Grigori. They looked like pale, overfed oafs.

"EWS agents officially fall under a special branch of Homeland Security." The ambassador stifled a cough. "Unofficially, they work for the Brotherhood."

"The team you see here monitors the entire Earth World," Uxa explained further.

Ambassador Kasey said, "Rest assured, the Brotherhood is here to help. We'll get those demons under control yet."

Van noticed a tenseness to Uxa's shoulders.

"Um, Uxa. Can I talk to you for a sec?" Van glanced at Ambassador Kasey. "Privately."

The two walked to a quiet area near the wall of the large room.

"I'm unclear. Who has higher authority, the Brotherhood or the Elders?" Van eyed the busy EWS agents, her mind already spinning with tactics on how to get rid of them.

"The Elders own Providence Island. We have ultimate control. However, it would be infinitely more difficult to keep the island a secret from terrigens if we did not get help from the United States government. The island's classification as a tribal reservation and national wildlife preserve is because of the Brotherhood."

Van narrowed her eyes at Uxa. "Have you told them the secrets of how to use the portal?"

"Of course not!"

Van recalled the suits she had overheard at the Dock Side Cafe. "It's obvious they're using us. Spying on us and trying to uncover the island's secrets. To figure out our technology, and to steal resources from the Living World. Once they do, they'll exploit the knowledge for profit, regardless of the damage it could do to both our worlds."

Instead of being angry, Uxa appeared pleased. "The Brotherhood has assigned top quantum physicists, cellular biologists, engineers, and a host of others who all secretly tried to unravel our portal technology, genetic differences, and to figure out ways to mine the resources abundant in the Living World. They are also trying to learn how to make energy weapons by using our gemstone technology."

"You're allowing them to *dissect* us?" Van didn't understand why Uxa remained calm and smug.

"They have failed." Uxa grinned. "And will never succeed, not as long as they continue to vibrate at such a low frequency. They are like rats on a running wheel. They can run as fast as they want but will get nowhere."

Uxa placed a hand on Van's back and applied a bit of pressure, telling her it was time for them to head back to the ambassador.

"The Grigori stick to eliminating demons who wreak havoc in the Earth World," Uxa said. "We leave the security of the island to the Brotherhood and their agents, and let them deal with the bureaucracy of the mainland government. It is a good balance, and we work in harmony together."

Uxa could make all the excuses she wanted, but Van still didn't like it.

"You are thinking of the Brotherhood as the enemy," Uxa said. "But the opposite could also be true. They could be our ally."

"Pfft."

"Vanessa, you must try to see the Brotherhood differently."

How could an enemy be an ally? Uxa had gone berserk.

Uxa grabbed Van's arm, clamping it tightly, and stopped their walk.

She roughly turned Van, so they were face to face and whispered fiercely, "Vanessa, you must learn to combine both good and bad to form a new synthesis, if not, stagnation will occur. You will be like water in a collection pond, motionless and stuck."

Before Van could retort, loud blaring sounds echoed throughout the room. Red lights flashed across the ceiling.

Ambassador Kasey came bounding over, cheeks flushed.

"What is it?" Uxa asked.

"That damn speedboat is back," the ambassador said. He took them over to view a large rectangular monitor.

A speedboat bobbed in the ocean. The same one Van had seen earlier while doing yoga.

"Your magic hiding the island isn't working." The ambassador's eyes bulged. "Fix it."

Van grimaced out of compassion for Uxa. The HG already had the Balish Council claiming her Grigori weren't doing their job. Now the Brotherhood insinuated the same thing.

If the ambassador was right about the magic on the island being faulty, then he just validated Van's concerns. The Brotherhood and their interference were destroying the fabric that held together the magic of Providence Island and the Living World. *Why couldn't Uxa see this?*

Everyone in the room watched helplessly as the speedboat reached the rocky coastline. Driven by a figure appearing blurry on the screen.

"How did this guy find us?" a suit asked.

Ambassador Kasey huffed. "Bring him in."

CHAPTER 8

"Sir, it's Myles Dinkle," a suit holding a handset said to Ambassador Kasey.

"Who's Myles Dinkle?" Van asked.

"Only the most persistent, snooping terrigen alive," the ambassador grumbled. "The number one thorn in our side."

"He is at the top of the EWS's watch list." Uxa frowned.

Van stared at the monitor. Four suits shoved a man in his early thirties into a military buggy.

To Van, the buggies looked like a golf cart had mated with a jeep. They were specially made vehicles used for transportation on the island. The non-military buggies were painted in bright colors. The military ones were black, boxy, and sturdy, giving them a sinister appearance. Whenever one drove near Van, she ducked out of sight.

"He's a nuisance. Nothing more." The ambassador's tone implied hope rather than fact.

"How did he get on the watch list?" Van asked. "Has he tried to reach the island before?"

"Myles operates a conspiracy theory website," a nearby suit said, holding his stare on the monitor. "Unfortunately for us, he's posted accurate data about Providence Island, the portal, and the Living World."

"Bah." The ambassador waved his hand. "Mostly junk. He thinks the US government created the portal."

"Recently, he has gotten an increase in followers," Uxa said. "His life's mission is to find proof and expose our world."

"He's recruiting more and more terrigens to help him in his quest," the suit said. "His followers agree the government is hiding a dark secret. They believe Myles is a crusader trying to protect their world. He's on the right track, which makes him a threat to the island."

"How does he know about our world at all?" Van asked.

"We'll find out once they bring him in," the ambassador said darkly. "How the hell did he find the island in the first place?"

"Timing," answered the suit. "Myles happened upon the island as it shifted out from behind the membrane-like veil. The island's moving on its own due to a malfunction in its magical protection."

"He's searched for us so many times in the past," another suit added, "he was bound to find us by dumb luck, eventually."

Ambassador Kasey's face flushed red. "How is this happening, Uxa? I need answers."

Uxa calmly replied. "The increase in violence, desecration of the environment, and economic turmoil in your world is interrupting the magic protecting Providence Island. We are losing the ability to cloak it from the Earth World's navigation systems and the ability to move its location from one world to the other."

The ambassador waggled his fist. "Do your job and fix the magic thing. My ass is on the line!"

"*My* job?" Uxa asked, unable to hide her annoyance. "You are the terrigen ambassador to the Living World. If you had done *your* job, this would not be happening right now."

Ambassador Kasey muttered to himself as he clustered with several suits to devise a next-step strategy.

While they were alone, Van asked Uxa, "What exactly is his job?"

Uxa kept her eyes on the ambassador as she answered Van.

"The Brotherhood and the Elders decided the terrigens needed protecting not only from unseen evil creatures but also from themselves. So, the Brotherhood recruited a terrigen ambassador to the Living World about two decades ago. The ambassador's job was to come here and learn about the delicate balance of our worlds and then go back and promote peace in the Earth World."

"Who was it? What happened to him?" Van assumed Kasey wasn't the first one.

"Decades ago, the Brotherhood fixed the US Presidential election so a top member of the Brotherhood would win. They saw value in his running mate, a good man, a terrigen, and they recruited him to become the first ambassador."

"As a sort of consolation prize? Sounds like they felt guilty." Van had pegged the powerful men in the Brotherhood as valuing only money, power, and control. It surprised her to hear about a display of empathy by the group.

"He proved a perfect candidate. He was politically influential and had served in office. The Brotherhood wanted someone the public already trusted and respected to spread the word of peace. Alvin Gormond accepted without hesitation."

"Al Gormond?" Van took in the enormity of this newest bit of information. "I'm not surprised he accepted. It meant he'd learn all our secrets."

"Exactly," Uxa said. "However, only having access to the island dissatisfied him. He insisted on traveling through the portal."

"Why was that a problem?" In his position, Van would want to see the Living World too. "It would've inspired a more passionate message about protecting the Earth World."

"We resisted allowing his travel-through," Uxa said. "We tried bringing a terrigen US President through the portal in the 1980s. Back in those days, they briefed presidents who were not already part of the Brotherhood. Afterward, he insisted on seeing the Living World. As you know, the only way to transport a terrigen through the portal is by using the Twin Gemstones. It turned out poorly. The portal rejected him and he suffered severe brain damage resulting in Alzheimer's disease."

"You're talking about—?" Van's jaw slackened.

Uxa nodded glumly. "That is why the Brotherhood does not brief the POTUS anymore. Anyway, we finally agreed to send Ambassador Gormond to Lodestar, since the situation in the Earth World was so dire. Even back then, the terrigens were on the verge of self-destruction. Like you said, we believed sending him to the Living World would make him a more convincing messenger."

Van struggled to recall any information about Al Gormond.

"We successfully brought the ambassador through the portal to Lodestar Station and showed him around Lodestar Village," Uxa said. "He returned without brain damage. He went back to the mainland with a message of peace and ecological balance, to be 'green,' to help protect their planet."

"But something happened with him, if I remember correctly."

"Yes." Uxa nodded grimly. "A few years later, Ambassador Gormond spoke of that which must be kept secret. He told a handful of top government officials everything. However, unbeknown to him, all of them were members of the Brotherhood. They discredited the ambassador publicly. It didn't take long before he agreed to stop talking, so there was no need to eliminate him. Oh, but they were close."

Van heard the shuffling of feet.

Wild grunts echoed in the room, coming from a man that looked on the brink of insanity.

"I knew it! I knew this place existed." Myles staggered past Van and the others, handcuffed and flanked by six EWS agents. His black hair was an uncombed mess, his hazel eyes crazed.

Van noticed he wore a gold bracelet with an ornamental design around a half moon.

"Where're they taking him?" She asked Uxa as the agents shoved Myles through a door.

"Let us leave them to do their job." Uxa walked toward the exit, the opposite direction the EWS agents had taken Myles. "Come. Let us discuss your mission."

Van followed but twisted around, taking one last look at the closed door. A sudden awareness encroached on her thoughts. Her current situation and Myles's were eerily similar.

Both of them were obsessed with getting answers and with protecting their worlds. Both of them were being taken away without a choice.

And both of their fates hung in the hands of people beyond their control.

CHAPTER 9

"I am sorry you had to witness that," Uxa said to Van as they entered her office in Marble Hall.

"Sorry? It's her fault Myles found us." Tussel Fynn leaped from his chair as they entered. He had been waiting in Uxa's office for his boss's return. "The ambassador told me." He flicked his head at the IIC phone on Uxa's desk.

Fynn dressed similarly to Uxa, except for a darker blue uniform. He had a mop of curly blond hair and a crooked nose. If he didn't act like such a jerk, he would be cute. Despite being impressed with Van's retrieval of the Coin of Creation last summer, Fynn's attitude continued to convey the message Van was unworthy of carrying the Anchoress bloodline.

"*My* fault?" Van's hand snapped to her chest for emphasis. "How so?"

"Your presence. Your Anchoress light. It's raising the island's vibrational frequency and drawing terrigens here." Fynn's words carried a tone of hostility. "The increase in Myles's followers is resulting in more and more terrigens searching to find the island."

"Darkness always seeks to destroy the light." Van understood his point.

"I'm worried." His tone softened once Van agreed with him.

Uxa sat at her desk. "Our problems run much deeper than Myles." She indicated for Van to take a seat.

By the grim look on Uxa's face, Van would need to sit down before hearing what she had to say next.

"Last year, Solana conjured demons by tapping into the power of her 'Dark Master,' as you call it. We have classified this master demon as a Class III, one strong enough to reach our world. But *how* did this master demon gain enough strength to reach Solana in the Living World?" Uxa rested her clasped hands on her desktop. "The terrigens' negativity, although strong, is not enough to generate a demon with that kind of power. It is different from any we have encountered before. I fear it is gaining more strength."

"If Solana's Dark Master is hiding somewhere in the Earth World, I'll find it." Van mentally packed her bags for a trip to the mainland, finally able to work in the field as a full-fledged Grigori.

"No." Uxa flattened her palms and leaned forward, her eyes on Van. "I have a more important task for you. I need you to check a seal during this Alignment."

"A seal? In the Living World?" She had expected Uxa to send her on a demon hunting mission, but Van liked seals. They were cute. Especially the fluffy, white snow seals with their dark, round eyes. "Does my mission have something to do with Lilla?"

She hoped not. Last year Van had met Lilla's sister, Lady Loka, the Elemental who guarded the Coin of Creation with her wily traps and monsters. Van dreaded having to face another Elemental.

"Lilla?" Fynn raised his brow.

"Lilla, the Elemental Guardian of All Animals," Van said.

Fynn shook his head. "I'm not following."

"Not that kind of seal," Uxa said.

Fynn rolled his eyes at Van's display of stupidity. "You thought she meant a *seal*? Not the animal—"

Van's cheeks flared.

"Fynn, enough," Uxa said, cutting him off. She turned to Van.

"Three seals secure the veil that separates the Living World and the Earth World. I fear there is a crack in one."

"Do we know what caused the crack? Is it because I connected to my Anchoress light?" Van's stomach knotted.

Her ancestral curse was no secret. It was the sole reason her father illegally went out of bounds the night Solana's demons murdered him. The curse originated a thousand years ago, around the time of the Dark War and, to this day, loomed over Van like a storm cloud. In a wild rage, her ancestor Amaryl accidentally cursed her family line. Van used this story as another reason to suppress her feelings. Based on Amaryl's history, emotions were dangerous and led to misfortune.

"An increase in vibrational frequencies in either world would not crack the seals." Uxa's eyes expressed deep contemplation. "But there is so much negativity building in the Earth World, I believe the pressure fractured one of them." Uxa looked grim. "I fear Solana's Dark Master may be strong enough to break through the damaged seal and reach our world."

"Then all the demons in the Earth World will follow," Fynn added, tensely.

"As I understand it, even if demons break through the seal, they won't be able to survive in the Living World," said Van. "Their vibration is too low."

"We believe the negativity of the Earth World is seeping through the crack, lowering the vibrational frequency in our world to match that of the demons." Fynn shifted anxiously. "If the master demon, or any demon, breakthrough, their presence would trigger more negativity, eventually lowering the vibration in the Living World to where demons could survive."

Uxa left her chair and began pacing. "The first seal is in the House of Lacus. It is the portal. I have checked, and there is no crack. Now, I need you and your team to check the second seal. You will head west."

"Why west?" Van asked. "Why. the second seal and not the third? How many seals are there? Shouldn't I check them all?"

Fynn snorted. "Why is working with you always like swimming upstream?"

Uxa threw Fynn a warning look to behave and then answered Van, "Based on information gathered at Lodestar, I have noticed a pocketed increase in negative vibrational frequencies in the west. It is also the location of the second seal." Uxa stopped pacing. Her demeanor turned even more serious. "Vanessa, I need you and your team to mend the crack before demons gain enough power to break it and reach our world. Do you accept?"

"On one condition." If Van couldn't go to the mainland and fight demons, then going to the Living World would have to serve her own agenda.

Fynn snorted again.

"Which is?" Uxa asked.

"I want to use the Coin to find a counter-curse." Van's father believed the solution lay hidden somewhere in the Living World and she needed to find it before her luck got worse. But the curse gave Van more than misfortune. It caused her to die during childbirth. As the Anchoress, her duty included passing down the Anchoress bloodline to her first-born female child. She deemed finding a counter-curse a critical objective to accomplish during this Alignment, more so than looking for a potential crack in the second seal.

"Oh, please," Fynn said. "You're not planning on having a baby on the trip, are you?"

Van couldn't decide what infuriated her more. That Fynn had called her mission a 'trip,' or suggesting she was weak enough to let romance get in the way of duty. She took a breath to calm down and then said, "Removing it will make me a stronger warrior. It's imperative to the safety and security of my people."

"Our people," Uxa corrected.

"And Brux wants to find Daisy," Van added.

His determination to find his sister was driven by emotion and would lead to disaster. But she hoped to use Brux's search for Daisy as an excuse to spy on Ferox. Van wanted to make sure Ferox wasn't following the path of his sister and conjuring demons.

"Vanessa, I sent a team to find Daisy." Uxa's expression remained stoic. "I believe her to be dead."

"Find her body then." Van threw her hands in the air, exasperated. "The Coin will show me the fastest way to the seal, then I can use it to find Daisy—dead or *alive*—and then search for the counter-curse. The Coin may be the only hope for me to remove this damn curse." Van took a deep breath and let it out slowly. "The Earth World is where the demons are. That's where I should be. On the mainland fighting demons to make sure none get strong enough to break the seal."

"We have Grigori trained to do that," Uxa said with some impatience. "You are not ready to fight demons in the Earth World or anyplace else. You are certainly not emotionally ready to use the Coin again."

"Pfft."

Uxa's expression grew stern. "Vanessa, you must integrate your feelings about your father's and Solana's deaths. Process the pain you are feeling. It is the only way you can become a competent warrior."

"Telling me I can't use the Coin is an emotion-based decision on *your* part. The wrong decision." As Van stewed, she wondered about Uxa's real motive for not letting Van use the Coin.

For years, high-level information leaked from Lodestar to the Moors. Yet, the spy remained a mystery. Everyone thought it was Van's father until she uncovered the truth about his innocence. The culprit who framed him—Solana.

"Until you learn how to control your power," Uxa said, "you will not be ready to use the Coin."

Van prickled with annoyance. She had gone back and forth, suspecting Uxa was the spy. Right now, she thought yes.

"Why can't you send someone else to check the seal? Like Pernilla."

"Pernilla is part of your team," Uxa said.

Van's irritation skyrocketed.

Fynn added, "All members of your team—"

"Must stick together," Van continued his sentence, rolling her eyes, "because of the collective balance of skills. Blah blah blah…"

"I would go with you if I could," Uxa said, trying to temper the situation. "But we have not found the device your father used to throw off the Balish squawker system. The Balish would track me the second I crossed out of the Salus Valde boundary."

Uxa began pacing again. "You must use your time wisely. Tensions remain high between the Lodians and the Balish."

"They're still trying to overthrow Manik's law?" Van asked. "I mean, the part that magically protects Salus Valde from being taken over by the Balish?"

Uxa stopped pacing and turned toward Van. "The Balish continue to gather evidence, hoping to prove we have violated the law so they can have it overturned, yes. Their primary focus is still to convince the Elementals that the Grigori are not doing their job."

"A cracked seal will only help further their cause," Fynn said.

"The Balish know that I'm real and have access to a magical weapon—the Coin," said Van. "They know I'm underage and can legally go out of bounds—"

"Not anymore." Fynn's lips turned downward.

Van paled. "What do you mean?"

"The Balish Council appealed to the Elementals," Uxa said. "They asked to change Article 57 of Manik's law, the section that allows children under the age of eighteen to leave the boundary of Salus Valde. The Balish claimed there is no reason for our Anchoress to go into Balish occupied territory now that she has established herself."

"They won?" Van's confidence—and stomach—plummeted.

Uxa nodded. "The Elementals approved the decree. The Lodian's Anchoress may not leave the boundary of Salus Valde."

"So how will I get around the squawkers?" This added a measurable difficulty to the task.

Uxa's eyes sparkled. "The Elementals didn't agree to track the Anchoress."

"So I can leave the Salus Valde boundary without the Balish being alerted." Van inwardly hid her relief.

"But if you're caught outside our boundary," Fynn said, "the Balish will assume we're seeking to make allies of other tribes. They already believe we're in cahoots with the terrigens, planning to rise against the Balish rule, in a foretold war they call Solmor."

"Right," Van said. "Their version of Dishora."

Fynn gasped; Uxa tensed. Apparently, neither cared for the comparison.

"If you are caught, the Balish Council will claim it an act of war. An obvious violation of Manik's law." Uxa paused, deep in thought. Then continued. "If you are found on their soil in possession of the Coin, which is a known powerful weapon... they will have won."

"But the Balish don't know my identity," Van said. "Or that I'm Goustav's descendent and the true heir to the Balish kingdom. That bit of information died with Solana."

"The Balish know the Anchoress exists," Uxa said. "And the spy in Lodestar remains a mystery. We have to assume the Moors know your identity, even the Balish Council. This will make your mission that much more dangerous."

"Wait." Van tensed. "I haven't agreed to check the seal."

"Mending a cracked seal is the best way for you to protect your people," Uxa said. "You must go."

Although, earlier, Uxa had asked Van if she accepted the mission. Now it seemed Van had no choice. "Do you at least know the exact location?"

Uxa shook her head, looking as if she had failed.

The door to Uxa's office burst open. Ambassador Kasey arrived, looking flustered.

Uxa and Fynn straightened, standing alert and ready for action.

"Maren's illness," he said. "It's worse than we thought. And it's spreading."

CHAPTER 10

"Medical is using colloidal silver to slow progression of the illness," Ambassador Kasey said.

"Are more children getting sick?" Uxa stiffened.

"Eight more have come down with the same symptoms. All terrigens, all on the island."

Ambassador Kasey turned to Van. "We have to mend the seal to prevent an outbreak in the Living World."

Van's hunch of something more than appendicitis afflicted Maren had proven correct. "What does Maren's sickness have to do with the seal?"

"The illness will find its way through the crack and reach the Living World," the ambassador said.

"Right now, it seems to be contained on the island." Uxa shifted her eyes, deep in thought.

Van asked the ambassador, "You're using medicines to get my classmates better? You *can* get them better, right?"

The ambassador glanced at the floor, then looked at Van. "None of our antibiotics are working. Colloidal silver will ward off the virus, but not for long. The situation is critical."

"Why aren't the children on the mainland getting sick?" Fynn asked.

"Perhaps the terrigens on the mainland are immune." Uxa leaned back against her desk and crossed her arms.

Ambassador Kasey shifted back and forth. "Well, uh—"

Uxa narrowed her eyes at the ambassador. "Yes? What is it?"

"It seems," he cleared his throat, "for the past several years, common bacteria in the Earth World have been mutating and becoming unresponsive to antibiotic treatment. Viruses have also been getting stronger, new strains discovered every year. First, we attributed this to adaptation. The bacteria and viruses getting smarter." He cleared his throat again. "Now, we believe our superbugs are getting stronger because of the increased number of demons."

Uxa's nostrils flared. "You. Kept. This. From. Me?"

Ambassador Kasey took a step back. "I, uh, didn't think it was important. We have crazy viruses all the time. Got top men working on it. It's under control. Nothing to worry about."

Uxa took a deep breath, probably to keep herself from throttling the ambassador. "This illness… you think the demons are getting so strong they have generated an illness that is afflicting Providence Island's terrigens?"

The ambassador gave his head a quick bob. "Yes."

"Why is Maren's illness different from the mainlander's viruses?" Van asked.

"We think the virus mutated, raised its vibrational frequency and changed form," the ambassador said.

"That's why it's here," Fynn said. "It would move toward the highest frequencies in the Earth World—the island."

"The illness travels to the easiest, closest match first, terrigens. They vibrate at the lowest frequencies on the island," Uxa said. "Then, once it gains strength, it will spread to those with higher vibrational frequencies."

"Same as demons," Van said, proud she understood the concept. "This illness isn't afflicting the mainland terrigens the same way because they're vibrating at a lower frequency than the virus."

"You're saying the disease will get stronger?" the ambassador asked.

Uxa nodded. "It went to the children first because they are innately more open to new frequencies and offer less resistance. The virus will gain strength and spread to terrigen adults. Eventually it will afflict all vichors."

Fynn tensed. "If the virus is seeking higher vibrational frequencies, then it's headed straight for our world."

"It's imperative we contain this illness on the island," Uxa said.

"If the Balish catch word of this, it will fuel their case for voiding Manik's law." Fynn wrung his hands. "The Grigori not doing their job—"

"Ugh," Van said. "Don't they ever stop it with this takeover-Salus-Valde stuff?"

"No," Fynn and the ambassador said at the same time.

"Our Grigori will immediately increase their efforts to reduce the demon population in the Earth World." Uxa turned to the ambassador. "Your people need to find a cure for the children in critical condition." She turned to Van. "You must mend the second seal."

Van sighed. "How am I supposed to mend this seal?"

"Use your Anchoress magic to connect to the power of the Coin," the ambassador said.

Van brightened. "I get to use the Coin?"

Uxa shook her head. "You are not emotionally equipped to handle the Coin again."

"Yes, yes," the ambassador said, waving his hand dismissively at Uxa. "You've expressed concern about the Anchoress's mental condition. However, the Brotherhood regards her emotionless state as a good thing. We believe it's a sign of maturity."

"I'm not emotionless." Van pouted.

"She is *not* ready." Uxa's entire body tensed. "She is not a weapon you can take out and use at your disposal."

The ambassador tightened his jaw, apparently sick of Uxa's menacing stares and ready to stand his ground. "Vanessa has the qualifications and experience to mend the seal." He curled his hands into fists. "She *will* use the Coin."

The moment had arrived when Van would discover who had more authority. Uxa, who spoke on behalf of the Elders, or the terrigens' Brotherhood.

Uxa remained quiet for what seemed like a long time. Then her eyes darted to Van. "I don't want you using it to search for Daisy's body or to look for a counter-curse."

The ambassador's entire body relaxed. "The Coin will show you the correct path. I'm sure you can connect to your powers to get the specifics on how to mend the seal." He patted Van on the shoulder.

"Could you be any more vague?" Van muttered as a way of hiding her newfound hesitation.

Ambassador Kasey and the Brotherhood's approval for her using the Coin made Van wary. She reconsidered Uxa's concern. Maybe Uxa was right. She wasn't emotionally ready to handle the Coin again. A wave of uncertainty washed over Van, making her sick to her stomach.

When she had used the Coin last year, its power had overtaken her, resulting in damage to her soul when she used it to kill Solana. If Van remained incapable of handling the Coin's power, it would corrupt her soul even more. She would be driven to insanity, like her ancestor Amaryl, which would lead her to worshipping darkness. She would end up evil like Solana.

"You must prepare," the ambassador said, interrupting Van's thoughts. "The Alignment begins at midnight tonight, and you only have a thirty-day window until... the... that monster is released by... who? The Elementals?" He stared at Uxa.

Van had momentarily forgotten about the Quasher. The horrific shadow-wolf that never stopped hunting her. Van rubbed her arms to ward off a chill.

"I guess the Brotherhood's not as informed as you think," Fynn said in response to Ambassador Kasey's bumbling.

"Tell me, then." The ambassador stretched his palm toward Fynn to emphasize his words. "What exactly is this *Quasher?*"

"Before recorded time," Fynn said, basking in superiority, "the Creator sent the Elementals—deities—to the land of humans to instruct them on the ways of the light."

The ambassador sighed. "Really? Going back to the beginning of time?"

Fynn ignored him and continued. "Instead, against the will of the Creator, the Elementals frolicked with humans and inadvertently formed the Lodian race, including the Anchoress. Since humans seemed to be doomed to failure, the Creator allowed the Anchoress to exist, along with her Items of Creation. These weapons were to be used by the Anchoress to restore order in the worlds when necessary. To give humanity a shot at surviving."

"And the Quasher?" The ambassador impatiently tapped his foot.

"The Quasher is the balancing force of the Anchoress," Fynn said. "Formed by nature at the time of her birth. Upon its creation, the beast was immediately bound by the magic of the Elementals to protect their daughter so she, the Anchoress, could live in peace."

"Because of the Elementals' misbehavior," Uxa interjected, "the Creator banished them to live forever on the physical plane."

"Mt. Altithronia, to be exact," Fynn said. "The Elementals didn't like this one bit. Angered by the seductive nature of humanity, they tied a condition to their magical containment of the Quasher."

"The Anchoress must keep her bloodline pure of the contamination of humanity, to mate only with descendants of Elementals, Lodians," Uxa said. "The purer the bloodline, the better."

"If the Anchoress brakes the purity of her bloodline," Fynn added, "the magic binding the Quasher also breaks."

"This protection ended a thousand years ago," Van said, who didn't like being spoken about as if she wasn't in the room. She was the current Anchoress, after all. "When my ancestor Amaryl, who carried the Anchoress bloodline, frolicked with the Balish Prince Goustav and had a baby."

"It's rumored the Balish are descendants of terrigens," Ambassador Kasey said, raising his eyebrows. "So, Amaryl definitely tainted the Anchoress bloodline." He tsked.

Fynn nodded. "After Amaryl's folly, and knowing from experience how irresponsible humans were, the Elementals took away the Anchoress's protection from the Quasher with a caveat. They created the thirty-day window. During this window, Luxta, as the ancients called it—"

"We call it the Alignment," Van chimed in.

"The magic of the Elementals contains the Quasher," Fynn continued. "This is the only time the Anchoress can safely set foot outside Salus Valde."

"It can't cross into my world? Can it?" Ambassador Kasey sounded nervous. "What keeps it in the Living World?"

"The beast cannot enter Salus Valde," Uxa said. "The Elementals magically protect our land, which means it cannot get to the portal, so it cannot come here."

"During the Alignment, the Quasher can't track the Anchoress," Fynn said.

The ambassador asked Van, "What did you do—or, I should say, what did your ancestors do—to make the beast want you so badly?"

Van shrugged. "My light is a threat to its existence."

"As long as the Anchoress lives, there will always be light in the worlds," Fynn said. "The Quasher hates this."

Ambassador Kasey shook his head, looking sad. "I guess the Anchoress's one great flaw is that she's part human and therefore fallible."

Uxa scowled. "I can take it from here, ambassador."

He bobbed his head, eager to leave. "I'll check on Dinkle's status. Find out what we're going to do with him."

He dashed out of Uxa's office, closing the door behind him.

Uxa turned to Fynn. "Please go update the rest of Vanessa's team."

Fynn gave a compliant nod and scurried from the room to do her bidding.

Uxa unrolled a large parchment on top of her desk. It was a map of the Living World.

"The Coin is with me," she said. "I brought it here so we could use it to confirm the second seal is in the west. I was not going to let you take it but—"

"The Brotherhood," Van finished her sentence.

"No," Uxa said. "Because it is reasonable to let you take it. Because you are certain you need it to complete your mission, and you claim you are ready."

"I am ready," Van lied.

"Use it to find the exact location, nothing else. Practice now, here, and see how you feel."

Uxa held the Coin on a black cloth and extended it to Van.

Overwhelming anxiety surfaced as Van reached to take the shiny gold relic. As soon as it touched her fingertips, she felt a jolt of energy. Van connected to a spiritual pulse cascading back through her entire ancestral line of Anchoresses. The capacity of their blood magic filled Van with hope, wonder, and dedication to the light with such intensity her eyes glistened.

Van's fingers trembled. She dropped the Coin onto the map. Not to find the seal's location, but because the power of her bloodline combined with the ability of the Coin frightened her.

The Coin shifted and pointed to a location on the map.

"Ah," Uxa said. "Location of the second seal—confirmed."

"Are you sure?" Van asked. "I don't think I did it right."

Uxa nodded. "The Coin jumped from your fingers, eager to pinpoint this spot."

"Great." Although Van remained unsure.

Now, after feeling the surge, Van didn't want to use the Coin to complete her mission. She believed Uxa was right; she wasn't capable of handling its power. Finding Daisy, Ferox, and a counter-curse were part of her own agenda and therefore optional. If she felt ready to use the Coin to find them, she would. Otherwise, she'd keep it safely tucked in her pocket.

Van focused on the map and stared in disbelief at the location shown by the Coin. Its triangle design clearly pointed right smack in the middle of a sea.

"Wait a minute," Van said. "The Coin's pointing at the ocean. To a place called the Bottomless Sea."

"That is correct. The seal lies on the seafloor."

"You're telling me *I*," Van swung her index finger to her chest, "have to *swim* to the *bottom* of the *Bottomless* Sea to stitch together a broken seal? Do I have that right?"

"Here." Uxa busily gathered more parchments. "The information in these scrolls will help. Let us figure this out together." She placed them on her desk next to the map, then turned and stretched to reach the top of her bookcase. "We need this reference book."

With Uxa's back to her, Van brushed the Coin with her fingertips to see if she got another jolt.

She didn't, but the Coin vibrated.

It shifted its direction to a different location on the map. To an island called Cortica.

Van squinted at the map. She noticed penciled-in scribbles near the island.

She realized the Coin wasn't pointing to the island of Cortica.

It pointed to a drawing of an ankh accompanied by ancient words Van's Anchoress abilities interpreted as "the Cup of Life."

CHAPTER 11

Uxa turned around, holding the reference book. She dropped it on top of the mess of parchments and scrolls covering her desk, shifting the map.

"Vanessa," Uxa scolded. "Pick that up. Put it somewhere safe." She pointed to the Coin, unconcerned with its change in direction, probably assuming the book had pushed the parchments into the map and moved it.

Van didn't understand why the Coin had moved, so she kept quiet about the Cup of Life.

"Tell me about Cortica," Van said.

"People call it Outlaw Island. It is a dangerous place on the fringes of society. There is no law or order there."

"They're not ruled by the Balish?"

Uxa shook her head. "The Moors have no power in Cortica. The island is full of pirates, cutthroats, and thieves. You will do well to stay away from there and focus on the Bottomless Sea." Uxa stood behind her desk and opened the reference book. "Let us get started."

Van took a seat on the firm, no-nonsense couch near the wall, away from the desk. "Why wait so long?"

Uxa reluctantly raised her nose from the book.

"The seal's been cracked for a while, I would guess," Van said. "Why didn't you tell me earlier that my mission would be to fix it? I've been asking you for almost a year. We could've poured over these documents for months instead of a few hours."

Uxa paused as if scrutinizing Van. Then said, "For security reasons. It is best if you and your teammates do not know your assignment until right before you leave." She slid into her desk chair. "Besides, I was unsure if we were dealing with a cracked seal. I am still not a hundred percent certain."

Van grunted as if accepting Uxa's poor excuse for an explanation. But her mentor's mysterious ways only raised more questions in Van's mind about whether Uxa secretly worked on behalf of the Moors as a spy in Lodestar.

Van's eyelids were already feeling heavy, and she knew she'd get no further explanation from Uxa. She got up and swiped a scroll from Uxa's desk, went back to the couch, and began reading.

They spent hours hashing over the information in the ancient writings until Van couldn't stop yawning. She stared at Uxa with glassy, tired eyes.

Uxa closed the ancient book they had been reading together on the couch. "I think it is best you get some rest. Fynn already informed Iphigenia, along with your other teammates and their parents. Of course, we did not fill the parents in on the details. All they know is their children will be working on a summer project on the reservation for a month."

Van wearily raised from the couch and yawned. "The Alignment begins at midnight. Are we leaving soon?"

"Your journey will be long. You need rest. Be back in my office at five a.m.," Uxa said. "You and your team will do a quick pack and prep and depart shortly thereafter."

Van refused an escort home. She needed time alone to absorb the challenge of facing yet another impossible mission on behalf of Uxa.

When Uxa fussed, Van said, "If I need an escort to walk home safely on Providence Island, then I don't stand a chance of conquering the Bottomless Sea."

Apparently, Uxa couldn't argue with that reasoning and conceded to let Van walk home on her own.

Once Van arrived at Mt. Hope Manor—and after Genie's interrogation—she went straight to her bedroom, took a long shower, and settled into her comfy queen-size bed, exhausted.

Annoyed that she didn't fall asleep right away, Van took a deep, relaxing breath to stop the chatter in her mind. She grabbed one of her pillows, hugged it to her chest, and curled her body around it in a fetal position. She loved the coolness of the smooth sheets pressed against her skin and the softness of the mattress as it cuddled her body.

She neared sleep when a peaceful amethyst mist filled her mind.

Jacynthia, Van said in her mind's eye.

Her spirit guide appeared, complete with amaranthine dress and matching cape, hovering several feet above the ground.

"Hello, my little warrior," Jacynthia said.

What's up? Van's words sounded casual, but they masked her dread. Her mission seemed insurmountable and the Quasher looming the background waiting to pounce didn't help matters. Yet she needed to act like nothing bothered her. To show her true feelings would make her weak.

"The Quasher provides you with an important lesson," Jacynthia said.

What? Why?

"No phenomenon is devoid of its opposite state. Every positive force must be balanced by a negative one. This is part of nature," she said as her waist-length, silvery-white hair flowed in an ethereal breeze. "The Quasher challenges you to exist in an equal state with destructive energy. It teaches you to create harmony between darkness and light. You must accept the duality of all things, even the Self. Make peace with your dark side. By doing so, you aid the will of the Creator."

Okay, sure. Van didn't understand Jacynthia's point and didn't care. The lull of sleep became too intense. She would mull over her spirit guide's words of wisdom tomorrow.

"Shed your mask of perfection and accept your new reality."

Jacynthia's words faded as Van succumbed to a dream state.

In her dream, she and Wiglaf were in a dark hole, a dungeon? No, they were on a ship headed to Cortica, both enveloped by the darkness in the crew's quarters. She watched Wiglaf's little white paws as he stretched and grasped the rung of the ladder leading to the above deck. His coiled tail bobbed as he climbed each step.

"Where're you going?" Van asked in her dream.

His answer filled her mind. "To find the truth."

Wiglaf disappeared above deck into the bright light of day.

THE BLARE of Van's alarm clock abruptly woke her. She shot up in bed, not surprised four a.m. had arrived so soon.

To Van's dismay, Genie and Rummie had woken early too, so they could say their goodbyes, both dressed in pajamas and bathrobes. Van endured their fussing and hovering, counting the minutes until she could break free and head back to Uxa's office at the complex.

"Stop," Van pleaded as they jabbed glazed orange scones at her. "You're going to make me late."

Gratitude surged when Providence Island Taxi pulled into the driveway and honked.

"Be safe," Genie shouted from the front steps of the manor, Rummie by her side.

Van leaped into the backseat of the classic yellow six-seater buggy with her backpack.

"Hey, Urvi."

The driver grunted a hello and stepped on the gas. The jolt of the buggy slammed Van back against the nylon seat.

She twisted around to see Genie and Rummie out of the back window, waving goodbye. She gave them a half-hearted wave, rolling her eyes at their lame, overt attention.

Van had scheduled the buggy to pick up her friends, too. First stop, the Gables to get Paley.

"Hey," Paley said, as she slipped in next to Van. She wore sky blue contact lenses and looked like she had gotten little sleep. "Sorry if we upset you yesterday, you know, after that thing with Bicycle Bob."

"Sorry, I ditched you guys." Van slid over to make room.

"I came by last night to sleep over, and you weren't there."

"I stayed with Uxa until late," Van said. "We were reviewing old parchments to help with our m—summer project." They weren't allowed to talk in front of anyone not directly involved with the mission. Although Urvi seemed disinterested in their conversation, Van knew better than to take any chances. Uxa might've been right to withhold details of their mission until the last minute.

On their way to pick up Brux, Van told Paley about her step-mother's secret boyfriend, Uncle Rummie.

"Are you sure you're not imagining him, like your 'friend' Jacynthia?" Paley giggled.

"As if." Van scrunched her face, then said, "I'm happy for Genie. Old people need love too."

"Really?" Paley raised her eyebrows. "So you're okay with some old dude walking around at breakfast in his tighty-whities?"

"Ugh." Van's shoulders slumped. "It really is quite disgusting."

"Is he your new father now?" Paley teased.

"Not funny." Van didn't think she was going to like Rummie hanging around her house. Now that she thought about it, he had no right to be there. She wondered if Genie allowed him into her father's private study in the basement, the room with the secret portal. The thought tormented her.

She calmed, remembering Uxa had her people put a new lock on the door. No one could get in there. Not Genie. Not even Van.

Paley crossed her arms. "Genie has some nerve dating so soon after your father died."

Although Van had said otherwise, she silently agreed with Paley. Genie's desperate need for love made her weak and exposed Van, her house, and everything in it to a stranger. Van considered Rummie's presence a security breach.

The taxi halted at the gate to Sweet Bay Drive, the part of the reservation where vichors from the Living World moved to after being stationed on Providence Island. Brux and his father, Professor Lake, lived in the bungalows there.

The security guard staffing the booth asked them to state their names. He turned to a computer screen and clicked the keyboard.

"Okay," he shouted, leaning out of the doorway. "Go on through."

The gate opened, and Urvi stepped on the gas.

They pulled into Brux's driveway.

"Maybe the rumors of her being loose are true," Paley continued to talk about Genie.

"Meh." Van's anguish had dissipated. "I don't really care."

"Care about what?" Brux asked as he hopped into the passenger seat, carrying his backpack.

"Nothing," Van mumbled.

Brux twisted around to face Van. "Did Uxa tell you it was okay to bring Paley?"

"I'm not going without her." If Van went to the Living World on her own, she was certain to never hear the end of it from Paley, to where it would destroy their relationship.

Paley wrapped her arm around Van's shoulders and gave her a hug. "Aw, thanks pally wally."

When they arrived at the complex, the trio scooted from the taxi and entered Marble Hall. They strode through the lobby and up the stairs to Uxa's office, where they got a different story.

"Paley can't go," Ambassador Kasey said, red-faced. "The Brotherhood put the Reagan rule in place for a reason. It clearly states no terrigen transports."

"But..." Paley trembled, her eyes watering. "I want to learn about my parents."

Uxa turned to Fynn. "Please take Brux to the equipment room. Make sure the team gets their supplies together. Take Van and Paley's backpacks."

Fynn readily complied and escorted Brux out of Uxa's office.

"It's too dangerous." The ambassador's eyes bulged.

"I survived the mission last year," Paley said.

"No, no." The ambassador shook his head; Van swore she

witnessed sweat flying from his brow. "Not the mission. It's too dangerous because of the Twin Gemstones."

Van didn't like this man making decisions for the Grigori, for Uxa, or for her.

"Grigori decide who goes through the portal." Van knew both she and Paley could survive using the gemstones again. "Uxa can give the okay for Paley's travel-through."

Uxa brushed imaginary dust off her desk and said sternly, "The Twin Gemstones are a dangerous and unpredictable way to transport a terrigen through the portal, and you are but children."

"We've already used them once—"

"The gemstones drained your energy and almost killed you," Uxa said to Van. "We still do not have enough data to know who can make it through the portal using them and who cannot."

"Or how many times the same terrigen can travel-through," the ambassador added. "If you try bringing Paley through the portal again, she could bounce back. It could addle her brain or cause memory loss. Not to mention the energy drain on you, Vanessa. It's not worth the risk."

"If I had brain damage, I'd know it." Paley stomped her foot.

"The damage isn't always immediate, it can worsen as you age," Uxa said.

Van twisted her lips in disappointment. Adults always found problems to put in the way of getting stuff done.

The ambassador seemed like he could sense Van's disbelief.

"Miss Nutting and Paley are both examples of travel-throughs going right," he said.

"*What?*" Van and Paley exclaimed at the same time.

"Miss Nutting transported?" Van's jaw hit the ground. *Miss Nutting had known about the risks of the Twin Gemstones from personal experience.* Just as Van had suspected.

"It is true," Uxa said. "Miss Nutting and Paley are called blunts." Her eyes turned to Paley. "You were both born in the Living World without ichor. Both orphaned babies, sent here to be raised on the island."

"I'm familiar with the word." Paley scowled.

"We needed to learn if the gemstones worked better with a blunt-vichor transport, as opposed to a terrigen-vichor transport," Uxa said.

"You used Miss Nutting as an experiment? To see whether she got *brain damage*?" Van got a better idea of the diabolical goings-on supervised by Uxa.

Paley clamped her jaw, her eyes widened, her cheeks flushed.

Van had never seen her friend this angry before.

"You picked her because she's an *orphan*?" Paley looked as if she were about to explode. "Disposable?" Her nostrils flared.

Ambassador Kasey took a step back.

Uxa waved her hands. "No, no. All the trial runs were done with volunteers. Strictly volunteers."

Van wondered if Uxa's statement contained any truth. She recalled Miss Nutting telling her and Paley that Uxa manipulated people into accepting her proposals, which meant Uxa's requests weren't voluntary. In hindsight, Van believed Miss Nutting regretted her decision to transport.

Paley seemed to simmer down at hearing the experiments were voluntary. Apparently, she didn't remember Miss Nutting's comment about being manipulated into transporting.

"Miss Nutting's travel-through went fine. So did mine," Paley said. "I don't see the harm in sending me again."

Uxa turned to Paley. "Another failed attempt involved a former US Senator who also was a member of the Brotherhood. His popularity with the terrigens made him an influential and powerful figure. His unsuccessful travel-through is something we islanders have to relive every time we see him."

"Yes, yes. We controlled the situation," the ambassador said. "Made it look like he died in a plane crash."

"What do you mean by 'see' him? We don't know him." Paley furrowed her brow.

"But you do know him," Uxa said. "You see him around town all the time."

Van filtered through her mind everyone she knew on the island and came up blank.

Uxa cleared her throat. "The Senator who supposedly died in a plane crash is Robert B. Miller."

Van understood. Her eyes darted to Paley, who stared blankly.

"Uxa is saying that we could end up like Bicycle Bob."

Paley gasped and ran her hand over her face. "I need some air." She rushed out of Uxa's office and took off down the hallway as if able to outrun this newest revelation.

Van sighed. "I'll be right back."

She hurried down the hall in the same direction as Paley. She had trouble finding her friend with all the different branches of corridors with their many doors. Van stopped when she stepped around a corner and entered a dimly lit, expansive room with a handful of desks piled with papers. Multiple jail cells filled the far wall.

Van stepped back and hid behind the corner. She peeked around and peered at Paley conversing with Myles Dinkle through the bars of a holding cell. They both sat on the floor.

"I don't think they'll let me go." Paley's eyes were downcast; her cheeks streaked with tears. "Uxa has no problem sending orphans, just not me. She's keeping me from learning about my parents."

"Now, now." Myles sat close to the bars, so he and Paley were mere inches apart. "I'm searching to uncover my family secrets, too."

Paley raised her eyes to Myles's. "Really?"

"My father, his name was Ruben." Myles reached his hand through the bars and clasped her hand. Their eyes interlocked. "He was born in the Living World, had no ichor in his blood."

"A blunt," Paley informed him.

"Is that what you call it?"

Myles's fascination with anything related to the Living World radiated from his expression.

Van was about to make her presence known when Myles continued.

"The Janus monster swallowed my father. Same thing happened to you."

CHAPTER 12

Van ducked behind the corner of the wall before either Paley or Myles glimpsed her.

"Eaten b-by the *what?*" Paley gripped the bars of the cell.

Yeah, by the what? thought Van.

"You don't know? I'm not surprised." Myles tsked. "I know from my research the Elders are tight-lipped about the flow of information." He leaned closer to Paley, speaking through the bars. "Most of the Living World tribes—"

"Balish, Balish-occupied tribes?" Paley asked.

"Yeah," Myles said, although by his reaction Van didn't think Myles had known about the Moors's monarchy of the Living World before Paley mentioned it. He seemed eager to take mental notes on any bit of information Paley inadvertently gave him.

Myles continued. "They believe in the myth of the Janus monster. A silent, invisible creature that sneaks into babies' rooms while they sleep and devours them whole, leaving nothing but an empty crib. They think crib death is the baby refusing to leave, fighting against the Janus to stay with his or her parents in the Living World."

Paley clasped her hands over her mouth, and muttered, "That sounds awful."

"Relax." Myles rested his back against the cell wall. "What really happens is a tear in the membrane between the worlds opens around the blunt baby. Large enough to drop them into the Earth World, usually at about one to six months old. Sometimes older. Once the baby lands in the Earth World, the tear closes, but not before it's detected by the Grigori. They use their multi-tracks to locate them and pick them up."

No wonder Myles is a security threat, thought Van. *He knows a lot about the Living World.*

"And the babies?" Paley chewed on her cuticles. "What happens after the Grigori pick them up?"

"Sometimes a terrigen finds the baby first." Myles shrugged. "We hear it on the news. Babies found in dumpsters. More often than not, they're blunts. Discovered before a Grigori can get to them. Babies retrieved by the Grigori are brought here to Providence Island."

"And raised in the Gables." Paley's hand dropped from her mouth.

Hopefully Paley found comfort in finally discovering her history. As Van did, learning more about what her father's duties were as a Grigori.

"This whole thing is... is... *terrible.*" Paley's eyes welled with tears.

Myles shook his head, so fiercely he practically hit the bars of the cell. "Listen, the Janus is a natural protective device created by the universe to help the babies who are born without ichor in their blood survive by being expelled into the Earth World." He rested his forehead against the bars. "It's a good thing."

"Then why call it being eaten by the Janus monster?"

"Lodians know the truth." Myles leaned back again.

Paley grasped a bar. "So that's another reason the Balish don't allow them outside Salus Valde."

Myles' face lit up as he absorbed this detail about the other world. His eyes gleamed as if he wanted to rattle off a hundred questions, but held back as to not scare away this fountain of information.

Paley scrunched her face. "Is the Janus monster the same thing as getting the call?"

Myles shrugged. "When a terrigen gets the call, they vibrate at a higher level than the standard terrigen. This increase in vibration creates a doorway, a pathway from the Earth World into the other world. They're going in the opposite direction as the babies swallowed by the Janus. But, yeah, kinda the same thing."

"Ah." Paley nodded. "I get it. Both happen because of a change in vibrational frequencies."

"The Grigori brought my father to the Gables at the late age of four." Myles shifted his eyes and stared above Paley's head as if recalling a painful childhood story. "He arrived on Providence Island with nothing but the clothes on his back, his baby bracelet, and vague memories of a different world. After he graduated from Canterbury Bells, he left the island. Settled down in Seattle. Married and had a family—*moi*." Myles patted his chest.

"Wow." Paley said, wide-eyed. Then she tiled her head. "What bracelet?"

"Some tribes in the Living World put their family crest bracelet on newborns, in case they get eaten by the Janus. But the people in these tribes know their children actually get transported to the Earth World. The bracelet allows the kids to identify their tribe as an adult."

Paley leaned forward. "So they can find their way home if they ever make it back to the Living World."

By her friend's tone, Van knew Paley's mind spun with ways of how to find her own bracelet.

Myles continued his story, his eyes staring unfocused as if seeing into the past again. "When I was eight, my father changed. He became disgruntled with life on the mainland and wanted back on the island."

"No one is allowed to return." Paley sounded like a child reciting rules laid out by the adults.

Myles snapped out of his trance and wrapped his fingers around the bars of the cell. "Despite knowing the island's exact location, my father could never find it. As a result, he became obsessed with doorways and eventually lost his job as an insurance agent."

"I'm sorry." Paley placed a comforting hand over his.

Myles smiled weakly. "My mother was a psychiatric nurse. She couldn't understand why my father wasn't able to find the island where he grew up, and realized his obsession with it was unhealthy. She dealt with his crazy theories and absences as best she could, all while continuing to work long hours to support the family—my father, me, and my sister."

"What happened? Did he ever find us—the island?"

"He moved us to Woods Hole, Massachusetts, and became a realtor. The perfect job that allowed him to continue with his obsession."

"How so?"

"Doorways. My father constantly searched the houses and buildings on his listings, looking for his big break. Finding a building that held a portal back to the island, or to the other world." Myles shifted his body toward Paley, creating greater intimacy as she continued to hold his hand. "I would sit with him for hours and listen to his stories of the mysterious island and of the strange faraway world. I believed, whereas my sister and mother dismissed his stories as silly conspiracy theories."

"Where is he now?"

"He died years ago from what the doctor's called 'failure to thrive.'" Myles' eyes misted. "But he really died from a broken heart." He pulled hand from Paley's and turned away. "From not being allowed back to his home."

"I'm so sorry." Paley's eyes filled with tears again.

Myles took a moment before he continued. "My father created a website before he died. Posted everything he knew about the Providence Island, searching for others with similar experiences. I pledged to carry on my father's quest."

He gripped the bars and pushed his face close to Paley's. "I, too, became obsessed with finding this island." His knuckles whitened from the tightness of his grasp. "But unlike my father, instead of wanting to live here, I vowed on his grave to expose whatever secrets it holds. It was the island's secrets that *killed* him."

Paley leaned back at his intensity. "D-do you keep in touch with your mom and sister?"

His knuckles gained some color as he bobbed his head. "Oh, yeah. My sister lives in South Tampa, Florida with her husband who works on MacDill Air Force Base." His tone had become softer. "My mother's retired and lives in St. Petersburg. It's a town near my sister. I talk to them daily." He looked at the ceiling and shouted, *"They'll want to know where I am!"*

Paley ignored his outburst. "You've inspired me." She sprung to her feet, looking cheery. "Now I *have* to go through the portal. I need to get to the Living World and search for my parents. They might be alive, and sad thinking I got eaten by the Janus monster. I have to find them and let them know I'm okay. So we can be together." Paley brushed off her bottom. "I'll try to get information about your relatives while I'm there, too."

"Wait," Myles cried. "If you bring me with you, I can tell you more. I can help you find your parents."

"Um." Paley hesitated.

Sure the conversation had ended and, not wanting to get caught snooping, Van scooted back to Uxa's office. The only people in the room were Uxa and Fynn.

"How is Paley doing?" Uxa asked.

"Fine. Just pouting. She'll be back in a sec." Van had no intention of ratting out Paley for making friends with their prisoner.

"Fynn, please escort Van to the breakfast room," Uxa said. "I will wait here for Paley's return."

Fynn led Van into a nearby conference room, where Ambassador Kasey hovered next to a long buffet table filled with bagels, fried potatoes, scrambled eggs, and pastries. His hand clasped a plate piled high with an assortment of goodies as he chatted with Brux.

"Drink." Fynn pointed at the buffet table to several pitchers filled with water shimmering with sparkles of silver.

"Don't mind if I do." Van grabbed a pitcher and glass. As she poured, two sets of women's gear and clothes laid out on nearby arm chairs caught her eye.

Brux came over, holding a heaping plate of fruit, oatmeal, and toast. "We're going undercover as marketeers' scouts again."

"Excuse me, *teammate*," said a condescending voice coming from behind Van.

Her skin crawled. She knew that voice.

"Pernilla." Van stepped aside so her nemesis could grab a pitcher. Van hadn't even noticed Pernilla in the room. But of course, being part of the team, she would be there.

The ambassador meandered over, desiring more gab time with Brux.

Van pointed at the two sets of gear. "Does this mean Paley is on my team?"

"Sorry. But no," the ambassador said. "Sending one of our people is the best way to go. And we have someone here, under eighteen, who is already prepped for the journey."

Van's hope crashed. They had laid the other set of clothes and gear out for Pernilla, not Paley.

"A terrigen?" Brux asked. "What about the Reagan rule?"

"An attempt seems warranted due to the urgency and importance of this mission."

"Meaning, you're sending someone to spy on us?" Van narrowed her eyes at the ambassador.

"Uh, no. No. We—"

"Who's going to bring this person over?" Van interrupted. She had no desire to hear his flimsy excuses. "Who else is on our team?"

Last year there were five kids on each team, plus Paley, making Van's team six. Between the two teams, only three of them made it back to Lodestar.

"My son, Ixl." Uxa had swept into the room, followed by a handsome bronzed skin boy around Van's age. "He is a vichor."

Van gaped at the boy, who was dressed in marketeers' scouts' clothing.

Ixl nodded at the crew.

Van nodded back, having a hard time picturing Uxa as his mother, or anyone's mother.

"Paley has not shown yet," Uxa said.

Van scrunched her face. "That's weird." She wondered if Paley reconsidered going on the mission. Then remembered how excited

Paley got over finding her parents. Van wriggled her shoulders. Something didn't feel right.

"She's probably down at the Clam Shack stuffing her face," Pernilla said.

Ambassador Kasey cleared his throat, as if to soothe over Pernilla's rude remark. "Ixl will transport using the Twin Gemstones. With one of our junior agents, Brad Davis."

A dark haired boy, who looked older than eighteen, had entered the room after Ixl.

"Junior Agent Brad Davis," he said, making his name and title sound like one long word. He firmly shook hands with Brux, and then Van.

"Are you sure you're underage?" Pernilla asked, as she shook his hand.

"I'm seventeen years and nine months old." He grinned.

"He gets to go, but Paley can't?" Van huffed and stomped away.

"Not so fast," Fynn said. "You three need to change." He opened the conference room door. "Restrooms are down the hall to the right."

Van, Pernilla, and Brux each grabbed their marketeers' scouts' clothes—worn khaki cargo pants with lots of pockets, ribbed tanks, and shabby, oversized, button-front shirts—and dashed into their respective bathrooms.

While in the stall, Van heard Pernilla bustling, as if changing their clothes was a contest. Van tsked. Yet, picked up her speed, entering the unspoken race to see who could change the fastest.

When Van and Pernilla returned to the breakfast-conference room, Brux was already there.

Ixl and Brad were prepping for transport through the portal by checking their backpacks, supplies, and gear. Uxa handed each of them a Twin Gemstone. They held the egg-size gems in their open palms and moved their hands next to each other's.

Both gemstones flashed a variety of vibrant colors until synchronizing with each other, settling on a deep orange. The stones pulsed in harmony with each other.

Van gazed at the door, shifting her weight from foot to foot. "I wonder what's keeping Paley?"

Since Paley wasn't part of the mission, the group collectively decided she had run back to the Gables to sulk in private, or, according to Pernilla, she was headed to the Clam Shack.

Van was about to dash out of the conference room to revisit the place with the cells when Uxa commanded Fynn, "Go check on Paley."

Fynn nodded and scurried out the door.

Uxa led everyone else into the hallway and led them through a winding corridor and down two flights of stairs.

They came to a door. Uxa typed in her passcode to open it. They entered a circular atrium made of granite and marble with a high, domed ceiling. The House of Lacus.

Against the far wall, a dais held an enormous black disc bordered by a band of granite lined with symbols and pictographs. A set of curved stairways protruded from the wall, one on each side of the disc, extending two stories high from the floor to the platform holding the portal.

Brux, Pernilla, Uxa, and Ambassador Kasey headed in the control room's direction, while Brad and Ixl made their way over to the stairways leading to the portal.

When Van passed through the center of the atrium, she stopped to gaze at the fountain with a statue honoring Queen Amaryl of the Dark War. She admired the toga-clad woman, her ancestor.

Amaryl's right hand held a torch. She had a sheathed sword in her belt, and around her neck she wore a coin pendant necklace. Water continuously poured into the fountain from an urn tucked under her left arm—*wait*. It wasn't an urn. It was a chalice with a barely noticeable marking on the rim.

Van stepped closer, peering.

The chalice had an engraving of an ankh.

Before Van could comprehend the meaning of this discovery, through the corner of her eye, she caught movement behind one of the many Doric pillars. Her head snapped in that direction.

Van squinted but saw nothing.

Hm. She tiptoed over to the pillar, to be sure.

"Vanessa, come along," Uxa called from the door of the control room, startling Van before she could investigate the pillar.

Van spun around and headed to the control room.

Once there, she studied the monitors, searching for anything out of the ordinary in the atrium. All she saw was Ixl and Junior Agent Brad Davis climbing the stairs and reaching the landing of the dais.

The granite stone band surrounding the black disc moved clockwise, rotating faster and faster until it became a glowing reddish-orange. A thin strip of sea-blue water filled the layer below the fiery band and rotated counter-clockwise at a steady pace.

Waves of sparkles twinkled in the eternal blackness within the disc and began to swirl. The portal was ready to transport.

With everyone caught up in preparations for the terrigen-vichor transport, they missed seeing a man scurry out from behind a pillar and dash toward the nearest stairway.

Except for Van. She gasped.

Uxa's eyes darted to the monitor. She scowled as she watched Myles sprint up one of the stairways.

"What the—" Brux said.

Van rushed to the door of the control room. "Paley, no!"

Pernilla elbowed Van out of the way, and screamed, "Stop him, you idiot!"

Paley stood next to a pillar at the foot of the stairway, gnawing on her cuticle. She released her finger long enough to yell, "Myles, go!"

Ixl and Brad jumped into the swirling blackness, just as Myles reached the dais and leaped through with them.

CHAPTER 13

Sparks flew from the black disc. Loud snaps and crackles echoed throughout the atrium in the House of Lacus.

Three bodies came shooting out of the portal as if being expelled from the gaping mouth of a monster.

"Ixl!" Uxa rushed up the stairway, her eyes wide with terror as Pernilla, Brux, and the ambassador followed behind.

Van ran to Paley.

"What did you do?" She gripped her friend's shoulders and shook them. "Did you free Myles?"

"He said Uxa lied to us about the Twin Gemstones." Paley looked perplexed. "He said he knew a safe way to get through the portal. That he'd come back for me." Her words were high pitched and stressed.

"What were you thinking?" Van resisted the urge to smack her friend in the head.

"If he could make it through without a gemstone, then I could, too."

"All three of them could die!" Van released her grip and threw her hands in the air. "Or suffer brain damage!"

"Myles said that wasn't true."

"And now, what do you think?" Van pointed up at the three bodies sprawled on the platform.

Paley's shoulders slumped; she cast her eyes downward. "I'm sorry."

"How did you even get in here?" Van asked. "It's locked with a passcode."

"The same way we got in last year. From the outside, through the main door."

Van and Paley walked to the bottom of the nearest staircase. The others were at the top of the platform checking on Ixl, Agent Davis, and Myles.

"Myles pretended like he had caught the illness," Paley said. "I called for an agent. When he opened the cell to check, Myles tackled him, grabbed his ID card, and we took off."

Fynn returned. He dashed across the atrium and skidded to a stop at the bottom of the stairs. "What happened?"

"We had an accident," Uxa cried from the platform. She knelt next to Ixl. "Call emergency medics."

Fynn turned around and sprinted into the control room.

Van looked up at the platform. "Let's go see if we can help."

She and Paley started up the stairs.

Paley hesitated.

Van clutched her friend's wrist and tugged to keep her moving. "Time to face the music."

As they reached the landing at the top of the stairs, Van heard Pernilla ask Uxa, "Why would you risk sending your son?"

"He volunteered." Uxa sat on the floor, cradling her unconscious son's head in her lap. Blood dribbled from Ixl's ears and nostrils. His facial skin looked badly burned, and his singed clothes smoldered.

"He is strong. Testing placed him as the most competent to complete this task." Tears welled in Uxa's eyes. "He is strong," she repeated.

While the ambassador tended to Agent Davis, Brux collected the Twin Gemstones and checked on Myles. All three men were in a similar condition. Unconscious, singed, and had blood streaming from their ears and nose.

Pernilla shifted. "If Van took Paley through last year, that means Van is strong."

Van paused, stunned by Pernilla's words. They sounded almost like a… *compliment*.

No one noticed she and Paley had reached the landing. Van knew Pernilla would've died if she realized Van had overheard what she'd said.

"Why can't she take Paley this year?" Pernilla asked Uxa. "The more hands on deck, the better."

"Paley is of very little help to the team on these missions. She compromises Van's energy and diverts Van and the other team members' attention away from completing their task." Uxa tore her eyes away from Ixl, waved her hand at the other two seriously injured boys caused by Paley's interference. "My case in point."

Paley whimpered at Uxa's cruel, yet accurate comment, causing Pernilla and Uxa to notice Paley and Van on the landing.

"I am sorry you had to hear that," Uxa said.

Pernilla sneered at Paley. "Nice work, doofus. You took out two members of our team."

Fynn and a bunch of emergency medics rushed up the stairs, carrying stretchers. They stabilized their patients and took them away. The ambassador left with them to oversee their care. Uxa refused to go.

"You should be with your son," Brux said.

"There is work to do here." Uxa straightened the top of her uniform and threw her shoulders back, ready to carry on. "I will be of no help to the medical team."

Van beamed, proud of Uxa's resilience. She considered her mentor's emotional control an asset that made Uxa a good leader. Van strived to emulate that level of control.

"What now?" Pernilla asked.

"Now that the ambassador has left us, I can tell you my son," Uxa's voice cracked with despair for a split second, "had an ulterior motive to go on this mission."

Uxa headed down the steps. They all followed, not wanting to miss a word. Except for Fynn, who rushed ahead of them.

"I asked Ixl to see what he could find about the master demon. To search for documents written by our ancestors and condemned by the Balish, to see if our Grigori had encountered it in the past. To listen to any folklore that would give me more data. Anything. So I can figure out what this evil is and how to fight it."

Uxa led them toward the control room. "Since my son and Agent Davis are out of commission, it is up to you to gather this information."

They entered the control room to find Fynn fussing with their gear, backpacks, and supplies.

He looked up and greeted them. "Check, check, and check. All is in order and ready to go."

Van had planned on talking her way into getting Paley on the team again, but after this fiasco, she didn't think Paley stood a chance.

Then Brux declared, "I think Paley should join us. She should go on the mission."

"Why would you want to that to yourselves?" Fynn asked.

"She helped us carry Maren to the hospital," Brux said.

"So?" Pernilla sauntered over to Fynn and snatched her backpack.

Van couldn't figure out where Brux was going with this idea. So far, his reasoning came across as pretty inadequate.

"Doing what's right isn't enough to be rewarded with a trip through the portal." Pernilla inspected the contents in her pack.

Brux continued, "Paley's at risk of catching the illness. Chances are, she's sick already."

"That's why she made the poor decision to help Myles," Van said, catching on.

Paley pressed the back of her wrist to her forehead. "I do feel a bit feverish."

Van perked up. "She has to go with us."

"Still not following." Pernilla pulled out a black ribbed tank, sniffed it, and then stuffed it back in her pack.

"I'm not either," Fynn said.

"The Twin Gemstones will raise her vibration higher than it is on Providence Island," Brux said.

"Keeping her in the Living World will slow the progression," Uxa said, sounding like she agreed.

Fynn grimaced. "You'd let her go? Even after what you just witnessed?"

"We'll keep an eye on her," Brux said. "Make sure she doesn't do anything else... uh..."

"Stupid," Pernilla said, finishing his sentence as she continued checking her pack.

"I'd feel better with her on the team." Based on the objections Uxa made earlier, Van added, "Otherwise, I'll be preoccupied with worrying about her."

"I have to go. I'll die quicker if I stay here." Paley scrunched her brow, probably from realizing what she just said.

"For Paley's health." Brux gave a curt nod. "And to help Van stay focused on completing the mission."

Van remained flabbergasted when Brux continued to campaign for her cause. Van wanted her best friend along for company and support. She also believed, despite making bad choices, Paley deserved the chance to learn about her parents. Van resigned to the fact she would always be there for Paley. However, she had no idea why Brux wanted Paley to come along. Maybe he sincerely cared about what Van wanted.

"But someone else should carry the Twin Gemstone, not Van," he added.

And there it is. Van knew he couldn't be entirely helpful.

Pernilla zipped her backpack. "I'll do it."

Brux and Pernilla both shocked the heck out of Van. Since when were they on her side?

"If it helps the mission and gets us going," Pernilla said like a trooper. "Let's do this."

Fynn gawked in disbelief at Uxa while she mulled over the idea. "You can't seriously be thinking of letting—"

"To prevent any more harebrained schemes," Uxa interrupted. "I think it is best Paley joins the team."

"Yay!" Paley clapped her hands together. "I'll get changed."

Van gave her pal a hug.

"Brux will carry the other gemstone," Uxa said. "Not Pernilla."

Brux and Pernilla stared at each other with quizzical expressions, but neither challenged Uxa's decision.

"Drink this." Fynn handed Paley an ampule. "Colloidal silver. You'll need to take one daily as a precaution to keep the illness at bay, or progressing if you're already sick. And it'll keep you from spreading the illness. I'll go grab more from medical." He dashed out of the room.

Brux picked up his backpack and slipped it on. "We're already down to a skeleton crew. We all need to keep fit and healthy."

Van checked her pack and in no time Fynn returned with Paley's ampules, a stuffed backpack, and a set of female marketeers' scouts' clothing.

Paley tucked the ampules into her newly arrived backpack. Her eyes darted around the room as she held khaki cargo pants in her hands.

"Right now, the demon illness is contained to Providence Island," Uxa said. "However, it could still spread. All of you are required to take colloidal silver as a precaution. You were given a dose at breakfast."

Van had an *a-ha* moment as she recalled the shimming water in the pitchers.

"You will take additional doses while on your journey," Fynn added.

"What symptoms should we be on the lookout for?" Brux asked.

Uxa's eyes darted to Brux. "Good question." She addressed the team, "Changes in behavior. Aggression, anger, depression. Fever, lack of appetite—"

"Crazy eyes." Van flashed back to Maren's crazed look as she attacked Van.

All eyes turned to Van.

"I've got experience with it." Van shrugged. "Just saying." Her cheeks flared.

"Where can I change?" Paley held up a white ribbed tank.

Fynn raised his index finger for Paley to wait a minute. "Speaking of change. I think it best if we change the team leader from Van to Brux." He held up his palms as if to ward off the expected verbal attack. "Wait. Hear me out. It should be a male to make it easier to move about in patriarchal, Balish occupied territories."

"It has to be Brux, then. He's the only male on our team." Pernilla glared at Paley. "Now that *someone* took out two of our teammates."

Van clenched her lips. Rejection and betrayal surged inside her. First the Twin Gemstones, now this. No one appreciated her and it made her feel alone. But when the team took a vote, Van raised her hand in agreement.

With Brux in charge, he'd be responsible for Paley and Pernilla. With him carrying the Twin Gemstone, he and Paley had to stay together while in the Living World. That would give Van time to sneak away and focus on her side projects like finding a counter-curse and checking on Ferox. No worries about Daisy, not with Brux leading the team. She knew finding his sister would be on the agenda.

"It is settled then," Uxa said. "Brux is the team's leader."

Fynn directed Paley to a nearby restroom, where she could change.

Uxa handed Van a handstitched coin-sized cloth pouch. "Use it well."

"I will." Van tucked the Coin of Creation into one of the many pockets in her cargo pants.

Paley returned, dressed and ready to go.

The team's departure time had arrived.

As Van climbed the stairway to the portal, she realized Uxa hadn't given the team a name this year. She wondered if this was a bad omen and hoped Wiglaf would make another appearance on this journey. The little bunfy provided them with luck and comfort. Every time she thought of Wiglaf, her chest got that annoying warmness. She rubbed her palm against her sternum. She didn't need Wiglaf. The little critter would be nothing but a distraction, another worry.

Everyone appeared solemn, bracing for the expected challenges waiting for them on the other side of the portal. When they reached the dais, Uxa suggested they take a moment to remember last year's teammates who didn't survive the journey.

Van warded off a chill as they also said a prayer for the three injured boys. Two who never even got to start the mission. She took this as another bad sign. What happened was her fault for not keeping a better watch on Paley. Van redoubled her commitment to find a cure for the Anchoress curse. By removing it, she could stop bad things from happening to her.

The portal's borders hummed to life. The black disc swirled with shimmers of silver.

Brux and Paley held the gemstones in their palms to attune them. Then leaped into the blackness, followed by Pernilla.

Van entered next. Unsure if she had the skills to pull off another victory. Wondering which of them wouldn't make it back this year. Including herself.

CHAPTER 14

Van, Paley, Brux, and Pernilla made it through the portal and safely landed on the platform at Lodestar Station in Salus Valde, Living World.

Van noticed the gigantic clock hanging above one of the large archways. Four hands with different phases of the moon adorned its face. Under the clock, the engraved stone sign read Lodestar Village. She felt like she had come home.

"Wow," Pernilla muttered.

Van smiled at Pernilla's reaction. It was like the first time Van had seen Lodestar Station. She had to keep in mind everything would be new to Pernilla.

Last time Van and Paley had walked through the station, it was deserted. Today, Van saw a good number of Grigori and what looked like the well-dressed citizens of Salus Valde. They casually sat on the white stone benches, leaned against the Corinthian columns, or milled about while waiting for their transport time.

Some had their eyes glued to their MTs, some watched the glassy gemstone screen hung on the wall broadcasting news bulletins and advertisements. Some had their nose in a newspaper called *Daily Acts*.

None of them paid any attention to the four teens marching toward the high-arched exit under the colossal clock.

"All the news feeds are owned and controlled by the Balish," Brux said.

"Really?" Pernilla rubbernecked every which way.

"How can they control the news?" Paley asked.

"Yeah." Van peered at Brux. "Manik's law protects Salus Valde from Balish rule."

"We're protected from invasion by the Balish and allowed to have our own belief system," Brux said. "But Lodians still have to abide by Balish law."

Van muttered, "They have to control the story. Sounds familiar."

The team hastily exited Lodestar Station and entered Lodestar Village.

Pernilla gawked at the fairytale cottages, the elaborate fountains, and the spectacular greenery of the quaint village. She paused and squinted at the majestic mountain towering in the distance.

Van answered Pernilla's unspoken question. "Mt. Altithronia."

"I know that. I'm well studied on the Living World." Pernilla's sharp tone exposed her true feelings. She felt uncomfortable being the only person on the team with no experience.

"Since when?" Paley asked.

"Since last night," Pernilla snapped.

Van had no time for Pernilla's insecurities. They had a mission to accomplish and only twenty-nine more days to do it.

"Come on." Van directed them off the cobblestone streets and into the forest outside the village.

After walking through the thick woods for some time, Paley asked, "Is this the same path we took last summer?"

"Yup," Van said.

"How do you know?" Brux asked Van. "Did you use the Coin?"

"Not yet."

Brux stopped short; Van kept walking.

He dashed forward and grabbed her by the elbow.

Pernilla halted.

Paley took a few more steps before she stopped. Her eyes turned to Van and Brux, a confused look clouded her face.

"How do you know what direction we need to go?" Brux asked Van, again.

"I'm taking us to the trunk-a-vators," Van said, irritated at Brux for challenging her decision.

"Without checking with us first?" Pernilla's knuckles turned white from gripping her backpack's shoulder straps. "And what's a trunk-a-vator? It sounds stupid."

"I'm team leader," Brux said. "I decide how we get there."

"Listen." Van poked him in the chest. "You do what you want. I'm going this way."

Van turned to walk away, but Brux tightened his grip on her elbow and yanked her back.

"If I'm not searching for Daisy, then you're not doing any personal stuff either," he said in a low voice.

"You mean Daisy's *body*."

Brux looked both pale from grief and flushed from anger. "You believe she's dead?" He released his grip; his hand fell to his side.

Van hesitated. She didn't want to give him hope. But she also couldn't lie to him.

"I…" The devastated look on Brux's face drained away all Van's stubbornness. "Screw death. Daisy's alive." She resumed walking. "And don't tell me you weren't planning to sneak away and go search for her," she cried over her shoulder.

"I wasn't!" Brux called from behind. He hurried and caught up with Van. "I take my responsibilities as your protector seriously. You should too."

Van shifted her shoulders, as if she needed to fix her backpack. "Don't tell me what to do."

Pernilla shook her head and said under her breath, "Spoiled. Little. Baby."

"Oh, no. You didn't just go there." Paley panted from the exertion of keeping pace with the team.

"You're the spoiled one," Van said to Pernilla. She kept her focus on the path ahead. "Whining so much, Uxa put you on the team to shut you up."

Pernilla stopped, shrugged off her backpack, and threw it on the ground. "Come on." She raised her fists. "Uxa's not here. There's no Grigori to interfere. Let's go."

Van sighed. It was going to be a long mission.

"Hey," Brux said. "Let's keep focused on our task."

Van faced Pernilla, needing to address the issue, since Brux, despite being team captain, didn't know how to handle this situation.

"I'm not going to fight you, Pernilla." Van didn't want to injure her teammate. Especially not in the first few hours of their journey. They were already down by two, thanks to Paley.

"Why? Chicken?" Pernilla made clucking noises.

"Shut up, Pernilla," Paley growled, ready to join the brawl.

"Oh, the little sidekick wants some action," Pernilla sneered. "I haven't seen you this excited since Beachside Cafe had a two for one donut sale."

Pernilla took a swipe at Van.

She ducked.

"You know what?" Van's teammates were sucking all the energy out of her. She didn't need this grief. This was Brux's team. He could deal with them. Van had other, more important things to worry about. Like how to find the seal, mend it, and get back to Lodestar before the Quasher ripped her to shreds. "Bite me," Van said to Pernilla and stormed off. She needed to get away from all of them.

Van picked up her pace and dashed deeper into the woods. Leaves swished against the exposed skin of her hands and face. An occasional twig snapped back, slapping her bare skin. "Ouch."

She carried on, which was significantly more difficult this year. The weight she had gained made running harder on her body. Her hips and lower back already ached, and she was panting.

At least it gave her a chance to clear her head. No matter how hard she tried, her feelings kept bobbing to the surface. Displaying moodiness in front of her teammates exposed her weakness as a warrior. Knowing this made her even more cranky.

Exhausted, Van had to slow down to catch her breath. As she did, her ankle gave out, causing her to stumble and fall face-first into a muddy puddle.

She lifted her head from the muck and spit out dirty water.

Van rested on her elbows, stomach down, in the mud. Drained and defeated. She strained her ears, listening for sounds revealing her teammates had followed.

She heard nothing but birds chirping and leaves rustling in the wind. Van raised herself to her knees. She wiped her muddy face and wept.

Wet and mud-covered, she staggered over to a rock and sat down. Tears streamed from her eyes, making pathways along her dirt stained cheeks. Her backpack dug painfully into her shoulders. Van shrugged out of it and placed it next to her on the rock. She tore open the zipper and rummaged around until she found an orange-date nut bar. She ripped into it as if she were starving.

She chewed and sobbed, coughing occasionally from getting bits stuck in her throat from shoving huge bites into her mouth.

Her sobbing calmed, and she observed her surroundings. The stillness of the woods echoed back at her. She could choke to death on the bar, and no one would know. Her body would lay there until it rotted into a mushy mess. Eventually absorbing into the earth, going back to the place from which it had come.

And no one would care.

"Mrwp!"

Startled, Van almost dropped her nut bar wrapper.

By her feet sat a furry, glowy-white critter. Staring up at her with his large, soulful eyes.

"Hi, Wiglaf," Van said to her only friend.

He stretched his long ears as high as they could go. "Rrpt weep ef."

Although happy to see her bunfy, Van didn't respond. Instead, she stared into the trees.

Wiglaf hopped onto the rock and rubbed his cat-like head against her thigh.

"Rrrpt. Rrrpt. Erp."

"Your paws are muddy."

"Wrrpt." He raised his whiskered nose and blinked at Van.

His adorableness won her over. "Okay, okay." She couldn't resist scratching him behind the ears. Her body suddenly surged with energy. Wiglaf always brought Van out of her funk.

She stood, recharged, and ready to get moving. If the team didn't care enough to find her, then she would take it upon herself to find them.

Pfft. So much for Brux's dedication to being her protector.

Van grabbed her backpack. She gazed to her left, then to her right. She twisted around backward and then looked forward. All the trees looked the same. She didn't know where she was or which way to go.

She panicked until remembering she had the Coin.

As she reached into her pocket for the pouch, voices emanated through the trees. Sounds of twigs snapping under rushing feet came closer.

"Van!" Paley's voice carried through the trees.

The brush parted, and Brux appeared. "There you are." He let out a sigh of relief. "You scared me to death."

Pernilla and Paley followed.

"I figured you guys wanted to go your own way," Van said.

"I will never leave you." Brux pulled a tissue out of his pants pocket and tenderly wiped dirt off Van's muddy face.

Paley placed a hand on Van's shoulder. "I'm glad you're okay. Muddy, but okay."

Brux stared into Van's eyes and said in a husky voice, "Don't run off like that again."

Van's heart whirled.

"Or if you do, hide better," Pernilla muttered.

Van swatted away Brux's help. "I'm fine." She snatched the tissue from Brux. "I can do it." She finished wiping her face.

"Wiglaf!" Paley screeched. She plunked her butt on the rock and scratched behind the bunfy's ears. "Look at your little muddy paws. Aw. You're *so* cute."

Because of his frequent appearances over the past year, Wiglaf had grown used to Paley's over-the-top affection. He basked in her attention.

Pernilla gazed at Wiglaf.

Van could tell she longed to touch him. "Don't even think about it."

Then Van dashed behind a nearby cluster of trees and changed into fresh clothes. Thankfully, Fynn had made sure they packed spares.

Brux rubbed his hands, full of pep. "Let's get back to task. Van, if you think the TAV makes sense, then that's what we'll do."

A rush of uncertainty filled Van. She hadn't consulted the Coin before deciding to use the TAVs. Now she questioned herself. She didn't even know if their connections to the west were working.

Wiglaf broke free from Paley's grip. He turned to face the group, chirruped, and then hopped into the woods to the east.

Van's head cleared. She smiled. "We follow Wiglaf."

They rushed to catch up with the bunfy and followed him until he stopped in front of an enormous tree.

"Looks like a TAV." Van gazed at its bulky knots.

"Let's see if it's working." Brux placed his hand on the biggest knot and pushed. A panel slid open, exposing a circular compartment large enough to fit all of them.

Wiglaf dashed inside.

"Whoa." Paley gaped. "Jorie's magic from last year must still power the TAVs."

"Wait. You want me to go in *there*?" Pernilla took a step back. "What exactly is this?"

"TAVs are magically imprinted trees." Brux entered the compartment.

"It's an elevator in a tree," Paley added. "Except it doesn't go up and down, it goes from tree to tree. Well, only to other magically connected trees in a network. Am I making sense?"

Brux held his hand over the doorjamb, the same way terrigens held the door to an Earth World elevator. The gesture struck Van as funny. She giggled.

Paley smiled at Van as she entered along with Pernilla.

Brux released his hand and the door slid closed. "King Nequus had one of their government-sanctioned wizards block the magic in the network, making the TAVs inoperable. Jorie, our team leader last year, used magic to get them to work."

"They're still working?" Pernilla looked unsure about trusting this new contraption.

"They're powered by the Universal Energy Grid, an energy source that comes from nature, not Jorie's magic," Van said. "All she did was reconnect some of the TAVs to the grid."

An illuminated embedded flat panel screen displayed a map of the landscape. Van pointed to the only lit area on the panel map. "This TAV will only let us go north to Altithronia."

Brux squinted at the map. "There are even fewer routes now."

"Maybe Jorie's magic is wearing off." Paley's finger shot to her mouth and she gnawed on her cuticle.

"I thought it wasn't dependent on Jorie's magic," Pernilla said, sounding stressed.

"The Balish probably discovered some were working and shut them down again." Brux pushed the tree icon on the screen. "Here we go."

Pernilla clasped the grab rail and braced for a wild ride.

Van snickered, having done the same thing the first time she rode in a TAV. But unlike last time, Van suffered no anxiety from being inside the enclosed space. For that, Van was grateful.

The TAV hummed and vibrated. Then came to a smooth, uneventful stop.

Excited to see Altithronia again, Van eagerly stepped from the TAV onto an expansive grassy area that seemed to float in the sky. She stood on a natural elevation on the earth's surface, perhaps a small mountain, since they were in a mountain range. High enough so that when she walked to the edge, the tops of giant pine trees reached up from the valley below and were still beneath her. Lush forestation and rolling hills spread for miles in every direction. In the distance, purple-pink leaves of weepy trees fluttered in the gentle breeze, creating a spectacular landscape. Altithronia remained as beautiful as ever.

Van closed her eyes and breathed in the unique woody fragrance of pine mixed with fresh mountain air. Her ears caught the familiar sound of a nearby crashing waterfall. In the distance, she heard Pernilla gasp and say, "Oh my gosh."

Van opened her eyes and walked around the TAV to the other side of the elevation. She stood on the ledge next to Pernilla and also gazed across the open area.

"It's amazing." Pernilla gaped.

A grand waterfall, edged on both sides by green vegetation, crashed off the jutting rocks in a steady flow.

Van peered down to see the waterfall's wide stream plummet into the base pond. She lifted her eyes to the top of the white-watered falls, and on the side, she recognized the enormous oak tree. The tree's massive, gnarled roots reached in and out of the earth, twisting down all the way to the pond below.

Wiglaf merrily chirruped by her feet.

"We're supposed to be here," Van said, lost in the natural beauty of her surroundings. "We stopped at the same place last year."

Pernilla responded by turning toward Van and pulling out a dagger. "Van," she said in a severe tone.

Confused, Van took a step back. She glanced at Brux and Paley, who chatted next to the TAV, about thirty feet away, hoping to get answers.

Paley looked over at them, and her eyes grew wide.

Wiglaf let out several rapid squeaks.

A worried look clouded Brux's face. He stepped forward. His mouth opened as if about to say something.

Strong hands roughly grasped Van from behind and pulled her close. Her back pressed against a warm, solid body. Sharp metal dug into her throat. A dagger.

A deep male voice growled in her ear, "Who are you?"

CHAPTER 15

Van's neck twinged as the stranger pushed the dagger deeper, pricking her skin.

"What are you doing here?" the stranger growled, addressing all of them.

A soft female voice rang like the chimes of an angel. "Kopius, put the knife down."

His grip lessened, and Van took a much-needed breath.

Kopius reluctantly lowered his dagger and released Van.

Van stumbled away, clutching her throat.

She expected Brux to dash to her out of concern. Instead, he halted. His eyes grew wider; his jaw slackened. "D-daisy?"

"Hello, brother."

Van twisted to look behind Kopius, and her jaw also dropped.

Daisy emanated a soft, feminine presence. Though a mere wisp of a girl, she seemed to awaken the hearts of all those around her.

Brux rushed to his sister. They wrapped their arms around each other in a loving embrace.

Van waited until they were done and then she gave Daisy a hug, careful not to squeeze too hard. Brux's sister always had the pallor of someone who could use a good meal, and today was no different. In

Van's arms, she seemed delicate as a flower petal and felt frail and bony. "Uxa told us you were dead."

"Nope." Daisy shrugged. "I guess not."

Daisy's wide, pale-blue eyes drew onlookers into her simple beauty. Yet, even as Daisy grinned, she still seemed sad.

Seeing Brux's sister standing before her, alive and well, caused Van's mind to spin a web of suspicion that, at worst, Uxa could be the spy in Lodestar or, at least, manipulative. Uxa could've told Van and the team Daisy had died with the hope they wouldn't go searching for her. But Van couldn't shake the feeling of Uxa being shady.

Paley and Daisy hugged.

"Good to see you," Paley said.

"Same."

Pernilla hadn't yet met Daisy. While they made introductions, Brux looked bothered, as if struggling against wanting to wrap his sister in an eternal protective embrace or giving her the freedom to live her life.

Daisy looked down at Wiglaf. "Good to see you again."

Wiglaf, already in love with Daisy, rubbed his face all over her ankles and purred. Daisy, enamored with the critter, bent down and scratched him behind the ears. "Ever since my torture—"

Brux winced.

"—I've formed a bond with animals and nature." Daisy took in a deep breath and let it out slowly. "So, *connected*." She shook her head. "I don't know if I make sense. But… I'm one with mother earth. Her creatures, and her bounty."

"Bounty means plants," Kopius added.

The team turned their attention to him, who, until this point, stood silently to the side, observing the newcomers while keeping a tight grip on his dagger.

"She developed an intuitive skill for using plants to make medicines," he explained. "Fascinating."

Daisy beamed at him.

"Kopius, right?" Paley batted her eyelashes at the blue-eyed Adonis.

To Van, he seemed older than anyone on the team. But she knew he was under eighteen, or he wouldn't be allowed outside the border of Salus Valde. And, by his coloring, he looked Lodian.

"Kopius DeTata," Daisy said in her airy voice as she made the introductions.

When Brux and Kopius clasped each other's wrists in greeting, Van expected thunder to rumble and lightning to crackle in the sky as each assessed the worthiness of the other.

Paley kept flipping her hair over her shoulder in a flirty manner. So much Van thought it an impressive feat for her to stop for a moment and clasp Kopius' wrist.

Daisy turned to Brux. "Father hired him to find me."

"Find her, I did." Kopius' eyes scanned their surroundings, as if on alert for trouble. "Of course, there was never any doubt that I wouldn't. I can do anything when put to task."

"Anything?" Brux looked skeptical.

"His special skill is making use of objects on hand to create something needed," Daisy said. "Come. I'll show you." She gestured across the open area, toward the gigantic oak tree at the top of the waterfall.

The team followed Daisy and Kopius onto a path in the woods. They descended downward until the trees ended and they entered the clearing by the base pond. Then they headed upward, climbing the terraced rocks of the waterfall that were intermingled with the tree's immense roots.

Wiglaf hop-scurried along with them.

During the climb, Kopius warily glanced at the bunfy. "What is that thing?"

"Sfft errt!" Wiglaf said, sounding offended.

"Bunfys are magical creatures native to Altithronia." Daisy smiled at the critter.

"But they can't perform magic," Paley said, using her response as an excuse to move closer to Kopius. "Like, he can't turn you into a carrot." She threw him a big smile.

Kopius didn't return the gesture.

"A bunfy's magic allows them to change their vibrational frequency and travel to different realms," Van said.

"Oh, right." Kopius seemed more appreciative of the bunfy now. "I've heard of them, but they're rare."

"Yes, and they attach to one person and watch over them for a lifetime," Daisy said. "This one has chosen you, Van. They bring good luck, and their purrs heal the soul."

Kopius seemed to store the information for future use in his mind-bank of data.

They reached the top of the waterfall. Kopius slipped inside a cave-like opening in the roots, which were about three times wider than him and twice his height. Daisy followed, then Brux, Pernilla, Paley, and Wiglaf.

Van entered next, surprised to see a cozy nook.

The tree's roots made natural walls. Light filtered in through the entryway, casting a triangular highlight on Kopius as he knelt by the unlit fire pit in the center of the dwelling. He smashed two stones together until he got a spark and lit the fire.

They sat on logs, except Brux, who sat on the ground, since there weren't enough seats.

"You can share mine," Paley suggested with a sly grin.

Seashells, stones, and twig figures, looking like hand-crafted dolls, were placed with care in the natural bumps and knots of the root-walls, acting as little shelves around the nook. Thoughtful gifts exchanged between Daisy and Kopius, to decorate their tiny home inside the tree trunk.

Van brushed aside the warm feeling in her chest. *What fools.* Wasting time making figurines for each other when they could've been honing their fighting skills. Or, back at Lodestar relaying to the Elders the intel gained from their time in the Living World.

Wiglaf sauntered close to Paley's legs. She scooped him up and placed him on her lap.

"You must be hungry," Daisy said. She gave Kopius a nod.

He passed around a wooden snack bowl filled with dried golden mushrooms, nuts, and apple-date jerky, along with a wineskin filled with a sweet amber liquid.

Van wanted to ask a million questions, but etiquette dictated she take part in their casual talk.

Brux and Daisy caught up on family matters. He informed his sister the Elders had named him as Van's assigned protector. This position required him, their father, and now her, to live on Providence Island.

"Ah." Daisy smiled at Van. "I knew if I didn't carry the Anchoress bloodline, it would be you."

The conversation turned to Kopius.

"Tell us how you freed Daisy," Pernilla said.

"I spent most of my time trying to pinpoint her location. That was the hardest part." Kopius tossed a nut in his mouth. "I focused on Balefire Palace in Aduro, but it turned out Merloc had her at Windermere Castle in East Alga. Took me another three months to infiltrate that place. Observed the goings-on, studied the patterns of traffic. I ended up sneaking in dressed as a servant. Bribed a few guards to get into the dungeon. Picked the lock."

"He rescued me." Daisy gazed dreamily at him.

Brux scowled.

"Didn't even get to kill any anyone." Kopius shrugged. "It was easy. Too easy."

"No matter." Brux placed his hand on Daisy's knee in a gesture done to get his sister's attention away from Kopius and back on him. "I'm glad she's here now. Safe."

"That's a lot to take on for someone so young." Paley tucked her chin under her shoulder and made googly eyes at Kopius.

"It was my first mission. Now I'm all about mercenary-style hires." Kopius shoved apple-date jerky in his mouth. "Loved it." He chewed with his mouth open.

"How did Professor Lake find you—a teen mercenary—to hire?" Pernilla asked.

"I met him at Lode-con." Kopius grinned.

Van and the others stared blankly.

"The *Lodian Consilium.* I'm placed on track to become a Grigori. In Salus Valde, we don't have to hide it like you do on Providence Island.

We do internships with the Grigori at Lodestar. Get to mingle with the top officials, senators and the like. Ran into him one day after a chamber meeting. He's a teacher, I'm a student. We got to talking."

"So that's why I've never met you before." Paley stopped petting Wiglaf for a moment so she could flip her hair over her shoulder.

Kopius didn't seem entranced by Paley's flirting and continued speaking to the group. "I've spent time in the Earth World." He shrugged as if were nothing big. "I've been to Providence Island. It's part of our classroom studies."

"Why weren't you placed on our team?" Pernilla asked.

Van swore she caught a sparkle in Pernilla's eye and wondered if a come-hither look would surface next.

"His skills probably weren't complementary to our team," Brux said.

More like not complementary to him. He and Kopius on the same team would spell disaster. Uxa would have known this and prevented it.

"How long ago did you rescue her?" Brux asked.

As Brux interrogated Kopius, his stare betrayed his discomfort about his sister's close relationship with this pompous, overly self-confident boy who looked more like a man.

Van wanted to tell Brux he needn't worry about a relationship between Kopius and Daisy. This guy had *player* written all over him. Despite Kopius's heroic rescue of Daisy from the dungeons of Windermere, Van couldn't believe she was stupid enough to fall for his act. Paley, yes. Daisy, no. Thus, proving once again emotions led to a person's downfall.

"A few months," Daisy answered.

"Couple of weeks," Kopius said at the same time.

"Which is it?" Brux leaped to his feet. "What's going on here?"

"Daisy's still recovering from her experience." Kopius put down his snack and visibly shifted to fighter mode, although he remained seated. "We're waiting for her to heal before we go back."

"It's protocol for you to get back right away." Pernilla seemed to not like him so much now that he had broken the rules.

Kopius frowned at Pernilla. "You Balish? You convert to Lodianism?"

"Why would you ask that?" Pernilla asked, taken aback.

Kopius shrugged, looking a bit more relaxed now that Brux had sat back down rather than pounce on him. "You've got tanned-looking skin. Looks kinda like a Balish skin tone. Your eyes, though. I can't figure out your eyes. Icy, light-blue like Lodians."

Pernilla proudly puffed her chest. "I'm a descendant of the Native Americans in the Earth World. I got the call last year."

"Mixed race. Fascinating." Kopius peered at her. "I assume Uxa figured your bronzed skin would be an advantage in the Living World. People will think you're Balish. Except for the eyes."

"I earned my spot based on my skills." Pernilla slapped her thigh for emphasis.

"Too bad you can't make them brown," Kopius continued to squint at Pernilla. "You'd have it made here."

Paley perked up. "I have brown-colored contact lenses. I can give you a pair."

As Paley shifted to get her contacts from her backpack, Wiglaf jumped from her lap and meandered over to Daisy. He rubbed against her ankles.

Daisy smiled, scooped him up, and placed him on her lap.

Pernilla appeared so perplexed by Kopius and so out of her element she mindlessly accepted Paley's contacts.

"I think we should spend the night here," Brux said. "Before we move on."

"We can't." Van began to stress out. "We only have twenty-nine days left of the Alignment." The wolf-like beast that hunted Van hunted her alone, not any of them. She took it as her personal imperative to keep the team moving before time ran out. "It's too early in the journey to lose a day."

Paley raised her hand and chimed in. "I vote we stay with Kopius and Daisy."

Van glared at Paley. "We can't do that and succeed."

Pernilla rested her knuckle against her chin, deep in thought, and then said, "Maybe we can leave Brux here. He can catch up later."

"I'm fine with that." Van fantasized about leaving all of them, and their emotional baggage, behind.

"It's my duty to stay with Van," Brux said. "So we're not splitting up."

"What about the Twin Gemstones?" Paley said, alarmed. "I have to stay with Brux."

"Oh, right," Pernilla said.

"That too." Brux smiled at Paley. "I haven't forgotten." He turned to the group. "As team leader, I think it's best we take a vote. Stay or go. I'll do what the group decides."

Van cast her eyes downward, unimpressed with Brux's leadership. He wasn't fit for the role. He was too soft.

"We stay the night. Hands up." Brux raised his hand along with Paley.

"We leave now."

Pernilla and Van's hands shot into the air. They stared at each other, both astounded to agree for the first time.

The team faced a tie.

No wonder Uxa formed five-member teams. Her son would've been the tie-breaker. Too bad he wasn't there. Being a well-trained warrior, he would've voted in favor of Van's idea.

Daisy continued to stroke Wiglaf as she watched the interaction.

The bunfy lay in bliss, curled on her lap. His long ears flopped down over the side of her leg.

"No need for a vote," Daisy's soft voice rang through her cozy home in the tree.

All their heads turned in her direction. People always seemed surprised when Daisy spoke, as if someone so delicate and serene couldn't make that much sound.

Daisy stared, looking at no one in particular. She threw back her shoulders to enforce her words. "I'm going with you."

"What?" Brux cried.

"No." Kopius leaped to his feet.

Their outburst shook Daisy and startled Wiglaf enough that he popped back into his magical animal realm.

Daisy also stood. "I want to complete the mission I started last year."

"Daisy," Brux said as he raised himself from the dirt floor. "We completed that mission. Van retrieved the Coin of Creation. Van's the Anchoress."

"Well…" Daisy paused. "What's the new mission?" She looked each team member in the eye, attempting to extract an answer.

No one dared speak if it meant suffering Brux's wrath.

"There is one," she continued, "or you wouldn't be here."

"We're going to the second seal," Van said. "Uxa believes it's cracked. Our mission is to mend it."

Daisy looked like she was about to ask a question.

"Not the animal," Van added.

"Ah." Daisy bobbed her head.

Brux shifted his body weight back and forth. "You need to get back home. To rest. Heal from your ordeal of being stuck in the dungeons of Windermere for almost a year."

Daisy ignored him. "Tell me more about the mission."

"The seal binds the two worlds together," Pernilla said. "The pressure caused by negativity in Earth World might've cracked it."

"And there's the illness," Van said. "There are so many demons being generated by the terrigens, a sickness formed. Right now, it's confined to Providence Island, but it could seep through the crack and reach the Living World."

Kopius positioned himself protectively closer to Daisy. To Van, it seemed habitual.

Daisy appeared to reflect on this information. "Mending the crack will prevent an outbreak in the Living World, and stop the demons in the Earth World from breaking through the seal," she said, to make sure she understood.

Brux had a close relationship with his sister. So close, he seemed to know what was on her mind.

He nodded. "Similar to when the seal broke a thousand years ago."

"During the Dark War."

Kopius wrapped his arm around Daisy. "How do you know that? Your father?"

"Our father. Yes," Daisy said.

"Having one who's a philologist at the Royal Lodian University, it's a given he taught us Lodian-Balish history," Brux said.

"How does the cracked seal fit in with the Dark War?" Kopius asked.

"The war was ferocious and bloody," Daisy said.

Van squirmed, hearing those terrible words coming from Daisy. It seemed odd and made a more significant impact.

"It lasted so long, it caused an imbalance of nature." Daisy hesitated, as if shaken by the blasphemy of anything disrupting the harmony of the natural world.

Brux took over. "The war started between the two most powerful tribes: the Lodians and the Balish. The Balish didn't care for the Lodians, the tribe favored by the Elementals, and sought to conquer their land, secrets, and access to the portal."

"The Balish were trying to rule more and more of the Living World," Kopius said. "The tribes fought back. I know the basics about the war."

"But did you know the Balish didn't fear the Anchoress or the Lodians?" Brux asked. "The Anchoress heir back then was a queen, a ruler. Her powers remained legend and folklore."

"All tribes had to choose a side," Daisy said. "The negative vibrations were strong and quickly reached the point where they could crack one, if not all three seals. This would allow the demons generated in the Earth World full access to the Living World, which we know eventually happened."

"Now it's happening again," Kopius said, answering his own question. "And there's no war in either world to create negative conditions to crack a seal."

Daisy glanced at her surroundings. "This tree acted as a resting place during the Dark War. A neutral place, a place of peace."

"How do you know that?" Van asked.

"I can feel it." Daisy gazed into space as if seeing something they didn't. "My connection to nature is telling me this is so."

Van resisted the urge to roll her eyes. *Another emotional basket case.* All the more reason to leave Daisy there and get the team moving.

"I'm joining your team," Daisy snapped out her reverie and said with gusto. "I want to help prevent the spread of this illness."

Daisy could command a room when she put her mind to it. She stood firm in her decision, claiming that as a newfound healer, it was her duty. None of them could talk her out of it.

By the time they had worked out the details about Kopius, who went on record against Daisy's decision, and Daisy joining the team, dusk was soon to set in and they decided to stay in the tree for the night.

Once they settled the particulars, Daisy and Kopius broke out their rations and they all ate a dinner of saffron rice and beans. Afterward, Van wanted to revitalize her spirit with a walk and some fresh air.

She twisted around before reaching the door-like opening in the root-wall, expecting someone to question her.

No one did, but Brux appeared torn about to who to care for: Van or Daisy. He chose Daisy, who continued to act a bit too familiar with Kopius.

Van gave them one last glance before she departed. The team looked like two couples gathered around a fire pit. Kopius and Daisy; Brux and Paley. Pernilla, the odd one out for once, looked forlorn, as though she longed for a multi-track to call Ken.

Van climbed down the terraced rocks. Tomorrow, she would make sure they nixed the melodrama and refocused on completing the task. She reached the collection pond at the base of the waterfall.

In the waning evening light, Van glanced at her reflection in the shallow edge of the pond. She frowned and used her palms to smooth her hair, mostly out of habit drilled into her by her step-mother rather than caring about her appearance. She hadn't transported to the Living World to enter a beauty contest. Van was there on a mission to protect her people.

Calmed by the steady rumble of the waterfall, she gazed at her reflection rippling in the waves.

Her image blurred.

The reflection of a woman stared back at her. She looked in her twenties and had long, wavy golden hair.

Van blinked. She looked again and saw her own reflection staring back at her. Van closed her eyes and shook her head, hoping to stop her mind from playing tricks.

She opened her eyes and gazed into the water, and saw... *blood?* She squinted. *That's not blood.*

Van reached into the pond and used her fingertips to pick up the flat, translucent, orange-red colored stone. *A carnelian*—was her last thought before her vision faded and grayed around the edges.

A wave of dizziness overcame her.

Her body crashed to the ground just before she lost consciousness.

CHAPTER 16

Van gripped the stone so tightly her knuckles ached.

Her fingers were long and thin, but they weren't her hands. They were a young woman's, perhaps in her early twenties. A woman from another time. From a thousand years ago.

Zurial. One of the four warriors of the Dark War. Amaryl's sister.

Van felt Zurial.

She was Zurial.

Zurial smelled the fresh scent of pine as she traveled through the woods at the foot of Mt. Altithronia. She gently rocked back and forth on the hard seat of the horse-drawn carriage, alert and tense. Next to her sat her mother, Queen Cordelia, who had just retrieved the four Items of Creation from the Elementals.

Zurial rubbed the orange-red carnelian worry stone with her thumb to calm her nerves.

Soldiers burst from the woods on horseback dressed in black uniforms with a red and gold crest—the Balish—and descended upon their wagon.

"Stick with the plan," her mother cried.

Zurial's heart raced as she leaped from her seat.

Her companions also jumped from the wagon. Her sister Amaryl's husband, Rowen, and his brother, Romet.

The four royals, who each concealed an Item of Creation, had planned to flee in different directions in case of a Balish attack. So Zurial dashed into the woods away from them.

She gripped her satchel to make sure she still secured the Cup of Life and hid behind a nearby tree to catch her breath.

Commotion coming from the wagon caused her to peek around the tree. She watched as her mother stayed put, along with several of her men. They unsheathed their swords.

The soldiers advanced.

Swords clanked.

Zurial's knuckles turned white from gripping the bark as she watched a Balish soldier knock the sword from Cordelia's hand. The queen's men struggled for their own lives, unable to help.

Her mother lunged to the side of the wagon, reached in and withdrew the Staff of Fire, her Item of Creation.

The massive soldier stepped forward, sword raised.

In one motion, Cordelia twisted, swiped the Staff, and blocked the soldier's attack.

Zurial jolted as she recognized the soldier battling her mother. The Balish Prince Goustav.

Goustav slashed and jabbed at Cordelia. He came down with a hard blow. The Staff tumbled from her hands. He swooped down and picked it up.

Goustav grinned as he held the Staff; his eyes widened.

Zurial believed they would take her mother hostage. Her heart sank as she saw the glint in Goustav's eyes. His grin, not one of victory, but of insanity. She knew by merely touching the Staff he had become corrupted by its power.

Goustav twirled the Staff and then stuck the tip into Cordelia's breast bone. With little effort, he plunged the Staff through her chest.

Blood spurted from the wound. Cordelia's eyes opened wide in surprise, then froze right before her light faded, and she slumped to the ground.

Zurial needed to go to her mother's side. As a trained healer, she could use her knowledge along with the power of the Cup, and mend her mother.

She took a step out from behind the tree. Someone clasped her arm, stopping her.

Her heart skipped a beat before the man said, "This way. Hurry."

To Zurial's relief, it was Romet. He had returned for her.

"But, my mother—"

"She is gone, and we will be next. Goustav has the Staff of Fire. Our men cannot hold him off for long. We must flee."

His grip tightened, giving her no choice but to go with him.

Branches swiped her face as she and Romet dashed through the woods.

They heard the rush of footsteps echoing behind them.

Romet paused. "Go!"

Zurial halted, stunned. "What?"

"Go. I will meet you back at Lodestar."

"No."

The determined steps of Goustav's soldiers grew closer.

"Go." Romet turned his back to her and faced the direction of the oncoming soldiers. He raised his sword.

Zurial dashed away. Branches snapped back and slapped her face and arms. Her eyes, widened in terror, occasionally got lashed with twigs and leaves. She didn't care. She ran.

The muscles in her legs became stressed, and she stopped to catch her breath. She gripped a tree and scanned her unfamiliar surroundings. She was lost.

The steady rumble of a nearby waterfall filled her ears. The sound comforted Zurial and, like a beacon calling to her, she followed it.

She entered a clearing. Water cascaded down the side of a cliff surrounded on both sides by lush vegetation. Here, she could see Mt. Altithronia and determined her general location. Afraid if she kept wandering she might run into Balish soldiers, Zurial climbed the falls, to the enormous tree that grew at the top.

She wedged herself into the tree's roots to hide and found it made a cozy nook. "This will do."

She settled in and curled into a ball, hoping no one would find her. With the Cup tucked securely in the satchel around her waist, perhaps she could get some rest.

Someone splashing in the base pond at the foot of the waterfall roused her. Romet!

Fearing he might be wounded, she bounded down the terraced rocks along the side of the waterfall.

A man lay face down in the shallow rim of the pond, dressed in a black uniform, dirty and bleeding.

Zurial's healer instincts kicked in and, fearing he might drown, she gently rolled him onto his back.

He blinked as if to clear his vision.

"Am I dead?" he asked with a croak.

Underneath the grime, bruises, and blood, Zurial could see the man was about her age and strikingly handsome. Her heart fluttered from instant attraction.

She helped the stranger to his feet and got him up the side of the falls and into the nook.

They had barely squeezed between the roots before he collapsed to his knees and passed out.

Zurial tore a piece of cloth from the hem of her robe and began wiping the blood and dirt from his face. The man's cropped haircut provided a clear sign of his royal status.

He opened his eyes; Zurial jerked back in fear.

"Where is my sword?" He struggled to sit up.

Zurial placed her hands on his shoulders and gently pushed him back down. "It is here. But you are safe. There is no need for your sword."

He blinked at Zurial as if processing her words. "My name is... Nick."

To protect her identity, but also not wanting to lie, Zurial gave him an abbreviation of her real name. "Zuri."

His eyes darted. "What is this place?"

"A mother tree, I think."

The vision blurred for a moment.

NICK LOOKED PALE AND SWEATY. He lay on the dirt floor in the mother tree, disoriented and semi-conscious.

He tried to lift himself.

Zurial gently pressed his shoulders, settling him back down. "Stay still.

You are sick with fever. Your injuries have become infected." She believed he hovered close to death.

She patted his forehead with a damp cloth. Warmness radiated in her heart as she gazed at Nick's face. She barely knew this man, yet feared to lose him.

His breathing became shallow. He stopped fidgeting and lost consciousness.

In a fit of desperation, Zurial grabbed the gold chalice, the Cup of Life.

Her training hadn't included handling its power, and, though a royal Lodian, she was not the Anchoress heir. Using the Item could make her fall into insanity as the Staff had done with Goustav.

Zurial said a prayer to the Creator and took her chances. She dipped the Cup into the closest water—the waterfall. Then, she placed the Cup on a nearby rock and cast a simple healing spell.

She left the Cup overnight to absorb the beams of the moon, as she had learned to do as a trained healer. At first light, she grabbed the Cup and dashed back into the nook.

She placed it to Nick's lips and poured the liquid into his mouth as best she could.

Immediately, his skin color improved, and breathing stabilized.

The vision blurred again as Zurial moved Van through time.

NICK LOOKED STRONG AND HEALTHY. Even his abrasions and bruises had healed.

Zurial's heart swelled with love for this man, but with this love came trepidation. By using the Cup of Life, Zurial had exposed her true identity to him as a Lodian royal. His enemy.

"You know who I am." Zurial backed away from him.

His warm brown eyes pierced hers. He nodded and stepped closer. "And you know who I am."

"Why did you attack our wagon? We were trying to bring a peaceful end to this war." Her back bumped against the root-made wall as he advanced closer.

"Following orders. Like now. I have orders." He reached for Zurial.

She pressed her back against the wall as if to move as far away from him as possible. "What orders?"

He wrapped his hands around her neck. "To kill you."

VAN WOKE WITH A START.

Zurial had released Van from the vision before finding out what had happened. But she knew the Lodian princess hadn't died. Later in her life, she had married the Balish King Manik.

The memory engram annoyed Van. Zurial had held her captive, forced to experience the pain caused by the death of the princess's mother, Queen Cordelia. Then Zurial left her hanging with impressions of both love and confusion for the Balish royal, Nick. A man who tried to choke her to death.

By recalling the memory engram, Zurial's love for Nick flooded Van. Then she remembered a certain detail from Zurial's vision and it replaced her warm fuzziness with raging anger.

CHAPTER 17

"There are *more*!" Van screeched as she rushed back into the nook. "More Item*s* of Creation!"

The four holders in the Celestial Tower made sense to her now.

"The Coin of Creation was just the first one! Did any of you know this?"

"Well, yeah," Brux and Daisy said in unison.

"I kind of figured based on the ancient stories," Daisy said.

"Along with the plural translation issues in the ancient language," Brux said. "And the four holders in the Tower. I thought you knew."

She stomped her foot. "I wasn't sure." Again, Van wanted to throttle Brux. "Would've been helpful to get confirmation."

Van took a deep breath in and let go of her anger as she breathed out. She updated everyone on her ability to receive memory engrams. Messages and impressions of events that had happened in the past by touching an emotionally charged object. She relayed Zurial's story.

"The carnelian worry stone belonged to Zurial." Van slapped her hands against her pockets, already knowing the stone wasn't there. "Ugh. I left it by the pond."

"No matter," Kopius said. "You got Zurial's message. Not sure what it means."

"It's a warning," Daisy said. "Cordelia retrieved the Items of Creation with the intent to use them to defeat the Balish. They're only to be used against what the ancients call *true evil,* not each other."

"So, if the Cup's magical ability is to heal and we can only use it against evil... doesn't that mean we're only supposed to heal evil people?" Paley asked. "Is that why Zurial didn't go insane after healing Nick, the evil Balish soldier?"

"Or do injuries count as evil and we use the Cup to heal wounds?" Pernilla pondered aloud.

"The Items of Creation are weapons," Kopius said. "How is healing an injured person a weapon?"

"The Cup can heal warriors injured in battle." Van shrugged. "It can keep your army strong, I guess."

"You *guess?*" Paley asked. "Aren't you the Anchoress? Shouldn't you *know?*"

Van glared at her friend. How dare Paley challenge her abilities in front of the team.

"Listen," Brux said. "Zurial used the Cup's powers to heal a person who was dying from battle injuries. She used it correctly."

"Did she?" Kopius asked. "Maybe Nick was destined to die and Zurial saved him against the will of the Creator."

"Sounds evil to me." Paley batted her eyelashes at Kopius.

"Queen Cordelia never should've retrieved the Items of Creation to begin with." Van made an effort to sound in control after Paley's awkward questions. "So the users are more likely to become corrupted, or driven insane."

"Why would she do that?" Pernilla asked. "Even if the Elders asked her to, it wasn't worth the risk."

"Order needed to be restored," Daisy said, in defense of Queen Cordelia. "The Great War between the Lodians and Balish wouldn't end quickly or easily. As the Anchoress of their time, she believed the only solution was to journey to Mt. Altithronia and retrieve her Items from the Elementals."

"Back then, the Quasher was still entombed beneath the earth by the Elementals, so there was no time constraint," Van said, still haunted by thoughts of the shadow-creature's large clawed paws and snapping jaw.

"Queen Cordelia took three other royals with her." Brux had learned the same story as Daisy from their father. "One to be responsible for each Item. Cordelia's husband, King Halldor, stayed behind at Lodestar to guard over their eldest daughter, Amaryl, the heir to the Anchoress bloodline."

"Princess Amaryl was too valuable to the Lodians to go on such a high-risk mission," Daisy added.

"Cordelia's reasoning made sense," Brux said. "Once she had her Items, she could tap into her magical powers as Anchoress, wield her weapons, and easily defeat the Balish. She took responsibility for ending the war. If the violence had continued, demons would've reached the Living World, causing Dishora. It's just... her plan failed thanks to the Balish ambush."

"Demons rose, and the Great war between the Lodians and Balish turned into the Dark War. Humanity versus demons," Kopius said. "Common historical knowledge."

"It's dangerous to retrieve all the Items of Creation." Daisy stared into space. "Too much power in the hands of mortals."

"It's a moot point." Pernilla shook her head. "I'm not sure why Zurial showed Van the Cup of Life. But our mission isn't to get another Item. It's checking the seal."

"We don't even know where the Cup is," Kopius said, in a way that implied he was thinking about retrieving it.

But Van knew the Cup's location. Cortica. They were headed straight for it.

Now she understood why the Coin pointed to the ankh on the map in Uxa's office. The Coin showed Van the best path for success. It had directed her to the Cup of Life.

Maybe it wasn't a coincidence Uxa picked the second seal, the one closet to the Cup. Van was the only person who could retrieve it from its hiding place, and only during the Alignment.

Did Uxa use a cracked seal as an excuse to bring Van close enough to Cortica that her magically activated Anchoress homing device would kick in, and she would be irresistibly drawn to the Item? Did Uxa plan for Van to retrieve the Cup all along?

Van shook her head to clear her thoughts.

Uxa had no ulterior motive. Van's dark thoughts were the byproduct of her damaged soul. It made sense for the Coin to point to the next Item of Creation. All four Items were probably seeking to reconnect to their collective power.

However, every Item placed in the hands of Uxa meant more power for the Lodians, and more personal power for Uxa. With the possibility of another war between the Lodians and Balish, it made sense Uxa would want them.

Then why not outright tell us the mission is to retrieve the Cup?

Paley broke Van's musings. "Has anyone figured out how we're going to check the seal if it's at the bottom of the Bottomless Sea?"

"Kopius will figure it out." Daisy smiled and lovingly gazed at him. "He can figure out anything."

"My special skill is creative problem-solving." Kopius smiled back at her.

The team's conversation faded. Several of them yawned, and they settled in for the night.

* * *

AT DAWN, Van took out the Coin and used it to find the best path to the Bottomless Sea. It pointed west.

"Ah!" Kopius raised his index finger in the air. "Toward Cortica, also known as Outlaw Island."

"And the seal," Pernilla added.

And the Cup. But Van kept this piece of information to herself.

The team left the mother tree and headed west. They took trunk-a-vators as far as the network would allow and then walked the rest of the way.

During their journey, Van occasionally consulted the Coin to keep them on track.

"You can give the Coin a rest now." Kopius' feet squished with each step. "We can follow Swampy Creek to the west coast."

Van threw him a questioning look.

"I memorized this region when I went searching for Daisy. Can't carry a map around. It's a dead giveaway I'm unfamiliar with the area. Might as well put a bullseye on my back."

Although they used the Coin, the trunk-a-vators, and followed the creek, it still took them five days to reach their destination. An area called the Skeleton Coast.

Saltbox houses popped up along the dirt road.

"It's a rough area," Kopius warned. "Loaded with miscreants and degenerates. Anyone who thrives living on the fringes of society."

They came to a wharf area that, even during daylight, had the shadiness of a rundown waterfront.

People scurried along, none staying in one spot too long. They wore layered, loose fitting, dingy clothes and looked like they hadn't bathed in years.

"Is this the only place that offers ships to the Bottomless Sea?" Brux nervously glanced at Daisy. Her delicate fragility and beauty in the wharf area stood out like a sunflower growing out of a pile of manure.

"Not exactly." Kopius looked grim. "We have to go to Outlaw Island to get passage to the Bottomless Sea. None of the ships on the coast will go there. At least, not where we want to go."

"How do we get passage to the island?" Pernilla's shoulders were tense, her eyes alert.

"When in doubt, look about," Kopius said. Daisy appreciated his wit. When no one else did, he sighed. "Let's check out the local watering holes."

Van reached for her pocket; Kopius placed his hand on her arm. "Not a great place to take that out." He meant the Coin. "Any of these hovels will do. Trust me."

"Never trust anyone who says *trust me*," Brux muttered.

The team strolled down the grimy, dirt road in the wharf area, in silence so they wouldn't draw attention to their group.

"Here," Kopius said. "Let's give this one a shot."

Painted across the entire front exterior wall of the two-story structure was a faded, simplistic mural. It depicted a scary-looking skeleton wielding a sickle. The skeleton rode a white horse that had already trampled over a fallen king and drew close to a young woman clutching a baby. Wavy blue water flowed in the background. Below the picture, a hand-painted name read *Fisherman's Rest.*

The eatery, the mural, and the wharf gave Van the heebie-jeebies.

Daisy, alongside Van, scrutinized the mural. "The skeleton of death. A warning," she said. "No one is free from experiencing the pain of death."

Paley shivered and clutched Van's arm.

"It gives a whole new meaning to the 'rest' in Fisherman's Rest." Kopius chuckled. He walked up the creaky, rotted wooden porch steps.

"The flowing water behind the skeleton is symbolic of the constant circulation of life," Daisy continued. "A force that comes into materialization and flows out again. The cycle of life and death."

"Well, aren't you the cheery one?" Pernilla brushed past Daisy, bounded up the porch steps, and went inside, right behind Kopius.

Brux nodded his approval, and the others followed.

It's just a stupid drawing. Van ignored the prickles on her skin and entered the eatery.

CHAPTER 18

The Fisherman's Rest was packed with people, which helped mask the team's entrance. There wasn't a drinking age in the Living World, but from the looks of the place, age wouldn't have been an issue, anyway.

Round dining tables dotted the large open room, all taken, and a mob of customers stood cramped in the spaces in between. The patrons were unshaven, disheveled, and had a look of depravity about them. Van overheard several lewd comments as she followed the others, one after the other, as they squeezed through the throng.

They ended up at the bar.

Daisy appeared serene and unimpressed with the degenerate patrons and the dismal ambiance of the place. This prompted Van to wonder what experiences she had while kidnapped, and on her journey back to Salus Valde with Kopius.

Still, Brux shifted to shield Daisy from the eatery's customers.

"Best place to get info? From the bartender." Kopius clapped his hands together, ready for action.

"Good," Van said. "I need some food." She wedged her way between Brux and Paley and leaned on the bar's railing.

"Get something alcoholic," Kopius suggested.

Brux snorted in disgust.

Kopius gave him the side-eye. "It's safer to drink alcohol here. The water's contaminated."

Pernilla raised her index finger to her lips. "Shh." She tilted her head toward the group gathered next to her at the bar.

Everyone on their team stopped talking and listened.

"Be careful," a plump woman with ratty hair warned her friends. "The Balish are infiltrating this area."

"They're not supposed to be here," said a potbellied man wearing a sailor's cap. "This is just more upheaval in the Balish kingdom."

"They're pushing their boundaries," said another man with several missing teeth. "Trying to clean up the coast, make it more civilized." He grimaced at the last word.

"Bales better stay away from Outlaw Island," said a scruffy man. "They'll get shredded to pieces there."

"I heard the Balish Council put a kill order on Lodian children," said the potbellied man. "Rumored the Anchoress is floating about."

"If she's out of bounds, then the Moors will have what they want." The ratty-haired took a sip from her tin mug. "The Balish can take over Salus Valde once and for all."

"Not without going to war," the potbellied man said. "One that will bring about Dishora."

"You mean, Solmor," the man with missing teeth said.

The group narrowed their eyes at the potbellied man.

"You Lodian?" the woman accused.

The men grumbled as one shoved the potbellied man.

"What're you? A dirt lover?" the scruffy man asked.

"No... I—" The potbellied man tried to speak, but the others roughly dragged him toward the door.

Kopius watched as they left. "Brutal."

Van shuddered. Everyone there seemed ready to brawl.

"Dirt lover?" Pernilla asked.

Brux redoubled his effort to shield Daisy. "It's a derogatory term making fun of Lodians and our beliefs. Specifically, our Grigori."

"So they're making fun of how we care for and protect the weak and innocent?" Pernilla grimaced with disgust. She leaned on the bar and raised her hand to get the bartender's attention.

Paley eyed a cute boy sitting on a bar stool nearby. He gazed pensively into his mug. His calloused hands showed he worked on the docks, perhaps as a fisherman's apprentice.

"I think he's admiring his reflection in the mead," Van whispered to Paley.

Paley shrugged. "I'll go find out." She darted over and leaned against the bar next to him.

He immediately perked up.

Daisy slid away from Brux so she could stand closer to Kopius.

Brux's nostrils flared. He grabbed Kopius by the elbow and pulled him aside, away from his sister, but close enough so Van could hear.

"What's the deal with you and Daisy?" he asked.

"There's nothing going on," Kopius said. "Your father's paying me to protect her, not date her, and I'm still on the clock. Geesh, man." Kopius shook his head. "Get your mind out of the gutter."

Kopius jerked his elbow free from Brux's grip. "Now," he said, straightening his shirt. "If you don't mind, I'm going to go help your sister complete *your* mission."

He weaved into the crowd away from the bar and Daisy.

Brux went back and leaned next to Van. "He's lying, of course."

"Daisy will be fine. It's just a case of puppy love." Van placed a comforting hand on Brux's shoulder. "Kopius is an okay guy. He'll do what's right."

Pernilla continued to have no luck, so Brux stretched his arm to flag down the bartender.

Van glimpsed Kopius chatting with several women on the other side of the eatery and nudged Brux to look. "His charm seems to work well with older women."

Brux twisted around. "Charm? His personality oozes like puss from a zit."

Van chuckled, then whispered, "Seems like his relationship with Daisy might already be over."

Relief flooded Brux's face; Daisy looked defeated, like a wilted flower.

While Brux and Pernilla jockeyed for the bartender's attention, Van noticed Brux with fresh eyes. Although his focus was on keeping his sister safe, when Van stood close to Brux, his energy seemed to encircle Van like a protective shield. She gazed at his biceps... they were definitely bigger this year. When she breathed in, she caught his sweet masculine scent and it made her feel warm and safe. Her insides swirled like a million tiny tickles, which irritated her to no end.

Paley returned, sulking.

"What's wrong?" Van asked.

Paley flipped her hair over her shoulder. "I learned more about my parents."

"You did?" Van raised her brow. "That's great. And really random. How does a stranger know who your parents are?"

"Not like that." Paley's eyes welled up and darted to the floor. "It's just... I was so used to being an orphan."

Van waited patiently during Paley's dramatic pause.

"That guy made me realize what it means to not be one." Paley could barely get the words out. "It's—m-my parents. They... didn't want me."

Paley's unexpected comment threw Van completely off balance. Her heart ached over Paley's pain.

"That guy's a slimeball." Anger helped take away the uncomfortable warmness in Van's chest. "Don't listen to him. Why'd you tell him you were a blunt?"

"I didn't. I pretended I grew up here. I got him talking about when we were kids and being scared of the Janus monster and stuff. So I could get a better understanding, you know. Turned out to be a bad move."

"Why? What'd you find out?"

"The Balish adults and practically all the tribes know Janus is a transport system to the Earth World." Paley stuck her knuckle in her mouth to stifle a sob.

"So?"

Paley unclenched her fist from her teeth. "The adults… they *choose* to leave their children in the Earth World. They tell themselves the Janus monster only eats the sick babies. Parents who lose their babies believe it's best to let them go. So the remaining family can move on with their lives." Tears streaked down Paley's cheeks. "They know about the portal in Salus Valde. They know the Grigori will let them transport to see their children." Paley sobbed. "But none of them ever do. They leave us! They just… *leave us*."

"I'm so sorry." Van slid off her stool and wrapped her arms around Paley.

"S-some parents come to Providence Island," Paley continued between sobs.

Van could feel the back of her shirt getting damp from Paley's tears.

"The Lodian Consilium allows them to convert to Lodianism and live on Providence Island, if they want. They can even bring their vichor children." Paley let out a wet, sloppy sob. "I c-could've had a r-real family. B-but, my parents didn't love me."

Pernilla, Daisy, and Brux stared at them. Van was certain they could overhear her and Paley's conversation, but stayed out of it, respecting their privacy.

Paley released her from the hug. "You know what?"

"What?" Van asked, relieved that Paley seemed to perk up.

"I need to find my loser parents." Paley wiped her eyes. "Confront them for being such uncaring asshats. Let them know it was their loss."

"Yeah! You go, girl," Van said, happy Paley had resolved her parental issues. "Don't talk to that guy anymore. He's a jerk, like most guys. I'm never falling in love."

"Yes, you will," Paley said kindly, her eyes wide and soft. "It's just… you're all locked up right now. Some great guy will come along and unlock you."

"Pfft. Doubt it," Van said as she scanned the disgusting male patrons in the eatery.

"Sure he will. He just needs to be smart enough to know he's a key and not a hammer."

Van's mind moved away from the unlikely prospect of romance back to her personal mission. Paley stuck to hers, finding out more about her parents. Now Van needed to refocus on her first order of business, removing the Anchoress curse. She doubted the miscreants on the docks would be any help.

Kopius swaggered back to the bar.

Daisy brightened; Brux grimaced and walked away.

"What did you find out?" Daisy's tone implied answering the question would verify he had done recon and wasn't flirting.

"I'm over this place." Pernilla glared at the bartender who casually chatted with patrons at the other end of the bar. "Let's find passage to Cortica and get out of here."

"I'm all for that." Van couldn't wait to get this mission done and get home. She doubled her resolve to talk Uxa into letting her be a full-fledged Grigori fighting demons in the Earth World.

"It won't be easy," Kopius said. "Cortica is off the map, if you know what I mean."

"No." Van stared at him. "I don't."

"He means it's not on any maps," Daisy said, sucking the mystery out of Kopius's comment.

Van thought Daisy's response was unlike her and figured it came from Daisy's frustration with Kopius flirting with those women.

"So right, my brilliant little flower." Kopius kissed Daisy on the top of her head; Daisy beamed.

"Those who live on Cortica, refuse to live by Balish law." Kopius rested one arm around Daisy's back. "They're wanted criminals hunted by the Balish, some flat out reject society."

"Or society rejected them," Pernilla said.

"It can't be worse than this place." Daisy rubbed her arms as if to keep away chills despite the warmth inside the stuffy, overcrowded eatery.

Kopius rubbed her back, and Daisy leaned into him.

Van's eyes scanned the crowd, hoping Brux wasn't watching.

"The Balish don't go there because the island is too unruly for even them to control," Kopius said. "Looting is their primary industry."

"Hey." Brux had returned, too preoccupied with something to notice Kopius and Daisy's intimacy. "You guys, come with me." He took them to the back room of the eatery where a clean-shaven man stood on a wooden crate surrounded by a crowd of blackguards, who gave the man their full attention as he spoke.

"He's built a following by speaking in cafes, pubs, and eateries all over the region," Brux said in a low voice. "His name's Semjaza."

Van leaned close to Brux. "What's he talking about?"

Brux lowered himself to Van's height and whispered, "You."

CHAPTER 19

Brux's last word—*you*—sent a shiver of fear through Van.

She glanced at Semjaza, standing on his soapbox, and surveyed the crowd. They were rapt with attention as the man spoke about the Lodian's legendary Anchoress.

"She has revealed herself to those in power, but many of us remain skeptical," Semjaza said. "Rest assured, she walks among us."

The onlookers murmured as they mulled over this bit of information.

"Before the death of Prince Ferox's siblings, he had no desire to inherit the throne. He preferred to live life with carefree, wild abandon, like his father." Semjaza wriggled his finger at the crowd. "Now the boy's responsible side is coming out, like that of his dear departed mother, Queen Brigid."

The crowd appeared enraptured by the soapbox orator.

"The upheaval in the Balish kingdom caused by the death of his family members—Princess Solana, Queen Brigid, and Prince Devon—opens the door to others attempting to take over. There will be much turmoil. A time of darkness has come upon us."

The crowd shifted and grumbled.

"The Balish Council wants to kill the Lodian's Anchoress. Snuff her light out of existence because of her immense power." He smashed his fist into his palm. "I say no!"

The spectators murmured and several shouted "No!" in agreement.

"Um." Van tugged Brux's sleeve. "I'm going back to the bar."

Semjaza lowered his voice. "There's an illness spreading to our shores."

Van stopped and twisted around as the onlookers gaped at Semjaza.

"How does he know about the illness?" Van whispered to Brux; he shushed her.

"By word of the light, this illness grows stronger. It will consume our souls. This d*emon illness,*" he raised voice with added passion, "came from the Earth World and is afflicting our children and our compromised adults. Take my word, if we don't stop the spread, this disease will reach each one of us!"

The crowd gasped.

"We need the Anchoress to set this right!" he shouted. "She will vanquish the darkness and save us! She is our redemption!"

"Oh brother," Van muttered, hoping she never came face to face with this guy.

After Semjaza finished ranting, he made his pitch for the onlookers to join his group, called Crusaders of the Light. He stepped down from his wooden crate and mingled with his audience.

"He's taking a huge chance yapping openly about the Anchoress," Pernilla said.

Kopius shook his head. "Not here. Anything goes."

"That's probably why he's here," Daisy said. "Despite the darkness of this place, there's an undercurrent of freedom… of light."

Van almost resented Daisy for always seeing the good in everything. Although every part of Daisy appeared fragile, from her naive mind to her tapered fingers that looked like their grip could barely hold the weight of a napkin, Daisy seemed to gain strength from her connection to the unseen vibration of nature.

"Should we believe him?" Van asked. "About the illness reaching the Living World."

Brux nodded. "We have to assume it leaked through the cracked seal."

"We need to mend that thing, fast," Kopius said.

"I couldn't agree more." Van nodded. "Let's get moving."

Daisy, Kopius, and Pernilla had made their way out of the back room. But Semjaza caught Van, Brux, and Paley as they tried to edge their way through the crowd.

"What brings you young'uns to the wharf?" he asked. "You lost? Need help? The word of the light will guide you."

"Thanks, but no," Brux said. "We're here to book passage to Cortica."

"Oh, no. No." Semjaza visually cringed as he swept his hands back and forth. "I'm here to save people from that kind of life."

"It's not like that," Van said.

"Life of crime. Living on the run. It's no life," Semjaza counseled. "Whatever you kids did wrong, it's not as bad as you think. By word of the light, it can be fixed."

Paley put her hands on her hips. "We did nothing wrong."

"Listen." Semjaza placed a hand on Brux's shoulder. "No good comes from Outlaw Island. That place... it takes your light. Chews you up and spits you out."

Brux crossed his arms. "Can you tell us how to get there or not?"

"You said you'd help us." Paley turned on her special skill and twirled her hair. She flashed him a big smile.

Semjaza grinned, suggesting he had a soft spot for Paley. "You can get there easy enough by paying for passage on one of the ships at the docks here. Most make runs to Cortica off the books." He winked and then leaned in closer to the trio. "But once you get there, you'll need money, or strength, to keep from getting killed. From the looks of it, you all have neither. It might be best you walk in light and join my crusaders."

"What we're doing is important to your cause," Van said with bravado.

Semjaza raised his brow. "Is that right now?" He squinted at Van. "What did you say your name was?"

Brux stepped in front of Van, probably thinking along the same lines as her. They didn't need this blabbermouth to think for even a second Van carried the Anchoress bloodline. Talk about adding risk to the mission. Especially when out of bounds Lodians were marked for death by the Balish.

"We're fated by the light to go there." Brux used a phrase that would resonate with Semjaza. "That's all you need to know." He winked conspiratorially.

Semjaza rubbed his chin in thought. "Fairy trade's hot right now." He kept staring into Van's eyes.

Van knew why. He hoped to see the telltale phosphorescent violet glow, a distinguishing mark of the Anchoress. Too bad for him, the glow only appeared when Van connected to her magical bloodline. But she didn't want to take any chances and thought it best to get away from this guy fast.

"Despicable trade. Highly illegal," he continued. "A fairy's tear will get you anything you want in Cortica, though. If you can get one, it will prove your prowess as thieves. Get you street credibility. Then you can get anything you want. But you didn't hear it from me."

Semjaza edged his was back into the throng, many eagerly waiting to speak with him.

"How do we get one?" Brux called to him.

He twisted around. "Get what?" Semjaza disappeared into the crowd.

The trio made their way back to the bar where Daisy, Kopius, and Pernilla were waiting. As they relayed their conversation with Semjaza, the bartender finally waited on them.

Seizing the moment, they ordered food and drinks. Kopius volunteered to run down to the docks and book their passage to Cortica, as long as they promised not to eat his double saebal bomb with fries.

"Wha—never mind." Van didn't even want to know.

The team stuffed their faces while anxiously waiting for Kopius' return. Van had scooped the last of her Moss Almonds and Avocado

Pud dessert into her mouth when Kopius returned from his trip to the docks.

"Booked passage on the *Seahag*." Kopius waved a handful of tickets. "It's a grain barge. Captain will take us on and drop us in Cortica. We leave tomorrow at dawn."

"We still need to get a fairy's tear before we go," Brux said.

"Not to worry." Kopius sat down on the bar stool and smashed the double saebal bomb into his mouth.

They stared at him, waiting.

"Well?" Pernilla asked.

"Didn't I tell you I'm a problem solver?" Kopius said with a mouthful of his partially chewed sandwich. He swirled a potato fry in front of Daisy's mouth.

She smiled and turned her face away.

Van rarely saw Daisy eat anything. The girl had zero appetite.

"Enough with the show," Brux said to Kopius. "Spit it out."

"You're not going to like it." Kopius stopped eating and turned his attention to the team. "We need to catch a fairy to get her tear."

Pernilla laughed.

"Like… a real fairy?" Paley asked. "I thought Semjaza was being silly."

Pernilla's expression grew serious. "Wait—for real? Fairies exist? I was thinking the tear was a stone or a flower or something."

"It doesn't surprise me." Van remembered the strange creatures she encountered on her last trip to the Living World, which included trolls, gnomes, buffalroo, and an evil sorceress.

Kopius nodded. "Semjaza told you right. Fairies are real."

"I've heard they exist," Brux said. "I've never known anybody who's seen one. Never mind gotten their tear."

"Apparently, this area is ripe with them," Kopius said. "It's probably what drew the criminal element to settle here."

"How do we catch one?" Pernilla asked.

"We have to set a trap in the woods. Called a fairy spike."

Daisy gasped and turned paler than usual.

"That sounds awful!" Paley gnawed on her cuticles. "We can't spike the poor fairy!"

Van brushed aside Paley's outburst and focused on the mission. "How do we get the fairy to the fairy spike?"

"Well, it seems the fairy…" His eyes darted to Brux, and he grinned. "Has to be *seduced.*"

CHAPTER 20

"What?" Brux widened his eyes. "No way!"

"Okay, how about *beguiling* her?" Kopius laughed. "Most guys would kill to meet a fairy."

Daisy's blue eyes darted to him. "Why would anyone want to meet a fairy?"

"They're incredibly beautiful." Kopius shifted on his stool. Probably uncomfortable talking about the subject to Daisy. She had an air about her that made others want to strive to meet her expectations of decency and goodwill.

"So?" Daisy shrugged. "There's plenty of beauty in the world."

"Why is there a trade for them?" Van asked, unsure she wanted to hear the answer.

Kopius shifted again. "Fairies bestow small gifts of magic. If you win their favor. Fairy magic on a simple level is undetectable by the Balish." He struggled to find the right words. "Some people keep them as pets, forcing the fairy through starvation or torture to use magic for their personal advancement. Only sacred magic can kill them, so they're basically immortal."

"Someone could hold them prisoner for an eternity?" Pink tinges appeared on Daisy's cheeks. Her eyes looked haunted, perhaps from her own experience with being held against her will.

"Doing some jackass family's bidding, generation after generation." Pernilla clenched her fists, ready to punch somebody. "No wonder the trade is illegal."

"No wonder it's so lucrative," Brux added. "They provide magic on demand."

"And," Kopius said, "like we already know, their tears bring in big money. Can you imagine what criminals get for a fairy?"

"We're not going to keep her," Van said, helping them stay focused. "We just need her tear, then we set her free. No fairy-napping."

"From what I know, fairies are sensitive to energies," Brux said. "They can feel the emotions and intentions of humans. That makes them hard to find, never mind catch."

"Thank the light for that," Daisy muttered, looking more wilted than usual.

Van turned to Kopius. "You looked at Brux, so that means he has the right emotional vibration to charm the fairy? How does that work?"

"You call to them by performing a sacred ritual." Kopius eyed his near empty plate. "They catch the scent of the caller's sweetness and come flying in." He grinned and popped his last fry into his mouth. "That's why it has to be Brux and not me."

"Fine." Brux sighed. "What's the ritual involve?"

"You dance while reading a poem that professes how beautiful she —the fairy—is and how much sweetness and love you have to give her." Kopius' eyes sparkled with anticipation over Brux's level of discomfort doing the ritual. "And then, there are the offerings."

"Oh, that's all," Van said, sarcastically.

"No, that's not all." Kopius' tone turned serious. "Brux will need to clamp the fairy's ankle in a manacle that has a chain attached to a spike hammered into the ground. Once she's caught, she'll let out a high pitched wail. That's when the traders quickly cover her with a special soundproof fairy sack. If she's left alone to continue with her cries, they'll eventually catch the attention of any nearby wizard who will then come to her rescue. Only a wizard, or the person who set the trap, can undo the fairy spike and set her free. Once she's freed, it's customary she offers her rescuer a tear to show her gratitude."

"Brux has to do the beguiling fairy dance, love poem reading?" Van grinned so wide her cheeks hurt, while Brux had the look of someone condemned to take one for the team.

"Naw." Kopius shook his head, letting Brux off the hook. "I can do it. I can fake niceness."

"You said sweetness, not niceness," Pernilla said.

"Same difference." Kopius shrugged.

"There's a difference between being nice and being kind." Daisy cast her eyes to the floor, clearly disappointed in Kopius.

Daisy's words resonated with Van. Brux's essence undoubtedly comprised pure sweetness. No faking it there. But they had overlooked the sweetest, kindest person on their team.

"No, not Brux." Van turned to Daisy. "You have to do it."

"Fairies like girls?" Paley asked.

"Hm." Kopius rubbed his chin in thought. "My intel said they're attracted to sweetness. I assumed since fairies are female, a male would attract them. But I have to agree, the female gender is pretty sweet." He smiled at Daisy and pulled her in by the waist for a hug.

Daisy grinned, clearly loving the attention. "It makes sense fairies would be pansexual. They probably sense energies, not gender."

Kopius gazed at Daisy. "Hands down, my girl is the sweetest." He kissed the top of her head.

Her grin grew wider.

"She's a sure bet to attract one," Brux said, looking like he was doing his best to ignore Kopius and Daisy's relationship.

Van was proud of Brux. He put his personal feelings aside for the mission. She grinned at him, just like Daisy did to Kopius. Mortified by her lack of control, she stopped it at once.

"The problem is the fairy spike." Brux looked at his sister. "Are you capable of grabbing a fairy and shackling her to a spike?"

"How big are they?" Paley asked. "I'm thinking they're the size of a butterfly."

"They're like the size of an elf," Kopius said. "Or a mountain goat. Kinda like, maybe… that barrel."

Paley snickered. "I have no idea what you're trying to say."

Van stared at him. "Which is it? An elf, a goat, or a barrel?"

"It doesn't matter." Daisy's long, white-blond hair shimmered as she shook her head and lowered her gaze. "I can't do it."

"That's the conundrum." Pernilla flipped her hands in the air. "The sweetest person is the most unlikely to carry out such an atrocity. No wonder fairies are near impossible to catch."

"I can hide nearby," Kopius said. "I'll swoop in and grab her."

"No way," Brux said. "It will distract Daisy knowing you're there. It will show in her energy. A telltale sign someone is else is near." He stood tall. "I'll do it. I'll grab the fairy and clasp her in the manacle. Then Kopius can swoop in and save her."

"Daisy's energy will be calm knowing her brother is close." Van bobbed her head in agreement. "And won't scare away the fairy."

"Kopius saving her won't work," Daisy said. "None of you can. I'm sure the fairy will sense something's wrong. We'll have to wait for a wizard to save her."

The team agreed with the eventual plan.

"We need to get moving if we want to reel in a fairy tonight," Pernilla said. "Where do we start?"

They left Fisherman's Rest and Kopius led the team off the main road and into the woods. "Look for a circular grassy area."

Van had been told as a child these were fairy rings. Now she knew why.

"When you find one, shout out," Brux said. "If not, or if we can't hear you, then we meet back in this spot in an hour."

They spread out in teams of two: Van and Brux, Kopius and Daisy, Pernilla and Paley.

Less than an hour later, the team stood in front of the perfect fairy ring, found by Pernilla and Paley.

"This will work." Kopius bobbed his head.

With the location chosen, the team exited the woods and went back to the nameless wharf village on the Skeleton Coast.

"Another challenge." Pernilla glanced at the shanties lining the wharf area. "Where are we going to find the beautiful things needed to lure the fairy?"

"No kidding," Kopius said. "This town's an armpit."

"Maybe we should venture off the main road," Brux said. "To where the families live."

Van and the others gaped at him.

"There have to be families here," Brux said. "And they have to live somewhere."

Kopius snorted. "Doubt it. No matter, I know where I can score some candied ale. You guys work out the rest." He clasped Daisy's hand.

"How do you know that?" Pernilla asked.

"I met a guy." He tugged Daisy along as they hurried away.

Daisy twisted around, stumbling from being pulled, yet grinning, and cried, "I'll work on getting the bouquets."

"Yeah," Kopius shouted. "Don't worry about all that feminine stuff —perfume, jewelry, flowers. I got that covered, too."

"Meet us back at the fairy ring," Brux yelled as the two darted away.

"Brux is right," Paley said. "People live here. Someone has to bake cakes and make candles. We just have to find them."

They wandered away from the wharf area and headed deeper into the village.

There were no lights on the dirt roads and few buildings. Van expected a knife-wielding thief to leap out of the darkness at them any second. Her nerves flared, especially with the setting sun. Not only because it made the street darker, but it reminded her time was slipping away. They had barely three weeks left to complete their mission.

"Look." Paley pointed to a three-story structure. Given its dilapidated condition, it didn't seem out of place on a dirt road in the middle of the woods.

"Who goes there?" asked a thickly built man sitting on a stool by the door, gripping a rifle.

As they approached, the man slid to his feet as if ready to defend the entrance from intruders.

Van peered into the wide rectangular windows of the building. She saw boxes. "Is this a warehouse?"

"It's the warehouse." His shoulders visibly relaxed, and he slung the rifle over his back, as if Van had said a secret password. Or more likely, he believed they had been searching for this place and finally found it.

Pernilla looked up and squinted at the top story's windows. "What do you have in there?"

"What're you looking for?" He crossed his arms over his massive chest, another clear indicator he no longer considered them a threat, but customers.

"We need a lot of things." Brux stepped forward, ahead of the others. "We're ready to buy." He took out his money pouch and jingled it.

The man grinned. "Well, come inside." He pushed the door and held it open.

Van hesitated. Then shrugged. She had nothing to lose. They arrived with a long list of items, and this man had products for sale.

The dusty air irritated Van's sinuses, and she rubbed her knuckles over her nose to stifle a sneeze. Rows and rows of boxes covered the floor of the long, rectangular room, pushed together so that paths formed between them. The windows looked unlikely to open, even in an emergency. Van doubted the aged wooden walls would hold up in a strong wind. Shelves filled most wall space, stuffed with various items—pans, glassware, paintings—reminding Van of a flea market.

Paley covered her mouth as she sneezed. "What is this place?"

"Pirates' loot," the man said. "This here's the storehouse. We hold the goods before shipping out orders. Items for sale, first floor only. Everything else is spoken for, but," he ran his eyes up and down Van and licked his lips, "everything's got a price."

"Not her." Brux yanked Van behind him. He stood nose to nose with the man.

Van's skin crawled. She could take a million showers and never wash clean the scummy feeling brought on by this guy's leer.

The man gave Brux a respectful nod and took a step back. Yet, he held a dangerous glint in his eyes. "Look at your leisure."

Van and Paley scurried down the aisles. Brux stayed near the entrance to keep watch on the lewd man.

Van, in a rush to grab what they needed and get out of there, stubbed her toe on a rusted anchor resting on the floor. "Ow."

"Over here." Paley held a dust-covered wooden flute.

"Score." Van high-fived Paley, while favoring her throbbing foot.

"Look." Brux pulled two crystal goblets from a shelf near the front. He proudly held them up. "You think she'll like them, right?"

"They'll do," Van said, hiding how taken she was by his genuine interest in impressing the fairy. And that he was smart enough not to say they were for a fairy in front of the storehouse guard.

Pernilla wandered over from another aisle. "I found these." She held a net bag filled with seashells.

"Perfect." Van gave her a nod. "Grab a crate of them."

"We only need a couple more things," Brux cried from the front of the storehouse.

The girls picked through a good portion of the stock and found a box of gold candles.

"That's it." Pernilla knelt by the box to inspect the candles. "This place won't have the last two things on our list."

Brux and the storehouse man haggled over the seashells, the flute, crystal goblets, and gold candles.

"That's way too much." Brux begrudgingly handed the man payment.

As they walked toward the exit, the man stepped in front of them, blocking the door.

"You haven't paid the departure fee." His eyes turned to Pernilla and scanned her body.

"I'm sick of your crap." Pernilla stomped toward the man. Her eyes flared with rage.

"Hold up." Brux clasped Pernilla's arm. "I'll handle this."

"No," Van said. "I will." She roundhouse-kicked the man in the chest.

The man smashed into a stack of boxes, which came tumbling down, crashing to the floor, spilling their contents.

Brux grabbed the crate of seashells, Pernilla snatched the box filled with their other items, and they dashed out of the storehouse.

Pernilla smiled at Van. "That was *awesome*."

"We still need two more things," Paley said, nervously flipping her hair, as they rushed down the dirt street toward the main road by the wharf.

"Didn't the Fisherman's Rest have sweet cakes on their menu?" Van asked. "There has to be a bakery nearby."

They scoured the structures along the back streets in the village until they stumbled upon the Sugar Galley Bakery.

Pernilla pounded on the door until a woman with dark circles under eyes and messy gray hair peeked through the curtain.

"Store's closed," the woman grumbled.

"We need some sweet cakes, fast." Brux held up two loscs.

The woman's eyes lit up at the silver coins. She unlocked the door and swung it open. "Come inside. Lemme see what I can do." Her smile displayed yellow teeth.

Unfortunately, the baker didn't have any doilies. In fact, she had never heard of them. As a self-proclaimed expert on baking cakes, she snatched the stamped silver coins from Brux, legit money, and got to work.

As the baker placed bowls, butter, sugar, eggs, and a bag of flour on the worktable, Van took a stack of white napkins and grabbed a pair of kitchen scissors. While the baker whipped together the ingredients, she and Paley cut the napkins into doilies.

"Kudos to art class." Paley held up her creation.

"Except in art class, we called these snowflakes." Van giggled as she held up hers.

"They'll do." Brux grinned.

Within two hours, they left the bakery with twenty custom ordered sweet cakes decorated with multicolored sprinkles and plenty of doilies. The cakes looked so enticing, those alone would've been enough to ensnare Van in the fairy trap.

They returned to their prearranged meeting place in the woods, and Brux placed the crate on the ground. Then he leaned toward Van and whispered, "You have a little something here." He grinned and pointed to the corner of his upper lip.

Van's fingers darted to her mouth. She swiped away the telltale smudge of frosting.

"Save some for the fairy," Pernilla muttered, as she swept past Van and spread the seashells around the rim of the fairy circle.

Kopius burst through the trees holding a jug of candied ale, followed by Daisy who carried a gorgeous bouquet of orange roses.

"Did you get musk oil?" Brux asked. "We need to get every detail right to make sure our plan works."

"Yup," Kopius said.

Pernilla took the bouquet from Daisy.

"And look at this baby." Kopius tilted his head toward the dazzling piece of jewelry Daisy pulled from her satchel.

"Nice." Pernilla placed the flowers inside the fairy ring.

"Wow." Paley ran her fingertips along the multi-tiered chunky necklace.

"Made with amber cabochons," Daisy said.

"I got you a flute." Paley pulled the musical instrument from their box of items and handed it to Daisy. "I hope you know how to play, or will at least give it a try. For some music, you know?"

"Thank you." Daisy took the flute and gave it the once over. "I know how to use it. I learned in school."

"We got a bunch of these, too." Van pulled a thick gold candle from the box. "We can put them inside the circle and on the rocks to create ambiance."

"They love gold candles," Brux said, in a way that made Van a bit concerned. He seemed much too enthusiastic about meeting a fairy.

Kopius, being a polymath, worked out how to make a fairy spike based on what he'd gathered from the rogues he met on the wharf while booking their passage to Cortica.

"This stuff is surprisingly easy to find on the docks." He hammered a metal spike into a sturdy rock.

"Yeah, try finding doilies." Van watched as Kopius secured the spike and attached the manacle.

He sprinkled a gold powder over the contraption. "Bought this from a person who bought it from a witch. The last piece to the fairy spike—magic."

"Where did you get the other stuff?" Paley asked.

"Don't ask," Daisy said.

"Brothel." Kopius winked as he pretended to whisper.

"We've got another issue to consider," Brux said before anyone could ask Kopius more questions. "Wizards are usually in the company of Balish royals."

Pernilla stopped fussing over arranging the necklace and twisted to face Brux. "Why's that?"

"A wizard is a highly skilled job," Brux said. "The Balish Council chooses you. A wealthy patron sponsors the wizard's training and education. Once trained, they're required to work for their patron or the Balish monarchy, and their magic is restricted and monitored."

"Only royals and wellborns are wealthy enough to sponsor wizard training," Kopius said.

"What about witches?" Pernilla asked. "You mentioned a witch."

"Not allowed," Brux answered. "Balish society doesn't allow female wizards."

"Women who do magic are witches." Kopius poured the ale into the crystal goblets. "All witches are banned and operate illegally. That's why they're pretty easy to find here."

"Solana was a sorceress," Van said. "How's that different from a witch?"

"Royal blood." Brux lit a gold candle. "The palace wizard will train the royal family's females in the art of performing magic."

"Warlocks are male royals trained in magic." Kopius saved the last bit of ale for himself and drank it straight from the bottle. "They have few restrictions. Not many around. Most are too lazy to learn."

"Then what's a sorcerer?" Paley asked.

Kopius shrugged. "A man who's not permitted by the Balish Council to do magic. Never heard of one, though."

"A Balish wizard's job is to monitor the squawker system." Brux continued around the circle, lighting the candles. "To detect ripples in the energy of nature that happens when people use magic. It's the same system that detects when adult Lodians go out of bounds."

"A wailing fairy will cause a ripple," Daisy said in a way that made Van, and most likely the others, ashamed such cruelty existed in the world.

Brux finished with the candles and knelt by the fairy spike. He brushed his fingertips over the metal as if questioning whether he could carry out the plan.

"Remember, cuff her ankle." Van hoped to snap him out of it. "Then leave before a wizard arrives with a squadron of Balish soldiers."

"We'll be waiting in the brush, over there." Pernilla pointed to a grouping of nearby trees and bushes.

"Wait. If the fairy gives her tear to one of her rescuers, how're we going to get it?" Paley asked.

"I'm going to steal it from whoever she gives it to." Kopius punched a fist into his hand. "I'm extremely resourceful." He grinned.

"Whatever that means," Pernilla muttered.

"Not going to be a problem," Kopius said, full of confidence. "Daisy, you just work your beguiling magic and get the fairy here. Brux, you do your job. I'll be ready to do mine."

Daisy stood in the center of the fairy ring. Brux ducked behind a large rock near the fairy spike.

Van hid in the brush with the others. She visualized the entire operation going without a hitch. Every detail down to gripping the fairy's tear in her hand.

Daisy read the heartfelt poem she had written, expressing her love for the fairy with such tenderness and sincerity Van's eyes teared up.

Then Daisy played the flute, surprisingly well, while dancing.

The haunting scene enticed Van, never mind the fairy. Candlelight flickered over the rocks, the gifts, and Daisy, enhancing the romantic setting. The flute music soothed the soul. Van's foot had a mind of its own and tapped to the beat of the flute. She struggled against an overwhelming desire to dash into the fairy ring and dance. Her cheeks flushed at the thought until she noticed Kopius' foot tapping, too.

In less than twenty minutes, a stunning brunette fairy about four feet tall flittered out from the trees, darting this way and that. Then hovered inside the fairy ring, getting closer to Daisy.

The fairy looked like a petite woman who weighed no more than eighty pounds soaking wet. The wings on her back flapped so quickly they blurred, reminding Van of a hummingbird. She wore a tight-fitting, short-sleeved, bright-orange v-neck dress with a staggered bottom hem, and matching colored booties on her feet.

Daisy smiled and welcomed the fairy. She offered the fairy snacks.

The fairy darted over to a sweet cake, and then back to Daisy. She giggled and fluttered up and down around Daisy and then dived over to a sweet cake and took a nibble. Then, she zipped around the fairy circle several times until pausing to hover over the seashells arranged around the edge of the fairy ring.

When the fairy slowed to pick up a seashell, she held still long enough for Van to notice her wings were a transparent yellow and shaped like those of a dragonfly.

Brux leaped from behind the rock and clutched the fairy's ankle. She squirmed as he secured the manacle.

The fairy let out a high-pitched screech.

Van clapped her hands over her ears.

Brux and Daisy also covered their ears as they rushed into the brush to hide with the rest of the team.

They waited.

The fairy's cries ranged from low to high pitched. Her wails were heart-wrenching, like hearing the whimpering of a wounded puppy.

"A wizard can hear her cries, even from a distance," Kopius whispered.

The fairy's wings fluttered wildly. Panic emanated from her over-large silver eyes. She tugged and tugged at the chain attached to the manacle, trying to fly away in a hopeless attempt to escape.

Revulsion filled Van. The scene pushed the limits of what she could bear in the name of the mission.

Daisy collapsed to her knees. She curled into an upright, fetal position, hands clenched together over her heart. With her eyes closed, she muttered to herself and rocked back and forth. Tears trickled down her cheeks.

Brux crouched by her side, his face a grimace of pain.

Kopius placed a comforting hand on Daisy's shoulder.

"Geesh." Pernilla shook her head. She turned away, unable to endure the scene.

"Hurry up, wizard." Paley chewed on her cuticles.

The fairy's distress became so unbearable, Van contemplated calling the whole thing off. Suddenly, a figure dressed in a black tunic-styled military uniform burst through the trees wielding a sword.

The commotion inside Van's mind screeched to a halt as soon as she laid eyes on him.

Van's insides seemed to collapse, and then burst. She gaped at the wildly handsome boy wielding a sword. He looked the same age as Van, or maybe younger.

She caught her breath as his alluring details sank in. Unusually cropped brown hair, a style not worn by many males in the Living World. Almond-shaped, amber-yellow eyes peering from his swarthy complexion. His strong jawline and broad shoulders. He moved with such strength and confidence, every cell in Van's body trembled from her attraction to him.

Van's heart awakened, surging her blood as if it had pumped for the first time. Her response both scared and excited her.

As she gazed at the boy, Van became aware he had broken her life into two parts. Before she laid eyes on him, and after.

The sensations in her body caused her to ache. Yet she felt full of hope.

Her hope plummeted as she recognized the red and gold insignia on the upper left chest of the boy's uniform. The crest of a royal Balish officer.

Daisy gasped. "It's Prince Ferox."

CHAPTER 21

As Prince Ferox spoke to the fairy, a hurricane of emotions swirled inside Van.

She squelched them and got to work.

Ignoring her teammates' chattering about this latest hurdle, Van used her mind's eye to peer into Ferox's soul, to see if he had a dark thread like his sister. If he did, Van would have to take care of it. But how? Kill him?

If he became corrupted like his sister, it would be Van's only option. He'd come for Van, to take away her light, and she'd be forced to defend herself using the Coin, just like she did with Solana.

Doing so would cause another strike against Van for using the Item incorrectly. But a little more damage to her soul was worth it, if it meant protecting her people.

The Royal Balish Soldiers and the raven-haired man who had accompanied the prince distracted Van too much for her to connect to her energy, making her unable to determine if Ferox had a dark thread.

The stylish, raven-haired man wore a goatee and an elegant purple and gold robe. He pointed his index finger at the fairy spike and murmured words. With a crack, the spike popped from the ground.

He's the wizard. Van stared in awe at his powers.

The fairy's wailing stopped.

Ferox unclasped the manacle from around her ankle, freeing the fairy.

As expected, she didn't fly away.

She fluttered around Ferox, batting her eyelashes and making musical cooing sounds.

Why doesn't she give him a tear and leave?

The fairy ran her fingers over Ferox's cheek and spoke to him in her indecipherable, squeaky fairy language.

Van fumed. *Get on with it.* She resisted the urge to dash from the brush and shoo the fairy away from him.

"Who did this to you?" Ferox asked.

She responded in her language.

The wizard translated. "She says... a sweetness. A young blond girl. A... *sweet* young blond girl."

"If you saw her again, would you recognize her?" Ferox asked.

The fairy peeped and cooed.

"She says the girl looks like sugar sweetness." The wizard sighed, lacking patience. "The fairy wants you to stay and play with her."

The fairy danced around Ferox, sprinkling shiny silver and gold dust on his head and giggling.

"We'll get nothing from her." The wizard flapped his hands at the fairy. "Stop bothering the prince. Shoo."

The fairy glared at the wizard as she dodged his hands. She hovered, high enough to be out of the wizard's reach, and lovingly gazed at Ferox. She raised her palm to her face. From the corner of her eye came a single drop.

The tear landed on her palm. It formed a sparkling crystal. When caught by the light of the candles, it shamelessly flickered every brilliant color of the rainbow.

She brought the tear-shaped crystal to her lips and blew a kiss. The fairy's tear floated through the air to Ferox.

He easily caught it with one hand.

Van took note as Ferox tucked the fairy's tear into a satchel he wore dangling from his belt.

In the blink of an eye, the fairy was gone.

"Take everything," Ferox said. "Leave the forest clean as if no one was ever here."

His soldiers blew out the candles and stashed away the fairy's presents.

Kopius shifted his body as if he were about to make a move.

"No." Pernilla placed a gentle hand on Kopius's arm. "Not yet. You'll get us all killed."

Kopius settled down.

Once the clearing had no trace of trash, Prince Ferox and his crew meandered back into the woods in the direction they had come.

Van and her team covertly followed them.

When it became clear Ferox and his men were headed back to the wharf area, Brux spread his arms and stopped the team.

"Let's hang back," he whispered. "The prince is famous. We'll be able to find him again."

"You better hope so." Van stressed over the time constraint. Or was it she dreaded never seeing him again? Van shook her head. If she wanted to see Ferox again, it was to check his soul for a dark thread, nothing more.

"We need to figure out how to get that satchel," Brux said in a low voice, despite the squadron having moved out of earshot.

"Avoid his soldiers *and* a palace wizard?" Van saw their plan as ill-fated now. Prince Ferox, the most heavily guarded Balish royal in the Living World, had the fairy's tear.

The team unanimously concluded there was no way marketeers' scouts from Hod would ever get close enough to the prince to lift the tear. They debated if it was even worth sticking around with such a high risk of getting caught as Lodians out of bounds.

"We can go to Cortica without the tear," Pernilla suggested. "Use our strength and wits to get by."

"Or we could end up dead," Van said.

"You're such a little wuss." Pernilla glowered. "Pathetic."

Van opened her mouth to retort when Daisy interrupted.

"Stop it." Her airy voice gave light to the darkness of their situation. "We work together. As a team. Not against each other."

Daisy was right. Van felt her cheeks flush, glad the shadows of night hid her embarrassment.

The group voted yes to heading back to Fisherman's Rest and figuring out their next step while grabbing some food.

Back in the stuffy eatery, Van crammed several fried coral-flower puffs into her mouth. She washed them down with a mug of mead and then ordered another.

The rest of her teammates sat slumped on their stools, sulking. Even Kopius accepted an attempt at Ferox would be futile. They picked at their food, except for Daisy, who didn't eat at all.

Van silently finished her meal while her teammates threw around ideas about alternative plans. The dinner, dim eatery, long day, and mead caused Van's eyelids to droop.

"I need some fresh air to wake me up." She slid off her bar stool.

Brux caught her by the arm. "It's not safe."

"Really? I think I'll be okay." Van pulled away from him. "I'm just going to sit on the porch steps."

"Fine." His attention went back to his plate. His manner emanated defeat ever since the failure of their fairy plan. He dug his fork into the last bits of his seared deepwater stingray, and didn't protest again when Van headed toward the exit.

As Van stepped onto the Fishermen's Rest porch, a rush of cool night air refreshed her.

She knew without the fairy's tear, it would take longer to complete their mission and be markedly more dangerous. If they had the tear, they would've exchanged it for guaranteed safe passage to the Bottomless Sea.

Van rubbed her belly. Her stomach ached from overeating. She burped, covering her mouth with the back of her hand.

Ahh, that feels better.

Needing to stretch her legs and walk off the meal, Van strolled along the dimly lit dirt road. Her head throbbed. She rubbed her temples to dull the pain.

I need Jacynthia. I could use her advice. Where's Wiglaf? He could point us in the right direction.

The few people milling about on the streets minded their own business, probably up to no good and not looking to make trouble with Van. She wasn't in the mood for a confrontation and was happy no one bothered her.

As she meandered closer to the docks, fog rolled in from the ocean and enveloped her. Cold drops of moisture sprinkled her skin. She sat on a bench, away from the main road but not quite on the docks, and reached into her pocket for the Coin.

She glanced left and right to make sure no one lurked nearby, then held the Coin in her palm for a consultation.

"Show me the best path to reach the second seal."

The Coin turned in her palm; the triangle pointed to herself.

"Show me the best path to remove the Anchoress curse."

The Coin shimmied and, again, pointed to Van.

She snapped her fingers closed. "I hate when it does that."

Van tucked the Coin back into her pocket. She lifted her knees and crossed her legs into the lotus position.

She breathed deeply until her mind filled with the familiar amaranthine glow of her spirit guide.

Why doesn't anything ever go right? Van asked Jacynthia without using words. *We had a perfect plan. All my thoughts focused on a positive outcome. Our plan still failed.*

"You can manifest nothing without feeling," Jacynthia said. "It is why emotions easily overcome intellect and why we must put feeling into our thoughts if we wish results. When you become emotionally numb, you block the Creator from resolving difficulties in your favor."

I have feelings, Van said, defensively. *Brux irritates me all the time. I'm also hungry. Is that a feeling? What does it have to do with my mission? Should we cut our losses and head back? If we stay and attempt to mend the seal, we could all die.*

"Wanting something to happen before it is ready to happen exposes us to the danger of doubt and may cause us to depart from our path. Troubled times are drawing near. Dangerous situations cannot be avoided." Jacynthia paused, and then said, "I advise you to be strong and unwavering in your quest. Flow like water through difficult situations by staying true to what is pure and innocent within your Self. This is how to escape danger and reach a place of peace."

I'll accomplish nothing by flowing like water.

"Do not to fall into the trap of searching for an immediate and easy solution to your troubles. You must accept the situation. Do not act out of a desire to escape the circumstances or you will fall into an abysmal pit."

A hand roughly gripped Van's shoulder, snapping her mind back to the physical plane.

Her eyes shot open.

The most handsome boy she had ever seen stood before her.

Prince Ferox said, "You are under arrest for perpetrating the heinous crime of fairy trading."

CHAPTER 22

Prince Ferox ordered his soldiers to bind Van's wrists. As they escorted her back to the main road, the few passersby furtively glanced at them and scurried away.

The prince and his men led Van into a stacked duplex guarded by a handful of royal soldiers. She squirmed when the soldiers shoved her toward the stairway leading to the basement.

Instead of letting fear overwhelm her, Van decided to use this as an opportunity to get closer to Ferox. For no reason, other than getting the fairy's tear and checking him for a dark thread. At least, that's what she told herself.

Van compliantly descended the stairs. She stifled a cough as she entered the dusty basement with its low-ceiling and wisps of cobwebs hanging from the rafters. The room had no windows and the plaster walls were discolored and cracked. Gold candles, ones they had confiscated from the fairy ring, had been placed around the room by the soldier who carried them, giving them enough light to see in the dim basement.

A soldier roughly frisked Van.

The Coin! Her anxiety surged.

His quick pat down missed the Coin tucked in one of her many pockets. Or he passed it by, only interested in finding traditional weapons that could harm the prince, like a gun or knife.

Two soldiers forced Van into a solitary wooden chair in the center of the room. Each kept a hand pressed on her shoulder, presumably so she wouldn't rise from the chair and attack five plus soldiers and a wizard.

There definitely weren't any official law-and-order buildings on the Skeleton Coast. Ferox must've rented the entire dwelling for privacy, security, and so he could use the basement as a makeshift interrogation room.

"My prince." The wizard bowed to Ferox as he entered the basement. "Windermere Castle requests my presence. I must beg your leave."

He nodded, and the wizard scuttled up the stairway.

Ferox stood directly in front of Van. "What's your name?"

He didn't sound happy.

"Nessie," Van lied, playing it safe, just like Zurial did when she met Nick. Rather than tell Ferox the truth, *I'm Vanessa Cross the Lodian's legendary Anchoress. The one with access to magical weapons powerful enough to obliterate the Balish.*

Yeah. No.

As Ferox considered Van for a moment, she figured he and his men must be in the area searching for out-of-bounds Lodian teens. Specifically, the Anchoress. Van knew Balish royals grew up well versed in Lodian lore. She imagined Ferox as a child, surrounded by his scholars, telling him, "One needs to know their enemies." This meant he knew the Alignment was taking place right now. And the Cup of Life was on Cortica, a mere ship ride away.

He'd make his father, King Nequus, proud by returning home with the Lodian's Anchoress. Found on Balish land with her weapon, the Coin of Creation. It would give King Nequus the ammunition he needed to petition the Elementals to remove Manik's law. Then the Balish would engage in a war with the Lodians.

"Well, Nessie." Ferox bent down and stared at Van, eye to eye.

The soldiers gripped Van's shoulders tighter to keep her in place.

"Earlier tonight we rescued a fairy caught in a fairy spike. She gave a description of the person who set the trap. You're a stranger in these parts, and you fit that description."

Ferox acted more mature than his age. His eyes told the story he held many burdensome secrets. His demeanor implied he faced those secrets with dignity and responsibility. Ferox's combined confidence, masculinity, and damn fine looks intimated Van.

Yet, she knew Ferox lied to her. They were both lying to each other. Sort of.

Nessie was a nickname for Vanessa and she set the fairy trap, but she wasn't part of the fairy trade. And Van knew the fairy didn't give Ferox any specific information. The fairy's description—a young, sweet, blond girl—fit Van and Daisy, as it did any blond teen.

"Marketeers' scouts have good reason to catch a fairy." Ferox raised himself to full height. "They fetch a high price on the black market."

A soldier came pounding down the stairs.

"Excuse me, Prince Ferox." The soldier bowed to his superior. "A girl claiming to be your cousin is here."

"What?" Ferox asked, puzzled. "Which one?" He shook his head. "Never mind." He stomped up the stairs and left the basement.

Van heard a scuffle coming from the first floor.

The surrounding soldiers grew agitated. Two of them dashed up the stairs.

After a bit of time passed, the door to the basement opened.

A soldier bounded down the stairs, his face bruised. He carried a bunch of backpacks. Ones looking suspiciously like those carried by Van and her teammates.

Pernilla followed behind him, looking grim. She wore yellow-colored contact lenses. She obviously borrowed Paley's so she could impersonate a Balish royal, Ferox's cousin, since she had the swarthy skin and darker haired look of a Bale more so than anyone else in their group.

Behind Pernilla came Brux with a black eye, Paley with a fat lip, and Daisy looking disheveled and terrified.

Van groaned. "What harebrained scheme did you try to pull off?"

More thumping and scuffling came from the first floor.

Two soldiers struggled to come down the stairs while propping Kopius, who looked battered and bloody.

"Kopius!" Daisy tried to rush over to him, but a soldier held her back.

"You should see the other guy." His grin showed bloody teeth. One of his eyes was swollen and half open.

The soldiers tossed him onto the floor by Van and the others.

Ferox strode down the steps next. He scanned their ragtag crew.

"Well, marketeers' scouts from Hod, you've gotten yourselves into some deep trouble." Ferox paced similarly to his sister. "The fairy trade thrives in Cortica. Taking part in it is punishable by life in the dungeons."

Daisy quivered, presumably remembering her time there.

"Cortica, or *Outlaw Island*, isn't Balish territory, but what happens there affects the mainland. *My* land." He stopped pacing and swiveled toward them. "This heinous criminal offense must stop."

None of them spoke. The room remained quiet and tense.

"I know you've bought passage to Cortica." Ferox waved the *Seahag* tickets bought earlier by Kopius. "Which means you are meeting a broker there."

"It's true," Brux lied. "Our contact is on Outlaw Island."

"I demand to meet this contact." Ferox's eyes darted to Brux. "I will personally see to bringing this miscreant, and anyone they're associated with, to justice."

"And in return?" Kopius raised his bruised brow and then winced from pain.

Van tensed. She mentally willed him to stop talking before he got them into even more trouble.

"You hold up your end, and I'll make sure your penalty is lenient." Ferox gave him a curt nod.

"Good. First things first," Kopius said to Ferox, his words came strained due to the beating, and he remained crumpled on the floor. "You need to change your rags."

"Pardon me?"

"You go to Outlaw Island dressed like that, in full-out Balish military uniforms, and you'll get us killed," Kopius said.

"What he means," Daisy added, using her most angelic tone, "is criminals have an understanding not to interfere with Balish rule on the mainland. But only if the Balish leave them alone in their territory. Outlaw Island is their territory. So, it's safest for everyone if you and your men dress down."

Ferox squinted at Daisy. "Do I know you?"

Van noticed the slight tightening of Daisy's shoulders. It struck Van for the first time. While being held prisoner by Merloc, Daisy might've crossed paths with Ferox. Van held her breath.

"No," Daisy said. "I'm sure I would remember."

Ferox grinned at her. "I would remember too."

Van prickled. She could imagine Ferox, with his protector personality, being attracted to Daisy's vulnerability and frailty. Like a shark drawn to chum in the water.

By the look on his face, Brux didn't care for their exchange, either. Kopius seemed fine, even smug, as if proud Daisy had used her charms to help advance their cause.

"You haf to take all of us," said Paley, with a lisp from her fat lip. "We can't separate—"

Van cut her off with a warning look before Paley revealed the Twin Gemstones.

"I can't leave some of you here without leaving soldiers to guard you," Ferox said. "We're bringing everyone."

Then he dashed off to make arrangements for their journey to Cortica, taking along a few of his men.

At least several hours had passed when Ferox returned wearing marketeers' scouts' clothing. His soldiers had also changed and carried bundles of clothes for the others in the squadron.

"I've booked private passage to Cortica on a ship called *The Obelus*," Ferox announced to the room. "We leave tonight."

After the remaining soldiers changed, they headed to the wharf area.

On the way, Kopius held up his bound wrists. "Hey, Prince Royal. Can you do something about this?"

The soldier closest to him smacked him across the head. "You'll show Prince Ferox respect."

"Once you're onboard, I'll have the restraints removed," Ferox said, unperturbed by Kopius's discourteous nickname for him. "On the ship, you'll have nowhere to run, and we've confiscated your weapons and backpacks."

Paley sidled up to Ferox and said coyly, "You really chartered a ship just for us?" She batted her eyelashes. "That's *so* amazing."

"We need privacy. Too many mouths mean too many revealed secrets," Ferox said as the group made their way through the thick fog over to the dock. "No one on Cortica will know I booked the entire vessel. If anyone gets suspicious, we'll maintain our cover as marketers' scouts by mentioning we finagled our way onto a merchant ship."

Ferox leaned toward Van and whispered, "How's that sound to you, Nessie?" He winked conspiratorially.

Van grinned at him like an idiot and stumbled as she stepped onto the walkway to the ship. She inwardly scolded herself for it. They had a lot of work ahead. How would this play out if she kept acting like a lovesick fool? She resolved to stay focused on the mission.

But the warmth in Ferox's eyes when they met hers... the way he carried himself... the command he had over his soldiers... She tried to deny he had kick-started her heart, to lock away her feelings.

But her attraction to him came crashing down on her like a tidal wave.

CHAPTER 23

Ferox had his soldiers toss Van and the others into a cramped cabin below deck. As promised, he had his men untie their hands.

"He's the crown prince." Excitement sparked from Paley's gray eyes. "He's *so* handsome."

"He's Balish and we're his prisoners." Van rubbed the painful pink rings on her wrists caused by the restraints.

"He's harmless." Paley's cheeks puffed from her dreamy smile. Then she winced from the pain of her fat lip. "He won't hurt us. Or turn us in. He's a softy. I can tell."

"He thinks we're marketeers' scouts caught up in the illegal fairy trade. Once he figures out we're out of bounds Lodians, he'll have us killed. Remember that." Van reminded herself to take her own advice.

She scanned the drab cabin. The claustrophobic room reeked with a damp, musty stench that hung so thickly in the air it stuck to her taste buds.

The ship swayed as they pulled away from the dock. Once they were underway, Ferox allowed his captives to leave the cabin.

Van and the others went up several stairwells to the forecastle. She gaped at the massive wooden ship.

"First time?" Kopius asked.

Van nodded.

"It's two-masted, square-rigged on the foremast." He pointed to the tall cylinder structures rising from the deck to the sky, attached with chains, cables, and ropes tied in a way that made them look like checkered ladders.

Van lifted her eyes to the big, white sails billowing in the wind.

"It's got a fore and aft sail on the mainmast." Kopius seemed just as impressed with the ship as Van. "And a square topsail."

Ferox, also on deck, caught Van's eye and smiled. Her cheeks grew hot, and she darted her eyes away.

Van overheard the salty old captain tell Ferox. "Best case scenario, trip to Cortica will take a day or two. Maybe three."

"Is there any way to get us there faster?" Ferox asked.

"Taint nothin' good about these waters, son," said the captain. "More often than not, we've got to change routes 'cause of the dangerous currents or bad weather. Occasionally got to avoid a trade ship wandered off the traditional route. And then there's the pirates."

None of those things sounded good to Van, but Ferox took the news with a stiff upper lip.

"Just do your job, Captain Widsith." Ferox gave him a curt nod.

The captain bounded down the stairwell and headed toward the stern, shaking his head and grumbling.

Van, Pernilla, and Paley had spent their childhoods around water on Providence Island. Brux and Daisy came from a wealthy family in Salus Valde. All of them had experience with boating, except Kopius. Thankfully, he was unbothered by the rocking ship.

"I can handle anything," he informed the team.

Ferox's men didn't fare so well. As far as Van knew, they were soldiers from Balefire City in Aduro. A dry, hot, sandy region. They lacked sea legs and looked green around the gills. Several of them staggered to the railing and retched over the side of the ship.

Ferox not only looked well, but seemed to thrive.

Van's teammates settled on the main deck near the heavy rope wound around the bottom of the mast. They huddled, whispering, their faces serious.

She figured they were plotting their escape. Instead of joining them, she went to the tip of the bow, hoping the wind would blow away the ship's cloying smells from her hair and clothes.

Van leaned against the railing, next to the wood pole that extended forward from the bow, and breathed in the fresh salty air. She closed her eyes. The brisk wind rushed against her body, blowing her hair and sweeping her face, carrying away her worries. Nothing else mattered to her at that moment. Not the mission, not her handsome captor, not the spreading virus. Only the eternal power of nature.

"You're not thinking of jumping, are you?"

Startled, Van twisted around.

Ferox grinned at her. "Best part of the ship, right?"

"Uh, yeah. I guess."

"Come, sit. So we can talk." Ferox stretched his arm toward a large crate.

"Is that an order?" Van crossed her arms. "Because it sounds like an order."

"I understand you're nervous," he said kindly. "Being a prisoner must be scary."

He understood nothing.

"I won't hurt you or your friends. I need your help—"

"I'd rather jump over the side of the ship." Van winced. She had no idea why those harsh words shot from her mouth.

"Really?" Ferox chuckled good-naturedly. "I'm not that repulsive. Am I?"

He turned his charm on high and bent at the waist the way a gentleman bows before a princess and, again, extended his hand toward the crate. "I'd be honored if you'd care to sit with me for a moment."

And just like that, he reeled Van in.

She complied *slowly* to emphasize her reluctance and sat on the crate.

Ferox maneuvered himself next to her, sitting close. Too close. Yet, his presence generated an enticing warmth inside Van, making her wish he'd move even closer.

A confusing pull swirled inside her. She swore Ferox had gone sweet on her. But Van was a warrior, not a girlfriend. He was Balish, not Lodian. He was her captor, not her friend. She feared if her emotions clashed anymore, they'd create a thunderstorm inside her body.

Ferox's upturned lips showed he took pleasure in their closeness.

Van wanted to slide a few inches away from him, but she already sat by the edge of the crate.

His grin and stare didn't waver, causing Van's nerves to reach a breaking point. She blurted, "What's up with that haircut?" She immediately regretted the juvenile question.

Ferox narrowed his eyes suspiciously for a moment. Then, he must've realized children from Hod, an impoverished region, weren't well educated. He probably thought Van had never seen a Balish royal before, and it contributed to her being so nervous around him.

"Only royal or wellborn Balish males are allowed to cut their hair this short. It's a sign of status and privilege."

"All those trips to the barber can really add up." Van burst into a giggle with such intensity, spittle flew from her mouth. Her cheeks flared.

"*Barber*? What's a barber?"

"Oh, um," Van squirmed. "It's a new type of service we're offering in Hod. A person who specializes in cutting men's hair. Never mind."

"Well, the marketplace of Hod is the most *cutting edge* place in the world." His grin grew wide enough to show his perfect white teeth.

She caught the joke, but her brain remained paralyzed from being near him. Only someone as charismatic as Ferox could get away with lame humor and still maintain his appeal. He'd made the joke hoping Van would feel less intimated by him, so she forced a chuckle. It came out sounding stupid, causing her to blush deeper.

"So, Hod, huh?" Ferox asked.

Van shrugged.

"There's quite a melting pot of people there. That region borders Antares and Salus Valde. Balish-occupied territory."

Van kept still, trying to figure out what he wanted.

"Did your parents teach you the beliefs of the *Sanctus Novus?*"

Ah. Ferox was trying to figure out if Van and her friends were Balish Loyalists, orthodox Lodians, underground Manikists, Anti-Manik Rebels, or had beliefs somewhere in between. Or believed in nothing at all, like most of the hapless people headed to Cortica.

Was Ferox on a mission to recruit wayward souls into believing in the *Sanctus Novus*?

Van didn't fully understand the differences between Lodian and Balish beliefs. Since it was the primary cause of discord in the Living World, it seemed an important subject to become well-versed in.

"A little bit," Van said. "We also learned about the Lodian's *Victus Opuseulus.* Why?"

"I'm trying to understand why you'd choose a life of crime when there's so much opportunity for better work."

"What does that have to do with the *Sanctus Novus?*"

"Life's not so clear cut about what is good and what is bad. The choice is subjective. So how do you know what is good?"

Van stared at him. Did he expect an answer? She didn't know how to respond, and he was making her feel pretty awful about herself.

"Look at your belief system," he said, answering his own question. "Does your choice promote the good of the world, or does it promote you? The sacred teachings help us remove our ego and only then do we make our choices."

"You're telling me I'm a bad person because I'm a thief?"

"You're not bad," Ferox said. "You make bad choices."

Van wanted to be angry. To scream the truth into his face. She was the Anchoress! She, too, possessed wealth and carried a royal bloodline.

Yet, when she looked into his eyes, she could see he truly cared about her. It melted her heart. The Balish crown prince, who had a million duties and responsibilities, made time to help Van, a lowly thief, crossing his path for a flicker of a moment. Her eyes watered over the beauty of his selflessness.

The precarious situation taking place in the Balish monarchy now made sense to Van. Talk of an overthrow of the sitting Moors because of Ferox being decent, fair, and kind. She hoped he was also strong and cunning or he would never survive in a world dominated by the Balish.

"Does that mean you'll let us go?" Van asked.

He glanced down. "I have to follow protocol."

Van scowled.

"But if I'm convinced you're headed on a corrected path." He flashed her a wide grin. "I'll see what I can do."

There's no way he and Solana shared a bloodline. How could a brother and sister be so different?

"The best way to know what's right," Ferox said, "is to make choices so you don't win, but others do."

"From what I know, that doesn't sound very Balish."

"What do you mean?" He looked taken aback. "Tell me," Ferox said, interested, rather than angry. "Tell me what you know."

"Um." Van scrunched her face. She didn't expect to get put on the spot. "The Balish don't have Elemental blood like the Lodians. The Balish believe Lodians are heathens, obtuse and primitive. Their simple minds cause them to live in the past. Their heads, clouded by legend and myths." Van stared at Ferox. "Am I close?"

Ferox chuckled at Van's dramatic description. "We see Lodians as cowards who hide behind their magical ancestors, the Elementals, and Manik's law. Their warriors, the Grigori, are not strong like our Balish soldiers."

Van's anger rose. They certainly weren't cowards. She wanted to defend the Grigori, but couldn't. Ferox still thought Van was an uneducated marketeers' scout from Hod. Giving him a piece of her mind would blow her cover. She bit her tongue.

"They can't even do their job of killing demons," Ferox continued.

Nope. Van couldn't stay quiet any longer. "Manik's law drives the Balish crazy because it protects the Lodians." Her nostrils flared.

"Sounds to me like they're jealous the Elementals favor the Lodians. Being their descendants makes Lodians highly magical, and magic is power. Balish fear that."

"We don't value magic. It's foolish, just like the Lodians. They actually believe their Anchoress carries a piece of the light in her blood, given to her by the moon." Ferox snorted. "Lodians had their chance at running the Living World a thousand years ago and failed." He scrutinized Van. "You seem to favor the *Victus Opuseulus.*"

Van opened her mouth to retort, when the man in the crow's nest interrupted their conversation.

"Sail, ho!" he cried.

Ferox and Van shot to their feet and turned in the direction he pointed.

A wooden ship sailed directly at them with great speed.

Ferox dashed down the stairwell, Van followed. They sprinted across the deck toward the stern and up another stairwell leading to Captain Widsith.

The captain stood next to the crewman manning the helm. He peered through a telescope.

"Who is it?" Ferox asked the captain, as he caught his breath.

The approaching ship raised her flag.

Even without a telescope, Van could see it. At first glance, she thought it was a Balish ship with its black flag. But instead of a red and gold insignia, it displayed a white serpent winding around a white skull and crossbones.

"Pirates!" a crewman yelled.

"Prepare for battle!" Captain Widsith cried.

The crew rushed to gather their swords, cutlasses, and scythes. Some prepped the cannons, others rushed down the stairwells, most likely to prep other cannons below deck.

The pirate ship traveled closer with unwavering determination.

"They're in range." Captain Widsith raised his arm and then swooped it toward the deck. "Fire! Fire!"

The cannons blasted. They looked and worked similar to Earth

World cannons, except they used finely crushed gemstones instead of gunpowder.

Van's ears went numb. The souls of her feet vibrated as *The Obelus* rocked with an explosion.

"Berth's hit!" bellowed one of the crew.

Van's knuckles grew white from gripping the taffrail. The smell of hot metal filled the air.

Multiple booms from the pirate ship made her stomach churn. Her eyes widened in terror as cannonballs soared closer. She braced for another impact.

Blasts erupted from every direction, causing geysers of wood and debris.

The ship jerked. Van's body crashed against the bulwark as pieces of wreckage cut through her face and hands, stabbing her like a million cuts of death.

Crewmen wailed, drenched in blood from their wounds. Some writhed on the deck, missing an arm or a leg. Another ran by shrieking as he held a blood-soaked hand over his eye.

"What's happening?" Van screamed. She crouched down, hands over her ears.

More booms echoed from the distance.

A violent eruption blew Van from her feet. She skidded across the deck and slammed into the abandoned helm. She heard a crack; her back twinged with pain.

The mast closest to her exploded and shattered. Wooden debris crashed down on her.

The boat rocked again.

Van tumbled across the deck and crashed down the stairwell.

Out of nowhere, Brux appeared. He wrapped his arms around her, using his body to protect her from the falling wreckage.

Van peered from under Brux's embrace and glimpsed the bow of the pirate ship glide past. Its starboard side slid into place alongside *The Obelus*.

The scarfed head of the first pirate came into Van's view. Followed by another, then another. They stood on the main deck of the pirate ship and flung multiple grappling hooks tied to ropes onto *The Obelus's* deck. The pirate crew yanked the ropes and pulled the vessels closer together.

"Swords up!" Captain Widsith hollered.

Terrified, Van cowered under Brux's protective body.

She scolded herself. She was a warrior, trained to fight demons, yet she became a jellyfish over a pirate invasion?

The pirates threw down several planks between the ships, making walkways, and advanced onto *The Obelus* wielding cutlasses and swords, screeching like bloodthirsty animals.

Some pirates were human. Others had green or blue skin. Some had fangs and long faces. One pirate looked part woman-part cat.

Brux nudged Van, still covering her body with his. "Get below deck."

"Are they demons?" Van wriggled away from Brux's protective grip and dashed a few steps up the stairwell to get a better look.

"Danger, ho!" screamed the man in the crow's nest.

The ship rocked.

Van lost her balance and crashed back down the stairwell; Brux collided with the bulwark.

Van's body ached in at least five places. Yet she scrambled to her feet. "Why did they fire at us?" It made no sense since the pirates had already boarded the ship.

"They're too close to hit us with cannon fire." Brux looked baffled.

"Land!" the man in the crow's nest cried out. "Rising all 'round!" He sounded nervous.

"Forget the pirates," Captain Widsith yelled. "We're about to become fish food!"

"There's no land here," Ferox shouted over the commotion. "We're in the middle of the ocean."

"It's not land," the captain roared. "Batten down the hatches!"

The Obelus rose, as if something from underneath lifted it.

The ship dropped.

Van stumbled and crashed to her knees. She regained her footing and staggered across the deck, to the side not obstructed by the pirate ship. She peered over the bulwark. Brux gripped her waist with one arm and grabbed the rail with his other hand, to prevent them both from falling overboard.

Scattered lumps spanned the sea around the ships.

"Are we hitting those tiny islands?" Van asked.

"Those aren't islands." Brux gripped her tighter. "It's a sea monster."

CHAPTER 24

Eel-like creatures with many cephalopod eyes on its head and tentacle-like bodies covered with suckers rose from the sea. There must've been at least a dozen of them.

The word "laocoon" echoed around the ship, coming from terrified crew members.

Van gripped the rail as the sea serpents jerked their pointy heads forward, trying to snag seamen into their fang-filled mouths. Water crashed onto the deck from the powerful movements of their massive bodies.

Neither the pirates, nor the captain's crew, trusted each other enough to stop fighting until one monster lurched its ugly head and, mid-fight, snatched down, catching a green pirate between its jaws.

The serpent lifted the pirate into the air. His legs flailed as he hung from the monster's mouth. He screeched for a second, still clutching his sword, until green-colored blood spurted from his abdomen. In death, the pirate's fingers released their grip, and his sword crashed onto the deck.

The crew and pirates stopped fighting with each other and turned toward the sea creatures, weapons raised.

Van steadied herself as the deck rocked from the laocoons' bodies moving underneath the ship.

Snapping jaws of the serpents darted down on the pirates and crew, like beaks of chickens pecking at grain. All hands swiped their swords, cutlasses, anything they could to battle the sea monsters.

Several men screamed as they each got snagged in the jaws of the creatures. Their blood oozed across the worn wood planks of the deck.

Everything happened so fast Van and Brux remained cowered by the bulwark on the level below, looking upward to see the action. Van saw Pernilla and Kopius dash across the deck. Each picked up a discarded deadman's sword and joined the fight.

"I need a weapon." Brux released Van.

"Don't go," Van shouted over the ruckus. "I have a weapon."

Seawater crashed over the bulwark, soaking them. They ducked as a slimy head swooped its pointy snout and smashed into the deck a few feet away, cracking the wood planks. It rose toward the sky and moved to find an easier target on the ship.

"No." Brux clutched the railing as the ship rocked again. "You can't reveal yourself. Get below deck with Paley and Daisy."

Brux darted up the stairwell.

Van rushed after him and paused at the top of the stairs, taking in the terrifying scene.

A bulky pirate raised his sword high, exposing his belly to the monster he battled.

Van cringed, fearing for his life.

He stepped aside as the serpent dove. The pirate used his massive arms to slash his sword in a wide arc, going straight through the creature's tentacle-body, slicing the monster's head clean off. It thudded to the deck.

Blue blood spurted from the headless appendage. It flailed wildly, then slowed as it slid over the bulwark and back into the sea.

Brux zipped around the fallen debris toward a sword lying in a pool of red and blue blood streaked with swirls of magenta.

"Brux!" Van cried out when he slipped and tumbled.

He lay face-up on the deck, vulnerable for a split second, long enough for a creature to dip its snout toward him.

Van gasped.

He rolled away, leaving the serpent to snatch nothing but air. Brux jumped to his feet and continued his sprint toward the dead man's sword.

Ferox slashed his blade at an snapping eel-like head, keeping the creature at bay. His awareness shifted for a second, long enough for him to glimpse Brux rushing in his direction.

Ferox swiveled, turning his back to the sea serpent, thinking Brux was coming for him. He faced Brux, sword raised. The monster lowered its opened jaw over Ferox's head.

"Look out!" Van screamed.

Brux leaped onto Ferox, the force of his body knocked the prince out of the way.

Ferox tumbled backward and smashed onto the wood planks, his sword cascaded across the bloodstained deck. Brux crashed down, rolled, and hit the outer bulwark.

The serpent's head dipped again, making another attempt to snatch Ferox.

The prince rolled aside as the monster's jaw came chomping down. Its thick tentacle-like neck smashed the outer bulwark, leaving a gaping hole.

Brux leaped to his feet as the ship rocked again. He lost his balance in the slick blood coating the wood planks and crashed face down on the deck.

The ship swayed.

He slid toward the damaged bulwark. His hands flailed as his fingers tried in vain to grip onto an uneven plank.

"Brux!" Van dashed from the stairwell toward him as he continued slipping closer to the gaping hole in the bulwark.

She raced across the deck and flung her body toward Brux, landing hard on her stomach, arms outstretched, hands reaching for him. The momentum caused her to slide across the soaked deck, head first. Her body stopped. Her fingers a hair's reach from Brux's.

He grasped for her, almost reaching her hands. The ship pitched. His eyes projected panic.

More and more distance grew between Van's and Brux's hands as his body slipped away, through the opening in the bulwark, and overboard.

Van scrambled to her feet. Struggling to maintain her balance, she rushed to the bulwark and gripped the taffrail. She leaned sideways and peered through the gap in the damaged wall into the sea below.

Brux had disappeared under the ocean.

"No!" Van screeched. Not only was his life in danger, so was Paley's. If Brux vanished into the deep with his Twin Gemstone, Paley would also die.

Van released her grip on the taffrail and took a step to center herself in front of the opening in the bulwark, ready to leap in after him.

"Stop!" Ferox grabbed her by the arm. His eyes, frenzied. Streaks of red and blue blood spattered his face and clothes. "He's gone. Get below deck."

"Don't tell me what to do!" She threw him a look to kill. "He's not *gone.*"

He'd simply fallen over the side.

Into the sea.

Occupied by a dozen sea serpents.

"You can't help him." Ferox yanked her hard, pulling her toward the inner deck.

They both ducked and rolled hitting the bulwark, to avoid a serpent's deadly jaw as it swooped across the deck.

With no other recourse, Van reached into her pocket and pulled out the tiny black pouch.

The sea monsters weren't human. They were evil creatures trying to kill them. This was a correct use of the Coin.

Van had already come into some of her power, and although Brux was her assigned protector, her newly gained skills helped even out their roles. They needed to look after each other. Now it was Van's turn to help him.

She leaned her elbows against the taffrail for balance and pulled out the shiny gold object.

Ferox kept watch. He swiped his sword every time a serpent bobbed its snapping jaws near them as he kept an eye on Van.

She held the Coin in her hand, and, as expected, it disappeared into her palm. Van closed her eyes and used her will to connect her Anchoress magic to the Coin.

Unspoken information downloaded into her being from her ancestral line. She opened her eyes and pressed her hip against the bulwark to keep steady as the ship continued to sway from the serpents' attack. Her eyes tingled as they turned phosphorescent violet. Van raised her arms over her head and clapped her hands together. She had connected to her power.

As her hands separated, yellow-orange discs of light swirled in each of her palms like two mini-shields.

More and more pirates and crewmen screamed as they got snatched by the sea monsters, escalating Van's worry about Brux.

With great determination, Van pushed one hand toward the eel-like head hovering directly above. A flash of light blasted from her palm, blowing it to pieces.

Bits of tissue, fangs, and blue-colored blood rained down onto the deck, drenching Van, Ferox, and a couple of nearby pirates.

She used her other hand and did the same.

Again and again. One hand after the other. Dashing across the deck, blasting one serpent's head after another.

But more and more serpents rose from the deep in a seemingly never-ending supply.

"We're outnumbered." Ferox stabbed the underside of a serpent's jaw, its blood poured down on him. The serpent jerked away, injured but not dead. "Use your innate powers! *Reach inside!*"

The fleeting realization that Van had exposed herself as the Anchoress heir to Ferox, and he seemed well-schooled in her abilities, was something she'd deal with after the sea serpent attack. If they survived.

Van took Ferox's advice to heart and refocused on her inner Self, not on the Coin. She visualized blasting every one of the serpents' heads at the same time.

Her body heated. Her palms got uncomfortably hot as energy rose inside her, cumulating in a crescendo and then… releasing.

Lightning bolt-like flashes crackled from her palms and blasted the head of every sea serpent in her line of vision.

Fragmented pieces of tissue and blood deluged onto the deck.

The remaining crew and pirates cheered. So grateful, none bothered covering their heads to protect against the downpour.

The severed tentacles slipped back under the sea.

The ship held steady; the water calmed. No one said a word.

Van rushed to the gaping hole in the bulwark and peered over the side.

Brux floated amid the ship's debris and remnants of blasted sea serpents.

She smiled and breathed a sigh of relief.

"Get me out of this mess," he cried, sounding grumpy.

"I saved your life. Watch your tone," Van said. There was no pleasing him.

Ferox appeared next to Van and looked into the water. "Fish him out! Now!" he yelled to the crew.

Several of his men hurried to obey. They dragged a cargo net to the opening and hastily tossed it over the side.

Once Brux safely made his way up the rope netting, Van relaxed. If he was mad at her for exposing herself as the Anchoress to the Balish prince, that was his problem. She had saved all their lives, and that had to count for something.

She scanned the calm horizon and her heart rate came down.

In the distance, she heard Captain Widsith bark orders. He was overexcited about something, but Van couldn't make out his words.

Ferox and his men dashed to pick up weapons discarded on the deck by the dead. He commanded the surviving pirates to reload any undamaged cannons.

Van didn't understand the big rush. Until…

"What—what's that?" She pointed with trepidation to ripples on the water's surface near the ship.

"Oh, no," Brux muttered.

Captain Widsith dashed over and grabbed the back of Van's shirt. "It ain't over yet, girl. Get those powers ready."

A giant island came into view before her. Not an island, an enormous head. Squid-like with a large, single cephalopod eye staring directly at her.

"You made it angry." The captain gripped his sword as he and his crew braced for the fight of their lives.

CHAPTER 25

"Laocoon," Captain Widsith snarled at the sea monster as if calling it out. He craned his neck as the enormous, squid-like head rose from the sea.

Van's stomach dropped as she realized this sea monster's arms had attacked their ship, like an octopus's tentacles. Its remaining limbs, the ones with their eel-like heads still attached, rose from the water with it. All of its eyes glared at Van.

In unison, they opened their jaws, including the main head, whose beak-like mouth displayed multiple rows of sharp teeth.

The monster's tentacles lurched forward all at once, each head snapping its jaws, trying to grab one of the crew or pirates.

The laocoon's main eye held its focus on Van. Its long, forked tongue shot straight forward.

"Duck," Brux yelled.

Van hurtled herself out of the way, and the tongue snapped back like an elastic. She landed on a splintered piece of the deck, slashing her right flank.

The laocoon jerked its glossy head forward, extending its jaw and taking a bite out of the stern close to Van and Brux.

The ship dipped and rocked with the laocoon's bite, sending the crew and pirates sprawling.

Van rolled and crashed against the outer bulwark. She screamed in agony. Her blood seeped onto the wood planks mixing with seawater, green and blue blood, and chunks of sea monster.

Van twisted to inspect her laceration, a splice below the ribs. The movement caused tremendous pain. She struggled to sit upright, encouraged that none of her internal organs had spilled onto the deck. *Only a flesh wound.*

Brux rushed over. "Are you all right?"

Van's blood oozed, and Brux applied pressure, using his hands to help stop the bleeding.

Across the deck, Kopius and Pernilla appeared by Ferox's side, panting, and soaked with red and blue blood as he, along with the crew and pirates, regained their footing.

Van heard Pernilla tell Ferox, "We came from the other side. Pirate ship's gone. Obliterated."

"Plenty to do here," Ferox said in a strained voice as he and Captain Widsith raised their swords to prepare for the incoming attack by more of the laocoon's tentacles.

Pernilla and Kopius joined Ferox and the captain. They slashed and jabbed at the eel-like heads.

"We have to get the main head," Kopius yelled, as he swiped his blade across a serpent's snout.

"It's too far out," Ferox said. "We can't reach it."

"Van!" Pernilla shouted a pleading cry.

With unsteady legs and clutching her side, Van heaved herself onto her feet with the help of Brux.

Several of the remaining crew members, along with Brux, circled Van, protecting her from the snapping snouts, so she could gather her power again.

Using all her strength, Van focused on the monster's giant eye.

The laocoon leaned forward, extending its beak-like mouth, and opened its jaw, ready to bite a chunk out of the ship again.

Van raised her arms and clapped her hands, but this time she held them together. A bolt of light shot from her clasped hands and harpooned the main sea creature's eye.

The laocoon let out several ear-piercing screeches. Its tentacles flailed, even the stubs with missing heads.

Its tentacles slowed and then dropped into the water. Where its eye had been was now a charred black hole. The sea monster silently slipped beneath the surface of the sea.

Pernilla rushed over to Van, her wet hair matted to her head and neck. She panted from exertion and wiped blood-soaked sweat from her forehead. "You think we killed it?"

"We weren't worth the hassle to eat." Kopius gave a weak, lopsided grin. Sweat and splotches of red and blue blood stained his torn clothes.

Brux twisted toward Van with a clenched jaw. "You shouldn't have done that. What were you thinking?"

"You're welcome," Van said meekly, drained from her laceration and from using her magical power.

Brux glanced at Ferox, who worked nearby helping the injured crew. He lowered his voice. "Now Ferox knows we lied about being marketeers' scouts." His eyes bored into Van. "That we're Lodians out of bounds and—"

"You're the Anchoress," Ferox said.

He apparently saw them whispering and came to put a stop to their private conversation.

The look on his face made Van uneasy.

Oh, I really screwed up this time. Van wondered if the Lodians might be better off if she died, laid to rest at the bottom of the sea along with her powers and the Coin.

Ferox glowered at Van. One of his men handed him a sword. He seemed to soak in the reality of standing before the Lodian's fabled Anchoress. No longer a myth and undeniably the most wanted criminal in the Living World, according to Balish law.

"Touch her and you're done." Brux protectively stepped in front of

Van, ready to continue the fight, although his time, against a different monster—Ferox.

Several more of the prince's soldiers rushed over. They flanked Ferox, ready to strike at his command.

"It's not against the law for underage Lodians to be out of bounds," Pernilla growled.

"You harm us, and the Elementals will never allow your people access to Salus Valde," Brux said.

Ferox continued to glare at Van, gripping his blood-soaked sword, though not raised. "Your presence here gives my family the evidence it needs to void Manik's law. Then," he turned to Brux, "we *will* be allowed to take over Salus Valde."

"The Elementals would never agree to that," Kopius said.

"We do this by the book." Ferox glanced at his men and barked, "Detain them!"

A soldier grabbed Van. She twisted and cried to Ferox, as they dragged her away, "All that talk about the *Sanctus Novus*. Making the right choices. It was all *lies*?" The bleeding in her wounded abdomen hadn't stopped, and she felt weaker by the minute. Perhaps it was worse than she thought.

"You *lied* to me!" Ferox scowled at Van.

"No. *You* lied!" She could tell her eyes were on the verge of becoming phosphorescent violet, although the energy she exerted being angry weakened her even more. "And I thought there might be hope for you."

Brux's eyes darted to Van's bleeding flank wound. "Van, you're seriously injured."

"Van?" Ferox called to them with an angry-smug look. "What happened to 'Nessie'?"

"She needs medical attention," Brux cried. "Now!"

"You-you killed my *sister*!" Ferox stormed toward Van; his men halted so he could catch up to them. He kept his focus on Van and gripped his sword tighter.

"Solana was evil. You know it," Van said, using too much of her remaining strength. "A dark thread twisted through her soul. There was no redemption for her. She would've killed you too if you got in her way."

"So if you look at it, Van saved your life." Kopius tried to lighten the mood, but his eyes remained sharp.

"She was my *sister*!" Spittle flew from Ferox's lips. "The heir to the Balish throne!" He raised his sword.

"Only because she murdered your brother!" Van shouted, although they stood only a foot apart. "And your mother!"

"Wait a minute." Ferox lowered his sword. "Are you saying she killed my brother? My mother?"

The air hung heavy with silence, other than the lapping waves against the damaged ship.

Van nodded.

"It's the truth," Brux said.

"Solana's demons killed your brother, Devon. It wasn't from the Grigori not doing their job." Van rested most of her weight on the arms of the man holding her. "Your mother died because she cast a protective spell on Devon that bound their two fates together. When he died, she died."

"It makes sense now." Ferox looked as though the fight had drained from him.

"Solana… she was rotten," Van said, in a softer tone. "She had to be… stopped."

"No one deserves to die," Ferox said, gaining back some of his energy.

"Including us?" Kopius raised his eyebrows.

"The law is the law," Ferox said. "I recognize Daisy, now. I know she's an escaped prisoner."

A muscle twitched in Kopius' clenched jaw. He looked ready to attack the prince.

"Your law. Balish law." Van threw Ferox a mutinous glare. "A law you and your council created to control us." She felt the tingle of magic activating in her blood that came about when she felt threatened. "Daisy broke no law other than being Lodian." Exhausted, injured, and trying to do the right thing, Van shook her head in disappointment. Ferox made everything worse by not listening to reason. "You need to let us go so we can save the worlds."

Ferox could be truly evil, like his sister. Her thoughts became frenzied, detached. Van searched for ways to justify grabbing the Coin and using its powers against him.

As Ferox pondered the situation, everyone held quiet and still.

Van used the reprieve to satisfy whether Ferox counted as true evil before taking extreme action against him. She connected with her intuitive power and peered into his soul, sure she would get confirmation by seeing a dark thread like she had with Solana.

She focused, staring at Ferox as her teammates resumed their attempt to bargain with the prince.

Van gasped. Her eyes widened in surprise. She saw no dark thread inside Ferox's soul. Only white light.

"You're right," Ferox said. "There's no kill order on Lodian children out of bounds. But Daisy is an escaped prisoner." His eyes darted back to Van. "And there *is* a kill order on the Anchoress." He raised his sword.

Van eye's tingled with magical energy. She knew they flashed phosphorescent violet just before her energy dissipated, and she collapsed.

In her semi-unconscious state, Van felt her teammates lift her. They carried her into a cabin below deck. In her daze, she heard both Brux and Ferox's muted and distant commands, like they were bossing the others around.

Van needed to come to terms with why Ferox caused her such emotional turmoil. Her attraction to him provoked intense feelings of both love and hate. Getting rid of all her emotions was the only way for her to gain control of her powers. She needed Jacynthia's help to figure this out and called on her spirit guide.

My feelings for Ferox are... confusing, Van said in her mind's eye.

"Every idea or truth bears within itself the opposite idea or truth. When you display an outward dislike of Ferox, this is a denial of your true feelings, which are those of romance."

I'm attracted to Ferox and Brux. But I can't have a relationship with either. It's so frustrating. Brux is my protector. Ferox is Balish and a stubborn ass...

"Beware, my little warrior. All relationships have the potential for growth, or destruction."

Ferox and I are so different from each other... right now he wants to toss me in a dungeon... I don't see how our relationship can grow...

"Why are you going to Cortica?" Her spirit guide's voice mixed with a male voice.

"The real reason." Ferox's demanding voice penetrated Van's awareness.

Jacynthia faded away, and Van regained full consciousness, but kept her eyes closed so she could eavesdrop.

"To check the second seal." Brux sounded stressed. "It might be cracked."

Someone pressed their palms against her wound, trying to slow the bleeding, although her skin felt tight like it had been bandaged.

"The second seal isn't on Cortica. It's in the Bottomless Sea," Ferox said.

Van was right. Ferox was well versed in Lodian lore from his scholars and from reading the *Veridicus Libellus* or Manik's text. The same book Van had read last year. A relic locked in the archives in Balefire Palace for a millennium until Van's father stole it. It contained information about the Anchoress, her abilities, the ancient royals, the Dark War, and the Items of Creation. Too bad Ferox's sister destroyed it before Van killed her.

"Please, unless you plan on letting Van bleed to death, she needs stitches," Brux said.

"I don't plan on killing her or letting her die. As long as you tell me what I need to know. Why send the Anchoress?" Ferox asked in a frustrated tone.

There was a muffled answer.

"Uxa should've contacted the Balish Council," Ferox said. "We would've sent a squadron to check the seal."

Silence followed.

"We consider the Anchoress a weapon," Ferox raised his voice. "Only taken out of dormancy to attack the Balish."

Van opened her eyes to see him raise his sword and point it at Brux's chest.

Brux stopped tending to Van's wound and bravely stood to face Ferox.

"You're going for the next Item of Creation!" Ferox said with fury.

"No, we're not," Pernilla insisted.

"Then why, Cortica?" Ferox applied more pressure to his sword, pressing the tip into Brux's chest.

"Because the Coin is leading us there," Van said, startling everyone.

She opted to use Jacynthia's and Uxa's advice regarding dialectical thought. Perhaps Ferox could be an ally, not an enemy. She also decided to stop hating Brux because of her romantic feelings for him and turn him into a friend, allow him to do his job and be her assigned protector.

"We all know the Elementals hid the Cup of Life on Cortica." Ferox's cheek twitched. He twisted and pointed his sword at Van. "So, Lodians *are* attempting to overthrow my family and take control of the Living World. You admit it?"

The two soldiers guarding the doorway raised their swords.

"No." Van waved her hand for Ferox to move his sword so she could sit up.

Her teammates look stunned. As far as Van knew, they didn't know the Cup was in Cortica.

She struggled, Brux reached around and supported Van's back, helping her to get upright. Van instinctively wanted to push him away, then embraced her new outlook and accepted his help. "Thanks."

Brux furrowed his brow at her unexpected kindness.

"The Anchoress's Items of Creation are my tools." Van sat with her legs over the side of the bed and gripped the edge of the mattress. "I use them to harness my innate magical energy, so I can restore order when demons reach this world. Using the Items to fight against one another is an incorrect use and will cause harm to my soul. I'm not going for the Cup."

Ferox lowered his sword.

Standing took all of Van's energy, even with Brux's support. She breathed deeply and focused on staying conscious long enough to get Ferox onboard as an ally. "The Coin is leading us to Cortica. I'm not sure why yet."

"I do." Ferox said, looking grim. "They're back."

"Who's back?" Pernilla asked.

"Demons."

CHAPTER 26

"There's an illness spreading," Ferox said. "Right now, it's only afflicting children."

"We know about the illness." Brux hovered close to Van. He continued to rest his hand on her back. "We heard about it at the Fisherman's Rest."

And from Uxa and the Brotherhood. "What does the illness have to do with demons being in the Living World?" Van's laceration throbbed. Blood seeped through the bandage.

"Hey," Paley said. She and Daisy peeked into the cabin; the soldiers standing by the door blocked their way.

Ferox waved his hand. "Let them pass."

"What's going on?" Paley asked as she and Daisy entered the cabin. They both looked shaken and wet, yet unblemished from the battle with the laocoon. Not a blood splatter on them.

Daisy dashed to Kopius. "You're all right!" She wrapped her arms around him.

"Just a bit banged up." Kopius grinned. "I'm glad to see you're still in one piece."

"I stayed in the crew's quarters with Paley." Daisy craned her neck to look up at him; her arms stayed wrapped around his waist. "I prayed to the light for your—and the team's—survival."

Brux frowned at Daisy. "I'm okay, too. Thanks for noticing."

Daisy released Kopius and smiled at her brother. "I'm happy you are too—Van!"

"Oh my gosh, Van." Paley scooted over to her side. "You're all bloody. Are you badly hurt?"

"Enough," Ferox commanded.

His soldiers tensed at his outburst. Their knuckles whitened as they clutched the hilt of their swords.

"I'm fine." Van swatted Paley away. "Tell us," she said to Ferox, "earlier when we were talking on deck, before the attack, you mentioned you needed our help. Does this have something to do with the illness?"

Ferox looked dour. "This sickness extinguishes a child's inner light. It causes an infection, a fever, that forces the sick to attach to the dark part of their Self. Kids struggle to resist it... they fight to cling to the light as the darkness seeks to destroy it. As it progresses, it eventually consumes the child's soul." Ferox paused as if to collect himself. "After the kids die, their bodies to turn to dust. Then they rise, undead, as creatures from the earth."

"Do you mean...?" Daisy looked stricken by the news.

"The illness," Ferox said. "It's turning children into demons."

Daisy gasped. Van gaped at him eyed wide-eyed. The others shifted, looking frightened.

"That's why Semjaza called it the demon illness," Pernilla said.

"Demons on Living World soil." Van knew what this meant.

"Dishora," Daisy muttered. "There's no doubt. The Escalation has begun."

"That's why you need us," Brux said to Ferox. "You need the Anchoress."

"And that's why you were on the Skeleton Coast," Van said, with greater understanding. "You knew the Cup was in this area. You were looking for me."

"When I thought you were thieving marketeers' scouts, I wanted you to help me find the Anchoress," Ferox said. "Scouts are scavengers. They're known to be good at finding things."

Daisy's eyes darted to Ferox. "You're after the Cup of Life. You want to use its healing powers to save the afflicted children."

Ferox nodded. "We can work together, as a team. On one condition." Ferox reached his hand toward Van. "Give me the Coin."

The hair on Van's arms stood on end. *Give him the Coin?*

Everything seemed to stand still. The Coin was her responsibility. How could she give it away? She glanced at her teammates. Brux, Kopius, and Pernilla were injured, exhausted, and probably hungry. Daisy and Paley, despite avoiding the battle, didn't look fit either. None of them had any fight left in them.

"Help me retrieve the Cup. Otherwise, I will *take* the Coin and send you back to the Skeleton Coast as prisoners," Ferox said. "Lodian teens arrested for dealing in the fairy trade, along with their Anchoress, out of bounds with the Coin of Creation. Well, we all know what happens next."

"You know we aren't fairy traders." Pernilla looked insulted.

"I know no such thing," Ferox said, being obtuse. "Unless you help me. Start by giving me the Coin. It's obviously leading you—the *Anchoress*—to Cortica and the Cup." He extended his hand closer to Van. "Make the right choice."

"We have to check the seal." Van was stressed about completing the mission. She didn't need another task added to her thirty-day window, which closed in three weeks. Although, she found some reassurance, having already crossed two other items off her list. Finding Daisy and checking to see if Ferox had a dark thread.

"Once I get the Cup, I'll let you go," Ferox said. "Then you can do whatever you want."

"Van," Paley whispered, loud enough for everyone to hear. "Give him the Coin."

"You can't possibly believe him." Pernilla placed her hands on her hips and narrowed her eyes at Ferox.

"I trust him. His energy is pure." Daisy smiled at Ferox, shining like a ray of light in the dingy cabin.

Ferox grinned at Daisy's endorsement.

"Give it to him," Brux said. "It's our best option."

"Our only option, from where I'm standing." Kopius eyed the edgy soldiers by the door.

What choice do I have? They were in no shape to fight everyone on the ship. Going back to the Skeleton Coast would set them back time-wise, even if they escaped Balish imprisonment, making it near impossible to complete their mission before her protection from the Quasher ended.

Van called the Coin from her palm. It rose to the surface of her skin.

She had a déjà vu moment. Her mind flashed to last year when she tossed the Coin to Solana. The Balish princess caught it with her bare hand and then burst into a thousand shadowy pieces.

Although Ferox was the enemy, the thought of him exploding made Van uneasy. Ferox offered to work with them. Her soul didn't need any further damage. "Um. I think… maybe wear gloves."

"I'm well versed in the stories of the ancient royals and the Dark War." He wiggled his fingers for Van to hurry. "I'm royal and can handle touching the Coin without corruption."

Solana was royal, too. Van didn't move.

Ferox sighed. "I'm not conspiring with demons. I'm not planning on killing any of you. My only interest is in maintaining peace between the tribes." He stretched his arm toward Van, hand open.

"Okay, then." She gently placed the Coin in his palm and stepped back, cowering, expecting him to explode.

Nothing happened.

Ferox didn't even appear smug about getting the Coin. He tucked it into the same pouch that carried the fairy's tear. He looked as if he had mentally checked off another task on his long to-do list.

"We Balish are good people," he said. "We believe in the light of the sun. I want to prevent Solmor by making sure there is no war between the Lodians and Balish. Now that I know who you are, it's my duty to find the real reason Uxa sent you here."

"I've already told you. To check the second seal," Van said, striving to look honest. "Really."

"We need to put a stop to the demon illness," Daisy said, still shaken by the news. "Ferox is on the right path. The Cup of Life is the only way to cure those who are already sick."

Ferox turned to Van. "If the ancient writings are accurate, you're the only one who can retrieve the Cup. If this is true, once you do, you'll give it to me. And then you're free to check the seal. I'll see to stopping the illness."

"Okay. Yup." Van bobbed her head. But at the end of their time together, she had no intention of letting Ferox walk away from her with the Coin or the Cup.

"One issue with that plan," Brux said. "We have to mend the seal first, to stop the spread of the infection."

"Maybe we should split up?" Pernilla suggested. "I mean, since we're not prisoners." Everyone, except Daisy and Van, talk-shouted at once. Offering suggestions, fighting between what to do first. Get the Cup or mend the seal? Who should go where, and who should do what?

Van remained silent. After her ordeal with the laocoon, she didn't have it in her to join the argument.

"It's a what came first, the chicken or the egg scenario," Paley said.

Ferox looked perplexed. "Why, the egg, of course!"

"Where'd the egg come from if there was no chicken to lay it?" Pernilla asked.

Ferox looked at her as if her question was absurd and said, "From the eye of the sun."

"Didn't anyone think we might need the Cup to mend the seal?" Daisy asked in her airy, yet authoritative voice.

All eyes turned to stare at her. A moment of silence followed as they absorbed her question.

Ferox gave Daisy a nod. "We will retrieve the Cup, and then I will let you use it to mend the seal, if need be," he said, with finality.

With their discussion over, they turned their attention to their current situation. The group left the cabin and went on deck to survey the ship.

The remaining crew, soldiers, and pirates had already begun working together. They tended to the injured and took an inventory of the damage to the ship.

The laocoon had obliterated the pirate's ship. The pirate captain was dead, and only a handful of his crew remained. Three human men; one male, blue-skinned pirate with pointed facial features; and one humanoid fish-woman with coral-colored scaly skin and gill-like ears. Her face protruded outward with bulging, overlarge eyes, and she had a round mouth with pouty lips. To Van, she looked like a human-sized goldfish.

The fish-woman removed her newsboy cap when Captain Widsith introduced her as Thyra. Instead of hair, a gold-colored fin fanned across her scalp.

"Fascinating," Kopius said, clearly interested in learning more about the strange woman.

She gave them a curt, nervous bow.

The newly merged crew got busy repairing *The Obelus.*

Ferox allowed them access to their backpacks, and Brux dashed down to the designated cabin. He returned with a backpack full of medicinal supplies, a change of shirt for Van, and jackets for his teammates since the air had gotten much cooler.

As Brux and Daisy applied tinctures and better patched up Van's wound, she watched Ferox working side by side with the crew. Despite the cooler air, he was sweating from the repair work and had removed his outer shirt. He wore a tight fitted tank, displaying his muscular torso and tapering waist.

Van narrowed her eyes at Thyra working next to him, chatting away. She scowled. The fish-woman needed to focus on the work at hand, not flirting.

"Sorry, did I hurt you?" Brux pulled his hand away from patting down her bandage.

"No." Van took her eyes off Ferox for a second to glance at Brux.

Although Widsith was the official captain of *The Obelus,* and the

Balish didn't rule Cortica, there was an unspoken acknowledgment Prince Ferox was in charge. It seemed all people, even creatures like Thyra, deferred to him, and groveled for his approval.

Ferox required Kopius and Brux to pitch in with the ship's repairs. Since the ship was patriarchal Balish-occupied territory, human females weren't allowed to help with repair work.

"Seriously?" Pernilla shifted her weight to one side and placed her hands on her hips.

"That's okay with me," Paley piped in.

"We have to respect his beliefs," Daisy said in good stride.

"It's obnoxious." Van muttered a string of words. The most audible were "chauvinistic" and "dictator," as Ferox's men shuffled the girls down into the galley to help prepare dinner.

"I don't even know how to cook," Pernilla said with a huff.

"I do." Daisy smiled, happy with the arrangement. "I can show you."

The galley had minor damage from the attack and was bigger than Van imagined. They had it stocked with bags of grain and barrels of vegetables. Stacks of pots, some tin mugs, and a handful of iron ladles and spoons were secured in cubbies on the wall. Chains hung a small iron stove from beams, and the floor of the galley was lined with tin to prevent the coals from setting the ship on fire.

The girls got to work, with Daisy instructing them.

Before long, Ferox popped in to see how they were doing.

"Fine." Van answered with attitude while snatching another potato out of the bin.

Pernilla grunted and pounded her fist into the biscuit dough she volunteered to knead.

Daisy bobbed her head, humming.

Paley giggled while chopping carrots. "It's fun."

Ferox peered at Van as she aggressively peeled a potato. "You don't look so good."

"No, she doesn't." Paley frowned. "She's terribly pale."

"You need to gain your strength," Ferox said to Van.

"Stop fussing. I'm fine." Although her body ached from her wounds and from exhaustion.

Ferox gave Van a once over glance. "You're not recovered enough to be helping in the galley."

"I said I'm fine."

"Get to the captain's quarters and rest," Ferox commanded. "That's an order. Go."

Van tossed her potato peeler onto the butcher block table. With no desire to waste her energy arguing, she trudged up several stairwells and walked across the deck to the captain's cabin. While lying in the small wooden bed, Van heard people shuffling around, working outside. She raised her ear, hoping to catch some conversation.

She heard bits and pieces. Mostly boring stuff about the repair work being done to the ship. Her ears perked up when Van heard Brux ask Ferox if he could check on her.

Ferox denied him.

Van fumed. Of all the pompous, self-righteous—her thoughts abruptly stopped when someone tapped on the cabin door.

"It's Ferox. May I come in?"

"Sure." Van's cheeks flushed as she realized Ferox said no to Brux because he wanted to check on her. She snuggled into her bedcover to make it look like she had been sleeping.

Ferox entered the cabin with confidence. His presence engulfed the room, making Van's entire body heat up. Her attraction to Ferox was becoming an issue. One she couldn't comprehend or accept, especially since she thought he was a jerk.

But he also showed qualities of fairness and seemed reasonable. His charisma made him an influential leader. And those strong shoulders...

Van brushed away her physical attraction to him. He seemed to affect all females the same way. She vowed not to become one in the crowd.

Ugh. Her thought process wasn't helping at all.

Zurial warned Van about this in her memory engram. Don't get involved with a Bale. The ancient warrior's relationship with Nick turned out poorly. Van had no wish to repeat it.

She wanted her feelings for Ferox to be false. But her heart insisted otherwise. It twirled like a cyclone when Ferox grabbed the chair next to her bed and turned it so he could face her.

"How're you feeling?" He leaned in close, looking genuinely concerned.

Van closed her eyes and inwardly shook away the notion that he cared about her wellbeing. She reminded herself he was the enemy. He had taken the Coin from her and now wanted the Cup, nothing more.

Didn't Jacynthia advise me to see him as an ally?

"Are you hungry? I can have some food brought in."

Van opened her eyes. She gazed at Ferox and shook her head. For the first time in a year, she had no appetite.

She had to face it. Ferox was a good guy.

Embarrassed by her earlier outburst, and uncomfortable about lying to him about agreeing to retrieve the Cup, Van stared at him, unable to think of anything to say. She definitely couldn't tell him she had no intention of getting the Cup, never mind giving it to him. Her plan was to check the seal and get home.

"We'll be arriving at Cortica tomorrow morning," he said. "Are you able to walk?"

Van nodded.

"Good." He smiled.

Van's insides melted.

"There are healers on the island. I'll take you to one once we dock."

His words wrapped around Van like a warm blanket. She smiled, and managed a feeble, "Thanks."

Van slept for several hours after Ferox left the cabin. She woke to discover *The Obelus* had docked at Outlaw Island.

CHAPTER 27

It was late morning when they reached Cortica, also known as Outlaw Island. Van stood on the deck of *The Obelus*, viewing the shoreline, and couldn't see the end. If she hadn't been told it was an island, she wouldn't have known.

Ferox, five of his soldiers, and a pirate familiar with the territory prepared to disembark. The pirate was Thyra, of course.

Van rolled her eyes. The fish-woman was incapable of being more than three feet away from Ferox.

Ferox instructed the remaining crew to guard the ship and continue with repairs. He commanded Van, Brux, and Kopius to leave their backpacks and ordered Daisy, Paley, and Pernilla to stay on the ship for their own safety.

Pernilla looked like she was about to burst like a geyser.

Instead of pointing at her and saying, "Thar she blows!" Van took the high road and let it go.

"I'm not thrilled about going to Outlaw Island, anyway." Paley shrugged.

Daisy bit her lip. "I don't think we should split up."

Van turned to Ferox and said, "I agree. We're a team, placed with each other for a reason. They need to come on shore with me."

A muscle in Ferox's jaw twitched as he mulled over the idea.

She knew he didn't want them to go because they were human females, the weaker sex, in his mind.

"It's an Anchoress thing," Van added, hoping to seal the deal.

"Fine." Ferox sighed. "There's a lot about the Anchoress I don't yet understand."

Van squirmed under his intense scrutiny of her.

Although dressed as marketeers' scouts, Ferox allowed his soldiers to carry swords, but not the swords of the royal Balish soldiers. The ones left by the dead pirates. He took a dagger.

"Marketeers' scouts carry weapons," Ferox said, as if someone was going to object.

From what Van had heard about Cortica, no one in their right mind would object to them carrying weapons.

"Where's mine?" Kopius extended his hands.

Ferox grimaced at the ridiculous question.

"We're not prisoners," Brux said. "This place is dangerous, and we have no interest in killing you."

"You're our ride home." Kopius bobbed his head in agreement with Brux. "You could use us as back up."

Ferox considered their request, then gave them a curt nod.

"Yes!" Kopius punched his fist, making a winning gesture.

"Thank you for trusting us," Brux said, as both he and Kopius concealed their daggers.

Pernilla raised her eyebrows.

"Go on," Ferox said to her. "I've seen you fight. You'll be an asset."

"Yes!" Pernilla also snagged a dagger.

Daisy, Paley, and Van perused the weapon inventory.

Two daggers remained. Daisy and Paley reluctantly took them, urged by Kopius and Brux.

"Let's hope I don't stab myself to death with this thing." Paley tucked the dagger into one of many side pockets in her cargo pants.

"I don't want this." Daisy held the blade between her thumb and forefinger. "You can be my weapon." She beamed at Kopius.

He grinned back. "I will be." He took the knife and slipped into the long side pocket of her cargo pants. "But take the dagger, just in case."

The only weapons left were swords, cutlasses, and axes. "I'm not taking any of those," Van said.

All of them tried to give their dagger to Van, even Pernilla.

Van refused. "I'll be fine."

"You're not going on land without a weapon," Brux said.

"Stay close to me," Ferox said to Van. "I'll watch over you."

Brux scowled and shifted his weight. "Hold on." He rummaged through his pants pockets. "Here. Take this, at least." He handed Van a jackknife. "Put it where you can easily find it."

Van opened her mouth to say she didn't need a weapon. She was a weapon. When Brux cut her off.

"Just take it." He shoved the jackknife at her.

Van didn't have the heart to fight with him. They had no time to squabble, anyway. She tucked the knife into her jacket pocket.

With the weapons issue settled, Ferox commanded them to get moving.

The team disembarked. They walked past several sketchy ships in dock, plus a handful of smaller boats, and went over to the wharf master's cabin.

Ferox placed two bagocs in the wharf master's palm.

He greedily accepted the legit Balish-stamped gold coins and asked no questions.

As they headed down the wide dirt road, a murder of crows took flight from the surrounding trees.

The fluttering black birds made Van think of Solana. When the Balish princess burst into a thousand shadowy pieces after touching the Coin. Van couldn't shake the feeling the crows had appeared to remind her she had corrupted her soul by misusing the power of the Coin. That she danced close to darkness and needed to be careful.

Van rubbed her arms to ward off the willies and redoubled her intention of never laying a finger on the Cup. Uxa was right, Van wasn't ready. She couldn't be trusted to handle its power.

After walking along the winding dirt road for about a mile, they reached the outskirts of downtown Cortica.

They passed by saltbox shacks and tenements. But in a swampy area, the houses were built on stilts and set in far from the road. In front of one, water rippled and Van caught the snapping snout of what looked like a crocodile. She imagined it as a watery graveyard for cutthroats and thieves who had double-crossed one another.

They arrived at the less swampy, more built up downtown area. Even in the morning light, shadows filled the town. At first glance, Van thought the townspeople were dressed in costumes for a Mardi Gras-style festival. Like she had wandered into a dark and twisted carnival.

She soon realized the island's inhabitants always dressed this way. Van saw skin colors ranging from white to green to yellow to black, and all the colors in between. The outcasts and misfits of society, along with the criminals, came there to be free from the restrictive Balish law and from societal confines.

Thyra fit right in with the crowd, but Daisy's waist-length, shimmering white-blond hair stood out like a full moon on a clear, dark night. Van figured Daisy's hair alone would fetch a good price in Cortica, given the elaborate wigs worn by the inhabitants, both male and female, human and non-human.

Brux stayed glued to Daisy's side, as did Kopius.

It didn't bother Van to see Brux more focused on his sister than on her. Daisy needed to be protected. Van could take care of herself. She glanced at Ferox, who walked close to her, and grinned.

The town was hopping. The street sounds comprised music, chatting, yelling, clinking of glasses, blasts that sounded like gunshots. Lots of gadgets on display outside the shops twirled or spun, and looked like toys used for fun, or to hurt someone. The townspeople lived in a constant state of bacchanalian celebration.

Paley whispered to Van, "This place makes my skin crawl."

"Crawl?" Van said in a low voice. "It makes my skin want to *run*."

The group stayed close together as they passed an eatery displaying a dirty fish tank swimming with black eels.

"Fine dining on display," Kopius quipped.

Paley clutched Van's arm and pulled her closer. "Ask Ferox if we can use the Coin to find the best path. So we can get out of this place."

"Shush!" Thyra scolded. "Some things best not spoken here."

A disheveled, rotund man with flushed cheeks stood in front of five large wooden casks and at least twenty smaller barrels. Van peeked down the alley behind him and saw a bunch of card tables and chairs set up. His patrons were relaxing at the tables and enjoying drinks out of tin cups, though some were standing.

"Bootlegger Bill's Barrel Rum," he said, as the group passed. "Rum from the west, it's the best!" He waved them over. "Five b-stips. All you can drink!"

Ferox tugged Van's sleeve to keep her moving.

"I dunno," Van said, pretending to be interested in taking up Bootlegger Bill's all-you-can-drink offer. "I'm pretty thirsty this fine morning."

Ferox grinned. "So am I. But not for that."

Mischief filled his eyes, the kind Van wanted to dive into with him.

Some pedestrian traffic looked like ruffians or ne'er-do-wells. Those not dressed to impress, dressed dingily. It was a mix. Half of the people dressed like they were at a twisted carnival. The other half wore drab, stretchy hats and overcoats or jackets, and cast furtive glances as they scuttled along, minding their own business.

"Good thing my men and I dressed down," Ferox said.

"I would've preferred you in that." Van nodded toward a flamboyantly dressed man wearing a piled-high white wig, a ruffled shirt, a fitted long coat trimmed with gold braids, and striped knickers.

Ferox chuckled and gave her a hug around the waist.

Van's entire body hummed with excitement from his touch.

On Van's other side, Paley clung to her arm as they passed painted women wearing bustiers. The women lingered on the sidewalk and smiled at passersby, attempting to lure them into nearby shanties.

"Gross," Paley mumbled.

A handful of the painted ladies swamped Ferox, Brux, and Kopius.

Brux and Ferox hastily turned down their provocative offers, but Kopius rattled off questions as if fascinated with them.

Pernilla pulled him away. "Check your pocket to make sure you still have your coin pouch."

"Hey!" a woman called to Daisy. "You lookin' for work?"

A grungy man who appeared to be loitering outside a nearby tobacco shop hollered to Brux, "How much for the blond?"

Brux clutched Daisy even closer as Kopius moved beside her, blocking her from the man's view.

They passed another shop displaying human skulls for sale, along with a variety of dried body organs, powders, candles, and other bones Van hoped weren't human.

"People use those things for black magic," Ferox said to Van in a low voice.

"Do we need to buy some of this stuff?" Kopius asked.

"Let me look. Maybe I can use something for healing." Daisy went into the shop.

Van didn't want any connection to dark magic of any kind and quickened her pace as if walking faster would get her away from the horror of the skull store. Or, perhaps, the temptation? Van had no desire to stick around and find out why the shop evoked a jumble of emotions.

The others stopped to peruse the merchandise and to keep an eye on Daisy. As Ferox went into the store, two of his soldiers remained standing guard outside. They held a sharp eye on Van and got edgy went she went more than two shops away. So Van didn't wander any farther.

"Beautiful girl," a voice called to Van.

A middle-aged, dark-skinned man sat at a table for two on the wood-plank sidewalk. The man's brilliant purple turban pinned with an amber jewel caught Van's curiosity. He dressed much classier than anyone she had seen so far and was the most well-groomed. He had a stunningly elaborate goatee and wore a clean, white pressed jersey under flowing purple robes that matched his turban.

Van thought she glimpsed a bunfy sitting on his table. She did a double-take and could've sworn the critter dashed under the table before she could get a good look at it.

The man noticed he'd caught Van's attention. "Beautiful girl," he repeated. "Come." He passed his upturned palm over his table, draped in a silver and purple tablecloth. He wanted Van to sit with him.

Van stayed on the road, away from the man, and bent down to see under the table.

"Was that a… do you have a bunf—" Van stopped mid-word, realizing the absurdity of a bunfy being in this despicable place. Even if Van was in dire trouble, Wiglaf wouldn't set paw there.

"The spirits… they call to you," he said. "Please, sit."

Van resisted her impulse to stay and talk to the captivating man and turned away, headed back to the dark magic shop and the others.

"Beautiful girl!" he cried. "Your ancestors asked me to give you a message!"

Van halted.

"You want to know? Come," the man persisted and again indicated for her to sit with him. "How often do marketeers' scouts come across an advanced seer? Hm?"

His words reminded Van of Ildiss, the gnome's seer she had met on her prior trip to the Living World. Ildiss had given Van invaluable information. She reconsidered his offer.

The handwritten paper sign taped to the shingles on the outside wall of the building above his table read *psychic readings one b-stip.*

Van had learned that stips were illegal because they came from "chipping." When crooks chip away at the edges of good coins to get extra metal and then melt it together to get a new coin. A b-stip was a bronze coin made from chipping pecs. If you're caught chipping, the punishment was dungeon time. If the Balish caught you with stips, they confiscated all the money in your pocket.

"What are you doing?" Ferox clamped her arm and glared at the man. "Stick with the group. No wandering off."

She turned to Ferox, making her eyes big and round. "Please?"

He visibly softened and reached into his pocket.

Brux darted over. "What's going on?"

The others gathered behind, including Ferox's soldiers.

"Be careful," Thyra said. "Fakes and scammers here."

"I got this," Ferox said to her. He addressed the group, "Stick around the shops. We'll catch up."

Brux glanced at Van, who gave him a reassuring nod. He looked irritated, but he and the others meandered back down the street, accompanied by several of Ferox's soldiers. Two of his men stayed to guard the prince and Van.

Ferox handed the goateed man a legit pec.

Van sat at the table.

CHAPTER 28

The seer stared at the bronze coin in his palm.

Van tensed. A pec was a legitimate coin, not a stip. It had the Balish stamp and was worth two b-stips. A telltale sign they weren't riffraff, and didn't belong on the island.

She feared the seer may screech at her and Ferox, point them out as strangers who came to ruin the freewheeling lifestyle of the island's inhabitants. An angry mob of desperados would come and rip her and Ferox to shreds and then toss their pieces into the swamp, never to be found.

He squinted at Ferox. Then, tucked the coin into his pocket.

"Some privacy," the seer said to Ferox. "Please."

Ferox stood firm and crossed his arms.

"I cannot concentrate with you lurking over the table," the seer said. "Privacy. *Please.*"

Van looked up at Ferox. "I'm not going anywhere."

Ferox considered the request. He nodded and meandered a couple of stores down to where Daisy and Paley were looking at seashells displayed for sale.

The seer closed his eyes and took a deep breath, apparently satisfied with the newly gained amount of privacy.

His eyes popped open. "I am the great Brizo!"

He had tarot cards on his table, and yet he clasped each of his hands around each of hers.

His sweaty grip, along with his intensity, made Van squirm. She tugged her hands, trying to pull away from his grip.

Brizo grasped harder and held her there.

He mumbled something unintelligible, and then said, "The spirits of water, they are flowing through me."

Brizo stared directly at Van, yet he held a vacant look.

He turned her hands palm up. His haunted eyes shifted to her palms.

"The cycle of tide and time is washing to shore," he stated in a dramatic tone. "The spirits… they chatter about astrological signs." His brown eyes rolled upward into his skull, showing only the whites. "Signs are not exact. They vary by a lifetime. Your spirit ancestors tell me the seven year Escalation to Dishora has not yet begun."

It was like the message Ildiss had given her. Van didn't know what it meant, or what she was supposed to do with the information.

"You struggle against the pull of darkness. It writhes inside your soul," his voice changed to sound like the throaty voice of a woman. "Your struggle blocks the aid of the Creator."

The hair on the back of Van's neck stood on end. Not only from the creepy change in the seer's voice, but because the seer spoke the truth. Van always remained aware of her damaged soul. She struggled against the lure of darkness as it battled for dominance inside her Self.

"Cling to the light, to your inner good." His eyes, still white, continued to stare at Van. "Remain innocent and pure. Selfless and sincere. Only then will you receive the assistance of the Creator."

"Got it." Van relaxed, expecting the reading to be over.

"A troubling time draws near," Brizo said, back to his own voice, yet he spoke in an urgent tone. "An abyss cannot be filled to overflowing." He gripped her hands tighter. "Save your Self and return to the light. There is corruption. Darkness. Every step leads to danger."

He shifted in his chair. "Darkness is rising. There is much danger! Do not retrieve the Cup of Life!"

With a perceptible shift in energy, his brown eyes returned to place. His eyes opened wider, as if the spirit world had terrified him. Brizo released and pushed away Van's hands as if they had burned him. He leaped from his seat so fast he rocked the table.

Van knew in the pit of her stomach, this seer had confirmed her worst fear. He had looked into her soul and saw a dark thread, and it had spooked him.

"This reading is over. Leave!" he cried, waving his hands in a shooing motion. "Get out!" He disappeared down the dark alley next to his table like he'd be safer there than with Van.

She vaulted from her chair, intending to follow him to get confirmation about her soul, but a painful grip around her elbow held her back.

"Not the best idea," Ferox said.

Van collapsed into his chest and wrapped her arms around him, shaking.

"What did he say that made you so upset?" He hugged her tightly.

"Nothing." She pulled away. "I just need some food."

Van didn't want to think about how she killed his sister, knowing it would damage her own soul. She didn't want to think about her father who had died trying to save her from the Anchoress curse. Or his ill-fated effort to prevent Van from retrieving the Items of Creation, so she wouldn't fulfill her doomed destiny to fight against darkness in the coming war.

She didn't want to think about her dark thread. Or examine her feelings for both Ferox and Brux.

"What happened?" Brux rushed over, his hand hovered near his waistband, ready to grab his dagger. His eyes darted to the passersby and loitering rogues, searching for someone causing trouble.

"Relax. Just Van acting like her same old self." Pernilla pursed her lips.

"Excuse me?" Van got in Pernilla's face.

"It would help if you focused on the mission. Rather than begging for attention from every guy you meet."

"I wasn't—"

Daisy reached for Van's flank, interrupting her.

"—ouch. What are you doing?"

Daisy lifted Van's jacket, overshirt, and ribbed t-shirt to check Van's bandage. "It's bloody enough to show through your shirt. You might need stitches."

"I'm fine."

Ferox shifted his weight and frowned.

Brux peered at Van's bandage. "You're not fine."

Van noticed dark circles under his eyes. She worried about the drain he suffered from the Twin Gemstones. The energy Brux needed to keep Paley in the Living World was taking its toll.

"Where's Paley?" Van asked.

Kopius pointed to a food stand called the Savage Polder. Paley stood at the window, chatting with a sketchy-looking boy. Although enthusiastic, Paley seemed to lack her usual buoyancy, mostly likely from the adverse effects of the gemstones.

Ferox huddled with his men and Thyra, deep in conversation.

He broke from his huddle and said to Van and the others, "Stay here, in the downtown area." He instructed three of his men to stay and watch them.

"You're not going anywhere without me," Van said.

Ferox broke into a full smile.

Van blushed. Ferox had taken her utterance as a declaration of her affection for him.

"You have the Co—Item." Van agreed with Thyra. Mentioning the Coin in this place wasn't a great idea. "I don't want you out of my sight." Van's cheeks turned a deeper red as her words continued to betray her emotions. "I don't want you sneaking away and leaving me —us—here, on the island." She vowed to stop talking until she could form sentences that didn't have a double meaning. Everything she said made it sound like she would miss Ferox if he left her when her real concern was the Coin.

"Van's right," Daisy said. "We need to stick together."

"Does this have something to do with the fairy's tear?" Kopius asked.

Brux cut in before the prince could even ask. "Yes, we were at the fairy ring. We saw you get the tear. But we're not fairy traders. We needed her tear to trade for information about the seal, and to secure a ship that could take us to it."

Daisy furrowed her brow, worried Ferox might believe they were criminals. "We weren't going to hurt the fairy."

Ferox held up his palms before anyone else could chime in. "At this point, I know you well enough to believe you."

"You don't battle the laocoon without forming some kind of bond. Am I right?" Kopius grinned.

Ferox placed his hands over his heart. "Then, you can trust to me take care of this task. It works both ways." He glanced at Van but spoke to the group. "I have to go. Try to stay out of trouble."

"Tell that to Paley." Kopius tilted his head toward the Savage Polder.

Paley stuck to the boy like a barnacle to a hull. Van frowned as she noticed the wet hem on his pants. A telltale sign he had been up to no good, making him Paley's type. Edgy, cute, dangerous.

Brux also noticed the boy's hem. "Maybe he got back from dumping a body in the swamp." He gave her a lopsided grin.

"Probably." Van turned her attention back to Ferox, still unsure if she trusted him leaving with the Coin. "I can go with you," Van said to Ferox. "Help with your... *task*."

"No need for you." Thyra flapped her pouty fish lips. "I help the prince."

"She knows the area." Ferox touched Van's arm, a comforting gesture, as if to say he held romantic affection for her alone. "You stay here. You'll be safe with my men and your team."

The warmth of his hand, and his intense stare, caused a surge of thrilling tingles throughout Van's body.

"I'll be back." He smiled. "I promise." Ferox turned to the soldiers he instructed to stay with Van and the others and commanded, "Protect them with your lives." He said to Thyra, "Let's go."

The duo headed deeper into the island trailed by two of Ferox's men.

Van found it difficult to take her eyes away from his departing figure. Her gut twisted with the sinking comprehension that she wanted him back just as much as she wanted the Coin.

Daisy moved close to Van. "He left three of his men with us." She placed a hand on Van's back, a tender touch. "Ferox wouldn't have left them here if he wasn't coming back."

"Doesn't matter." Pernilla overheard Daisy. "We don't need him or his stupid ship."

Ferox's men scowled but said nothing.

The group meandered around the shops and stands, staying in the downtown area, as instructed by Ferox.

None of the island's inhabitants bothered them, and Van thought the rumors about Cortica were exaggerated.

They circled back to Paley, who remained at the food stand with the wet-hemmed boy.

Van went over to her. "Hey."

Paley smiled, her eyes glassy, most likely from the empty mug in front of her.

"Having some fun." Paley leaned into Van and attempted to whisper, "While we can." She gave the others a sloppy grin. "You never know when another kraken will jump out and attack us."

"It was a laocoon," Brux said. He extended his hand to the boy. "Brux."

The boy shook his wrist. "Jedrek."

The others made their introductions.

"You're only young once." Jedrek raised his mug to the group. "Have to live for the day."

Van didn't like him. Something seemed *off* about the boy. He appeared well-kept, yet Van couldn't shake the slimy vibe he emanated.

The stand's attendant slammed four oversized mugs down in front of them.

"What's this?" Kopius picked up a mug.

"A clap of thunder," said the barkeep. "House specialty. Looked like you all could use one."

"It's on me." Jedrek smiled.

Van grabbed a mug. It was the size of her head. It was so heavy, she struggled to get it to her mouth. She took a sip and choked. The potent drink tasted like a mix of cranberries, iced tea, and grain alcohol.

"I'm afraid to drink anything here," Daisy said.

"Let's go walk around." Van wiped her mouth with the back of her hand.

Paley shook her head and moved closer to Jedrek. "I'm good."

Van sighed. Nothing short of dynamite would get Paley away from an interested guy.

"Come on," Van persisted. "We need to... *go*." She raised her eyebrows, trying to get Paley to catch the hint and stick to the mission.

"You never want to have fun." Paley seethed. "We're teens. This is our time."

"We're not here to have fun," Van said. "We have work to do."

"Come on," Jedrek said. "Loosen up a little."

"You're a poop." Paley pouted.

"Yeah, you are," Pernilla said to Van. She swiped a mug from the counter, took a gulp, and coughed. "Wow."

Pernilla's comment caused Van's annoyance to escalate since Pernilla only agreed with Paley to rile Van.

"I dare you to have some fun," Paley said. "At least until prince fussy-face comes back and drags us away. Probably lock us up forever."

Paley and Jedrek leaned in toward each other and chuckled like co-conspirators.

"Paley, you need to keep your mouth shut," Kopius warned.

"There're tons of fun places to explore," Jedrek said. "Food stands, gambling, game rooms. Hey, there's even a wax museum." He pointed across the street.

"That's a weird thing to have on Outlaw Island," Daisy muttered.

"It's called *outlaw* because people are free to do what they want." Paley's eyes darted to Jedrek as if she spoke from his earlier words.

"Only about half the people here are actual criminals," he said. "And they're more freebooters, doing what they need to survive."

"Okay." Van clutched Paley's arm. "Let's go in there." She pointed to the wax museum.

"Ho, no." Paley wobbled and had to regain her balance from Van's tug. "I'll be staying here, with Jedrek. You guys go. Have some fun for once."

"What about the," Van lowered her voice, hoping Jedrek wouldn't hear, "gemstones? You have to stay with Brux."

Paley leaned in and said in a failed attempt to whisper, "It's right across the street. Close enough."

Van peered at Brux.

He agreed with Paley. "It's within the radius of our separation not to cause an additional drain."

Kopius glanced at the museum and raised his brow in interest. Daisy gripped his hand, ready to go with him.

"I've seen people going in and out," Kopius said. "Can't hurt to pop in."

Pernilla shrugged. "Could be interesting. We can kill some time while we wait for prince fussy-face to get back."

Paley snort-laughed.

"This is a dangerous place." Brux looked concerned. "There are twisted souls here."

"Maybe not," Jedrek said. "The sign says wax museum and *fun* house."

"Why does it have the word fun in parentheses?" Van asked.

"Don't be a party pooper," Paley goaded. "You're such a wuss."

Pernilla often insulted Van using the same word. Paley used it now to hit Van where it hurt.

"Fine. We'll go in. But when we get back, you'll leave Jedrek and come with us?"

"Yup." Paley bobbed her head.

Van and the others crossed the road and entered the enormous rectangular structure called Wild Willie's Wax Museum and "Fun" House.

Ferox's men waited outside as the five of them walked through the wooden double doors and entered the lobby.

Across the room stretched a counter spanning the wall. It reminded Van of an Earth World movie theater concession stand. Although this one had barstools on both ends and the concessionaire stood in the middle behind the counter's display cabinet, which was filled with boxes of candies and a popcorn bin.

The man had a long, white beard combed into a point, silver hair, and pointed ears. "Welcome. Welcome." He opened his arms wide and gave them a huge, over-the-top smile. "What's your pleasure?"

"It's a wax museum, isn't it?" Van asked, thinking this guy was crazy.

A teenaged boy scurried behind the concession stand. He scooped three boxes of popcorn, put them on a serving tray already holding several poured mugs, and then disappeared through a swinging door.

"I can get you anything." The concessionaire winked at Brux. "And I mean anything."

The few patrons sitting at the counter pretended not to stare, but their side-eyed glances were obvious.

One customer sitting near them tipped his head toward the concessionaire. "He's in a good mood because he finally found himself a wife."

"At last! He found someone who can stand him," said another customer. "It's a miracle."

The silver-headed man guffawed and, in good-nature, reached across the counter, grabbed the patron's shoulders, and gave him a shake. "So right, you are." He grinned and extended his hand to Brux. "Name's Willie Pria, proprietor."

Brux, Van, and the others introduced themselves.

When Daisy reached out her hand, Willie didn't clasp her wrist. He grasped her hand and kissed it. "Hello, my beautiful flower."

Kopius pulled Daisy's hand out of his grip and held her close.

"She's one for the demimondaines," he said to Kopius with a wink. "You looking to sell her?" He leered at Van and Pernilla. "Those two will fetch a price too."

Pernilla protested, insulted, then asked, "Wait. What are demimondaines?"

Willie ignored Pernilla's question and continued speaking to Brux and Kopius. "Here, they're not as choosy as the houses in Osney."

"We're not interested in selling our girls." Brux threw him an angry glare.

"Well, I'd keep an eye on them." Willie returned Brux's hard stare, all cheeriness in his tone now gone. "There's lots of bad people here. They could end up at the Treasure Chest. You might as well get paid for it, rather than killed."

Brux turned to the team. "We're leaving."

"No, no!" Willie's cheerful tone had returned. "All in good fun." Willie smiled and spread his arms wide again. This time, he pointed out two doors on opposite sides of the lobby. "Choose your adventure. On the house. To apologize for my remarks. Pick a door."

"It's free," Pernilla said. "Can't beat the price." She headed toward the door to the right.

Van and the others followed her into a poorly lit, black-walled room with no windows.

Brux entered last. As soon as he set foot inside, the door closed behind him, and the lights went out.

CHAPTER 29

Van heard someone patting the wall.

"There's no handle to get out," Brux said.

"Hey!" Kopius pounded on the wall.

"Let us out!" Brux yelled.

Dim lights turned on, highlighting a corridor on the opposite side of the room that led deeper into the museum.

Van locked her arms with someone. "Daisy?"

"It's me."

Someone clasped Van's other hand.

"It's me." Brux gave her hand a squeeze.

They moved down the gloomy corridor, single file, in one connected group.

"I think we entered the fun house," Pernilla said.

"I'm not having fun," Daisy said.

"Now we know why the word *fun* was in parentheses," Van muttered.

They entered a poorly lit room with about a dozen wax figures on display.

Kopius perused one of the female sculptures. "It's Queen Amaryl."

"They're warriors from the Dark War," Brux said.

"If they have artifacts from the ancient warriors here," Pernilla scrutinized the wax sculpture of Prince Goustav, "we might find something about the master demon for Uxa."

Van peered at the figure of a woman with long, wavy, golden hair. She held a gold chalice. "Here's Zurial."

After getting Zurial's memory engram, Van became interested in learning more about the woman's prominent and impactful life. Zurial had lived a thousand years ago and people still remembered her to this day.

Van leaned in and read the museum label.

The Lodian Princess Zurial married the Balish King Manik Moor, ending the Dark War. A wedding designed to make peace between their tribes... the caption revealed more about her life. Things Van already knew, and then went on to say the wax figure had genuine fragments of Zurial's dress and strands of her actual hair.

"Ugh!" Van stepped back. "This place is creepy."

"Let's get out of here." Brux's eyes darted around the room, searching for an exit. He turned to leave the room they way came, but the door had disappeared. Brux ran his hands up and down the black wall. "Where's the door?"

"Gone." Kopius sounded grim. "There's no turning back."

Van glimpsed the arm of someone wearing colorful, dotted material on their puffy sleeve moving among the shadows in the room. The hair on the back of her neck prickled. "There's someone in here."

Brux and Kopius dashed over to look behind the wax figures where Van thought she saw someone.

"I don't see anyone." Brux stood behind several wax figures.

"Nope," Kopius said. "No one's here."

"Look." Pernilla pointed to the far side of the room.

A wooden, arrow-shaped sign appeared. It read "this way" and pointed down another gloomy corridor.

"We have no choice," Brux said.

Again, they clasped hands and cautiously trod down the passage.

Van didn't like the fun house. She scowled as her heart pounded against her chest. None of them would be in this mess if Paley hadn't goaded Van into it.

The floor dropped from under her feet.

Van screeched as she and the others plummeted for several seconds and crashed into a ball pit.

Van got her bearings and stood. Her legs trembled from the unexpected fall.

"What the—?" Kopius mumbled, as he and the others rose from the pit.

Van grabbed one of the off-white fiber balls and held it up to get a better look. Something moved inside. "These aren't balls." She shivered and chucked it aside. "There's something inside them." She waded through the spheres, rushing to the side of the bin.

All around them, stick-like legs poked through the round, fibrous objects, tearing the fiber.

Van thought they were spiders until one hopped onto her neck.

"Ugh!" Her hand snapped up, and she threw the insect aside. The green bug had two large, round, yellow eyes and long, pointed, bent legs. *A praying mantis!*

Van's hair tugged as some bugs got tangled in it. She shook her head and swept her hand, trying to get them out. It caused the bugs to become more entangled.

More and more of them hopped on her.

The others yelped and scrambled to get out of the bin.

Van swung her legs over the side, still using her fingers to yank insects out of her hair as her feet hit the floor. She brushed the green bugs off her clothes, as Brux and Pernilla leaped over the side of the bin. Daisy and Kopius followed.

They used their hands to wipe themselves and shimmied to get the insects off their clothes.

Van opened her mouth to say something and one jumped inside. It wriggled as she used her tongue to push it away and pulled it out with her fingers.

She retched.

The bin rapidly filled with insects. They multiplied at an unnatural rate and crawled over the sides like water spilling from a bucket.

"We need to leave. Now," Kopius said, as he and Daisy stepped back from the bin.

The insects reached Van's boots. They began hopping onto her pants.

"Come on." Brux tugged Van's arm, as the others got moving.

They rushed down another dimly lit corridor.

Fog filled the passageway, causing Van to choke. The thick mist made it difficult to breathe.

"Keep going." Brux coughed, barely able to get the words out.

They outran the fog and stumbled into a room with black walls, no windows, and two arrow-shaped signs. One sign read "boys" and pointed to the left passageway. The other sign read "girls" and pointed to the right.

The fog rolled into the room as if following them.

Kopius and Brux dashed down the left corridor; Daisy and Pernilla hurried down the one to the right. With a split second thought, *I'm sticking with the guys.* Van sprinted down the hallway to the left.

Fog drifted into the hallway and surrounded Van, making it hard to see.

She slowed her pace and stopped. "Brux?"

No one answered.

Something moved behind her.

She whipped around. "Who's there?"

Silence.

"Kopius?"

Van could sense someone in the corridor with her, and it wasn't one of her teammates. Her heart raced so fast, the pounding filled her ears.

She dashed away, farther down the corridor.

The fog cleared enough for her to see.

Van had entered a barn's stall.

A reddish-brown horse stood before her, lengthwise, so she could see its protruding ribs. The horse appeared malnourished but was too busy eating to notice Van.

"Hey there." Van raised a quivering hand to give the horse's neck a comforting stroke, thinking this crazy place must scare the animal.

Her hand hit a rope. She noticed a blood-stained noose around the horse's neck.

She cringed and recoiled.

The horse snapped its head toward Van.

It didn't have one head. It had two. Malformed and conjoined.

Van gasped and stepped back.

Its fanged teeth from both mouths dripped with blood. Its eyes faded and muddled. On the floor, Van could see the horse was eating severed body parts. Arms, legs, a torso—human remains.

Van screeched and raced down another a corridor, searching for an exit.

She entered a darkened room and stopped. With the lights off, Van could only make out the shadowed forms of exhibits.

"Let me out of here," she cried into the darkness.

Silence.

She couldn't hear the others.

Faint lights turned on.

Van was in another room that displayed wax figures. But these sculptures weren't people from the Dark War. These figures were horrifying.

Several unshaven men hung from a brick wall chained by their wrists, their bodies emaciated, their faces twisted in agony. A pale woman dangled from the ceiling, locked in an immobilizing metal cage. She held an expression of terror and hopelessness.

A male figure lay face up on a wooden frame. His legs and arms bound. His abdomen sliced open, exposing his intestines which had slid out of his body, and dangled over the side of the wooden contraption. From the look on his face, the man was still alive, yet a wax figure.

They looked so real.

Van shuddered. The room resembled a medieval torture chamber.

Filled with a variety of sadistic devices, including whips, chains, collars, and metal masks.

An overweight, middle-aged woman wax figure sat on a chair in the corner. Some of the woman's rotten teeth were missing. Her dirty cherub cheeks had fresh scratches, as if those trying to escape her torture had clawed her. She wore a grubby butcher's apron and gripped a chain attached to a bloodstained meat hook.

Van bent to read the museum label. *Murderous Martha and her dungeon of fun.* Van peered at the wax figure. She crinkled her nose. The statue smelled like wet dirt and dried blood. She looked so lifelike—

Martha leaped off the chair and tried to snatch Van.

Van jumped back, eyes wide, in time to miss the woman's clutch.

Martha swung the meat hook like a lasso and cackled.

Van scrambled to get away, nearly tripping on her own feet, and raced down another corridor.

She skidded to a stop on entering a room with a plump child about nine or ten sitting in a school house chair. Not a wax figure. A live child.

Scribbled handwriting on the wall read Jacob's Play Room.

Wooden toys cluttered the room. Trains, dollhouses, horses. Also, stacked cages filled with either a live cat or a dog. The animal's eyes expressed sorrow, their bodies bone thin. None made any cries for escape, as if they'd been trapped for years and resigned to their fate.

It took Van a moment to realize the boy clutched the legs of a headless chicken. The chicken's body dangled from his hand. A fresh cut dripped with blood from its severed neck. The bird twitched. Not yet dead.

With his other hand, the boy took a bite out of the chicken's head. He smiled at Van with blood-drenched teeth as he chewed.

Van's hand sprung to her mouth. She dashed down another corridor, gagging, in a mad frenzy to escape the fun house.

She stumbled into another poorly lit room. Someone shuffled behind her.

Van twisted around. "Who's there?"

A creepy clown emerged through the darkness dressed in a white and orange polka dotted romper, with a red and white painted face exaggerating his features. He wore a thick, orange wig and rushed at Van, wielding a bloody machete. He laughed, high-pitched and maniacal.

Van let out a squeak-like scream, turned, and dashed away.

The madman chased her. His laughter echoed down the corridor.

She reached a room where a heavy-duty plastic clown's head occupied an entire wall. The clown's opened mouth formed a passage into another chamber. With the machete-wielding psycho close behind, Van dashed through the mouth of the plastic clown.

She entered the next horrible place. *Will this nightmare ever end?* Painted on the wall were the words Cotton Candy's Dining Room. Human-sized pink pods were scattered about that looked made with spun sugar strands from a cotton candy machine. Moaning came from several pods and moving lumps protruded out from the sides. The clown had trapped people inside the cotton candy pods, the same way a spider wraps cobwebs around its prey to make a cocoon. The lumps were the people moving inside, trying to get out.

Van gasped. The hair on her arms stood on end.

Echoes of the clown's skin-crawling laughter ricocheted off the walls.

She rushed out of Cotton Candy's lair and down another corridor. Her legs flailed in the air as the floor gave way and she fell through a trapdoor.

With a thud, she landed on her back, perfectly fitting into a cushioned wood coffin.

Before the coffin's lid slammed closed, she saw the oddest thing.

Spectators.

They sat in tiered seats surrounding a central space, looking down at her. Van figured the viewing area spanned the entire floor plan of the fun house, including the room where Van lay in the coffin.

The spectators wore metal goggle-like glasses and peered through what must've been a bewitched glass ceiling, watching Van and most likely the others as they fought a battle of life or death trying to escape the fun house.

Right now, Van couldn't see anything. The coffin offered no light. She slammed her palms against the cushioned lid. *Sealed shut.* She frantically pounded her fists against the coffin's sides and kicked with her feet as best she could with the little space available.

Her injured side ached from the fall, and her struggling made it worse.

Who cares? I'm trapped in a coffin!

She was going to die. Suffer a long, uncomfortable death. Her muscles cramped. She needed to stretch, *right now,* but couldn't. She needed air. *I can't breathe. I'm trapped—*

Stop.

She turned inward and halted her racing thoughts. She took control of her breathing and gathered her wits.

She listened, and couldn't hear any sounds. She was alone.

Think!

Van could only move a few inches in any direction without hitting the sides of the wooden box. The claustrophobia was enough to drive her insane. Perhaps that's what Willie wanted. For Van to go crazy and become a permanent figure in his house of horrors.

She thought back to when Willie gave them a choice between the two doors. Now, Van realized one door led into the fun house, the other went to the seats of the spectators. Without this prior knowledge, the choice was a roll of the dice, a gamble as to your fate.

The boy eating the chicken's head entered Van's thoughts. She gagged, setting off her anxiety.

The air was so thick, she couldn't breathe. *There's no air. I'm suffocating. It's so dark. I'm going to die.* She gagged again. And again. Her heart pounded so hard it felt like it would also suffocate her. *I can't breathe—*

Stop!

Van took a deep breath and cleared her thoughts.

It's okay. I can find a way out. How? Think. How?

She could've blasted her way out if Ferox hadn't taken her Coin. Frustrated, she beat her fists against the sides of the coffin.

Okay. Relax. There has to be a way out.

She didn't have the Coin but what did she have?

The jackknife Brux had given her!

She fumbled in her pocket, grasped the knife, and took it out. Her fingers trembled as she pulled the blade and locked it into position.

Van used her fingertips to feel the groove formed by where the lid met the side of the coffin. She ran her fingers along it, as far as she could reach.

She felt metal bumps—*a latch*—near her head.

Van tore away the silky fabric lining the coffin's interior around the latch. She stuck the blade of the jackknife into the joint and wriggled the knife, trying to jimmy the lock.

Her efforts seemed futile. Out of exasperation, she rammed the knife into the groove, over and over, hoping it would break the latch.

She heard a click and pushed the top upward.

The lid lifted by about three inches. Light and air rushed into the coffin.

Air!

Another latch by her ankles held the lid closed.

Given the limited mobility inside the coffin, Van couldn't bend down and reach the spot.

She focused on the partially opened section near her head. Van used all her strength to push the cover upward, praying sheer force would snap the other latch, or break the lid itself.

Her efforts gained her less than a foot of additional space. The section by her ankles remained locked.

Van couldn't fit her body through the opening. She didn't care. She squeezed her face and hands through it, anyway.

She rocked her body, throwing her weight against the side of the coffin as she shoved her head and hands into the narrow gap. The coffin wobbled. It seemed to be elevated on a flimsy table.

Every time Van pounded her body against the coffin's side, the box swayed.

Again and again, she rocked her body, smashing it against the side.

The table gave way.

Van crashed to the floor, along with the coffin. Its sides smashed apart; the lid popped open. Her flank laceration streamed blood from the trauma of the fall.

Van crawled away from the busted coffin and curled into a fetal position on the floor, clasping her flank. Her jackknife lay nearby. She snatched it and shoved it into her jacket pocket.

She looked up and saw the spectators. Blurred images through the glassy-looking ceiling. They stirred. Van glimpsed coins changing hands and knew they were placing bets. Who would make it out of the fun house alive? Who would go crazy? Wagers on her and the other's misfortune or death.

No wonder Willie let them in for free. He probably hoped they'd choose the fun house and provide entertainment. If not, they would be spectators, and perhaps buy refreshments and make bets. Either way, he'd benefit.

"You're despicable," Van shouted at the spectators.

With some effort, she got to her feet. Clutching her bleeding flank, she jogged out of the coffin room and down another corridor.

She entered a chamber filled with fun house mirrors.

"Van?"

"Brux?" Van caught sight of him.

He appeared blurred. No, wait. It was his distorted reflection in one of the full length mirrors.

Van dashed over, hoping to find him. Her eyes darted from mirror to mirror. Multiple images of her warped reflection stared back at her.

She peered into the mirror where she thought she saw Brux's reflection. Her own image gazed back. Van glimpsed a shadowy figure scurry behind her.

She twisted around and saw nothing but mirror after mirror.

Maniacal laughter of the clown filled the room.

She hurried away, dodging the mirrors in a frenzied search to find the exit.

Van caught sight of Brux again and raced to that mirror.

"Brux!" She placed her palms on the glass. Her hands fell through an empty frame.

Scuffling sounds drew closer. She hastily stepped through the frame, hoping to find Brux, and appeared in the room she had first encountered when entering the wax museum. The one with wax figures of warriors from the Dark War.

She dashed over to the wall with the door, hoping to find the exit. Her hands ran up and down the smooth wall, finding nothing.

Van sighed.

Her injury ached. Her body sagged with fatigue. No way was she going back into the fun house.

She surveyed the wax figures and stomped over to the sculpture of Zurial.

"Help me," she cried to the figure.

Every cell in Van's body tugged at her as if the figure were pulling her into it, consuming her, wanting her to become embalmed in wax forever, like her.

Van heard movement behind her and twisted around. *It's that damn clown again!*

Without thinking, she stepped backward and bumped into the wax figure of Zurial.

Van spun around, startled.

The figure smashed into the wall, then bounced forward. Van stumbled as the wax figure toppled on top of her. They both crashed to the floor.

Van's nose stung from the blow to her face. Her flank injury throbbed. Her vision blurred...

CHAPTER 30

Nick's hands wrapped around Zurial's neck.

She saddened, not from being strangled, but from the love of her life breaking her heart.

His hands glided over her jaw, to her cheeks, and into her hair. He gently caressed her scalp.

"I would never hurt you, my love." His lips touched hers.

Zurial turned away. "But I am a Lodian princess. Nick, you are a royal Bale."

He smiled. "Not a royal. The *royal." He reached his hand to her for an introductory wrist shake. "Prince Manik Moore."*

Zurial gasped and stepped aside. "The heir to the Balish throne?"

Terror gripped her heart at this threat against their newfound love. They could never be together. Their differences were too great.

"Not to worry, my love." He clasped her shoulders. "It does not change a thing about us. We have much to discuss... later." He leaned in. His lips caressed hers.

The image blurred.

Zurial took Van through a montage of their days, enjoying unbridled love and healing in and around the mother tree. Then, the fragmented images stopped.

"It has been weeks. Our families will be worried about us," Manik said. "It is time."

"They will never understand." Zurial desired to stay in the mother tree, to hold on to their bliss a little longer.

"If you can heal wounds, you don't have to fight," Manik said. "We will help our families heal old wounds, just as you have healed me."

"From what I have heard, emotions are something your brother Goustav will never comprehend."

"Then we will teach him. Teach them all a lesson in harnessing emotions to show strength, not force."

Zurial nodded. She mustered the courage and mentally prepared herself to go through with their plans. She slid her hands up Manik's chest. "Your father. He is the key to our truce... and marriage. How will he take the news?"

"Our marriage will end the war. If my father cannot see this as a contract for peace, benefitting both sides, then the future of both our tribes will be in jeopardy." He cupped Zurial's face in his hands. "I will gladly give up my kingdom for you."

The image blurred. Zurial again moved Van forward through time.

The vision cleared.

Zurial entered a pillared room made of white marble inside Lodestar Station, in the wing where her family lived.

Her father, King Halldor, and her sister, Amaryl, rushed into the room. They embraced Zurial, happy for her safe return and even more overjoyed that she had brought them the Cup of Life.

"Where is mother?" Amaryl asked.

Zurial's eyes darted to the floor. She shook her head.

"The rumors are true." King Halldor looked grief stricken. "But, we had hoped..."

Amaryl's eyes filled with tears.

"The Anchoress light has passed to your sister," King Halldor said to Zurial, keeping a brave face. "She is now queen."

Zurial turned to Amaryl. "The others?"

"Rowen survived. As did Romet."

"Do we have the Coin?" Zurial asked.

King Halldor beamed. "We have the Coin and now the Cup." His face grew darker. "Which leads us to presume the Balish possess both the Sword and the Staff."

"Romet did not know what happened to you." Amaryl placed a tender hand on Zurial's shoulder. "He came back to us injured by a Balish royal who had taken the Sword from him, only to find that you had not yet arrived. We feared the Balish had captured you."

"Speaking of being captured by the Balish." Zurial's stomach knotted. "I have something to tell you..."

A PUNGENT SMELL tore Van from her vision.

It burned her nostrils and the back of her throat, choking her.

Her eyes popped open to see Ferox kneeling beside her, holding an opened ampule.

"Get away from her." Brux roughly grabbed Ferox by the shoulder.

"It's spirit of hartshorn," Daisy said.

"Take it easy." Ferox held up his hands. "Daisy's right. I'm trying to help."

"Wh-what happened?" Van rested on the wood-planked sidewalk outside the "fun" house.

"Lucky my men were here," Ferox said, still bending over Van. "Otherwise, you'd be casualties of the fun house. One of them had the sense to call me back."

"His men stormed the place." Kopius bobbed his head, impressed.

"They saved us." Daisy beamed.

"What a nightmare," Pernilla said with haunted eyes.

Van sat upright and coughed. "Ouch!" She placed her hand on her flank. It came back blood-soaked. "My wound's reopened."

"I'm taking you to a healer." Ferox scooped her off the boardwalk.

"You're not taking her anywhere." Brux blocked Ferox.

"Don't try to stop—Brux? You okay?" Ferox asked.

Brux wobbled. He turned pale and collapsed to his knees.

"Brux!" Daisy squatted beside her brother.

Van squirmed, causing Ferox to gently release her. She knelt next to Brux, too, and put an arm around his shoulders. Her eyes darted to the Savage Polder. Paley and Jedrek weren't there.

"Where's Paley?" Van had a good idea why Brux had fallen ill. The same thing happened to her last year when Paley had gone out of range with her Twin Gemstone. Van scowled. Paley knew she and Brux couldn't be separated while in the Living World or they would both die from energy depletion.

Van figured Paley would never intentionally walk out of Brux's range. But Paley had been drinking… and that boy seemed a bit shady… "We have to find her!"

Ferox gave Thyra a curt nod.

"I find Paley." She dashed away.

Ferox motioned to his men. "Take them back to the docks. Keep watch on them."

Two soldiers helped Brux stand; he didn't resist.

"Hang in there. I'll find something that'll help," Ferox said to Brux.

Van went to join the others, who headed back to the dock, when Ferox thumped his hand on her shoulder.

"You're coming with me," he said.

Van was more than happy to oblige. Although worried about Brux, she knew Daisy would be there to care for him. And Van wanted to spend more time with Ferox, to get to know him better.

"Are you well enough to walk?" Ferox asked.

Van wanted to say no so he would hold her in his arms again. But she nodded.

Ferox led her away from the downtown area and deeper into the island.

"Where did you go?" Van scolded herself for sounding like a jealous girlfriend.

"I'll show you," he said with a sheepish grin.

They arrived at a sprawling two-story house. Large enough to be considered a mansion. The open front porch had fancy white rails and stately white pillars on the lower level. Van assumed the once private residence had been converted into the island's medical center.

Before Ferox took the first step up the expansive front stairway, a stunning dark-haired woman wearing a silk robe clinging to her well-endowed figure swung open the double doors. She slinked onto the porch. "Welcome back," she cooed.

Ferox clasped Van's hand and led her up the stairs.

He nodded to the brunette, as he and Van strode past her and went inside.

On the way in, Van glimpsed a discrete metal sign by the doorbell that read *Treasure Chest*.

CHAPTER 31

Van scrutinized the woman who had opened the door to the Treasure Chest, wondering if she posed a threat to her and Ferox's potential relationship.

She could clearly tell the woman wasn't wearing anything under her loosely tied silk robe. Van couldn't determine the woman's age, but if she had to guess, she would say mid thirties.

The entryway opened into a foyer, doubling as a casual living room. A candelabra and lanterns with candles cast enough light for a relaxed ambiance.

After the ordeal in the fun house, Van never thought she would want to see dim lighting again. But here it pleased her. The shadows hid her blushed cheeks as she took in the detailed paintings hanging on the walls. They depicted men and woman performing various sex acts, some showed two women and one man, others were of orgies. They also passed sexually explicit statues.

Ferox and Van followed the shapely brunette through the expansive foyer.

Colorful flowering plants gave the house a pleasant, sweet smell and toned down the scandalous artwork. Most plants had clusters of beautiful six-petaled blue and white lotus flowers. Hidden speakers played soft music that sounded like a blend of flutes and tinkling water.

They passed women lounging on fainting couches, sitting in cushy high-back chairs, or provocatively strolling the room. They wore bustiers and ruffled skirts with slits up the sides and other styles of lingerie. All of them wore spiked heels and sparkling jewels. Many displayed entirely bare chests or had one full breast showing. None of them paid any mind to the trio.

Van turned a brilliant shade of red to the tips of her ears.

Ferox gripped Van's hand as they continued to follow the woman to the back of the foyer, toward two spectacular stairways sweeping up to the second story that, together, formed the shape of a heart. The top of the stairs joined to form a balcony.

The woman directed them to an archway beneath the balcony.

On the wall above the archway, Van gawked at a stunning mosaic of a circle enclosing equilateral triangles intertwined to form a six-pointed star. Although the mosaic didn't illustrate naked people having sex—a welcome relief—Van still had no desire to encounter what lay beyond the archway.

She halted and tugged her hand out of Ferox's grasp. "Why'd you bring me here?"

The woman gasped in delight. "Oh!" She clasped her hands together. "She is as beautiful as an Elemental! Are you sure you do not want to sell her to us?"

The muscles in Ferox's jaw tightened. "No. Just medical treatment, as I prearranged."

"What?" Van took a step back. "I'm not letting her touch me."

The woman continued to gaze pleasantly at Van.

"This is Madame Vang," Ferox said. "Madame Vang, meet Vanessa Cross."

"Don't tell her my *name*." Van's jaw dropped.

"Pleasure, my child." Madame Vang reached out to shake Van's wrist.

Van recoiled. "You're not a doctor. You're a-a..." Van wasn't sure how to say it and not sound offensive.

"She's not a prostitute," Ferox said. "Not like the kind from the other world."

"Certainly not." Madame Vang retracted her meticulously manicured hand.

"They're demimondaines," Ferox said.

"They're what?"

"We're closed for training," Madame Vang said. "There will be no patrons visiting us until later tonight. You will be safe here."

Van had been so distracted by the establishment overall that she hadn't noticed there were no men present.

Ferox leaned close to Van's ear and whispered, "Relax, will you? I'm trying to help."

His warm breath on her ear and his throaty, masculine voice sent a wave of excited chills through her body.

"Come." Madame Vang offered Van her hand. "I will tell you about the demimondaines, and you will be happy."

When Madame Vang extend her hand, her robe opened, exposing a tattoo on her pelvic area, just below her belly button, of a red snake entwined with a gold snake rising upward to form one, larger serpent.

Van gasped and pointed. "That tattoo! My step-mother. She has the same one."

Madame Vang grinned. "I will tell you about your step-mother's tattoo. Then, perhaps, you will let me treat you. Your boyfriend has thoughtfully taken care of the expenses in advance."

Van stammered. No audible words left her lips. She had too many questions, and they got stuck trying to come out all at once.

Genie's a demimondaine? Is my step-mother a paramour? Why would Ferox think I'd let a prostitute give me medical care?

Why did she call Ferox my boyfriend?

"Perhaps she is much sicker than we thought?" Madame Vang looked concerned as she noted Van's inability to speak.

She gently clasped Van's hand and led her and Ferox down a long hallway to a room with a single bed covered with white sheets and a matching blanket. The predominately white room had the sanitized appearance of a hospital, but had accents of colorful trinkets, gorgeous coral, liquid-filled ampules, and many jars holding powders on the bureau, desk, and nightstand.

A hand-embroidered wall hanging read, "The treasure is within."

Madame Vang instructed Van to lie on the bed.

"But… I'm bleeding." Van lifted her shirt to show the madame her blood-soaked bandage. She didn't want to stain the woman's pure white sheets.

At the sight of Van's blood, Ferox growled, not bothering to hide his agitation, "Lie down and let Madame Vang treat you."

Van wanted to believe he truly cared about her and wasn't simply using her to get the Cup. This last thought caused her heart to wrench. She turned away from Ferox to hide the conflict reflected in her eyes and held her stare on a beautiful piece of peach-colored coral.

Madame Vang noticed Van's interest in the coral. She picked it up and held it in her palm, giving Van a better look at it.

"It is sometimes hard to think of corals as colonies of animals, but they are." She gazed at the branch-like piece. "In the sea, this coral is alive, using sunlight to make sugar for energy and nourishment. They build tiny calcium houses for themselves, stacking the houses on top of each other to form larger structures that look like stone."

She raised the coral to eye level with a forlorn expression. "In the Earth World these little animals are being destroyed by terrigens. It is heartbreaking how they neglect their environment. Their oceans. If terrigens continue on this path, our world will also become affected."

Van warmed to the madame. "No wonder the Balish want them… eliminated."

Ferox shifted uncomfortably at Van's statement, but he must've known Madame Vang told the story to win Van's trust. He seemed satisfied it worked.

"Please, lie down," Madame Vang said in a soothing tone as she placed the coral back on the shelf. "Next, I will tell you the story of the demimondaines and of your step-mother, whom I believe I am familiar with since we are a small circle. If you are satisfied, only then will I treat you."

Nothing could keep Van off the bed now. She had to learn Genie's story. She found it impossible to believe her step-mother had anything to do with this madame.

"The serpent tattoo is the mark of a demimondaine," Madame Vang said. "A woman belonging to the demimonde or social class of those who are kept by wealthy lovers or protectors."

"No." Van fiercely shook her head as she lay on the soft, white bed. "My father knew Genie as the palace healer at Balefire."

"Genie?" Madame Vang seemed deep in thought, trying to recall the name.

"Her real name is Iphigenia," Van said.

"I see." The madame gave her a nod. "Genie is her nickname."

"Iphigenia Prenda?" Ferox raised his brow.

Van nodded.

"She was no palace healer," he said.

Madame Vang flinched.

"Well, yes, she was the palace healer," Ferox backpedaled, not meaning to have insulted the madame. "But also much more. She tried to rip my family apart. I wasn't born then, but I remember hearing the rehashed stories when I was a child."

"Iphigenia Prenda." Madame Vang searched her memory. "Yes. She was King Nequus's lover."

Ferox already knew this but still looked stricken.

"She's your step-mother?" Ferox asked Van. "I always assumed my mother had her killed."

"So, that's why Genie was in the woods the night she met my father." Van turned to Ferox. "Your mother must have found out about their affair."

"If so, she was fleeing for her life…" His voice trailed.

"Demimondaines are often placed among the wealthy as healers," Madame Vang said with skilled timing, smoothing the conversation, so no one was made to feel uncomfortable. "We are not well liked in common society, but are highly regarded among wellborns and royals. We are exceedingly skilled at what we do."

"I still don't understand. You said you're kept by wealthy lovers. Doesn't that mean you're a… um… how does it fit in with healing?"

"Ah, yes, I see." Madame Vang activated her training mode. "Seduction is considered a form of healing."

"Great sex can be very healing," Ferox said, earnestly.

Van's cheeks flushed. She shifted on the bed.

Madame Vang placed the underside of her wrist on Van's forehead, checking for a fever.

"They're a magical faction, and their numbers are few," Ferox continued. "Because of their scarcity and high demand, demimondaines are employed by the upper classes, including the royals."

"The Balish allow us to use magic to enhance our skills in both sexual acts and for healing." She gestured for Van to turn on her side and face the wall. Then she carefully removed Van's blood-stained bandage.

"How do you use magic for… that?" Van winced from the pain.

"We change our personality and use magic to alter the coloring of our appearance in a chameleon-like way to make us more desirable to our customers." Blood streamed from Van's wound, soaking the white sheets.

"Do I need stitches?" Van asked.

"Stitches?" The madame sounded offended. "How barbaric." She applied pressure to the wound using both hands and holding a fresh cotton square.

Van twisted as she lay on her side, watching the madame and keeping Ferox in her line of sight.

"We create potions to block pregnancies and to make sexual relations more fulfilling for both parties." Madame Vang flashed a seductive glance at Ferox and then turned her attention back to Van. "We master many skills. Sexual prowess, acting, blending in, socializing, being a delightful hostess. Appearing non-threatening is also an area of our expertise."

"Some consider them dangerous." Ferox sat in a nearby chair, relaxing now things were progressing nicely. "Because of their ability to bend men to their will without the men knowing it."

"What brought you to Outlaw Island?" Van asked Madame Vang.

"Our kind comes here to be freed from the rules of society, to be our own women." Madame Vang reached for an ampule on the night table. "Parents or guardians sell their children into the life at a young age, most as babies. Some of us hope to escape our fate. But once trained, the lifestyle draws us. It becomes part of who we are and never leaves us. Here, we can choose to stay in the house and take many lovers. We ply our trade on our terms, outside Balish rule." She ever so slightly tilted her head in apology to Ferox.

Ferox gave her a curt, forgiving nod.

"I was once part of the great house in Osney, Antares. The most widely recognized and respected house for demimondaines. The Treasure Chest is not an officially recognized house."

Madame Vang poured a bright orange liquid over Van's wound, catching the drip with a hand towel.

"Ouch." Van flinched from the stinging liquid.

"I train my ladies until the age of nineteen, and then, when ready, they ply their trade."

"Why nineteen? We're adults at eighteen." Van made a painful grimace as the madame patted the excess liquid from her wound.

"Ah," Madame Vang raised her brow at Ferox. "Of course. She is Lodian."

"In Balish society, we come of age at nineteen," Ferox explained.

Madame Vang grabbed a different ampule and poured an amber-colored liquid onto a cotton square.

"You train them in healing?" Van wanted to smack her forehead over her stupid question as soon as the words left her mouth.

"Demimondaines are taught the lifestyle of companionship. This involves knowledge in the healing arts, including working with potions." Madame Vang again displayed her skill at smoothing over awkward bumps in the conversation. "We use this knowledge to create secret elixirs infused with magic to prolong our youth and vigor."

The madame dabbed the cotton square on Van's injury. The liquid soothed Van's throbbing wound.

"I am sixty-four years old."

Although flabbergasted by Madam Vang's age, Van's thoughts went to Genie. Now Van understood how her step-mother had remained uncannily youthful over the years. She realized Genie might be much older than Van thought. This spurred Van to add another item onto her list of things to do. Get the secret ingredients to that youth potion!

Madame Vang read Van's expression. "We are forbidden to share our secrets under penalty of death, as ruled by the great house." She gathered several jars filled with powders. "This rarely happens, as we are too selfish and competitive to share our secrets with women outside the demimonde."

She scooped small amounts of powder from each jar into a mortar.

"Most are ambitious and use their skills to advance their position in life by going after a long-term relationship with the wealthiest of men. We call these men *marks*."

Ferox snorted. "My father likes to drink. He looks for sexual partners who can also be drinking buddies. How could Iphigenia, or any demimondaine, be able to keep fit and healthy while handling his lifestyle?"

"We train to become immune to the negative effects of alcohol. If we choose, alcohol can have a mild relaxing effect. It never impairs our judgment. We are equipped to handle all situations."

Van remembered Genie's sudden interest in a special morning beverage with her new boyfriend. Her step-mother had told Van the drink was "not for children." Van realized the libation contained either alcohol or a magical youth elixir. Probably both.

"And my step-mother, Genie?" Van asked. "Did she target my father? Was he a mark? They had a long-term relationship. Marriage."

Madam Vang used a pestle to refine and blend the powders.

"Demimondaines are power hungry seductresses, full of selfish enthusiasm. But our lives are full of wonder and delight."

Ferox tightened his jaw and leaned forward in his chair. His hand moved ever so slightly toward his concealed dagger.

"Look what washed upon my shore today." Madame Vang's eyes darted to Ferox. "None other than the Balish crown prince."

She turned to Van. "And, I presume, the Lodian's fabled Anchoress."

CHAPTER 32

Van shot upright in the bed. She stared wide-eyed, terrified by what Madame Vang would do with the knowledge of her and Ferox's true identities.

The madame had already admitted ambition played a part in her trade. How would she leverage this information?

Ferox rose from his chair; his shoulder's tense. "What more do you want for your silence? I've already paid you well."

Madame Vang smiled serenely. "I have no desire to further myself any more than being here at the Treasure Chest. You have no need to fear me. Your identities are safe. And yes, you have taken care of me with abundance."

Her knowing stare at Ferox, like they shared an intimate secret, caused Van to glare at him with accusation.

"With coin," Ferox added, flustered by Van's unspoken claim. "Money. Nothing else. I paid her with money."

Madame Vang grinned as she watched their exchange. She held the mortar and pestle but hesitated to apply the medicine.

"I have more to tell you about your step-mother, Vanessa. If it makes you both feel more comfortable and trusting of me, I will tell you, although it is forbidden." She shrugged. "Here on Cortica, rules are bent, even broken."

Van nodded and laid back down on the bed.

Ferox took his seat, but stayed perched on the edge of his chair.

Madame Vang sprinkled what looked like gold dust over Van's wound. It began to heal before their eyes.

"It will continue healing over the next several days." The madame went to the desk and picked up a roll of tape, scissors, and a new bandage.

"At an early age, your step-mother's parents recognized the monetary value of her unusual beauty." She cut pieces of the tape. "They sold her to the demimondaines at age five. They fetched the highest price in history for such extraordinary prettiness. She did her training in the great house in Osney."

"Being betrayed by your parents... being sold... how do you ever get over it?" Van asked the harder question, uncertain she wanted to hear the answer. "*Did* she ever get over it?"

"The life of a demimondaine is good. We know no other way." She shifted hooded eyes toward Ferox. "Most of us find it quite pleasant."

Van had grown weary of Madame Vang's overt flirting with Ferox. "Getting attention from men makes you feel validated," she said, as the madame dressed what remained of Van's wound. "You're always trying to get power through a man rather than using your own power. Sounds like a sad life to me."

Madame Vang finished taping the dressing and grinned at Van. "Here." She clasped Van's hand. "I will show you. Stand."

Van rose from the bed with apprehension.

Ferox stayed seated, but leaned forward with curiosity, watching the scene unfold.

"Dance with me." Madame Vang swiveled her hips and swept her arms above her head.

Upbeat music filled the room.

Madame Vang's fluid movements artfully blended into the rhythm, creating an alluring dance of seduction.

Van had no desire to dance. Yet, she danced anyway, caught up in the moment. Madame Vang's hypnotic presence made dancing fun and, Van admitted, healing.

"Sway your hips. Like this." Madame Vang placed her hands on Van's hips to guide her.

Van followed the madame's instructions, worried the movement would awaken the pain of her injury. As Van swiveled her hips, she felt no soreness in her side.

Ferox remained silent. His eyes held steady, as if both intrigued and wary of the seductive show.

Van enjoyed herself until she became acutely aware of how she moved her arms, hips, and legs. Awkwardness overwhelmed her, especially with Ferox watching her dance. She stopped.

Madame Vang clasped her hand, reengaging Van.

Van's thoughts and concerns drifted away and she, again, found joy experiencing the motions of her body.

"Notice the life energy as it flows through you," the madame said with glee. "Accept it with your heart and soul. Feel. Create. Express your feelings through your movements." She blissfully twirled Van. "Feel your power as a woman. Laugh. Cry. Dance!"

A wave of embarrassment set in from Van's intimate dancing with the madame. She was no demimondaine. "My side aches." Van yanked her hand away from the madame's grip and sat down on the bed.

Madame Vang shrugged. She continued dancing and turned her attention to Ferox. She reached her hands to clasp his, attempting to lure him into joining her.

"Enough." Ferox stood.

Madame Vang ceased dancing at once. "As you wish." She submissively bowed her head.

"Tell us how to get the Cup of Life," he demanded.

Ferox's brilliant idea hit Van like a lightning bolt. As the madame of the Treasure Chest, she must hear a lot from her customers and probably knew everything about the area.

Ferox seemed to intimidate the madame, like he did everyone. And he had paid her a *lot* of money. She didn't put up a fuss.

"You must cross the River Shade," she said. "You will need to pay

Kharon, the ferryman, a fairy's tear. Beyond the River Shade, lies the Cup of Life."

If they needed a fairy's tear, they were in luck. Van had seen the fairy give hers to Ferox before she flittered away.

Ferox raised his brow. "The Cup is on Cortica?"

"I thought it was in the Bottomless Sea," Van said.

"That is all I know." Madame Vang demurely bowed her head.

Ferox had everything he needed to get the Cup. Van, who was the only one who could retrieve it, the fairy's tear, and now the location. But Van didn't want to waste time recovering the Cup. She needed to change his mind and get him to help her check the seal. Then, if the team had time, they could get the Cup. Which reminded Van of her other quest. Her personal one.

"Do you know how to remove a curse? Asking for a friend."

"Curse? What curse?" Ferox narrowed his eyes at Van.

"There are many ways." Madame Vang raised her brow. "What is the nature of your *friend's* curse?"

Van squirmed. They both knew Van was asking for herself. Her desire to find a counter-curse overrode her discomfort.

"Okay. It's me," Van confessed. "My ancestor Amaryl accidentally cursed her own bloodline. Now the Anchoress is doomed to die giving childbirth."

"And you're required to have a child who can inherit the Anchoress light." Ferox looked concerned.

"I mean, not soon." Van twitched. "Not that you meant now." Her cheeks flared. "I meant in the future. You know. Way future, like maybe—"

"Ancient magic is potent and binding." Madame Vang graciously interrupted Van's moronic babbling. "I am sorry to say its complexity extends beyond my training. However, as a favor, I will peruse our ancient texts and scrolls. I will send word by morning if I find something helpful."

Ferox remembered to ask the madame for a tincture that would help strengthen both Brux and Paley.

She got to work, mixing liquid drops into a small amber glass jar with a dropper. She handed it to Ferox. "Anything else?" She asked solicitously.

Van had enough of the madame and couldn't wait to get away from her.

"If you find anything more about the Cup, send me word," Ferox said. "You know where to find us."

The madame nodded graciously.

Van and Ferox followed her back through the dimly lit hallway and into the foyer. As they bounded down the porch stairs, Madame Vang shouted parting words of wisdom.

"The best cure for everything is love," she cried. "Love heals and love feels."

As they reached the sidewalk, Van whispered, "She's a bit… *different.* Don't you think?"

Ferox threw her an amused grin; Van's heart melted.

"How's your wound?" he asked.

"Great." Van patted her side and winced. "Still a bit sore."

"I wasn't sure, you know. Because of all that dancing you were doing."

Van grinned as her cheeks burned. She playfully whacked him on the arm.

He laughed, seeming to enjoy her company.

They passed a large fountain marked by age with grime and cracks. A stream trickled from the chipped mermaid's mouth. In the basin, golden-orange fish leaped in and out of the discolored water. Van wondered how such a beautiful fountain came to be in such an undesirable place.

While watching the dancing fish, Van remained acutely aware of how Ferox's powerful, masculine presence enwrapped her in a comfortable safeness… and made her excited.

Fairly certain Ferox had developed feelings for her, she worried his affection wasn't strong enough for him to let Van check the seal, instead of retrieving the Cup. Heck, his feelings for her might not even be genuine.

Retrieving the Cup with his help would only cause problems. He'd demand to bring it back to his family at Balefire. Van and her team would never let that happen.

She faced a dilemma.

Despite their growing connection, she decided the best path for her was to steal the fairy's tear and ditch Ferox.

CHAPTER 33

Van couldn't risk Ferox going for the Cup of Life on his own and possibly finding a way to retrieve it, or, more likely, die trying. To be safe, she needed to steal the fairy's tear from him so he would have no way to cross the River Shade.

Uxa, failing to mention the other Items of Creation, made Van so furious she didn't want to retrieve the Cup. The Grigori could find another way to cure the demon illness.

But the Cup wanted to be found. Van couldn't escape her inner pull toward the Item. It called to her like a beacon.

Which reminded Van, not only did she need to steal back the tear from Ferox, but also the Coin of Creation.

"So, Van." Ferox smiled at her. "I know a bit about your step-mother. Tell me something else about your family, or yourself."

Dammit. Ferox's interest in getting to know Van filled her with dread. It made her uncertain she could stick to her plan.

Didn't Ferox mention he was interested in peace? Maybe it was in Van's best interest to befriend him, rather than ditch him. Peace between their tribes was the best way for Van to protect her people.

She eagerly talked to him about her childhood. Van told him about her favorite memories of her father, like the time they went quahogging on Buzzard's Bay. About how she and Paley had become friends, living near each other on the island, and of Paley standing by her when everyone thought Van was a slow learner and placed in special classes.

She carefully avoided specific details about Providence Island, including its location. Van still didn't trust their relationship. Ferox might have ulterior motives, like getting secret information from her about her life and the Lodians to pass along to his family.

"Enough about me," Van said. "Tell me about your childhood."

Ferox opened up to Van. He talked about growing up with his twin siblings, Devon and Solana.

"My parents, the Balish Council, and the Balish Royal Court favored Devon, even Solana, over me to inherit the kingdom," Ferox said. "They tell me I'm too much like my father. Fun-loving, irresponsible." His eyes shifted to Van. "A heartbreaker."

Van could live with the first two adjectives, but the last one made her worry about his sincerity again.

"Truthfully, I was all those things." Ferox glanced at her. "I had no interest in running the kingdom until Devon and Solana died. Then, it became my duty."

"I'm sorry." Van's guilt about Solana came rushing back. She refocused on her mission and brushed her remorse away.

"I understand," Ferox said. "She was no angel. And if she killed my brother and my mother..."

His voice trailed off. They walked in silence for a while.

"They say I'm kind, nonjudgemental. Bad things for a king to be." Ferox gazed into the distance; the muscles in his face relaxed as if recalling a happy memory. "But my mother, she saw my true potential." He turned to Van and said with conviction, "I will be a righteous king."

Van gently placed her hand on his arm. "I know you will."

They reached the docks and reunited with Brux, Pernilla, Kopius, Daisy, and Paley, who stood by *The Obelus*, guarded by Ferox's soldiers and Thyra. All were impatiently waiting for their return.

"You look better," Brux said to Van. "Are you okay?" He cast a wary glance at Ferox.

Brux held a sack in his arms that Van assumed was a bag of potatoes. He stood close to Daisy and Paley, who were trembling from either the chilly evening air, the locale, or both.

"I'm fine." Van didn't want fists to fly between Brux and Ferox.

"Where were you two?" Pernilla asked like an angry mother. "We've been waiting for over an hour."

"He took me to the Treasure Chest."

"What?" Brux's face turned red with fury. He shifted his bundle to one arm and stomped toward Ferox; his other hand a clenched fist.

Ferox's men snapped to attention and extended their swords, crossing them in front of Brux to block him.

Ferox raised his palms in surrender. "No, no. Nothing like that." He tipped his head toward the soldiers, and they lowered their swords. "The demimondaines are healers."

"Sexual healing, baby." Kopius chuckled, not helping the situation.

"Brux, I'm fine. The madame healed my wound." Van lifted her shirt and pulled a piece of tape to expose a portion of the pink line, forming a scar.

"Wow." Pernilla bent to inspect it.

Van quickly reattached the tape, annoyed at Pernilla's keen interest in her wound. She said to Brux, "We got you and Paley a strengthening potion to help with the drain caused by the gemstones."

Brux and Kopius shifted their weight and furrowed their brows.

"I know about the Twin Gemstones," Ferox said. "I figured it out when Brux collapsed. Keeping the peace is what I want. Not stealing from you, or dragging you off to the dungeons." He reached into his pocket and took out the glass dropper jar. "Here." He handed it to Brux.

Van turned to Paley, who seemed withdrawn. She noticed her friend's clothes were damp. "What happened to you?"

Daisy pulled Paley closer in a comforting hug.

"N-nixe." Paley wrapped her arms around her herself to help soothe her shaking.

"Water spirit," Thyra clarified.

Van's jaw dropped. "That guy you were talking to at the Savage Polder?"

Paley nodded. "He-he was... he was... he lured..." She looked sickened.

"They lure victims into the sea," Thyra said.

"I knew I didn't like that guy." Van frowned.

"Males assume many shapes. Including human." Brux cradled his odd sack.

"How did you survive?" Ferox asked, looking both concerned and outraged that someone under his care had gotten into danger. "Those creatures are deadly."

"Sometimes," Thyra said. "Sometimes harmless and friendly."

"This one wasn't harmless," Kopius said.

For the first time, Van noticed he was also damp, Brux too.

"He-he took me to the beach." Paley trembled. "It was supposed to be romantic. He tried to drown me."

"No," Thyra said. "Not drown. He take you home to his world under the sea."

"Yeah, we call that being drowned," Kopius said.

"I-I used the d-dagger." Paley shook. "Stabbed him. I didn't mean to k-kill him."

"I'm so sorry." Van wrapped Paley in a hug. "Good thing we took weapons with us." Van shivered, remembering the coffin incident in the fun house.

"B-Brux and Kopius came," Paley said.

"We found her standing waist deep in the water, holding a dagger dripping with blood," Brux said. "The nixe was nowhere to be found."

"Do you think I k-killed him?" Paley said, still shaking. "I didn't mean to kill anyone."

"We would've found his body floating nearby if you killed him," Kopius said.

"It's okay." Van rubbed Paley's shoulder. "It's over now."

"No more fraternizing with strangers," Ferox commanded. "Let's keep our team together."

Ferox taking charge, comforted Van, until he barked at his men, "Sequester them to their rooms." He turned to Van, yet continued to speak to his crew. "For their own protection."

Van fumed. They were getting along so well until now. Locking them in a cabin wasn't about protection. It was to remind Van she was under his control, causing her to question her attraction to him.

Maybe it was an illusion to keep her off balance. She had crushes before, like on Brux and on Ken. But this ran much deeper. Ferox had done nothing special to cause Van to be enamored with him, other than being himself. She couldn't deny her romantic feelings for him. Though, when he acted like a jerk, it made it easier for her to squelch them. Warriors had no use for emotional attachments.

One of Ferox's men tried grabbing the potato sack from Brux's arms.

"No." Brux swung away from him, protecting his bundle. "I'm bringing Hiccup."

Van squinted in the darkness. She noticed a bone-thin puppy the color of a burlap sack. Apparently, she'd missed a lot.

"He was scrounging around for food on the docks," Brux said. "I'm keeping him. I think he's sick."

"It's fine," Ferox said to his men. "He can take the dog."

The puppy hiccuped and cuddled closer to Brux.

"I see where he gets his name." Van yearned to pet the puppy, but it looked so frail she didn't. "Does it have the demon illness?"

"I'm not sure," Brux said. "But I don't think it transmits to animals."

Van felt as weary as the puppy looked, even despite her healing session with Madame Vang. Her teammate's bodies drooped with exhaustion, too. After Brux got to keep Hiccup, nobody put up a fuss about being sequestered to a cabin.

Van was wrong to assume their rooms would be onboard the ship. Ferox's men shuffled them away from the docks.

She soon discovered what Ferox had been doing when he had gone off with Thyra, besides visit Madame Vang. He had secured a safe place for them to stay by renting the entire top floor of a nearby three-story inn, a term Van loosely used to describe the Wharf Lizard.

Ferox's men led Van and the others to an impressive suite, while Ferox and his crew occupied the remaining rooms.

The suite slept eight. Three bedrooms, each with a double bed, and two sleep sofas in the main area. Van and Paley volunteered to sleep in the same room. Daisy and Pernilla each took one of the other two bedrooms. Brux grabbed a sleep sofa, and Kopius nabbed the other one.

The soldiers had already taken their backpacks off the ship and had brought them to the suite. Everyone hustled around, settling in, taking showers, and getting ready for bed.

Paley wiped herself with a towel. "I'll never feel dry again."

Van sat on the double bed in their bedroom. "I'm glad you're okay."

"I'm fine," Paley said. "I've learned my lesson. No wandering off without Brux."

"There's more to the lesson than that," said Van. "And don't forget to take Madame Vang's drops."

Paley yawned. "I won't." She crawled into bed and instantly fell asleep.

Van lay awake, staring at the intricate Venus flytrap designs on the wallpaper. Her mind kept veering back to Ferox. His almond-shaped, amber-yellow eyes. His strong jawline with a hint of stubble. Everyone responded to his innate charisma and ability to command. That kind of power in the hands of a Bale, Van figured, would produce a dark thread. Yet, Van glimpsed inside his soul, and it was bright white. Meaning, Ferox championed for good, not evil.

But could she trust him?

Every time she thought about his light, his goodness, the dark part of her soul called to her. Van had damaged her soul as a consequence of murdering Ferox's sister, Solana, using the power of the Coin. Being such a good person, Ferox had forgiven Van for this transgression.

Or did he?

He could be leading her on, to ensure she retrieved the Cup. Van closed her eyes, but her mind continued to wander.

Zurial had crossed through space and time to show Van a glimpse of her life. She found it an odd coincidence Zurial's message was about her doomed marriage to a Balish king. And now, Van had met Ferox, the Balish crown prince.

He was a descendant of Manik and Zurial. Van was a descendant of Goustav and Amaryl. She quickly reminded herself they came from two different ancestral lines. The brothers, Manik and Goustav, had become romantically involved with the sisters, Zurial and Amaryl. Niece, nephews, cousins? None of that mattered now. The ancients mingled and married a thousand years ago. Ferox was safe for her to date.

Van's eyes shot open.

What?

She couldn't even think about dating Ferox. He was a worse romantic choice than Brux.

When Van got older and had to settle down, her requirement for a husband included marrying someone with the highest percentage of Elemental blood, someone pure-blooded, or from a "royal" Lodian bloodline. The rule stemmed from ancient times when kings and queens ruled Salus Valde.

The Lodian Consilium and the Elementals remained adamant about keeping Lodian bloodlines pure. The belief about mixing bloodlines being a treasonous betrayal to their people held true for both the Lodians and the Balish. As for Van, the Anchoress, this rule was unbreakable.

If Van ended up marrying Ferox and they had a child, Van would further dilute the Elemental blood from her Anchoress line. Last year she received a warning not to dilute her bloodline in a memory engram from her ancestor Amaryl.

Zurial told me the same thing!

Look what happened when Zurial married Manik. *Complete disaster*. Zurial had reiterated Amaryl's warning.

When Amaryl gave birth to Astrid, the baby she had with Goustav, she lost the Elemental protection from the Quasher for the entire Anchoress lineage, right down to Van. This was the reason for the

Alignment. The restriction of when Van could safely travel outside of Salus Valde without fear of a Quasher attack.

If the Elementals did that to Amaryl, what would they do to punish Van? Dread seeped into her bones.

She heard shuffling and a muffled commotion coming from the main room. Since she couldn't sleep anyway, Van slipped out of bed to investigate.

CHAPTER 34

Van entered the main room of the suite and discovered Kopius and Brux wide awake, attempting to sneak out a window.

"Looks like they're reinforced." Brux tugged at one of the two windows.

"They're designed to keep us in," Kopius said.

"I don't even want to think about what they use this place for." Brux shook his head grimly.

Kopius marched over to the suite's door.

"Don't." Van startled them.

"The door's guarded. Already tried it," Brux said. "Ferox isn't letting us leave the inn."

"We can take care of the guards." Kopius clenched his fists.

"No. We can't lose Ferox's support until we get Thyra on our team. We need her." Van came to this realization right then. "If the seal is at the bottom of the sea, we need Thyra to get there and mend it. She's part fish. I'm sure she can hold her breath underwater." Van tilted her head. "Why are you trying to leave?"

Brux pointed to his puppy curled up on a makeshift bed made of towels and pillows. "I need to get Hiccup to an animal healer."

"You mean a vet?" Van asked.

"Where's your bunfy?" Kopius asked. "Maybe we can use his Swiss Army tail to pick the lock on the window."

"Wiglaf's not a tool." Van scrunched her brow. If Kopius knew about Swiss Army knives, strictly an Earth World item, he must have spent more time there than he let on. Van looked at him in a different light, and for the first time, wondered if he was working as a double agent for Uxa.

His mention of Wiglaf caused an ache in her heart. Why hadn't her furry friend come to visit? Van assumed Cortica had something to do with it. The place was too dismal and dangerous for her beautiful little bunfy.

"He's getting sicker." Brux stared worriedly at Hiccup. "I gave him the rest of the strengthening potion you got from Madame Vang. It's not helping. Can she make a healing animal tincture? If you asked the guards to see Ferox, they'd let you. He'll let me go see the madame if the request comes from you."

"I don't think that's a good idea," Van said. "We have a long way to go to check the seal and we're almost halfway to the end of the Alignment."

"Van, he'll die," Brux pleaded with misting eyes.

"Maybe tomorrow. If we have time."

Memories of the Quasher terrified her. Its snarling, snapping jaws. Claws the size of swords. Hostile, unwavering red eyes.

Even after Van went back to her bed, the Quasher haunted her thoughts until she fell into a short, disturbed sleep. When she woke a few hours later, she checked on Brux and the puppy.

Brux cuddled Hiccup in his arms. "He's dead." Tears streamed down his cheeks.

"Oh Brux, I'm so sorry." Van slid onto the couch next to him.

"This will destroy Paley and Daisy," he said, as if his tears were for their pain.

Van didn't understand why she couldn't cry. She reached down inside and felt numb. She knew the puppy's death was heartbreaking, but that was the cycle of life. We live, we do the best we can, then we die.

"It was just a dog," Van said, to console Brux.

"How would you feel if it were Wiglaf?"

Van remembered being devastated when she thought Solana had skinned Wiglaf alive. But there was nothing Van or anyone could've done to save the poor bunfy who died in his place. She shrugged, unable to find words to describe how she felt or didn't feel. Why couldn't she *feel*?

"My mistake." Van shrugged again. "I'm getting something to eat." She went to the cabinets in the mini-kitchen. Glad to see Ferox had his people stock the cupboards.

"You need to care about *all* creatures, not just humans," Brux called from across the room. "We're all interdependent and interconnected. We're woven together to make up the fabric of the life force. When are you going to understand that?"

Van turned to Brux and stared blankly at him. She shoved a cream-filled sponge cake into her mouth, went back into her bedroom, and closed the door.

She paced her room, quietly as to not wake Paley. Brux infuriated her. Of course, she knew about the interconnectedness of life. It was the reason she was killing herself to protect the terrigens and her people. But his reaction to Hiccup's death caused Van to question if she had made the right decision by not asking Ferox for help with the puppy.

Hiccup's death was on her. Did that make her a bad person?

Van strained her brain, trying to fathom how the puppy's life was more important than their mission and her safety from the Quasher. Getting the puppy medical help would've jeopardized both. They were running short on time. Nobody seemed to care about that except Van.

After mulling over her decision, she concluded any good leader would've done the same thing. With the issue resolved in her mind, she tucked back into her bed.

Her mind continued to spin. She twisted and turned so much her sheets got tangled around her legs. *Ugh.* She tossed them onto the floor and sat upright. Wasting time in this hovel caused her anxiety to spike.

Van considered eating more snack cakes, then sadly admitted there wasn't enough food on the entire island to fill the void she felt inside. Her frustration grew. She got up and quietly paced the bedroom again.

She had vowed to always choose the good. To resist the dark pull inside her soul. It made sense for her to deny her emotions so she could make the best choices as a leader. Like she had done with Hiccup. However, what counted as a good decision had become increasingly unclear to her.

If I could remove this damn curse, I'd be able to save my soul, and everything would be fine.

The best person to hash over her issues with was a meditation away. Van plopped down on her bed and positioned herself in the lotus position. She controlled her breathing. Her mind quieted. Inwardly, she called out to her spirit guide.

"Greetings, my little warrior." Jacynthia hovered several feet above the floor. Her amaranthine robe flowed in an otherworldly breeze.

I didn't get Hiccup medical help, and the puppy died. Did I make the wrong choice? If I did, then maybe all my past decisions were wrong. Like when I used the power of the Coin against Solana.

"One can learn as much from doing something wrong as by doing something right. The Creator observes only how you respond to the challenges you face."

How am I supposed to respond?

"The empowered person notices how water changes its shape to fill any space it encounters. Rocks breaking the water's path is a warning to not resist change and not to cling to old approaches. We learn from this observation to bring flexibility into every situation."

I'm a bad person, right? My soul, it's dark. Isn't it? Tell me the truth.

"You cannot be whole or powerful until you make peace with your dark side," Jacynthia said. "When you exist in a state of duality, you remain connected to the physical world where your senses perceive opposites. Good, bad. Right, Wrong. Healthy, sick. Reconcile with the pull of opposites within yourself. Only then will you be in accord with the will of the Creator."

I don't want to make peace with my dark side.

"The two power idea is a creation made by humanity. When you believe in two powers, you must always upgrade your inner fight. The two forces within you will always be in conflict with each other. Stronger always defeats weaker."

So you're telling me my dark side is stronger?

Van's anxiety intruded into her thoughts and caused Jacynthia's image to falter.

She gained control of her breathing and grew calm, bringing her spirit guide into focus again.

"There is no such thing as good power and bad power. There is only one power, that of the Creator. The Creator took a piece of Itself and made space for your existence. You were born with the ability to re-connect with this force that created you."

Van found Jacynthia's advice confusing. She needed more clarity to comprehend her spirit guide's wisdom. But fatigue encroached on their conversation. Jacynthia faded away as Van slipped into a deep sleep.

CHAPTER 35

Someone banging on the suite's door woke Van.

She waited, lying in bed, hoping one of the guys would hear the knock and go answer it.

The thumping persisted.

Van groaned and lugged herself out of bed.

This better be important. Why isn't anyone else waking up?

Van shuffled across the main room. Through the windows, she saw the darkness of night. Brux and Kopius lay sound asleep, each on top of their own pull-out couch. Neither had bothered to expand their couches into a bed. Brux had wrapped Hiccup in a towel and cradled the dead puppy in his arms.

Van gazed at Brux's sleeping face. Peaceful now. A sharp contrast to hours ago when he was wretched with heartache. A sharp pang of regret caused Van to grasp her chest. She rubbed it to make the feeling go away. Compassion made her weak.

The knocking persisted.

"Not sure why this couldn't wait until morning," Van muttered. She swung open the door, eager to stop the tenacious rapping before it woke everyone in the suite.

A pretty woman curtsied, dressed in a tightly laced, elegant bustier gown with a matching cape.

The two guards in the hallway shifted tensely as they kept sharp eyes on the woman and Van.

"Sorry to bother you, miss." The woman wore glamorous make-up and looked to be in her mid-twenties.

"Oh, right." Van realized she must be one of Madame Vang's demimondaines. She was expecting to hear whether the madame had found a cure to the Anchoress curse. "Come in."

"Thank you, miss. But I cannot stay. I came to give you this." The woman held a hand basket filled with homemade soaps and offered it to Van.

She accepted the basket, confused. "Um…"

"Madame Vang regrets she cannot find a solution to your problem. Since your boyfriend has already paid for her work regarding this matter, she offers you these soaps in its stead."

Van prickled at the woman's use of the word boyfriend, but was pleased Ferox had taken care of paying the madame.

"Okay, thank you." Van accepted the basket, hiding her disappointment. But her father had searched for years to find a counter-curse and came up empty. How could she expect Madame Vang to do it in a few hours?

"Take a bath. Use them now. They will cheer you." The woman smiled. "Make you smell pretty for your beau. If not him, then someone else." She winked.

Van wearily eyed the soap. The woman hinted the madame had infused it with magic, or pheromones. Something making the user alluring to the opposite sex. Something Van had zero interest in.

Instead of asking the woman if she had any friendship soap, Van said, "Will do. Please thank Madame Vang for me."

The woman bobbed a curtsy again.

Van closed the door, surprised no one had woken from the demimondaine's visit. She placed the basket of soaps on the accent table by the door. Then wandered back to bed and snuggled under the covers.

. . .

EARLY THE NEXT morning Ferox pounded on the door, requesting they gather downstairs.

Everyone rose. Brux broke the sad news about Hiccup to the others.

Paley and Daisy shed tears. Pernilla and Kopius bowed their heads in grief but displayed fortitude.

Ferox and Thyra expressed their condolences. Ferox allowed Brux and the team to bury his puppy outside. Van hoped the funeral service would help Brux put the ordeal behind him.

Afterward, the team headed into the dining hall next door. They chowed down a prepared breakfast of sweet potatoes, sautéed river eel (Van and Daisy abstained), and colorful mixed fruits. Brux kept his distance from Van. She could tell he hadn't forgiven her about Hiccup.

After the team finished their meal, Ferox appeared behind Brux and Kopius, flanked by two of his men. Each wore a backpack and carried an extra sword.

"The journey will be dangerous," Ferox said. "Can I count on you?"

Brux and Kopius nodded.

"You have your weapons?" Ferox asked the guys.

They nodded again.

"I have mine too." Pernilla raised her hand. "In case you're interested."

Van could tell the patriarchal Balish society was getting on Pernilla's nerves.

Ferox nodded to her. "Of course."

"Take this as well." Ferox gave his men a nod, and they handed a sword to both Brux and Kopius.

Pernilla held out her hand for a sword, too. Although she still carried a concealed dagger, as did Daisy and Paley. Although Paley seemed more squeamish about her blade, now that it had been tainted with nixe blood.

Van patted her jacket pocket to make sure she had her jackknife, despite knowing koga-clava would serve her better in a fight. But, still. After the coffin incident, she wasn't taking any chances.

Pernilla scowled when Ferox didn't acknowledge her gesture and, instead, he turned toward Thyra and said, "Let's get moving."

Thyra knew the area, but didn't know the exact location of the River Shade. She figured the river was on the other side of the island, the undeveloped part. The place people were too afraid to explore. Not because of any lurking cutthroats. But because of the terrifying creatures living in the darkest part of the island.

Van clutched Ferox by the elbow and pulled him aside. Touching him felt right. Although she worried he would find the gesture inappropriate. In no world was it acceptable for a detainee to grab a crown prince.

Instead of being offended and defensive, he grinned at Van's touch.

Her heart whirled. She immediately put a stop to it. "Why not use the Coin?" Van asked in a whisper.

"It's an incorrect use," Ferox said.

"We won't be harming anyone."

Ferox gazed at Van without judgement. "It's disrespectful to the power of the Coin. We can find our way using our inner resolve. This is the correct action."

Van furrowed her brow.

"There's time." Ferox continued with his reasoning. "Two weeks before the Alignment ends."

Van didn't have time to spare. The Quasher lurked in the shadows, impatiently waiting to be released from its restraints so it could consume the Anchoress's light. Van shook her head and walked away. There was no reasoning with him. He was as stubborn as a rock breaking water in a stream.

Daisy laid her hand on Van's shoulder. "Don't fret. The forest will guide us where we need to go."

Van resisted rolling her eyes and instead grabbed her backpack.

Prepped and ready, they set out on their journey to the River Shade.

. . .

After a couple of hours, the trees became denser. The wide dirt road turned into a pathway through the woods.

"How much longer?" Paley's cheeks flushed from exertion.

"We get there soon," Thyra said.

Ferox used a hand signal to halt and silence the group.

A rustling noise sounding like many light paws trampling over leaves came rushing at them from the left.

"What is it?" Pernilla peered intently into the woods in noise's direction.

A scurry of squirrel-like creatures stampeded past them, dodging around the bottoms of the trees and past their feet.

"Kopidodens," Thyra said.

Daisy rested her delicate hand on Kopius's shoulder in relief. "They're harmless."

"Look at their long, fluffy tails." Paley smiled at the critters.

"They're good for food." Kopius grinned.

"We're not in need of food," Ferox said.

"Why are they running?" Van asked as the critters scooted past, dodging her ankles.

"Let them run," Thyra said. "Kopidodens bad."

"I dunno," Paley said. "They tasted pretty good when we ate them last year."

"They change." Thyra's large, fishlike eyes narrowed.

The scurry of kopidodens ended, and the group moved on.

The pathway through the thick woods grew narrower as swampy water edged in on both sides. Now and then, slithering black snake-like creatures revealed themselves on the surface of the murky water. As long as they kept to themselves and stayed off the pathway, Van was fine with them.

Ferox raised his hand to stop the group again. "Did you hear that?"

In the stillness of the woods, Van heard it.

The rattle of chains.

"What is it?" Paley gripped Van's elbow.

The chains rattled again. This time closer.

"Whatever it is," Brux said in a low voice, "the kopidodens were running away from it."

"Thyra?" Ferox raised his brow.

The chains clanked again.

"Kluddes." Thyra opened her abnormally wide eyes even wider. "This creature hide in shadows of swamp. Attack innocent traveler. Sound betray their approach. Is rattling of chain. Prepare fight."

Van searched the ground for a thick branch to use as a weapon.

"Swords up," Ferox cried.

Brux, Kopius, Ferox and his men unsheathed their swords.

"Can we outrun them?" Kopius asked.

"Faster we walk, faster they follow," Thyra said. "No one can outrun the kluddes."

The fin on Thyra's head expanded, causing her newsboy cap to fly off. Two fins popped from the sides of her neck, and her hands enlarged and grew webs between the fingers. Her fingernails lengthened into deadly blade-like claws.

Paley took out her dagger with shaking hands.

Daisy stood still, looking serene and not making any move to brace for a fight or to retrieve the dagger from her pocket. "I refuse to fear nature's creatures."

Kopius protectively stepped in front of Daisy. "I fear them. Stay behind me."

Van twirled her branch and entered a fighting position.

They waited for the attack.

The swampy forest remained silent.

All Van could hear was her pounding heart.

CHAPTER 36

All around them, skeletal creatures swung from the trees like chimpanzees.

They looked like human remains wearing grubby, shredded clothes, and draped in rusty, seaweed coated chains. Their heads, a hairless skull. Rotting flesh hung from their bones as if they were deceased pirates who had risen from their swampy graves. Yet, the creatures weren't human.

One dropped from a low-hanging branch like a spider attached to its web. It snatched one of Ferox's men. He let out a brief yelp as the kludde lifted him into the trees and disappeared from sight.

The kluddes had no weapons, other than their elongated skeletal arms and bony clasp. They swooped in and out of the surrounding trees and dropped on them, carefully avoiding the team's blades, Thyra's claws, and Van's baton.

Paley swiped her dagger at the swinging, bouncing creatures. A kludde dove from the trees, wrapped her in its bony grip, and lifted her up.

Brux leaped over and swung his sword, cutting the stretchy fiber supporting the kludde. Both it and Paley tumbled to the ground.

Paley rolled away as Brux used both hands to stab his sword into the creature. The blade went right through the creature's rib cage and into the dirt behind it with no effect.

A different kludde clutched Brux from behind and began to lift him.

In one swift move, Ferox swiped his blade through the top of the kludde's skull, splitting it in half, then ran his sword straight down along the creature's spine through its rib cage, careful not to hit Brux.

The kludde broke into pieces and collapsed; Brux crashed down onto the dirt pathway.

The harder the group fought, the more creatures dropped from the trees. To where it seemed to rain kluddes.

One dived to snag Van. She darted out of the way. It dangled in front of her, hanging by its weblike string, reaching its bony clasp at her.

Van twirled her branch and shattered the kludde's skull. Each bone detached before her eyes and the creature tumbled to the ground in pieces.

More and more creatures dropped.

"Get away from the trees!" Ferox cried.

"This way," Thyra said.

They dashed through the woods, smashing through kluddes, and veered off the dirt pathway. They waded through thigh-deep swampy water until the trees became spaced farther apart, making it difficult for an air attack by the kluddes.

They paused. The woods were still.

Van sighed in relief, as did most of her teammates.

"Not safe," Thyra said.

A kludde rose from the swamp in front of Van and wrapped its skeletal arms around her.

She braced, expecting to be hauled into the trees, ready to jab her stick upward and crack the creature's skull. Instead, the kludde changed tactics and pulled her under the water.

Van didn't have to time to catch her breath. The muddy swamp water enveloped her face, rushing into her nostrils and filling her ears. She released her fighting stick and used her hands to pry the creature away from her.

The kludde gripped its arms tighter like a boney clamp, crushing both Van and her backpack.

A coral-colored shape appeared in front of her in the murky water. *Thyra!* Van was right, the fish-woman could breathe underwater.

Thyra grabbed the kludde by the skull and yanked its head off.

It released Van.

She shoved away the skeletal body and scrambled to stand in the thigh-high water, leaving Thyra to battle against another kludde.

Van broke the surface and gasped for air. Her drenched backpack tugged heavily on her shoulders. Her stick floated nearby. She grabbed it and scanned the swamp.

White skulls atop of ribbed torsos bobbed all around them. The creatures' bony arms reached and clasped, trying to snag their prey. To drag Van and the others under the water, to make them corpses in a swampy grave.

A kludde attacked Pernilla. She jabbed at its skeletal body, hitting its rotting flesh and ragged clothes, missing its bones. It clutched her. They both dropped under the surface.

Another kludde snatched Daisy. They disappeared underwater.

Kopius dove in to rescue her.

Ferox slashed his sword through kludde after kludde. They shattered, collapsing into the water in pieces. But more and more rose in their place. His men were nowhere to be seen.

Brux reached under the water, searching for something. He hauled Paley to the surface. She stood trembling with terror in her eyes, clutching her dagger, soaking wet.

Brux twisted and sliced his sword through another attacking kludde.

Pernilla reappeared, gripping her blade. Her lip curled in fury.

Van twirled her stick and bashed the skull of an oncoming kludde. Her eyes darted from creature to creature. "There are too many!" She needed the Coin from Ferox. To connect to her power so she could blast the evil things. "Fero—"

A kludde snagged her from behind.

It pinned Van's arms to her sides and yanked her under the water.

Lying face up, with the kludde underneath her, she saw a sword zip through the murk, narrowly missing her head and cutting straight through the kludde's skull.

A hand grasped her chest and hoisted her to the surface.

Van gasped for air as she wiped water from her eyes. It was Brux.

"Duck!" he cried.

Van bent down. Brux swung his sword at another kludde leaping from the water to snatch her.

Van straightened and swung her stick, smashing another kludde's skull to smithereens before it caught her in its deadly grip.

She tried to access her blood magic without the Coin. She couldn't remain uninterrupted long enough to find out if she could connect to her power.

Brux struggled, looking exhausted, as he helped Van and Paley fight the relentless onslaught of the kluddes. Van could tell the gemstones drained his energy. He wouldn't last much longer.

None of them would last much longer.

Van yelped from an electric jolt as something long, thin, and black slithered past her in the water, brushing against her thigh. *An eel!* At least, it looked like an Earth World eel.

"Get out of the water!" Van shouted to her teammates as she swiped her stick at another kludde.

The next time an eel swam past Van, she grabbed it with her free hand. The eel's electrical current harmlessly ran through her body. She knew nothing about eels or electricity. Yet, her inner Self knew her Anchoress light protected her from the eel's strong electrical pulse.

Thyra rose to the surface.

"Get out of the water!" Van yelled. "I know what to do."

Thyra joined Van and the others as they made their way to a cluster of nearby low-lying rocks.

Van dropped her stick and gripped the eel in both hands.

The kluddes continued to pop up and down, in and out of the water, rattling their chains.

Van's teammates slashed their swords and smashed their feet into the creatures to keep them from climbing onto the rocks with them.

Van hastily enacted her plan before the kluddes resumed their aerial attacks.

The slippery eel wriggled and squirmed in Van's grip. She grabbed its head and forced its mouth open. She willed herself to connect to her magical bloodline, to the power of the moon, so she could increase the voltage of the electric eel.

Once her teammates were clear of the water, Van held the eel by the hinge of its jaw, making sure its fangs were prominent and shoved its head under the surface. The eel squirmed and released its electric venom, enhanced by Van's Anchoress magic.

The swamp lit up with a golden-orange electric current, as if glowing with underwater lights.

A plethora of skulls broke the surface of the water, followed by floating skeletal bodies, cluttering the swamp with dead kluddes.

Van heard their chains rattle in the trees again, and dread gripped her. But the sounds drifted farther and farther away, as the remaining kluddes retreated.

With the threat gone, the team waded through the swamp, except Thyra who swam under the water, and hauled out Ferox's men.

Brux, Ferox, Kopius, and Pernilla removed the soldier's backpacks and laid them on the rocks. Ferox removed their outer shirts and used the clothing to cover his men's faces.

"We lost some good people." Ferox lowered his head as he stood over his deceased men. "Let's say a few words to help their souls pass into the light. To help us process our loss."

"Now's not the time," Van said. "We need to keep moving and stay focused."

The silence hung heavy.

Brux clasped Van's hand and said, "You're not alone. I'll be with you when and *if* you have to face the Quasher."

Van burst into tears. All the tension she had been holding in came gushing out.

The entire team, all soaking wet, cradled Van in a group hug.

"I know your path is difficult," Kopius said, uncharacteristically sincere. "But you have us."

"None of us are going to face any challenges alone," Ferox said. "We're in this together."

"One team," Pernilla said.

Mortified by her emotional outburst, Van wriggled free and wiped away her tears. "I'm okay. Let's do this." She was fine with a prayer as long as it meant they stopped hugging her.

The team held hands and formed a circle standing in the murky swamp water next to the rocks with Ferox's dead men, and surrounded by the floating skeletal remains of the kluddes.

Brux said a prayer for the deceased men's spirits to have a safe journey as they made their way toward the light and back into the arms of the Creator.

Then the team moved on, deeper into the murky swamp.

CHAPTER 37

Despite Ferox having no soldiers left to defend him, everyone still defaulted to his authority, and he continued to lead the team.

As they waded deeper into the swampy woods, the water reached their waists.

"This is gross." Paley crinkled her nose. "It smells like rotten spinach."

Van kept her eyes on the swamp's surface and on the trees, flinching at the tiniest sway of a branch or ripple on the water's surface.

"We getting near," Thyra said.

"I hope so." Ferox glanced at Thyra. "We'll be reaching the sea soon."

"It doesn't make sense," Brux said. "This island's not big enough to have a significantly sized river."

"In this place?" Van meant the entire Living World. "The River Shade is probably some magical stream that drops into a cave or something."

A nearby splash caught their attention. All of them paused and turned in the sound's direction.

The slick, gray body of a marine animal broke the surface of the water and dipped back under.

Daisy and Paley gasped.

The water's surface grew calm and still.

"Maybe it went away," Paley said.

"Doubt it." Kopius moved closer to Daisy.

"It's just a harmless fish," Daisy said. Being the shortest in the group, the swampy water rose to her armpits.

Van frowned at her. The kluddes had dunked Daisy, like everyone else, yet she looked fresh and beautiful, like a golden flower growing out of a sewer.

"Swords." Ferox remained calm as he unsheathed his blade.

Van anxiously scanned the swamp. There were no sticks in sight for her to use as protection. She remembered the jackknife stuffed in her pocket, and then acknowledged it would be useless against most creatures, like it would've been against the kluddes. But she had her fists. She moved into a fighting stance.

They remained alert and ready.

A bearded man popped his head out of the water, though he wasn't entirely human. He had a man's face, but the rest of him was a hefty gray seal.

"Hello!" He greeted them cheerily, keeping his head and torso above the water and waving his fin. The creature warily gazed at their drawn weapons. "I'm a selkie." As if that explained everything.

"Selkie friendly." Thyra retracted her claws.

"You can call me Sammy," the selkie said.

Ferox, Brux, and Kopius lowered their swords. Pernilla continued to keep her dagger raised.

"What's a selkie?" Paley put her blade away.

Van recognized the look on Paley's face. It meant she wanted to adopt him as a pet. Van rested her hand on Paley's shoulder to keep her from wading over and scratching him behind the ears. Although Van had to admit, he was adorable.

"Selkie." Brux narrowed his eyes in contemplation.

"Male selkies are responsible for storms strong enough to sink ships," Daisy said. "It's their way of avenging the hunting of seals."

"It true," Thyra confirmed.

"Shouldn't you be in the sea?" Pernilla tucked away her dagger. "What are you doing here?"

Daisy looked concerned. "The water here is much too shallow for you to swim freely."

"I'm looking for my wife."

Kopius raised his brow. "In a swamp?"

"Not for nothing, but I met all of you here." Sammy grinned.

Van, Paley, and Daisy chuckled. No one else seemed to care for the selkie's sense of humor.

Ferox introduced himself and then everyone else to Sammy.

"Pleased to meet you all." Sammy bobbed his head good-naturedly.

"A female selkie can shed her skin and come ashore as a beautiful woman." Daisy eyed Sammy knowingly.

Kopius perked up. "Really? Tell me more."

Daisy threw him a stop-being-silly glance and continued. "If a human man finds her skin, he can force her to become his wife."

Sammy bobbed his head again, making him look more like a seal than a human. "If I get back her skin, she'll be able to leave the confines of her forced marriage and return to me. Her true husband. Can you help me?"

"What's in it for us?" Kopius asked.

Daisy gave him a swift elbow to the ribs.

"Humans." The selkie lowered his eyes. "Always in it for the gain."

"These human good," Thyra said, heatedly.

"It's not that we want something," Van said. "We're short on time, and we need to find the River Shade."

"So I heard." Sammy bobbed his head. "That's why I approached you. If you find my wife's skin, I can get you a map showing you how to get to the River Shade."

"We don't need a map," Ferox said. "The river has to be less than an eighth of a mile from here."

"The River Shade isn't on Cortica," Sammy said. "It's on another island. To find it, you must use a secret map. Which I will gladly show you if you get my wife's skin. It's the only way she can return to me, and we can once again enjoy the open sea."

"Can you ensure our safe travel to the other island?" Brux asked.

Sammy flicked his head. "I can promise no selkie will churn the sea around your ship."

"How will we recognize your wife?" Ferox asked. "Do you know who kidnapped her?"

"His name's Willie Pria. He owns Wild Willie's—"

"We know who he is," Pernilla interrupted, scowling. "Why am I not surprised?"

"All you have to do is get me her skin. Then she'll be able to escape. I can't go on land with you. Male selkies can't change form."

"We'll have it to you by sundown." Ferox struck a deal with the selkie.

They planned for Sammy to wait for them by the docks near *The Obelus.* There, they would reunite with the selkie after retrieving his wife's skin.

The team headed back through the swamp in good spirits. They cautiously and quietly moved through kludde territory, relieved the skeletal creatures chose not to tangle with them again.

Once they reached the dry path, they took a quick break to rest.

All their clothes were soaked from wading through the swamp. Van sat on a rock next to Paley, and they both took off their boots and wrung out their socks.

"Ugh, my back." Van rubbed her lower back. Then she stretched her hips. "I need to get back to my yoga."

Brux passed a wineskin filled with water to Ferox, who took a sip and passed it on. Everyone got a drink.

Ferox stood. "We need to get moving."

Van reluctantly pulled on her wet socks. She stuffed her foot back into her hiking boot without checking it first.

Something nipped at her toes.

"What the—?" She held up her boot and peeked inside.

A squirrel-like creature gaped at her. It had larger, more full ears than a squirrel, as if flattened by a rolling pin. Its nose came to a point, like a mouse. When the kopidoden saw Van peering at it, it leaped from her boot, let out a squeak, and scurried behind a nearby shrub.

"Are you hungry?" Van asked, using a baby-talk tone. "You were in my boot. I'm thinking you were looking for something to eat."

Van picked a peach-colored wildflower. She moved slowly so not to scare away the kopidoden, and brought the flower to the critter's nose. It scrunched up and backed away.

"Don't worry, the kluddes are gone."

Pernilla came over to see what held Van's interest. "For someone who always wants to get moving, you sure are taking your sweet time."

Daisy also wandered over. "They'll only eat out of your hand."

Van placed the flower on her palm and extended it to the little critter. Of course, Daisy would know since she seemed to be the nature and animal loving expert on the team.

The kopidoden stretched its nose as if to sniff the flower, or to test Van's trustworthiness, then began nibbling on the flower's petals.

"He's eating!" Van grinned.

Thyra came over to check out the kopidoden and nodded her approval. "Need to feed."

"Why?" Ferox asked with trepidation.

"Van, that's enough," Brux said. "Let's get moving."

Van remained crouched, letting the kopidoden eat out of her palm.

"They can change this time of year and become harmful," Daisy said. "If they eat, they won't turn. I'm not sure why."

"Eating calm them," Thyra said. "Still, behavior uncertain."

"But he's so cute," Paley whined. "I find it hard to believe this little guy would give us trouble."

Pernilla squinted at the tiny animal. "It looks like trouble to me."

"Let's not take any chances." Kopius peered into the trees. "It's too quiet. I have a bad feeling."

"Let's get going," Ferox said.

The critter finished eating the petals and happily scurried away into the woods, not glancing back.

Brux stiffened. "Don't kopidodens travel in a scurry?"

Everywhere Van looked, kopidodens creeped along the branches of trees or peered out from their hiding spots under the leaves.

"Uh, oh," Thyra muttered.

All the kopidodens hissed. Their fur lengthened and turned into sharp spikes like a porcupine.

"Swords up," Ferox cried.

The kopidodens leaped from their spots, hurtling themselves through the air.

"Ow," Paley yelped, as one impaled her chest with its spikes and bounced from her body.

Van ducked, covering her head. The creatures jumped up from the ground and dropped from the trees. Pins and needles stabbed her every time she got hit with a kopidoden.

"They're trying to stab us to death!" Paley wailed.

"Death by a million cuts," Pernilla cried.

Kopius batted away as many bouncing kopidodens as possible using his sword. "Daisy, stay behind me!"

Daisy curled into Kopius's backpack, tucking into it like a pillow.

The critter's needles continued to prick Van's skin with each hit—on her stomach, legs, face. "Ouch!"

"We deserve it for invading their habitat." Daisy covered her head with her arms.

"There have to be hundreds of them." Brux used his sword to swat the bounding critters. Bloody spots dotted his face and hands.

One after the other sprung from the ground, piercing them with their spiked bodies.

"Run!" Ferox shouted.

"Run," Thyra echoed.

They sprinted away from the kopidodens, but the critters spun and lifted off the ground, forming a swarm. It was like dashing through a swirling pin storm.

Van swatted one that twirled near her face. Its needle-like spikes cut deep into her hand. If it had hit her neck, it would've sliced her carotid artery.

"Damn gnats." Pernilla batted away the critters with her dagger. "Ouch!"

"Ow! Ow!" Paley yelped. "I feel like a human pincushion!"

"Circle around the girls," Ferox hollered to Brux and Kopius. "We'll hold them off as long as we can."

Van, Daisy, and Paley clung together, slightly less assaulted being surrounded by Brux, Ferox, Kopius, and Pernilla, who faithfully took a stand to be treated equally with the guys, and Thyra who also didn't include herself as a girl.

Van heard screeches of pain coming from her teammates as the spiked creatures continued to impale them.

Someone's blood splattered across Van's face as she breathed in. She swallowed some of the spray, triggering a coughing fit.

Over the noise of them being slowly stabbed to death, cricket-like sounds arose from the surrounding trees.

The kopidoden's attack slowed and then stopped.

Some zipped back into the trees, some hung in the air and clustered together, still spinning.

Van saw long, yellow snouts with pointed teeth break through the leaves in the trees above them.

Bright yellow creatures, each about the size of a monkey, appeared on the branches. But they looked nothing like monkeys. These creatures had parrot-like bodies and almost wholly round heads.

At least twenty of them swooped down from the trees. Using their wings to jerk forward, they snatched the twirling, spiked kopidodens in their snouts. They crunched them, one at a time, with their sharp teeth as if eating a delicious snack.

"Yellow heimwatt," Thyra said.

"To the rescue." Kopius lowered his sword.

The kopidodens gathered together, forming a massive swarm. They maneuvered away from the flying, snapping heimwatts, trying to escape.

The heimwatts spread their wings and followed them, lurching and catching the spinning kopidodens in their long snouts as if it were a game.

"Let's move," Ferox commanded.

Van and the others took off down the path, away from the kopidodens and heimwatts.

"I'm glad we ate them last year," Paley muttered.

From that point onward, the journey back to town was mercifully uneventful. Thyra's thick, fishlike skin somewhat protected her from the kopidoden attack. Everyone else continued to bleed from the innumerable pinpricks.

Ferox clutched a bleeding spot on his neck. "First stop, the Treasure Chest."

Madame Vang appeared on the porch as they marched up the stairs, dripping wet and splotched with blood. She placed her hand on her cheek. "Oh, my."

Again, Ferox paid the madame for her healing services, and she led them inside.

Pernilla and Paley cast furtive glances at the sexually explicit artwork as they walked through the foyer.

Several demimondaines clustered around Brux, trying to tempt him with their services.

The madame threw them a sharp look, and the women gracefully nodded and backed off.

Daisy clung to Kopius. Neither of them showed any reaction to the establishment. Kopius seemed more concerned with tending to Daisy's wounds.

Thyra's fishlike eyes opened wide. She stopped and said to Ferox, "I leave. Wait for you outside." She dashed out of the foyer.

Madame Vang took them to the back room and started with Daisy, who appeared to be the most injured.

While the madame treated each of them, the team formulated a plan to get back Sammy's wife's skin.

"Willie wouldn't leave it in his residence where his wife could find it." Kopius paced the room.

"Where then?" Ferox asked.

"He has a safe in his office at the wax museum." Madame Vang dipped a cotton swab in an amber liquid and patted it on Paley's injuries. The cuts healed before their eyes.

Kopius stopped pacing and twisted toward the madame. "I bet that's where he stashed the skin."

"He probably keeps all his valuables in there," Pernilla said.

"No." Van shook her head and waved her hands. "No way am I going back into that fun house."

"All right." Brux rubbed his chin, deep in thought, as he considered Van's stance. His face lit up. "How about going as far as the concession stand?"

Van narrowed her eyes at him. "What do you have in mind?"

He smiled. "Getting Willie to help me sell you and Daisy to Madame Vang."

CHAPTER 38

After Madame Vang healed each of them, the team went back to the Wharf Lizard.

They changed, dumped their backpacks, and then headed to Wild Willie's Wax Museum and "Fun" House to enact their plan.

Van willed herself not to vomit when she stepped through the wooden double doors.

A handful of male customers sat on stools at the concession stand, having a drink and chatting with each other. To Van, they looked like wharf rats. Thugs who crept around the docks at night looking for things to steal, or people to rob.

"Welcome Back!" Willie grinned and opened his arms wide as he greeted Brux. "Ready for another round?" His eyes darted to the fun house's entrance.

Brux took a seat at the concession stand. Daisy and Van obediently stood behind him.

An older man sat slouched on a stool, cradling his mug. "Adults are getting sick now."

"King Nequus has the illness under control," said the man sitting next to him.

"Not too many of the sick have turned, I heard," said a man wearing a black cloak.

"Not yet," the older man said in a panicked tone. "People are saying Solmor is here."

"Take it easy." The cloaked man shifted uneasily on his stool. "There's no need for that kind of talk."

Hearing news about the illness spreading to adults gave Van a massive anxiety attack and made her feel like she wasn't moving fast enough. Time was slipping away.

"Wait." Willie narrowed his eyes at Brux. "You didn't bring those thugs with you, did you?" he asked, remembering Ferox's men who had broken in and saved them from the horrors of the fun house. "Party poopers, the whole lot of them."

"I'm here for something else," Brux said.

"What can I do you for?" Willie asked.

Paley entered the lobby.

Willie glanced at her, looking eager to send her through the fun house. He turned away when Paley sauntered over to the concession stand helper and applied her best skill, flirting. She giggled and flipped her hair to distract the boy.

Paley hadn't recovered from her incident with the nixe, and after learning about her part in their plan, she said, "I'll do it, but I'm not leaving with *anyone*."

While Brux distracted Willie with the details of brokering a deal to sell Van and Daisy to the Treasure Chest, Paley kept the concession stand helper preoccupied. While this was going on in the front lobby, Kopius and Ferox were sneaking in through the back of the building. Madame Vang had drawn a rough blueprint of the museum with directions for them to find Willie's office and safe.

"Wonderful. It's settled." Willie leered at Van and Daisy. "Let's take them in the back so I can get a better look." He winked at Brux and jerked his head toward a door behind the counter with a sign that read "private."

Brux, a terrible liar to begin with, looked like a fish caught on a hook.

Daisy tensed.

Kopius and Ferox hadn't yet entered the lobby, which meant they were still in Willie's office stealing the selkie skin. Van fidgeted, wishing they would hurry. Kopius had boasted he knew how to crack a safe. She hoped he was right.

Not knowing what else to do, Van took action by using one of her all-time highest skills. She threw a fit.

"I'm not going anywhere!" Van stomped her foot. "How could you even think of selling me to the demimondaines? I thought we had something *special*."

"You'll do as I say! Both of you." Brux slammed his fist onto the counter.

"I'm doing as *I* say!" Van screeched.

"Me too," Daisy said. "You *lied to me!*"

Van found it eerie to see the usually serene Daisy acting upset.

"I'm the man," Brux pounded his fist into his chest like an ape. "I make the rules." He grabbed Van and Daisy by each of their elbows.

"Little spitfires." Willie licked his lips. "They'll be perfect once they're broken."

Van wriggled against Brux's grip. "Let me go!"

"Give her a little crack across the face." Willie suggested with a wave of his hand. "That ought to keep her in line." He gave Brux a knowing nod.

The other patrons minded their own business as if nothing was going on.

Willie walked to the end of the counter and opened the half door so Brux could bring Van and Daisy behind the concession stand. "Come on. Let's get to my office."

"Why do I need to go to your office?" Brux asked, stalling.

"I'm going to need a sample first before I introduce them to Madame Vang." He jerked his head, indicating for Brux to get a move on.

Brux dragged Van and Paley behind the counter.

Willie led them through the door marked "private" and down a dim, carpeted hallway.

They bumped straight into Kopius and Ferox.

"What—?" Willie exclaimed.

Brux released his grip on Van and Daisy.

Willie raised his fingers to his mouth and whistled.

Three burly men dashed around the far corner and marched down the hallway toward them.

Ferox, Kopius, and Brux grappled with the men.

Willie wrapped his arms around Van and dragged her toward a nearby door.

Thyra and Pernilla bounded down the hallway, coming from the lobby, and joined the fight.

Van struggled against Willie's grasp as he hauled her through his office's door.

Daisy followed and stomped over to them. "Stop."

Willie chuckled. He unwrapped his arms from Van, yet kept a firm grip on her wrist. He stepped toward Daisy. "Come here, girl." Willie grinned as he stretched his free hand to snatch Daisy. "The more, the merrier."

Daisy let loose and kicked Willie in the crotch.

He let out a pathetic squeak, released Van's wrist, and keeled over.

Van gaped, paralyzed, while processing what had just happened. Daisy tugged her arm, spurring her to action.

They turned toward the door of Willie's office, and halted seeing Brux standing there. He winced with empathy as he grinned. "I even felt that one."

They met up with the others in the hallway. Willie's three men lay unconscious on the floor.

"We heard you throwing a fit and peeked inside," Pernilla said to Van, as the team raced down the hallway back toward the lobby. Thyra and Pernilla had been stationed outside, on the lookout for trouble.

"We saw Willie take you behind the counter and followed you," Pernilla continued.

"Saw whole thing," Thyra said.

The group dashed past the concession stand. Paley ditched the helper boy and joined them.

The customers looked up from their mugs at the activity, but remained disinterested.

The team sprinted through the lobby, out of the building, and hurried down the boardwalk for several blocks. Then slowed to a brisk walk once they were sure Wild Willie and his men weren't pursuing them.

Van stopped.

The others halted to see what was wrong. They peered at Van, concerned.

"Are you all right?" Ferox placed a hand on Van's back.

Brux threw Ferox a dirty look, as if the prince was interfering in his job of taking care of her.

"That was awful." Paley shuddered.

Van bent down and grasped her knees, trembling. "That was… so… *gross*." She took a deep breath and pushed the sickening feeling aside. The event raced through her mind, including how she escaped Willie's clutch. She burst out laughing. Van reached up and gripped Daisy's shoulder. "You—you—"

"What's wrong?" Ferox pushed his eyebrows together. "Is she having a nervous breakdown?"

"You—kicked him," Van said between gasps of laughter. "Right in the *nuts*!"

Daisy let out a big belly laugh; Paley burst into giggles.

Pernilla grinned at Daisy. "Nice work."

"What are nuts?" Thyra asked.

Van used the back of her hand to wipe her eyes. "I'm fine."

"We need to go meet Sammy," Brux said, bringing the team's focus back to the situation at hand.

"Willie and his men won't be happy," Kopius said. "And they're probably on their way to find us."

"Let's go." Ferox seemed annoyed at the girls blowing off steam by laughing. Apparently, none of the guys thought it was funny to get kicked in the nuts.

"You got the skin?" Van asked, still wiping tears of laughter off her cheeks.

"Sure did." Kopius held up what looked like a tightly balled, light-brown velour blanket.

"Great job." Daisy wrapped him in a hug.

"Let's move," Ferox commanded. "My men will storm the area if I'm not back in a few minutes."

The team dashed toward the docks. When they arrived, Sammy bobbed in the water, waiting.

Ferox laid the skin on the dock in front of Sammy. "Is this all you need to get your wife back?"

Sammy peered at the skin. Being a selkie, and therefore part seal, he couldn't actually pick it up unless he used his mouth. "Yes! Yes! She'll be here any second."

"Now for your end of the bargain," Kopius said. "The map."

"The map is on my skin," a woman's voice came from behind.

They all turned to see a stunning woman standing naked on the dock. With blond hair so long, it brushed against the wood planks as she walked forward.

Kopius opened his mouth to say something. Daisy clasped his arm and shook her head.

"Ezili!" Sammy cried, practically leaping out of the water.

She bent over the side of the dock and kissed him on the lips. "My love."

Ezili took her skin and held it up to show them the map, partly covering her nakedness. "What location do you seek?"

"The River Shade," Brux said.

"The Cup of Life," Van added. Why not ask for what they really wanted? Ferox was there, so she had to ask for the Cup, rather than the second seal.

"We are here." Ezili pointed to a spot on the map. "You must sail across the Bottomless Sea." She moved her index finger slightly to the west and settled on an island. "Here lies the River Shade. On Insulam a Mortuis."

"Island of the Dead," Brux said.

Ezili continued, "Pay Kharon, the ferryman, a fairy's tear and he'll take you to the underground cavern that holds the Cup of Life."

"Told you it would be in a cave," Van muttered, glad she had conquered her fear of enclosed places last year.

Ezili wrapped her skin around her shoulders, and it magically stretched to cover her entire body, leaving only her pretty face. The covered parts transformed into a brown seal and she dropped onto the planks of the dock. The locations on the map were now nothing more than spots on a brown seal's fur. She waddled off the edge and splashed into the water.

Ezili turned her human face to the group. "Thank you."

"Good luck." Sammy bobbed next to her.

He and his wife swam away in the open ocean against the backdrop of a gorgeous peach sunset.

"We'll take *The Obelus* to the island," Ferox said. "Brux, Kopius, Thyra," he paused, and then said, "and Pernilla. Before heading back to the inn, can you help me check the ship's repairs and make sure it's stocked with supplies?"

Pernilla heartily agreed, happy to be included. Brux, Kopius, and Thyra no doubt expected to be asked.

"A-hem." Van placed her hands on her hips.

Ferox glanced at her and sighed. "Okay. Fine. *Anyone* who wants to help with the ship can stay and do so."

Van shrugged. "No thanks. I'm too tired."

Ferox shook his head as if he would never understand the female gender.

"It's nice to be asked," Van mumbled.

Daisy and Paley both claimed exhaustion and had no desire to help with repairs, so the team split up. Some went to the ship, others back to the Wharf Lizard.

Brux escorted Van, Daisy, and Paley back to their suite without incident and then headed back the to the ship.

Once inside the suite, Van and Daisy began packing the team's items.

Paley paced the room, unable to stay still. She looked clammy.

"Have you been taking the colloidal silver?" Van scolded herself for not getting extra from Madame Vang.

"Yeah, yeah," Paley muttered. "I've been taking it."

"Your immune system is being compromised by the Twin Gemstones," Van said. "And Brux might be too far away."

"No, it's not that." Daisy peered intently at Paley.

"We might need to up her dose," Van said to Daisy.

Daisy felt Paley's forehead with the back of her hand. "It's a fever." She looked worried. "I don't think the colloidal silver works anymore."

"What? Why?" Van asked.

Daisy sighed. "The colloidal silver only delays the inevitable."

"What are you saying?" Van raised her tone an octave higher with each word.

"I'm saying Paley has the demon illness."

CHAPTER 39

"I'm not sick," Paley said with a crazed look in her eyes.

"Why don't you lie down?" Daisy suggested.

Paley snapped her head at Daisy and glared. "Why don't you make me?"

"She's getting aggressive," Van said to Daisy. "It's another symptom."

"Don't talk about me like I'm not here." Paley stomped into the bedroom she shared with Van and slammed the door.

"I think it's the gemstones. Paley's too far away from Brux," Van said. "I'll go to the wharf and get him."

Van opened the door to leave; Brux stood there, about to enter.

"Twin Gemstone?" Van asked, knowingly.

He nodded. "I felt the drain. I might've been too far away."

"You felt the drain because Paley is sick," Daisy said.

They filled him in on Paley's behavior.

"If Brux is back, and he was close-by to begin with," Daisy said, "then Paley has the demon illness."

The clock began ticking on Paley's death and subsequent transformation into a demon. Van had to get her friend back to the medical wing at Lodestar where the Brotherhood could treat her illness, sure they must've found a way to cure terrigens. The pressure of completing the team's mission weighed more heavily on Van now.

She called for Wiglaf to come and help Paley with his healing purrs, but her bunfy didn't appear.

Van, Brux, and Daisy argued about how to handle Paley until Kopius and Pernilla returned.

"Thyra went to her own room," Kopius said.

"Ferox and his men are staying on the ship for the night," Pernilla added. "Talk about paranoid. Glad he let us leave, though."

"Where'd you go, mate?" Kopius asked Brux.

He pulled his gemstone from his pocket and waved it at Kopius.

"The ship's repaired and stocked." Pernilla rubbed her hands together. "We're ready for departure at dawn."

"Why not leave now?" Brux asked.

"Something to do with the tides, or the weather." Pernilla shrugged.

Van wanted her teammates to shift their attention away from Ferox and the Cup and concentrate on their mission of checking the seal and safely returning Paley home.

One problem.

Van needed to retrieve the Coin before convincing them to abandon Ferox. She refused to let him leave with it. The Coin was the only sure way to find the seal, despite Van's strong suspicion that the seal was near the Cup. But Ferox had the Coin tucked away in his pocket. Right next to the fairy's tear. Which gave Van an idea.

She strolled into her bedroom, tiptoed past Paley, who was asleep on the bed, and went into the adjoining bathroom.

Van brushed her hair and changed into her sexiest outfit, a white ribbed tank top and clean cargo pants. She cursed herself for not packing any cute dresses or any makeup.

She finished sprucing up and then remembered the scented soap brought to her courtesy of Madame Vang.

Dammit. Van forgot to use it and forgot to thank the madame for it while being healed after the kopidoden attack.

She'd have to remember to thank Ferox for paying the madame to search for a counter-curse. It would help gain his trust and aid in her seduction plan to get back the Coin. Van glanced at her reflection in the mirror and decided she looked fine. There was no time to take a shower using the soap and then get ready all over again.

Paley lay on the bed, looking worse than ever. Her face was pale, and she had a coating of sweat covering her skin. "What're you looking at?" she growled.

"Nothing." Van zipped from the room.

"I'm going out for some fresh air," Van announced to the others.

Brux leaped from his chair. "I'll go with you."

"No—uh, stay here with Paley," Van said. "I don't think it will help her condition if you move too far away from her, you know, because of the gemstones."

Kopius volunteered to escort Van.

"I'll go too," Daisy said.

"Well, I'm not going." Pernilla plunked herself down in a comfy armchair.

"None of you are going," Van said. "Daisy, you mentioned being exhausted. Stay here and rest. Take a bath or something." She turned to Kopius and Brux. "I need some alone time to think."

Brux scowled.

"I won't go farther than the front porch." With that settled, Van headed for the door.

No soldier guarded the hallway. Not only was Ferox short on men, but he was also smart enough to know Van and the others wouldn't run. They had nowhere to go, and he still had the Coin.

She bounded down the stairway and heard Brux call to her from behind.

Van stopped her descent and twisted around to face him. "What's up?"

"I could ask the same of you." He gave a knowing glance at her clothes, aware she had gussied up, something not done to sit on a front porch. "What are you up to?"

"I..." Van saw the look on Brux's face and hesitated. For the first time since Ferox had entered her life, she thought about Brux's feelings and how her closeness with Ferox might be upsetting him. "I'm going to talk to Ferox. But it's not what you think."

He looked pained. "Sure. Whatever." He turned and headed back up the stairs.

"Brux," Van called after him.

He paused on the steps and twisted to face Van.

"You know we can't be together," she said.

"You can't be with Ferox either. He's *Balish*. That's even worse."

"I have to be with someone," Van said, raising her voice.

"Yeah. You do." He continued up the stairs, shoulders slouched. "Go to Ferox," his voice trailed behind him. "Maybe he can be your assigned protector."

"I didn't mean Ferox," Van shouted.

Brux reached the top of the steps. He stopped but didn't turn around. "Yes, you did," he said sadly. Then disappeared down the hall.

Van stomped down the stairs, furious. She had no intention of getting involved with Ferox. In fact, the opposite was true. Why couldn't Brux believe that? Her only goal was to be a good warrior and to keep her people safe. Period.

Van headed for the docks. She didn't like Ferox controlling their mission. She didn't need his interference. They had less than two weeks before she would be forced to face the Quasher. If it came down to it, she knew Brux would be there to protect her, and it would end in disaster. Like it did for her ancestor Amaryl when her husband, Rowen, died trying to protect his wife from the shadow beast.

Van fantasized about Ferox leaping in and saving both her and Brux from the clutches of the Quasher.

Ferox, my hero? The thought mortified her.

"Coin. Fairy's tear. Seal," Van repeated over and over. She needed to keep her focus. She resolved not to let her emotions get in the way when she enacted her plan.

"Coin. Fairy's tear. Seal." Snag the Coin. Grab the fairy's tear, so Ferox couldn't try to get the Cup. Then ditch Ferox and mend the seal. "Coin. Fairy's tear. Seal." Get the job done and go home. Paley's life depended on it.

The soldier on the docks by *The Obelus* informed Van the prince's whereabouts were none of her business.

"I have to talk to him about our mission," Van said.

The soldier remained stoic. "It can wait."

Van, once again, relied on her skill of throwing a fit. "Take me to him right now." She stomped her foot.

"Or what?"

"Or I'll tell him you wouldn't let me talk to him, although you knew it was *urgent*. I'll make sure he leaves you on this island to *rot*." She stomped her foot again to make sure he knew she meant business.

The soldier reluctantly gave in and called to another to come and cover his post.

"Follow me," the soldier said, as if taking care of Van was a major chore.

He entered a path in the woods.

Van hesitated. "Where're you taking me?"

"You want to talk to the prince?" he said curtly. "Follow me."

She followed the soldier down a winding path in the dark woods. Van could barely see. Her anxiety rose. She heard the tinkling of water just before they entered a clearing.

Layers of rocks formed a small, semi-circular cliff. Five thin streams of water cascaded down into the natural collection pool at the bottom. The water appeared hot enough for wafts of steam to drift upward around the water lilies floating on the surface. Candles placed on the layered stones illuminated the hot spring.

"My prince." The soldier bowed. His voice rang across the serenity of the spring, causing a white bird to take flight. It looked like an Earth World dove.

In the candlelight, Van swore the bird carried a wafer in its mouth. Was Ferox feeding the birds?

Ferox stretched his arms wide as he propped his upper body against the side of the spring, fully exposing his chiseled chest. Van noticed his clothes—all of them—lying on a flat rock directly behind him.

Suddenly, her scheme seemed ridiculous, and her resolve crumbled.

"I'm sorry to bother you. But you have a guest." He tilted his head toward Van. "She demanded to see you."

"Demanded, huh?"

Van noticed every curve of his biceps, his deltoids, the blur of the submerged part of his six-pack and naked lower body...

Her eyes darted away. Part of Van wanted to flee. But the part controlling her feet made her stay. Her eyes hesitantly moved back toward the hot spring.

"Shall I remove her?" the soldier asked.

"No." Ferox glanced at his man. "You may go."

"Very good, my prince." The soldier bowed and then departed.

Ferox's sultry gaze turned to Van.

His lips curled into a seductive grin.

CHAPTER 40

Van forced herself to focus. "I..."

"It's called the Water of Life." Ferox swept his hand, meaning the hot springs. "Madame Vang told me about it. Very healing." He rose from the water.

Van quickly turned away. The shed skin of a snake lay in the dirt. Van shivered, wondering what slithering things moved through the woods in the night. Whatever this was, it had gotten bigger.

"Join me," Ferox called to her.

"Um..." Van's seduction plan flew from her brain. She panicked.

Get a grip! There was nothing to fear.

"Sure." She turned around, relieved he had sat back down in the spring.

Van marched to the edge. The air over the water was hot and moist, like a sauna. She really wanted to take her clothes off, but the thought made her blush. She gazed at Ferox.

He chuckled. "Come in with your clothes on." He waded across the spring to where Van stood, keeping his lower half hidden underwater. "You look beautiful, by the way. I understand if you don't want to get your clothes wet."

"Well, I..." His charisma drew Van in and made her both scared and thrilled. She glanced around the woods.

"No one's here. Just us."

A heavy pause hung in the air.

Ferox grinned. "I'll turn my back."

Van peeled off her tank with trembling fingers. She kicked off her boots, pulled down her cargo pants, and dashed to the edge of the spring wearing her panties and bra.

With her nerves on end, she hurtled her body into the spring, slipping on the slick rocks, and crashing into the water with an ungraceful splash.

She resurfaced, gasping for air and brushing her wet hair out of her eyes.

"I can turn around now, I take it?" Ferox said, obviously hearing her grand entrance.

Van wiped the droplets off her face and patted her hair, hoping she didn't look completely terrible.

"You okay?"

"Yeah." Van's face turned beet red. She bent her knees to make sure she stayed under the surface from her neck down in the jacuzzi-hot water.

"Nice, isn't it?" Ferox smiled at Van.

She wondered why he didn't demand to know what made her interrupt his private bath. No matter, she was certain he kept the Coin and the fairy's tear close to him, most likely in his discarded clothes.

Ferox waded back to his spot against the wall of the spring, which happened to be in front of his clothes.

Van paddled closer to Ferox with what she hoped was an alluring smile. "Very nice." She tried not to twitch and to keep her voice steady, to conceal any telltale sign she was up to no good.

Ferox seemed entertained as Van moved closer to him.

"It's not here." He grinned.

Van pretended to look confused.

"You're after the Coin," he said. "Perhaps even the tear. They're not here. They're safely hidden. Elsewhere."

Ferox's perceptiveness stunned Van. With her plan now dead in the water, she should storm out of the spring and go back to her suite.

But she didn't.

He caused Van's thoughts to pull in two different directions. Do the right thing by leaving. Or stay and get closer to the enemy.

"Stay," Ferox said, as if seeing the battle going on inside Van. "There is much we can learn from one another."

He had a point. If Van stayed and got to know Ferox, she could gather intel to use against him later. She might even get him to say where he hid the Coin and the tear. Any good warrior would do the same. Plus, the heat and minerals in the spring water made her cuts from the kopidodens, now a healing pink, feel even better.

"What do you want to talk about?" Van settled into a nook on the edge of the spring close to Ferox, but not close enough for him to touch her. "I mean, we have nothing in common."

Ferox gazed into the distance, deep in thought.

"Tell me about my sister," he said with a pained expression.

Van took his words like a punch to the stomach. Again, Ferox wanted her to explain why she had murdered his sister. Van figured he must struggle with the justification of it and needed more details to keep him from drowning her on the spot.

The spring suddenly seemed to turn up the heat.

He must've noticed Van's discomfort, and said, "We Balish see the death of my brother Devon as a bad omen. We believe death of a royal twin *splits* the bloodline. Solana also died. Death of both royal twins." He cast his eyes downward. "Our *Sanctus Novus* mentions a split bloodline preceding a great battle for power, where control of the lands will be at stake. The Balish Council is using my brother and sister's deaths to start a war with the Lodians."

"A preemptive takeover?" Van asked. "Before the Lodian's Anchoress gets too strong?"

Ferox turned to Van. "I don't want war."

A moment of reflection passed, then Van said softly, "She wanted to be queen, your sister. To rule the Balish kingdom. She took out anyone in her way, including her twin brother."

"Devon," Ferox said, pensively. "People said he was born to rule. Being king was his destiny. Nothing could stand in his way. He had the fortitude and desire to rule our kingdom, but he was also ruthless." Ferox grunted. "He had this air of superiority about him." Ferox turned to Van. "He would've taken charge and got the kingdom running in good order. Now the council has placed that task on me." He made it sound like a burden.

"I thought you wanted to be king?"

He shrugged. "Word is, the Balish Council and most of the Balish people don't think I have what it takes to rule the kingdom."

"Why? Because you're fair and nonjudgemental?"

"They say I'm blessed with nothing but good looks—"

Van snorted.

Ferox grinned. "Hey, I'm simply repeating what I've heard."

Van smiled back.

He continued in a more serious tone, "I have charisma, but lack discipline." He struggled to tell her the rest. "They say Solana, a mere *girl,* had more grit than me."

"Oh, boy." Van shook her head. "Are they confused?"

Ferox seemed pleased with Van's response. "I take the advice of the council into consideration, but my word and my mind are my own. I do what I think is best for all. That's what makes people say I'm too compassionate. It's why the council encouraged me to roam the countryside with my squadron. Toughen me up. A soft heart makes a poor king." He snorted. "Well, I've got news for them." He leaned closer and whispered. "I'm already king."

"What'd you mean?"

"Everyone... our people, the Balish Council, the Balish Royal Court, love my father, the *Great King Nequus*. You've already heard me mention my father's a drunk. The bigger secret is... my father only goes through the motions of being king."

"I don't understand." Van leaned closer to him. Interested, and flabbergasted, Ferox shared such a private glimpse at the inner workings of his family with her.

"He attends social events and parties and spends money. My

mother had no problem covering for him. She loved running the kingdom, albeit from behind closed doors. Now and then, she'd catch my father being unfaithful and threaten to leave him. It was all for show. My mother never would've left. My father didn't care about any of his mistresses, until..."

"Until...?"

Ferox said nothing.

"Oh." Van caught on. "Genie."

Ferox nodded. "That indiscretion, my mother couldn't tolerate. My father had genuine feelings for Genie, that's why my mother placed a kill order on her. I don't blame your step-mother for running to Salus Valde and converting to Lodianism. It was the only way she could survive."

Ferox had validated what Van always sensed about her step-mother. "So Genie never loved my father." *Or me.* "She was just being a demimondaine."

"It's her nature, Van," Ferox said with soft eyes. "She got dealt the hand of being a master companion. She had little choice. It's all she knows, and she's doing the best she can with it. You can't fault her for that." He inched closer to her. "I choose to believe there was true love between Genie and your father."

"Pfft." The whole situation depressed Van. "Genie didn't marry my father for love. She married him for security." How could her father be so stupid?

She recalled Genie's beauty and how her training included tricking men into falling in love with her, molding herself to suit her mark. Her father never stood a chance. It also explained why Genie didn't have a mother's bone in her body. Demimondaine training didn't include motherhood classes.

But Van was grateful for Ferox's kind words. "I meant it when I said your sister would've killed you, too, if she thought you were a threat to her ascension."

"The council would never have allowed a female to sit on the throne."

"I wouldn't be so sure about that," Van said. "Solana had the skills to get what she wanted."

"Her sorcery, you mean."

Van nodded. "She would've poisoned the entire council if it came down to it. Or put them under a spell."

"Impossible," Ferox said. "The palace wizard constantly monitors for unauthorized magic."

"Seriously, Ferox. She was bad news."

"Do you think I'm bad news?" Ferox shifted to a sultry tone.

His intense stare reached into Van's soul and grabbed her heart. She looked away. "From what I've heard about your cousin Merloc, he's someone you should be worried about. He might want the throne."

Ferox grinned. "You're worried about me?"

He leaned back against the wall of the spring, his tone turned somber. "Merloc can be dangerous, I know, but there's a difference between force and strength." He turned to face Van. "I'm sorry about your friend, Daisy. As soon as I found out, I ordered Merloc to release her. That's how Kopius got into Windermere Castle so easily."

Van tried to conceal her surprise, but her jaw dropped.

"Merloc's good at what he does. I give him a lot of control and autonomy, and that keeps him happy. He respects blood lineage and order and has his sights set on inheriting the Alga region once his father passes into the light."

A dark thought crossed Van's mind. "Why are you telling me this?" She became certain he planned to kill her.

"You seem like someone I can talk to. You have similar family obligations placed on you."

Van agreed with him. It was a relief to talk to someone who understood the burden of family. The more Ferox opened up to her, the more they connected on a deeper level.

He slid closer to Van. "I wanted us to get to know each other. You know, because it's good for tribal relations." He grinned.

"Oh, uh, of course. Yeah." Van flinched, flustered by his intensity. She became disheartened when he pulled away.

"I don't wish to make you uncomfortable," he said, giving her an explanation.

"You're not. You won't—aren't," Van sputtered, a bit too eagerly. She flushed, wishing Genie had taught her some moves from the demimondaine handbook.

Ferox glided closer to Van. Desire glistened in his amber-yellow eyes.

This time, Van didn't flinch.

CHAPTER 41

Light from the candles caught the droplets on Ferox's shoulders, making his skin glisten.

As he inched closer, Van's lips tingled in anticipation. His unwavering stare caused her to believe she was the only person in the worlds to him.

His lips touched hers, and a burst of delight flooded her insides. The Balish Council had it right. He was soft. But in good ways. His skin, his lips, his heart.

Van's hands glided over his chest. Her touch conformed to each ripple of muscle. Her fingertips slid over his hard nipples and up the sides of his neck, over his strong jaw, and into his damp, silky hair. She leaned her body into his. Van desired more of him. All of him...

She pushed away and gasped.

"What's wrong?" Ferox gazed at her inquisitively.

"We can't."

"We're kissing, nothing more. I agree, we should take it slow."

"We can't... date," Van said. "We can't... *like* each other."

"Why not?"

"We're... *different*."

"You mean from different tribes," Ferox said, as if he understood Van's concern. "I'm not bothered by it. Why are you?"

"Your people want to kill me."

Ferox brushed his fingers along Van's jaw. "I won't let that happen."

"Don't you know the story of our ancestors?" Van knew he did.

Ferox leaned close to Van and whispered in her ear. "How Manik and Zurial fell in love and got married. A Balish King and a Lodian Princess. Hm, sound familiar?"

Ferox's sincerity about marriage made Van's insides swirl with glee. As he laid butterfly kisses on her neck, she asked, "And how did that turn out?"

Ferox leaned back, grinning. "Tell me."

"I want to hear your version of the story." She needed to convince both Ferox and herself no good would come from their being together.

"Okay," Ferox said, playing along. "Manik and his proposal of marriage to Zurial was a blessing and came with a plan to end the war and bring peace to the land. When demons reached our world, both our tribes banded together to defeat them. But instead of stopping there, the war between the Balish and Lodians resumed." Ferox shook his head in disgust. "But Zurial and Manik arranged a truce with your queen's approval."

"Queen Amaryl, the Anchoress," Van said. "She had a great incentive to end the war because her husband, Rowen, was on the front line fighting. She was happy about the marriage and believed in Manik's sincerity because he let Zurial return to Salus Valde with the Cup of Life."

Ferox nodded in agreement. "The war was bloody and ferocious. No one wanted to lose more loved ones. Each side had two Items of Creation, a sign of balance."

"Amaryl's intuition told her Manik could be trusted, but the Balish could not," Van said, challenging Ferox. To see if he agreed *he* couldn't be trusted. "But Amaryl did what was best for her people and agreed to the terms of the wedding."

"The wedding went off without a hitch. It was a grand time, filled with love and joy. The end." Ferox moved in for another kiss.

Van backed away, scrunching her face.

He shrugged. "Didn't think that would work." He grinned and settled back against the side of the spring.

"Manik's brother, Goustav," Van said. "His infatuation with Amaryl led to his ultimate betrayal and the rebellion."

"Unfortunately, yes," Ferox said, grimly. "I've read the ancient scrolls. Many royal Lodians came to Balefire to celebrate the birth of Zurial and Manik's baby. Their child would join the two tribes forever. But Goustav didn't approve of their wedding or agree with the truce."

"He and his underground followers rose and slaughtered every Lodian in sight right after Zurial gave birth to Mehal," Van said. "Including Zurial."

Ferox gazed at Van and caressed her cheek with his fingers. "I'm sorry. It was a terrible thing."

Van pulled away. The pain of the bloody event seemed to throb in her veins. Her eyes welled up, and she wanted to cry.

Ferox sensed her discomfort and changed the subject somewhat. "I read there are six goblets. Five replica goblets. One given by Zurial to each of the guests at the wedding table. One went to Amaryl, which is rumored to be in the possession of Manikists. The underground network of people who oppose the current Balish rule." Ferox grimaced. "They don't understand. I want peace as much as they do. I believe in my ancestor Manik's truce."

Van knew the location of Amaryl's replica goblet. Noam and his son, Zane, proprietors of The Troll's Foot Tavern in Araquiel had it in their possession.

"Manik's goblet is with my uncle King Mador, in East Alga," Ferox continued. "Goustav's Bloody Rebellion destroyed King Halldor, Rowen, and Goustav's replica goblets. Zurial became obsessed with her goblet, which was, of course, the Cup of Life." He turned to Van and said softly, "Goustav didn't kill Zurial. She suffered massive blood loss from childbirth."

"Oh." Van wasn't sure what to do with this newest insight, or if it even mattered. Zurial's death took place before Amaryl cursed her own bloodline, and Zurial wasn't an Anchoress.

"I am sorry," Ferox said again. "I understand your point. It was a terrible time. But that won't happen again. We've learned from our ancestor's mistakes. Together, we can make our world better. We can find peace."

Despite Ferox's positive outlook, rehashing the story of their ancestors made Van more determined than ever *not* to get involved with him. She had come to Ferox for the Coin and the fairy's tear. She needed to get them. Then she could ditch him, check the seal, and get back to her normal life. But Ferox claimed he had hidden them somewhere else, and flirting with him was leading her down a path to disaster.

Van pushed away from the side of the spring, ready to leave. She remembered something and twisted around to face him. "Oh, I wanted to thank you for paying Madame Vang extra to search for a cure to the Anchoress curse."

He jolted upright. "I haven't paid Madame Vang for that yet. I will. But I haven't yet."

"Well, I mean you paid Madame Vang for something. She sent one of her demimondaines to my room."

Water rippled as Ferox rushed to her. He gripped her shoulders. "Did this woman give you anything? Did you eat or drink anything?"

"No, no. I..." A chill ran through Van's body. She recalled her encounter with the woman. "A basket of handmade soaps from the madame. To make up for not finding a counter-curse. I thought nothing of it. Why are you looking at me like that?"

"Van, those soaps weren't from Madame Vang. I think someone is trying to kill you. Where are the soaps now? Did you throw them away?"

Her heart battered against her chest. *Where did she put the basket?*

"Van, that soap is deadly. We have to get rid of it!"

Both Ferox and Van leaped from the hot spring. They grabbed

their clothes, hastily dressed, and dashed down the path through the trees.

Several of Ferox's soldiers lurking in the woods nearby caught the movement and rushed over on alert.

"Follow me," Ferox commanded.

So much for them being alone, Van thought fleetingly.

"Maybe housekeeping threw them away," Van suggested. With dread, she knew no one had cleaned the suite, and a maid would never mistake a basket of handmade soaps as trash.

They raced back to the Wharf Lizard and stormed up the stairs.

Ferox burst into the suite, followed by Van and his men.

Brux and Kopius leaped to their feet, as did Pernilla.

Van turned to the accent table by the door. She clasped the handle of the soap basket. "There's one missing."

"One what missing?" Pernilla asked.

Ferox's eyes darted around the room. "Where's Daisy?"

"Taking a bath." Kopius' shoulders tensed. "Why?"

Van rushed over to the suite's main bathroom. She tore open the door.

Daisy sat in the tub. She clasped the soap, rubbing the bar on her arm and chest. Her wide, innocent, pale-blue eyes shifted toward Van, startled by her friend's brazen entrance.

"Daisy! No!" Van cried.

The soap dropped from Daisy's grip and slipped into the water. Her eyes went blank; her jaw slackened.

Daisy's body went limp, and she sunk under the bath water.

CHAPTER 42

"Daisy!" Van rushed to the side of the bathtub along with Kopius.

He propped Daisy upright and placed his index and middle finger on her neck to check for a pulse.

"Is she dead?" Van dreaded the answer.

He took his thumb and opened one of her closed eyelids. "Not dead. In a coma."

Brux whipped around and stomped toward Ferox. "Did you have something to do with this?"

He didn't get close. Ferox's soldiers restrained him.

"No, he didn't," Van said.

Kopius, who couldn't have cared less about the commotion, lifted Daisy from the tub. He held her in his arms, dripping wet, brought her into the main room of the suite, and gently laid her on the couch by the window. He covered her naked body with a blanket and turned to Ferox. "Open it."

Ferox nodded to one of his men. The soldier used a forked key and unlocked the window.

Kopius opened it all the way. "She would want fresh air."

"Who's making all that noise?" Paley's meek voice emanated from her bedroom.

"Where'd this soap come from?" Pernilla reached into the basket to grab a bar.

Van dashed over and swatted it from her hand. "Don't touch it!"

"It's poisoned." Ferox used a towel to pick up the soap from the floor and tossed back it into the handbasket. He handed the basket to one of his soldiers. "Get the soap from the bathtub. Then get rid of the whole thing."

"A woman came to the suite and told me Madame Vang had sent me a gift," Van said.

"Maybe Madame Vang has an antidote to the soap's poison." Brux settled down enough for the soldiers to release their grip on him.

Van nodded. "She might have more colloidal silver for Paley, too."

"Pernilla, Kopius," Brux said. "You two stay here and watch over Paley and Daisy."

Kopius hovered over Daisy, looking devastated. "It's my fault. It was my responsibility to watch over her." He knelt and took one of Daisy's hands in his own. "I'm so sorry. I should've done better."

Pernilla knelt beside Kopius. She wrapped an arm around his shoulder for comfort.

Van stepped in front of Brux. "You can't go to Madame Vang's." He had the other Twin Gemstone. He couldn't leave Paley.

"I don't care. I'm going." Brux jutted his jaw. "I'll be close enough."

Ferox listened to their exchange but didn't pry.

"Brux, you can't go." Van stared into his eyes. "Being hell-bent on doing whatever it takes to save your sister will kill Paley."

His shoulders slumped. "You're right."

"Good. It's settled," Van said, relieved. She went into the bedroom to check on Paley and their supply of colloidal silver.

It surprised her to see Wiglaf sleeping on Paley's belly. She had called for Wiglaf to help Paley, but didn't think her bunfy had responded to her plea. Van thought it odd Wiglaf didn't greet her when she entered the suite, or the bedroom. Her internal alarm blared. She dashed to the bed and examined her bunfy. He wasn't moving.

"Wigalf?" Van picked him up. He drooped like a wet noodle in her hands. "Wiglaf!"

"Van?" Paley muttered. She looked like death.

Wiglaf let out a weak chirrup. The bunfy half-opened his eyes and feebly raised one ear in an arc.

"Wurp meep," he said in an apologetic tone.

"What's wrong with him?" Brux asked gently from the doorway.

"He tried to comfort Paley. Being near her is draining his energy." Van's desperate eyes turned to Brux for an explanation. "You told me last year it wouldn't hurt him to use his purrs to help sick people."

"Bunfy's purrs raise the vibrational frequency of the sick and injured, helping them heal." Brux grimaced, deep in thought. "It makes no sense he would get drained from trying to help Paley."

Wiglaf squirmed in Van's arms.

She carefully laid him back down on the bed next to Paley, who had already fallen back to sleep. Her stomach rose and fell with each shallow breath.

Wiglaf struggled as he attempted to climb onto Paley's stomach, but lacked the strength. He settled on lying next to her, stretched lengthways against the side of Paley's torso.

"Is it okay if I leave him there?" Van watched as her little bunfy settled in. "I think he wants to stay."

His tiny face pointed into Paley's armpit, surrounded on the other side by her arm. He wrapped his ears around his head like a blanket and closed his eyes.

Brux stood in the doorway. His expression bleak. "I think this proves the illness is like nothing we've seen before."

Van took in the enormity of what he meant.

"There's no longer a question whether the seal is cracked," Brux said.

"Demons could break through it at any minute," Van said. "We need to get to the Bottomless Sea. *Now.*"

Brux shook his head. "No, first Daisy. Go to Madame Vang."

For a second, Van thought, *hell no*. The seal was more important. She needed to repair it to prevent the Earth World demons from breaking through, and to save more people from getting sick. Then, after completing their mission, they could get Paley and Daisy back to Lodestar for medical treatment. Brux based his decision on emotions, on saving one person right now. His sister. Warriors made decisions using their heads, not their hearts.

Van opened her mouth to object, but the pain in his eyes distracted her. "Of course. First, Daisy." She knew his sister's condition sickened him to the bone.

They left the bedroom, closing the door behind them. Ferox and his soldiers had left, most likely to give their group some privacy and to prevent any more drama with Brux.

Kopius and Pernilla watched over Daisy. Neither had moved from their position by her side.

"Be safe," Brux said to Van. He looked drawn from the gravity of the situation, and from the gemstones sapping his energy. Van could see it in the dark circles under his eyes. He joined Kopius and Pernilla kneeling by the couch.

Pernilla twisted around as Van grasped the doorknob to leave the suite.

"Does Paley need anything?" she asked.

Van shook her head. "There's nothing we can do for her right now. Wiglaf is sleeping with her."

"I heard what you said about him being sick, too. Will he be okay?" Pernilla asked.

"I hope so." As a magical creature, protected by Lilla, Van believed he would be fine. Besides, she had an enormous task in front of her. The lives of every person in the Living World *and* the Earth World depended on her mending the cracked seal. She could hardly add another concern to her plate.

Pernilla nodded, not a trace of hope on her face, and turned back to stare at Daisy.

Van hastily left the suite. She hurried along the sidewalk, dodging intoxicated passersby and ignoring the calls of the peddlers and the plentiful merchandise displayed on their carts. Van easily found her way back to the Treasure Chest.

She dashed through the doorway, but didn't see Madame Vang in the foyer. Since the establishment was open for business, Van thought the madame might be busy with a customer.

One of the demimondaines noticed Van. "Wait here," she said and darted through the archway under the stairs.

Within minutes, the madame meandered through the foyer to greet Van.

Van blurted out her situation and what she needed. More colloidal silver for Paley and an antidote to the poison for Daisy.

"I see." Madame Vang led her down the hallway and into a sitting room with comfy couches and high backed chairs.

"Given the condition of your friend Paley, I must conclude the demon illness is escalating." The madame clasped her delicate hands together as if the reality of this news brought her great distress.

"Light is self-sustaining, darkness exists at the expense of weakening others." As Madame Vang moved to grab some ampules, tiny flickers of light gleamed from the strands of gold threaded throughout her gown. "This illness is emotionless. It attacks everyone without prejudice or sympathy. It consumes the souls of those afflicted, extinguishing their light." She handed Van an amber dropper jar. "Colloidal silver will help delay Paley's eventual death."

"And Daisy?"

"Dark magic created Daisy's poison. She is under a spell. There is only one way to save both Paley and Daisy's life." Madame Vang paused, as if reluctant to continue.

"Well?" Van wished the woman would just spit it out.

"No," Madame Vang shook her head. "I must not speak of that which must be kept secret."

"Tell me!" The sheer power of Van's words was enough to shake the truth from the madame.

Madame Vang's eyes met Van's. "The Vas Ansata. Ankh Chalice. The Gold Goblet."

"What're you talking about?" If Van wanted a cryptic response, she would've asked Jacynthia.

"The only way to save your friend Paley's life, to cure her illness, is the same thing that will treat Daisy's poison. You must—"

"Retrieve the Cup of Life," Ferox said as he entered the room.

CHAPTER 43

"Do you live here now?" Van glared at Ferox.

"The madame was telling me about the Vas Ansata when you arrived." He turned to the madame. "I'll pay you for your help."

Madame Vang's lips curved into a grin. "Of that, I am aware." She lightly ran her fingers over his jaw. They lingered on his lips long enough for Van's annoyance to escalate.

"The Vas Ansata will solve your problems. It allows the holder to command the power of water to heal." As the madame spoke, she moved behind Ferox. She brushed her hands along his shoulders, ran them down his back, and rested them on his hips.

Madame Vang's appearance had changed. She looked younger, like a teenager. Apparently determined to lure Ferox into being one of her many customers.

The madame moved her lips close to his ear as if she might kiss him. "The Cup," she whispered. "Is life."

"Where's it hidden?" Ferox asked. "You told us to cross the River Shade. You failed to tell us the river isn't on Cortica."

His raw, masculine sexuality—or perhaps his wealth—seemed to capture Madame Vang's full attention. It made Van wonder if the madame had a greater interest in retaining Ferox as a permanent lover. The idea wasn't far-fetched. It's what Van's step-mother had done with Van's father, and then with her new boyfriend, Uncle Rummie.

"You know," Madame Vang cooed. "We are taking customers tonight." Her lips brushed the skin on Ferox's ear.

"Okay," Van blurted. "Enough." She balled her hands into fists and rested them on her hips. "I can't help but think how convenient this is for you, Ferox. You keep bugging me to get the Cup. I didn't want to do it. Now Paley and Daisy are sick, and the only cure for *both* of them is for me to retrieve the Cup, or the *Vas Ansata*." Van's eyes darted to the madame. "If you knew more about the Cup, why didn't you tell us before?"

"Nay." Madame Vang stopped caressing Ferox and stepped away from him. Her lips tightened into a straight line. "Since then, I have done research to get the information you need. Finesse, along with bribery, takes time." The madame held her stare on Van. "To retrieve the Cup of Life, you will face the trials of the Water Elemental."

"Naturally." Van sighed. "Do you know what she uses to guard the Cup? What kind of monsters?"

The madame glanced at Ferox.

He gave her a nod. "Go on."

"When you near the Cup, you must face challenges presented by your inner Self. You must walk in faith."

Great. Van didn't know what that meant, but didn't like the sound of it.

"The Cup? What does it look like?" Ferox asked.

Van already knew what the Cup looked like. Last year she had seen it in a mural called *The Wedding Celebration* while in the Grotto. She also drank from Amaryl's replica Cup at the Troll's Foot Tavern, and had seen it in Zurial's memory engram.

"It is a breathtaking bejeweled goblet made of pure gold," Madame Vang said. "It fills with any ingestible liquid. But those who touch the Cup face the difficult task of combating gluttony as the Cup must be used wisely and with respect."

"How is that a weapon?" Van asked. "Can it be used to poison people?"

The madame gasped. "Only by one whose soul has been corrupted by darkness. This is why the tests to retrieve the Cup are great. One must be ready to wield its powers for healing."

"It can endlessly supply water for soldiers in battle," Ferox said. "And to heal those injured. Making it a great weapon to have during a war."

"To gain the Cup's healing powers," Madame Vang added, "you must place it under a full moon. When the water turns orange, it will heal all who are injured or sick. Those who are but one inch from death."

"Can it heal people from..." Van hesitated, not sure if she should ask the question. "Quasher wounds?"

"I am uncertain what animal you speak of, but yes. It can heal all wounds." Madame Vang nodded. "But it cannot bring people back from the dead."

Madame Vang ran her fingertips along Van's cheek. "The Cup only heals the body, not the soul. The soul, my darling, is something you must work on yourself."

Van pushed the madam's hand away. "I have to mend the seal first."

"Van," Ferox pleaded. "We have to get the Cup. Use it to create the healing potion and save Daisy and Paley."

"If the seal breaks, it will expose the entire population," Van argued. "Great numbers of people will become infected and turn. A demon army will rise, and the worlds will collapse. My chief priority is to save as many people as possible."

"But Daisy and Paley will die," Ferox said. "The Cup will save your people—both our people—by healing those who are sick. I'll have my father allow your Grigori to cross the boundary so they can take care of any demons here."

Van scowled at Ferox. He was basing his decisions on emotion, just like Brux.

"We get the Cup. Then, we mend the seal. We'll use the Coin to find it." Ferox paused, observing Van's surprised expression. "That's right. I agree with you about repairing the seal. But it's our responsibility to save Daisy and Paley first."

Van was astounded Ferox offered to help mend the seal. He had already agreed to let Van and her team mend the seal, but now he, too, had taken on their mission. A task ordered by Uxa, the Head of the Grigori, a Lodian, and his family's nemesis. *Why is he being so reasonable?*

Madame Vang hadn't been able to uncover the exact location of the Cup, but she confirmed Ezili's claim it was on Insulam a Mortuis.

Ferox thanked the madame and paid her.

She wished them luck and looked saddened to see Ferox leave.

Van and Ferox headed back to the Wharf Lizard, rehashing what they had learned about the Cup.

Before Ferox dashed away to his room, he said, "Gather the others and meet me at *The Obelus*. We leave immediately."

Van agreed. She swung open the door to the suite and gaped at the scene before her.

Daisy now wore a pretty dress, and at least a dozen critters had joined her. Animals similar to Earth World squirrels, raccoons, cats, wolves, mice, owls had come through either the open window, or, presumably, someone let the larger ones through the door, knowing Daisy would want her animals friends around her.

The critters surrounded Daisy on the couch, perched on the windowsill, floor, and on the backs of nearby chairs. The animals watched over Daisy, their Princess of the Forest, along with Pernilla, Brux, and Kopius.

The animals had placed flowers and ferns around Daisy and had made a crown of colorful blooms, berries, and leaves they had put on her head. Daisy's hands were clasped over her stomach. In them, she held a bouquet of pink and purple flowers.

Van peeked into the bedroom to check on Paley and Wiglaf. Their condition hadn't improved and was perhaps worse. The animals had also placed flowers and greens around them, too. Van put drops of colloidal silver given to her by the madame into their mouths and then went back into the main room.

Kopius remained in the same spot as when Van had left.

"He hasn't moved." Brux rose from his chair by the couch; the nearby animals shifted from his movement and then settled in again. "Pernilla went into town to get the dress for Daisy at his request. She traded Daisy's dagger for it."

"I brought him back food." Pernilla waved her hand toward a cup of soup on the coffee table. "Didn't touch it."

"Did you get an antidote from Madame Vang?" Brux asked, like he already knew the answer.

Van shook her head. Her eyes turned to the critters. "What's going on with the animals?"

"Animals are connected to nature, like Daisy," Brux said. "They can feel her pain and are here to offer her their support."

"Went to check on Paley and a few of the critters followed me," Pernilla said. "They put those flowers around her and Wiglaf. I guess they care about Daisy's friends, too."

"I should've made my feelings for her more clear." Kopius stared at Daisy, almost as if talking to himself. "I was too much of a coward to show her how much I cared. Now it's too late."

Van rubbed his back. "I'm sorry, Kopius."

"Don't worry," Brux said. "We'll find an antidote."

"She'll get better," Pernilla said.

Their words of comfort made no difference. Van wasn't even sure Kopius heard them.

"There's no time to delay," Van said with renewed vigor. "Grab your things. We're setting sail right now."

As Pernilla, Brux, and Van gathered their backpacks, Van relayed the details of her visit with Madame Vang.

"I'm not going," Kopius said, dimly. "I'm not leaving Daisy's side."

At that moment, Van realized she would be the only member of her team going.

Brux bent over Daisy to whisper goodbye. The animals shuffled and bobbed, as if unsure of his motives, but didn't block him as he kissed her on the forehead. "Be well, sister."

The animals calmed, satisfied he posed no threat.

"Brux," Van said with apprehension. "You can't leave Paley, you have the Twin Gemstone."

"I can't leave you either," he said. "I'm your assigned protector. And you have to go. You're the only one who can retrieve the Cup."

"But I won't die being separated from you," Van said in a kind tone. "If you leave, both you and Paley will die from energy depletion."

Brux looked defeated, like he knew Van spoke the truth.

Next, before Van left, Paley's condition needed to be addressed. Kopius was in no shape for instructions. Brux… she couldn't be sure he was ruthless enough to do what needed to be done, worst-case scenario. Van turned to Pernilla. "Paley's getting worse."

Pernilla set her jaw and crossed her arms. "It's not my fault."

"I know." She pulled Pernilla aside, so the others couldn't hear. "It's not that. It's…" Van needed to word her request carefully. All the things Van hated about Pernilla—her brutality, stubbornness, confidence, lack of compassion—Van now saw as valuable assets to the team. She was grateful Pernilla had warrior blood, and the ability to block her feelings and get the job done.

"You have to stay too," Van said.

"What? No way!" Pernilla said heatedly. "I'm not letting you hog all the glory."

"No, it's…" Van shifted. "Paley. She might turn. Do you know what I'm saying?"

Horror flashed in Pernilla's eyes. She gave a grim nod.

"Kopius is in no shape to help… Brux doesn't have it in him. It will be on you. Do you have—"

Pernilla unsheathed her dagger. "I'll ritualize it so it can kill demons." Before Van could ask, she continued. "Uxa taught me."

Pernilla's haunted eyes and sloped shoulders belied her reaction to this recent development in their mission. Pernilla never thought she'd have to use her fighting skills against a teammate. Especially not a consecrated dagger.

Van had honed her warrior skills, becoming a thinking-acting machine. Yet she couldn't push away her sadness for the task that lay before Pernilla—to kill Paley after the illness turned their friend into a demon.

"You can go," Pernilla said. "I'll take care of… business here."

Brux stomped over to Van. "I'm going."

"And how's that going to work?" Van asked.

"We take Paley with us. We can't risk her turning near Daisy, not with my sister in this condition. I need to go with you."

He really cares about me.

"It will anger the Elementals if I don't carry out my duties as your assigned protector. Plus, I'm the leader of our team."

And there it is. His desire to accompany Van was about the mission. *Good.* It meant he was learning to become a fierce warrior.

Van considered his request. She knew from experience when the moment came, when training became a reality, things were much different. Pernilla might be unable to kill Paley. If she left all of them in the suite, the fate of all four—Brux, Daisy, Paley, and Kopius—would rest in Pernilla's ability to get the job done. It was too much of a risk.

"We all go," Van said. "Except Kopius and Daisy."

When Pernilla didn't put up a fight, Van knew she had made the right choice.

Satisfied, Brux draped Paley over his shoulder. Van slid Wiglaf into the front of her jacket, swaddling him against her belly like a baby. They bid farewell to Kopius, Daisy, and her critter following, although Daisy's condition still rendered her unconscious and she probably didn't hear.

Kopius remained hunched by Daisy's side. He didn't turn away from her as he mumbled, "Walk in light."

Van, Paley, Brux, Wiglaf, and Pernilla left the suite. Deep in Van's gut, she knew not all of them would return home.

CHAPTER 44

The waning crescent moon hung in the clear night sky, floating in an ocean of twinkling stars.

Van thought it looked like the universe's mouth. Mysteriously grinning. Aware of the deception and unforeseen perils among the mortals below. Yet keeping its secrets to itself.

It cast enough light for Van to see Ferox on the dock, impatiently pacing as he awaited their arrival. Like Van, he knew the stakes and time was running out.

Brux had Paley draped over his shoulder. "We'll need to keep an eye on her." He shifted her weight to emphasize his point.

Ferox led them up the walkway onto *The Obelus*.

Once on deck, Van held out her palm. "Let's use the Coin to find the best way to the Island of the Dead."

"We don't need the Coin to find the island or the Cup." A muscle flexed in Ferox's jaw. "We have enough to go on from Ezili's map."

"But you have the Coin with you, right?" Van asked, ready to sprint back to his room and grab it before their hasty departure.

Ferox patted his chest pocket. His teasing grin implied, if Van wanted it, she would have to get through him first. Or at least through his clothes.

Her cheeks flushed as her stomach did an exhilarated flip.

Ferox helped Brux carry Paley to a quiet cabin below deck. They laid her on a cot-like bed. She mumbled, semi-conscious.

Van peeked into her jacket at Wiglaf. Her bunfy hadn't moved since she had tucked him inside. She pulled him out. His body drooped in her grip and he felt warm to the touch. She gently placed him on the bed next to Paley. Again, he stretched his body along Paley's side, getting as close to her as possible, and settled in for a nap.

"Maybe he could use a break," Brux suggested.

"He has free will. If he wants to leave, he can," Van said, annoyed. His tone implied she didn't care about Wiglaf, and by extension—Paley, Daisy, and the Lodian people. It seemed she couldn't muster enough caring energy to please him.

Pernilla volunteered to resume her duty watching over Paley. She patted her hip where she hid the dagger. "I'll perform the consecration ritual right now."

Van accepted. She was too busy to concern herself with Paley or Wiglaf. She had two missions to complete and little time to do it.

Ferox directed Brux toward a different cabin; Van followed.

Brux crashed onto his bed, dark circles under his eyes. "I need to rest for a minute."

Brux didn't even wince when Ferox placed his hand on Van's back and whispered, "Now, to your quarters."

Ferox led Van to an expansive cabin that looked suspiciously like the captain's quarters.

"Wow." Van gaped. "This is nice."

Ferox wandered over to the small, four seat dining table secured to the floor with bolts. He glanced at the basket of crawfish and picked up the decanter. "Care for some rockwine?"

"Just water." Van grabbed the pitcher on the nightstand. Mostly as a distraction from Ferox being in her sleeping quarters. He emanated so much sensual energy, Van's hands trembled as she poured the water into a tin cup.

"Well." Ferox cleared his throat. "Good night."

He paused with his hand on the doorknob. "I'll be on deck keeping watch, in case you can't sleep." His invitation thickened the air as he slipped out, closing the door behind him.

Now how am I supposed to sleep? Van needed rest to strengthen her energy for the challenges she and her team would face. Who knew what horrors awaited them? If it was anything like when she retrieved the Coin, they were in for a rough time.

Van considered drinking some rockwine to help her sleep, but decided against it. She needed to be in top shape to get the Cup. First, she would save Daisy and Paley, which would please Ferox and Brux. Then she would use the Cup to mend the seal, which would protect her people.

Plagued by the tasks ahead, Van tossed and turned in her bed. The wonderful state of sleep eluded her, so she decided to get advice from Jacynthia on how to best deal with the Water Elemental guarding the Cup.

Van controlled her breathing, calmed her mind, and connected to her spirit guide. But when Jacynthia appeared, Van asked about a more pressing concern.

How can I get rid of this attraction I feel toward Ferox? It's getting in the way of my mission.

"You will not find your way out of danger and difficulty if you remain in an emotionless state of mind." Jacynthia floated in her mystical breeze, hovering several feet above the wooden floor. "When the soul is locked in the body, you are not internally free. You must confront your feelings and integrate them to be in accordance with the Creator."

But the more I feel, the greater the darkness rages inside me. I'm worried my damaged soul is leading me down the wrong path.

"Your soul can never be permanently diminished. It is part of the Creator. As such, it will return to the Creator after leaving the physical body."

If I fall for Ferox, Brux will think less of me. My people will think less of me. Ferox is Balish. He's the enemy.

"It is in accordance with the time to acknowledge not everyone is like you, and to accept other's differences."

The Lodian Consilium will never allow our relationship. The Elementals will retaliate like they did in Amaryl's time. But I fear the darkness inside me is pulling me toward Ferox. It's making me choose wrong. It's making me... evil.

"Everyone has light and dark inside themselves. You must strive to balance this duality within the Self and in all things. Know the dark part of the Self does not make you evil. Evil does not have power on its own. Refuse to feed negative thoughts as it makes them grow. Instead, commune with the positive eternal presence within."

How do I balance my darkness when I fear it?

"All fear is a lack of faith in the Self. Make peace with your dual nature by drawing on all energies available, the dark as well as the light. By embracing your shadow Self, you can be healed."

Van decided it was time to get down to business. *Is retrieving the Cup and healing my friends before mending the seal the correct path?*

Jacynthia paused.

Van wasn't sure if her spirit guide was done imparting her cryptic wisdom, or if she was thinking about what to divulge next.

"It is necessary for you to face the tests of the Water Elemental," Jacynthia said. "To retrieve the Cup of Life, so you can learn how to conquer the second plague of humanity. The Plague of Death."

Death? The word upset Van so much, she was surprised it didn't break her connection to Jacynthia.

"Death is the great letting go." Jacynthia remained serene. "It prepares the way for the new, for what is to come. Even if this acceptance of our new Self is painful, we cannot escape it. Do not attempt to avoid it or you will be doomed."

True to Jacynthia's nature, her answer gave no cheat notes.

"It is time for me to leave." Jacynthia faded. "Good night, my little warrior. Good luck."

Van fell into a disturbed sleep, aware time was running out for her to stay in the Living World without facing the Quasher. But she had to fulfill her mission for Daisy and Paley.

For her people.

For humanity.

CHAPTER 45

Van woke to find she had twisted the thin sheets on her cot-like bed and crunched them into a ball. Her pillow lay on the floor.

Unable to fall back to sleep, she thought about taking up Ferox on his offer for a midnight visit.

Van recalled Zurial's memory engram. Manik had told the princess if they healed wounds, they wouldn't have to fight. It made sense for Van to build her relationship with Ferox. Unlike what happened during the time of their ancestors, she and Ferox held the potential to heal the differences between their tribes.

Van had trouble holding onto the idea of Ferox as the enemy. He was younger than her by eight months, but she didn't consider Ferox a boy, more of a man of extraordinary power. His radiance attracted Van so much it scared her. She believed he genuinely cared for her, too. Yet, the depths of his feelings remained a mystery.

Van didn't want to be like her demimondaine step-mother, so she promised herself to keep her promiscuity under control. With this self-imposed restriction firmly in place, she allowed herself to get out of bed and go to Ferox.

Van found him standing on the bow, gazing across the dark,

moonlit sea. His strong shoulders and tapered waist silhouetted against the moonlight.

"Hey," Van said.

He twisted around. A pleased look spread across his face. "I'm glad you came."

"I couldn't sleep." She leaned against the bulwark next to him.

Neither spoke at first. They both gazed at the magnificence of the sea against the starlit night. Waves splashed noisily against the bow as the ship cut through the vast ocean. The cool mist of seawater brushed against Van's face.

Ferox leaned sideways, facing Van. "I see your spirit, Van. It looks familiar to me." He shifted closer. "Who are you?"

"Who *are* you?" Van's knee-jerk reaction embarrassed her.

"I want to know who *you* are." Warmth emanated from his eyes. "Truly." He placed his hand on hers.

Van cast her eyes downward, as if the worn wooden planks would offer her answers. Reaching deep inside, he forced her to admit, "I don't know."

Ferox placed his fingertips under Van's chin, lifting her face. His lips touched hers. Hesitant at first, then greedily.

She tilted her head back slightly and ran the tip of her tongue along his lips. He tasted salty from the sea air. She wondered if the skin on other parts of his body tasted the same.

Ferox's passion grew; his kiss deepened. This time, Van returned the hunger. Their lips and tongues locked in an epic battle for pleasure. Their bodies seamlessly melted against each other's.

A thought corrupted Van's bliss. She pushed him away. "We can't."

Ferox gazed into her eyes. "This again?" It was a throaty whisper.

Seductive enough for Van to want to throw her cares about saving her people and their friends overboard. For her concerns to sink into the depths of the dark blue sea, never to be seen again.

Her desire to engulf Ferox with her whole body and mind bubbled inside her soul. But she remembered the vow she had made before leaving her quarters. Van pushed her feelings down, hiding them below the surface, the same way the ocean conceals her many secrets.

"We're... different. Impossibly different."

Ferox settled back against the bulwark. His arms stretched along the grab rail. His manner patient. "So, let's talk about them. See if we can work something out."

Again, Van looked inside herself. An emptiness echoed back at her. She didn't know what to say or how to start this kind of conversation. "You go first."

"Okay. Let's see." He twisted his lips in thought, taking her request to heart. Obviously caring about the honesty and integrity of his answer.

"Well, us Bales worship the sun, sunlight, the day," Ferox said. "We believe the night is full of danger. Only evil things lurk at night."

"Like Lodians?" Van smirked. "We worship the moon, moonlight, and believe the sun worshippers are susceptible to falling into the shadows. Going bad because they don't know how to handle encounters with darkness."

"We believe in technology and science." Ferox continued with good-natured banter. "Come on. Let's get it all out."

Van grinned. "We believe in harnessing the energy of nature for power."

"There is only one power, an overcoming power. Survival of the fittest, smartest, and strongest. A single dominant principle, the strength of one. One family. One person who rules over the rest."

"There is only one power. Balance," Van said. "We don't exist individually. We're all interconnected and interdependent. Those who thrive are adaptive, inclusive, and loving."

Van recognized repartee as the best strategy for this kind of discussion. *Sensitive*. A way not to accuse, or try to put their own spin on each other's beliefs.

"When we come of age, those worthy become Sun Initiates," Ferox said. "They're trained to accomplish in our kingdom the same as what the sun accomplishes, giving life and warmth to all."

"When we come of age," Van said. "Some are moved into Advanced Studies, including Grigori training. Grigori vow to protect the weak and innocent from evil. That includes terrigens."

"Balish vow to protect our world from all enemies, including terrigens if need be. Especially if their energy generates too many demons for the Grigori to handle and they rise into our world."

Van flinched, expecting him to mention the second seal. He didn't. Although he knew, as well as Van, an increase in demon activity in the Earth World had cracked the seal, and it was the Grigori's responsibility to keep demons under control.

"We would do well to be rid of the terrigens," he said.

With that last comment, Ferox sounded a lot like his sister Solana. "The Lodians are your rivals, the only tribe with enough power to overtake the Balish kingdom," Van said, blowing their camaraderie. "You're using the terrigens as an excuse!"

She cringed over her own words. She had brought up *taking over his kingdom!* Was she trying to get thrown overboard? She inwardly sighed, resigned to her bad habit of acting like a compete idiot around him.

"Killing off terrigens would create an imbalance between the worlds," Van said, trying to smooth over her outburst. "The veil separating us from them would break down and cause Dishora, which translates to mean the end of time."

Ferox appeared unbothered. "We don't believe in Dishora. The *Sanctus Novus* warns of Solmor. A time when demons gain enough strength to gather and form armies in the Earth World. Then, they will rise into our world, alongside terrigens, to swallow the sun and bring darkness to all the lands. Meaning, they go after the royal family, my family."

"The Lodian's *Victus Opuseulus* says Dishora is a natural phenomenon that occurs when the two principles of good and evil rise and oppose one another. Whenever a new cycle of creation takes place, with it comes a battle for power. A great war. One of two things comes from this. Balance of one another, or an overcoming of one another."

"Who gets to decide what's good and what's evil?" Ferox shrugged. "It's subjective."

"Demons are evil."

"No doubt." Ferox shifted toward Van. "I'm trying to understand your beliefs, Van. They're important to me. But, I mean, come on. Lodians believe the Balish descended from the mud, same as terrigens?"

"From what I can tell, the terrigens and the Balish have a lot of similarities." Van expected him to get upset and dash away, putting an end to their fledgling relationship once and for all.

He didn't.

"All vichors are made from a piece of the Creator," Ferox said. "It means we all have the light of the Creator flowing through our veins. Terrigens were created from the mud. That's why they generate demons and why their world is dirty, violent, overpopulated, and diseased."

"So, we're back to hating on terrigens again," Van said edgily.

Their conversation had turned awkward. Van worried trying to understand and tolerate each other's differences might've propelled her people into a war with the Balish.

Still, she knew Ferox better now that they had shared their thoughts. She was unsure if she should be angry about his beliefs, but Van glared at him, anyway. Annoyed by her attraction to him, growing like a rising tide and just as inevitable.

Before she could decide what to do next, Ferox took the matter into his own hands.

"Don't be mad," he said in his smooth, deep voice, probably unaware of the confident curl to his lips.

He softly cupped Van's chin in his hands.

Her insides instantly turned into lovesick mush.

"I respect your right to believe anything you want, even if I can't understand it myself." His kisses landed lightly on Van's cheeks and neck.

Her anger washed out to sea. Van couldn't remember what had made her so upset.

Ferox gazed into Van's eyes. Little flecks of moonlight highlighted the tips on his cropped, brown hair. His soft breath brushed against her face.

"Let's not fight." He crushed her lips with his.

She wasn't sure if it was the romantic moonlit ocean, the heady sea air, their intimate conversation, or a combination of all three. But her body's response to his kiss filled Van with such overwhelming passion she gave in completely.

For about a minute.

Then she got a grip on her emotions and pulled back again, afraid.

Ferox, once more, patiently leaned back against the bulwark.

To Van, their differences seemed insurmountable. Confusion about their relationship caused a swirling sense of turmoil inside her. Then, a dominant thought rose to the surface.

Did their differences really matter that much?

Neither spoke for a moment.

Then, Ferox confessed, "I'm still grieving over my mother, brother, and sister's deaths."

It surprised Van as he took the conversation even deeper. She expected him to be insulted and angry for pulling away from him again.

"It's... I still can't believe they're gone. I'm struggling to do right by my people and my remaining family."

"Aren't they the same thing?"

"Not always." Ferox lowered his eyes. "I'm worried about the growing upheaval in my kingdom. As I mentioned before, the council will seek war with your people, to take over Salus Valde, including the portal and the Grigori's responsibilities, in the name of preventing Solmor." Ferox wrapped his arms around Van.

"Is that what you want?"

"I want what's best for all." He shifted his weight as if the conversation made him uncomfortable. "But sometimes what's right isn't so clear cut."

"Your council's beliefs have the power to set in motion a war between our tribes based on expectations and superstition." Van shuddered over the thought and sank deeper into his embrace.

"A war I'm not sure if I—or anyone—can stop." He hugged Van

tighter and whispered close to her ear. "But whoever wins can create a better world."

Ferox's optimism, his husky voice, and his warm body pressed against hers set off an unquenchable desire in Van for more of his touch. With great courage, she peered deep inside her Self. She acknowledged her feelings for both Brux and Ferox, but only one could hold a place in her heart. Ferox.

She no longer wanted him there so she could steal back the Coin or the fairy's tear. Having them wouldn't change anything. She would still want him to accompany her on the mission.

Her forbidden romance with her assigned protector, Brux, seemed in the distant past and was no longer an issue. Now, she faced a greater challenge. A romance with the enemy. But she and Ferox were two parts of a whole. Like darkness to light. Night to day. Good to evil.

Yet Van couldn't shake a nagging thought in the back of her mind. Once she retrieved the Cup of Life, would Ferox take it from her?

Van suspected Ferox knew she was Goustav's heir. Besides the spy in Lodestar feeding his family secrets, it clearly stated this in Manik's text. Something Ferox admitted to being well versed in. This made Van the true heir to the Balish kingdom and a threat to Ferox's throne. Giving him a solid motive for wanting Van dead.

She also wondered if Ferox would be a worthy ruler or if he would succumb to the call of darkness like his sister Solana. He would be especially susceptible to corruption by possessing two of the four Items of Creation. Misuse of those Items would poison his mind and send him running into the arms of darkness.

But Van had decided. Right or wrong. Good or bad.

She was willing to bet her life on Ferox.

CHAPTER 46

The earliest rays of sun peeked over the horizon, promising a bright dawn.

Van and Ferox disentangled their bodies and meandered down to the galley. Together, they made a breakfast of fruit and oatmeal. They ate in blissful solitude, enjoying each other's company. They talked about their school years. Their funny classmates, teachers who were mean to them, dumb things they did or didn't do.

Once finished, they went topside to check in with the captain.

"We're getting close," Captain Widsith shouted from behind the helm. "Steady as she goes."

The others woke and began trickling onto the deck.

The ship bobbed as it cut across the ocean. The masts creaked, and sails noisily flapped in the wind as they neared land.

They came to a narrow opening between two cylindrical stone structures. One on each side of two land masses stretching far into the horizon.

Van gaped in awe, craning her neck to see the top of the two towers as the ship glided between them. The whitish-gray stone tower to the ship's the left had striations as if a giant had stacked round, flat stones one on top of the other, reminding Van of a jenga game.

Ominous-looking black rock comprised the other tower. It had a glossy, melted appearance, as if lava had shot from the ground and solidified, forever reaching for the sky.

As the ship passed between the stone towers, the air cooled and the sea quieted in a calm-before-the-storm kind of way. The message sent by the towers rang loud and clear. Enter at your own risk.

Van rubbed her arms to ward off a chill that had nothing to do with the drop in temperature.

"All's well," cried the man in the crow's nest.

A raindrop hit the back of Van's hand. Little drops pitter-pattered on her hair and jacket. She dashed inside, went down the stairwell, and into Paley's cabin.

"How're they doing?" Van asked.

Pernilla twisted around and raised her gaze to Van. She looked pale and had dark circles under her eyes. She shook her head, letting Van know her friends had made no improvement.

Paley lay motionless on the cot-sized bed, tucked under the sheet with her top torso, arms, and head exposed, giving Van the impression of how Paley would look in a coffin.

Wiglaf rested next to Paley, his body also half-tucked under the sheets. The bunfy's ribcage rhythmically flowed up and down as he breathed. But Van didn't notice any respiration in Paley's chest.

"She's breathing, right?" Van placed a finger under Paley's nostrils to check for expiration of air.

"Barely," Pernilla said. "We have little time."

Van placed a gentle hand on Pernilla's shoulder. "We're almost at Insulam a Mortuis. We're all going to make it."

Pings echoed off the walls so loud it sounded like millions of thundering pellets hitting the ship.

"That's some bad rain." Pernilla rose from her chair as if ready to go out there and stop it.

They left Paley's cabin, walked up the narrow stairwell, and peered at the deck. The rain came down so hard it seemed like there was more water in the sky than in the sea.

Waves rocked the ship, reaching upward like giant wet fingers striving to climb aboard. Van and Pernilla crashed against the doorjamb.

"If this rain keeps up, it'll sink us," Pernilla shouted over the noisy storm.

"I'm going on deck to see if Ferox, or anyone, needs help," Van cried. "Go back to Paley." She crouched with her arms overhead and dashed into the rainstorm.

Pernilla followed.

"Tidal rains!" Ferox yelled through the thundering downpour; Brux and Thyra had joined him on deck.

"Sammy promised us smooth sailing!" Van said, saddened the selkie had betrayed them.

Strong waves rocked the ship. Salty seawater splashed on them.

"Rain not caused by selkie." Thyra held herself steady by gripping the taffrail.

"Just bad weather," Brux shouted through the downpour.

Van's drenched clothes clung to her body.

"We entered a marginal sea after passing the Towers of Good and Evil." Ferox gripped the base of the mast. "It's a division of the ocean, partially enclosed by islands."

"No predictable weather here," Thyra said.

The ship violently rocked as a wave crashed onto the deck, causing Van to slip. She tumbled, knocking into Pernilla, sending them both sprawling across the deck.

Van's tailbone crunched as she smashed down onto the hard planks. "Ouch."

Brux weaved his way over to her, slipping and sliding as he went. He grabbed Van around the waist, got her upright, and held her steady. He stretched his other arm for Pernilla, who struggled to stand on the slippery deck of the swaying ship.

"Get below!" Ferox grasped onto a nearby rope hanging from the mast. "All of you."

"What's that noise?" Pernilla coughed and spit rainwater.

"The turbulent weather is creating mini-tidal waves." Ferox looked grim. "Get below deck!"

"No." Van choked as seawater splashed into her mouth. The roiling of the ship made her stomach queasy. It felt like being trapped on an endless roller coaster ride. "We're staying here. We want to help."

Just when Van thought it couldn't get any worse, lightning streaked the sky, followed by an eardrum-busting thunderclap.

The rain pelted them, feeling more like small stones than water.

"Rain, now hail," Thyra yelled. "Condition getting worse."

"Get below!" Ferox ordered.

Golf ball-sized pieces of ice crashed onto the deck, smashed against the mast, and plummeted through the sails, causing holes that looked like little dots.

"Ow!" The ice-balls bruised Van's skin. One slammed into her head, she felt dizzy from the sheer force of its impact.

The ship rocked from another powerful wave. Seawater splashed onto the deck.

Pernilla gripped the taffrail. Brux struggled as he dragged Van toward the stairwell leading below deck.

Even if Van wanted to go back inside, between the slick wooden planks, the incoming ice-bombs, and the rough sea, there was no way she'd be able to get there. Brux wrapping his arms around her didn't help.

Lightning crackled across the sky; thunder boomed. The ship rocked again, slammed by another wave. It seemed the ocean wouldn't be satisfied until it pushed them all the way back to Cortica.

The downpour increased. Or was it water crashing on deck from the sea? Van couldn't tell.

"Scylla!" the crow's nest man shouted.

An unholy screech cut through the commotion.

Brux lost his footing and released Van. He tumbled and crashed against the ship's bulwark.

Van grabbed hold of the nearest stationary object, a round, knob-like protrusion used to wind excess rope. Once she got a firm grip, she turned her gaze toward the others' terrified stares.

Lightning lit the sky. Thunder boomed.

A naked woman rose from the sea.

The creature had pale, yellow skin and cascading coral-colored hair down to her belly button. Ten times the size of a human woman, the creature's lower half remained underwater. Her mouth opened to an unnaturally round O, and she belted out a hollow, demonic screech. As she flailed her arms above her head, her hair also lifted into the air and thrashed wildly.

Van thought she wet her pants from fright, but couldn't tell because the torrential rain and the seawater had already drenched her.

"Scylla!"

Cries of the sea monster's name rang through the wind, hail, and thunder. From the waist up, the monster looked like a human woman, but her lower body emerged, made of seaweed-looking tentacles.

At least ten tentacles broke the surface of the water and slithered through the air toward the ship. Their tips had protuberances that reached like fingers.

The tentacles grasped the bulwark with their sticky hand-like grip. The surface beneath its clutch dissolved away as if acid had been poured onto the wood. Another curled into a fist and smashed into the deck, causing an explosion of busted planks.

Scylla made their previous battle with the laocoon seem like a warm up act.

A seaweed-hand stretched and reached. It swooped down to nab Van. She let out a sharp, piercing cry as she ducked and rolled away from its grasp.

Wiglaf responded to her scream and appeared on the top railing of the outer bulwark, close to Van. His fur wasn't glowing white like usual. His ears flopped down the sides of his face. Already drenched from the rain, his tiny paws gripped the railing as the ship recklessly swayed. With a direct hit, the hail alone would kill him.

"Wigl—" Van tried to tell the bunfy to go back to his magical realm. When she opened her mouth, water sloshed into it. She choked and coughed up the salty sea. Hard, icy rain pummeled her as the ship dropped and rose again.

All around her the crew swung their cutlasses, axes, and swords to fight the reaching, gripping seaweed tentacles, while still getting pelted by the hail and soaked from the rain and the seawater.

Van stumbled as she reached for Wiglaf and crashed to the deck.

A tentacle missed clutching Van and nabbed the crewman fighting next to her. It wrapped around him and lifted him into the air by his waist. The monster's seaweed grip corroded his abdomen. He shrieked in pain as his blood splattered down onto the already soaked deck.

Her bunfy gripped the railing as the ship rocked. The deadly tentacles twisted and swirled around Wiglaf, darting with their acidic grip, dissolving more and more of the ship and snatching more crew members.

Van rose and took several steps. The ship lurched and sent her sprawling, away from Wiglaf.

With Van's limited visibility, she could only catch glimpses of Thyra, Brux, Pernilla, Ferox, and his soldiers as they battled the sea monster's tentacles alongside their shipmates.

Ferox gripped a rope to steady himself as he slashed and swiped his sword at a seaweed tentacle stretching its finger-like projections at him.

Brux dodged a tentacle-hand that clamped the bulwark inches from him. His movements lacked energy and Van knew the Twin Gemstones weakened him. She feared for his life as he slashed his sword and cut clean through the tentacle. Green liquid gushed onto the deck, burning holes through the wood planks. Some splattered onto Brux's arm. The monster's acidic blood ate through his jacket down to his skin. He yelped in pain and dropped his sword.

Pernilla moved into Van's view. She bent to grab a fallen crewman's blade but slipped across the roiling deck and slammed against the outer bulwark where Wiglaf clutched the railing.

The ship heaved to the side. Wiglaf's grip on the railing slipped. His tiny paws scrambled to keep him balanced.

"Wiglaf!" Van shouted to Pernilla.

The weakened bunfy couldn't keep hold. Wiglaf lost his grip and toppled over the side.

"No!" Van reached her arm, her hand grasped for Wiglaf, though she was nowhere near him.

Brux flew into view. He stretched over the side to catch Wiglaf. His hands came back empty.

A tentacle swooped down, Brux leaped out of the way and crashed against the bulwark, near where Pernilla crouched.

Thyra dashed over to help. The tentacle-hand twisted and wrapped its seaweed fingers around her waist, raising her high into the air. Her legs flailed for a moment before the corrosion ate away her body, splitting her in two. Thyra's lower half dropped onto the deck, a flood of her orange-colored blood mixed with the downpour of rain. Her head and upper body splashed into the sea.

A seaweed hand reached for the two targets cowering behind the bulwark. Pernilla and Brux stabbed at the tentacle, keeping it at bay. Each nick sent a drop of its green blood burning through whatever material it landed on, be it skin, metal, or wood. Van knew when droplets hit either Brux or Pernilla by their screams.

The tentacle turned and gripped the outer bulwark. Its acidic touch sunk into the wall, inch by inch, eating away the wood. The appendage dropped into the sea, leaving a gaping five-foot hole in the bulwark inches from Brux.

Scylla screeched again and continued to flail her arms and wild coral-colored hair.

Van wrapped her arms around a mast and braced for another tidal wave to hit the ship.

The boat raised several yards and then swooshed as it dropped back down.

Brux lay sprawled on his stomach. His feet pumped back and forth, trying to grip the slippery deck. His fingers curled and uncurled as he attempted to catch onto the slightest uneven plank on the deck.

In a sickening déjà vu, Van watched as Brux slipped over the side.

"Brux!" Pernilla rolled onto her stomach and reached through the jagged opening in the bulwark in time to clasp his hand.

A tentacle rose from the sea, water dripped from its seaweed-like fingers as it darted straight at Pernilla and Brux.

Sickened and terrified by the scene, Van tried to connect to her blood magic, but there was too much chaos. She needed to focus… she needed the *Coin*!

Van glimpsed Ferox stabbing his sword at a reaching, gripping tentacle with one hand and clutching onto the rope with his other hand. She released her clasp on the mast and carefully made her way to him.

Pernilla struggled to pull Brux back onto the deck. The blue-skinned pirate with the pointed face, along with several other crew-mates, stabbed and sliced the seaweed-like projections whirling above Brux and Pernilla, protecting the two of them.

Dripping acid spurted from the wounded tentacles as they thrashed in the air above. Cries rang out as the liquid burned into those below.

The ship rocked. Van lost her balance. She slipped and smashed onto the hard planks. She slid closer and closer to the opening in the bulwark, the same one where Pernilla grasped Brux. Van curled her fingers, trying to dig into the deck as she glided straight for them. If she crashed into them, all three would plummet over the side.

Her fingernails caught on an uneven wood plank, halting her slide. She crawled the rest of the way to Ferox, rolling once to avoid the crashing fist of a tentacle, all while getting bruised and battered by the hail and soaked from the rain and the seawater. She grabbed the rope next to Ferox and stood on shaky legs.

Pernilla slipped lower by the second as she struggled to keep her hold on Brux.

Deadly tentacles twisted all around.

"Give me the Coin." Van reached out her palm while clasping onto the rope with her other hand.

Ferox swiped his sword straight through an attacking tentacle. Its severed fist dropped onto the deck and began burning a hole through the wooden planks.

"This is a losing battle," Ferox yelled in a survival haze. "Every time we wound one, we hurt ourselves. The creature's blood is destroying our ship. We're going to sink."

Van wasn't sure if he knew who stood next to him.

"Ferox, the Coin," Van sputtered through a mouthful of rain. "I need the Coin!"

Through a lull in attacking tentacles, Van's words penetrated Ferox's attention. His gaze turned to her. "Van?"

He reached inside his chest pocket, pulled out a small satchel, and handed it to her.

Van wrapped her arm several times around the rope and fumbled with the satchel. Another tentacle stretched its reaching fingers to grab them. Van stayed behind Ferox as he jabbed and sliced the tentacle. They both struggled to maintain their balance as the ship rocked and rain and hail pelted them.

Lightening streaked across the sky, followed by a deafening thunderclap.

Pernilla had gotten Brux back on deck, but Van could see massive burns from the sea monster's blood on her back, shoulders, and arms.

Van pulled out the shiny gold object and held it in her palm. She expected the Coin to sink into her hand so she could use it as a weapon.

It didn't.

Van closed her fingers over it. "Show me the best way out of this mess." She hesitated to open her hand, afraid the ship would toss, and the Coin tumble into the sea, never to be seen again.

"Van!" Ferox hollered, his voice conveyed his exhaustion. "Use your power! *Hurry!*"

Van wound her arm more around the rope, ensuring a semi-stable grip and crouched into a fetal position to better hold her steady.

She opened her fingers. The Coin pointed to her.

"Oh, for the love of—" Van snapped her fist closed.

A tentacle met its target and wrapped its stretchy seaweed fingers around Pernilla's waist, raising her from the deck.

Brux reached up and clasped her hands in a sick reversal of fortune.

The tentacle's toxic grip ate away Pernilla's abdomen. Her feet flailed back and forth like she was running, trying to twist out from Scylla's grip. Blood dripped from her torso. She gripped Brux's hands, raising him into the air along with her. Then Pernilla's life faded, and she released her hold.

Brux plummeted. He bounced off the wooden planks of the deck as he landed. The ship lurched. He tumbled through the blown out bulwark and dropped into the sea.

The fingers tightened their grip on Pernilla, severing her body in two pieces. Her legs and lower torso splashed into the water. Her head and upper body thudded against the bulwark before slipping overboard.

Van scrunched her eyes closed and turned away.

Pernilla... *dead*. Pernilla. *Dead*. Van hyperventilated. Tears streaked her cheeks, mixing with the rain. But, Brux. He could still be alive.

Ferox cried out in pain.

Van's eyes shot open. Ferox's sword crashed down and skittered across the deck. A tentacle had nicked his arm. Thankfully, Scylla didn't get a full grip. Ferox's blood oozed into the cloth of his tan jacket.

Scylla screeched again.

Van gripped the rope, ready for a tidal wave to rock the ship.

Her eyes darted across the battle zone. Scylla's acid-blood had corroded huge chunks of the deck. Human blood stained the damaged, soaked wooden planks. Most of the crew were dead. Now Ferox stood defenseless, quickly unwinding his arm from the rope as the tentacle-hand returned to deliver its final blow.

Van was the last hope to save the ship and everyone who remained on it.

Do it!

She closed her eyes and concentrated on her mother's love and the strength of her ancestor, Amaryl. Her eyes tingled, turning phosphorescent violet, as she connected to the power of her ancestral Anchoress line.

Van opened her eyes, full of determination, strength, and hope.

Until Paley walked on deck.

On seeing her friend, Van lost the connection to her power.

Paley stared with black eyes. Her cheeks hollowed and her skin sallow. She looked like a living corpse. Died and come back to life.

In her hand, she held a lit stick of dynamite.

CHAPTER 47

The ship rocked, blasted by another wave caused by Scylla.

Van slammed against the mast. Her hand jolted, the Coin flew from her grasp. It twirled through the air as if in slow motion.

Paley lost her footing as she tossed the stick of dynamite. It soared upward toward the sky.

The Coin landed on the drenched, blood-soaked deck as the dynamite twirled through the air, rising higher as the ship dipped lower.

The violent movement of the ship hurled Ferox across the deck, out of range of the reaching seaweed-like hand, but closer to the plummeting stick of dynamite.

Van hastily uncurled the rope from around her arm, keeping her eye on the Coin.

She dashed forward. The ship shifted. She crashed to her hands and knees, got her bearings and scuttled toward the Coin. She stretched her arm, her fingers reached... so close... she almost had it...

Van heard Ferox shout, "Charybdis." But didn't know what he meant.

The dynamite landed and exploded.

The blast blew Van across the deck. She heard a crack in her back as she smashed against the bulkhead. Fragments of rope and sail, along with bits of wood, crashed down around her like rain.

The ship lurched again, but not in an up and down movement.

This time, the ship locked into a smooth, forward motion, hurtling round and round as if being flushed down a gigantic toilet.

Van slid toward the opening in the blown-out bulwark. She frantically scanned the deck where she last saw the Coin and caught sight of the shiny, gold disc gliding toward the opening a few feet in front of her.

The Coin slid over the side.

Unable to stop her momentum, Van slipped through the opening too and dropped headfirst into the sea.

She got caught up in the swirling water, but drowning wasn't her primary concern. The teeth were.

Many curved rows of pointed teeth, in a circle, conformed to the sides of the whirlpool.

I'm in the mouth of a sea monster!

Charybdis. The name Ferox had yelled. A warning that came too late.

Van tumbled, sprawled like a starfish, as she hurtled round and round in Charybdis's gaping circular jaw. Van realized the sea monster created the whirlpool to get travelers into its enormous mouth.

She choked on the water cascading into its throat like a massive waterfall and mercifully missed its pointed teeth as she dropped deeper into its mouth.

The light from the sky became edged out by darkness as Charybdis closed its mouth.

The watery environment enveloped Van, congealing enough to slow down her rapid descent. She breathed normally, though surrounded by gelatin-like, bluish-white water.

Her support ended. Van splashed into the sea, plummeting deep under the water. She waved her arms and kicked her legs, swimming upward, until she broke the surface and gasped for air.

She took in her surroundings. They made no sense. She expected to be in the monster's belly, deep under the Bottomless Sea. Instead, in front of her, she saw land.

She scanned the horizon. Aqua water surrounded her, so calm it appeared glass-like. A beautiful peach sunset was visible in the sky. *The Obelus,* nowhere in sight. The land stretched for miles on both sides.

Van swam to shore. She dragged her aching, exhausted body onto the beach.

She lay on her back, on the soft sand, panting. Without a doubt, Van believed she rested on the shore of Insulam a Mortuis. Charybdis's mouth, a passageway to the hidden island.

Her back ached from a rock wedged underneath her. Van leaned to her side and reached around to remove the hard object. She pulled it from the sandy ground. *A human skull!*

She chucked it aside, repulsed. Then noticed the entire beach was littered with human skeletal remains, and dead fish in various stages of decomposition. Confirming she had indeed washed ashore onto the Island of the Dead.

Van needed to venture into the creepy island and find Kharon the ferryman to take her across the River Shade.

The fairy's tear! Her anxiety escalated. Ferox had it. She didn't know where he was, or if he was even alive. She needed the tear to pay the ferryman.

Wait a minute.

She pulled out the satchel, hoping Ferox still had it stashed with the Coin. She held her breath and checked inside.

She turned the tiny sac, dumping its contents into her palm. Nothing came out. She shook the satchel, hoping against hope, and... out tumbled the fairy's tear.

Yes! She thanked the light, and Ferox for trusting her with both the Coin and the tear.

With work to do, Van leaped to her feet. She brushed off the beach sand from her butt and scanned the sinister woods encroaching on the island.

Fear twisted her gut.

The woods had the look of whoever entered, didn't leave. And the trees seemed to acknowledge her presence. The leafless branches, arms with claws, waved in the windless breeze. Like long, pointed fingers beckoning her to come and stay for a while, or forever.

The ominous sensation of dread weakened her resolve. Van shook it away by remembering what brought her there. The Cup of Life.

If anyone on *The Obelus* had survived Scylla's attack, they'd need the Cup's healing properties. Daisy and Paley, too. Both of their lives hung in the balance, along with all those who were sick from the demon illness.

Van snorted, disgusted with herself for being afraid. *Fear*. A useless emotion, even for a junior warrior. Jacynthia had told her fear was a lack of faith in your Self.

Pfft. *I got this.*

She needed to keep moving. Once Van completed this part of her mission, she still needed to find the second seal, and time was running out.

First, the ferryman. Van shook away her jitters. Focused on her inner Self, trusted in her power, and stepped forward.

No path led through the trees, so Van aimlessly meandered through the woods. She hoped the island was small enough for her to stumble across the River Shade.

The temperature dropped, chilling Van to the degree where she could see her breath. Now and then she passed aged bones partly covered by dirt and protruding from the ground. She told herself they were animal bones, which was still bad, but she needed to divert her anxiety about walking alone through the dark woods on the Island of the Dead.

CHAPTER 48

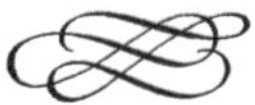

Van's eye caught a small, round, flesh-colored object lying on the ground ahead. It stood out among leaves and dirt and seemed out of place in the woods. Curious, she bent down and picked it up.

Ugh! A baby doll's head!

Someone had poked its eyes out, and it had no hair. The doll's body was nowhere around. The head was lying on the ground, not covered with dirt and leaves, giving Van the impression someone had recently placed it there. Some nutjob was running around the island decapitating baby dolls.

She chucked the head aside and shuddered, wishing she had the Coin to lead her in the best direction.

Aware someone else was in the woods with her, Van moved forward with her nerves on edge. The sky darkened, making the woods shadowy and even creepier.

Droplets of rain pitter-pattered down on her hair and jacket. She dreaded another downpour. Van used her fingertips to wipe the droplets from her eyes and cheeks. When she pulled back her hand, her fingers were smeared with a bright red fluid. Not rain, *blood*!

She looked up. A half-eaten chimpanzee dangled from a tree

branch by its feet. Its entrails hung downward, dripping with blood. A fresh kill.

Aargh! Van sprinted. Her heart pounded against her chest. She wanted to get as far away as possible from the chimp's blood rain. Whoever did that to the chimp might be nearby, lurking behind the trees. Probably the same person, or creature, who gets off decapitating baby dolls.

She raced through the woods into a clearing. She stopped short at the sight before her. A group of people dressed in animal costumes sat in a circle on folding chairs playing poker with tarot cards, using a cut-off tree stump as a table. Or were they animals that looked like people?

The disturbing creatures halted their game. Every one of them turned and stared at Van.

She gasped. The hair on the back of her neck stood on end. Van twirled around and dashed back into the woods the way she came.

Her arm struck something. It yanked her backward, forcing her to stop. A low hanging vine had tangled around her elbow. She struggled to break free, but became more entangled. The harder she tried to undo herself, the more vine wrapped around her. Now it encased her body and crept upward toward her neck.

The animal people were coming any minute. Terror made Van wriggle enough to grip the vine. She pulled and wrenched, rushing to rip her way free. Except it wasn't a vine. It was a hangman's rope!

Van screeched in horror. She twisted and tugged at the rope. It coiled around her body even tighter, as it snaked around her neck.

The jackknife Brux had given her! Van maneuvered her hand into her jacket pocket and pulled it out. She hacked at the ropes, frantically sawing. The ropes loosened. Finally, she broke free, tore the noose from around her neck, and sped away.

She aimlessly dashed through the woods. Branches whipped against her face and snapped against her body. She didn't care.

Van came upon the clearing again, except this time the animals playing poker weren't there. Just the stump, the tarot cards, and five empty folding chairs. *Where are the animal-people?*

Van bit the back of her knuckles to stifle her scream. Instead of going back the way she had come, she dashed across the clearing and into the woods beyond.

The stars and moon in the night sky offered dim lighting, making it difficult to see. Van slowed her pace and still smashed into a tree trunk.

Her nose and mouth hit a sharp nub on the tree. She stepped back, rubbing her stinging face.

The nub wasn't part of a broken tree branch, as she had thought. Nailed to the tree was a human thumb!

Ugh! Van's feet hit the dirt as she raced away in a panic. She ran until she became so winded she had to stop and catch her breath. She thought of the thumb. A weird image crossed her mind of a bodiless hitchhiker, thumb out, pointing to the desired destination.

Van gathered her courage and went back toward the bodiless thumb. She peered at it and followed the direction in which it pointed. Soon, she heard the rushing water of a river. She stepped out of the woods onto a riverbed. She had arrived at the River Shade.

She walked to the river's edge. Fog covered the river, so Van couldn't determine its width. Her boot brushed against a weathered piece of wood. She bent down and saw writing carved into it. She picked it up. Someone wrote the inscription in Latin, a language in which Van was fluent.

In flumine et puellae iacet. Mortuus oculos conspiciunt hyacinthino pallio. Et aqua fluit sanguine eius ruber est.

"In the river lies a girl. Dead violet eyes stare. The water flows red with her blood."

The inscription sent shivers up her spine. Scowling, Van flung away the morbid carving. She was done being frightened. She was the Anchoress. A warrior of the light. She breathed deeply, ready to face Kharon the ferryman and get on with the mission.

Where is he?

The repetitive swishing of water caused by an oar rolled through the fog.

The ferryman appeared.

A single lantern hung from a pole on the bow, casting a dim light. Kharon stood in the back of the rowboat. Hands, nothing but bones, grasped a single oar. His skull face stared from its black hooded cloak. The only sounds in the quiet woods were the swoosh, swoosh, swoosh of Kharon's paddle as he steadily rowed closer to shore.

The bow of rowboat arrived directly in front of her. One skeletal hand gripped the oar. He extended the other toward Van. Each phalange opened, one by one, exposing his bony palm.

Terrified and wondering what this personification of death wanted from her, Van didn't dare move. Then her brain snapped into gear and she dug into her pocket, eager to retrieve the satchel. She waded into the knee-deep water, next to the rowboat, and placed the fairy's tear into Kharon's bony palm.

One at a time, each of his bony fingers curled closed around the tear. He retracted his hand into the wide cuff of his cloak. Then it reappeared as he extended his arm and pointed a finger to the single bench in the rowboat.

The boat swayed under Van's weight as she climbed aboard. She gripped the sides of the rowboat to hold steady, but it was unnecessary. The foggy ride across the River Shade was as smooth and unperturbed as Kharon's demeanor.

The rowboat came to a stop at the opposite riverbed. Kharon turned his frightening skull face toward Van. His permissive nod wasn't necessary for her to leave the rowboat. She leaped out the second he turned his hollowed eye-sockets at her.

Van's shaky legs surprised her. Kharon had unnerved her more than she cared to admit.

In front of her, partly hidden by the fog, she glimpsed a path.

She cautiously followed the winding dirt trail deeper into the flourishing woods. Unlike the dead, leafless trees she had passed through earlier, green vegetation covered the branches. Ferns, vines, and other foliage.

Van stayed on the main path, avoiding its many branching trails, until she passed a swampy area and heard the splashing of something in distress. She veered off the main path and trekked in the commotion's direction.

Van recoiled seeing a young alligator tangled in vines, thinking of it as another sea monster. She considered leaving, but it was young, not more than a baby, and in distress. It wasn't fair to let the poor animal pay for the laocoon and Scylla's sins.

She skimmed her way around the edge of the swamp. Her feet sank into the mud up to her ankles. She mumbled baby talk to calm the alligator. The closer she got, the more the young gator wriggled and snapped, trying to escape the vines, and Van.

The alligator's mouth, not entirely ensnared, had enough leeway to bite. Van paused and again considered turning away. She sighed. Since she had come across the young alligator, her gut told her it was her responsibility to do something about it.

She bent down, careful to keep away from its snapping snout, and used both her hands to break away the vines. She tore each one, stopping occasionally to avoid getting bitten. The squirming gator soaked Van with stinky swamp water. Mud permeated her boots down to the skin of her ankles and feet. Finally, she broke the last vine and set the young alligator free.

It stopped struggling, but didn't leave.

Van perused the gator. It had no injuries. She pulled her foot out of the muck and took a step back, monitoring the gator, while wondering what was wrong with it.

The alligator waddled out of the swamp and onto the mud, right up to Van's feet. She didn't flinch, eager to know what it wanted.

The gator opened its mouth and uncurled its pink tongue. At the tip lay the Coin of Creation.

Van gasped with joy. *The Coin!* She swooped down and seized it before the alligator changed its mind.

The gator closed its jaw and shuffled back into the swamp, disappearing under the murky water.

Van held the Coin between her thumb and forefinger, inspecting the shiny gold object to make sure it wasn't a fake.

It wasn't.

Studying it was unnecessary. Van's connection to the Coin vibrated in her blood. She tucked it into her pocket and continued down the main path again.

She paused. *I have the Coin.*

The young alligator had given Van the Coin for a reason, especially since she thought she had lost it at sea. Van pulled it from her pocket and asked it to show her the best path to the Cup of Life.

Van followed the twisting path, taking direction from the Coin until she reached a beautiful blue lagoon. It didn't surprise her when a divine voice addressed her.

"Vanessa Cross," said a woman sitting on a decorated throne carved from the cliff surrounding the lagoon. "I have been expecting your arrival." Though she sat some distance away, her voice carried clear across the water.

"I am Thalassa, the Water Elemental. The Guardian of the Cup of Life," she said in a not-so-friendly tone. "I heard you coming from miles away. Smashing through my habitat like a clumsy oaf. Intruding into my peaceful state of meditation."

The Elemental rose from her throne and stepped onto the multicolored pebbles that had washed ashore by her feet.

Thalassa peered at Van with pursed lips. "Are you ready to die?"

CHAPTER 49

Van became acutely aware she wouldn't get along with this high and mighty Water Elemental.

She strode along the curved shore, getting closer to Thalassa, half-expecting a monster to leap out of the lagoon. "I'm not going anywhere." Van had a lot to live for. She resented Thalassa for even suggesting it was her time to die.

The Elemental observed Van, unmoving, except for her shoulder-length, dirty-blond hair that undulated as if she were underwater. Thalassa wore her gold crown just so and had adorned her silver robes with intricate detailing made from actual coral.

"If you wish to retrieve the Cup, you must pass my test," Thalassa said, implying it was impossible.

The Elemental's overlarge sea-blue eyes, with hardly any sclera, didn't blink. She possessed beauty, but in a nontraditional way.

Thalassa stood in front of her remarkable throne. Sculpted into the chair were detailed images of fish and sea nymphs with a large scallop shell for the backrest. The throne's arms ended in conch shells. On the cliff surrounding the lagoon, hundreds of colorful wooden masks hung neatly. All different in shape, size, and design.

The entire scene gave Van the impression this Elemental was finicky and difficult. Nothing like Lady Loka, the Guardian of the Coin, who was warm and friendly by comparison.

The Elemental extended her arm, palm up. An archway appeared in the side of the cliff. Thalassa stood silently as she waited for Van to catch on and walk through it.

Van readied herself for the Elemental's test and strode through the archway. The stone rumbled as the opening closed behind her.

She entered a cavern that took her breath away in its magnificence. Six-petaled lotus flowers, some white, others light blue, and some a mixture of both, dotted the walls of the cavern. A handful of thin waterfalls cascaded onto rocks. However, in the collection pond, she witnessed an odd sight. A bunch of naked children playing.

They splashed each other, giggled, and climbed on the low lying rocks. Some swam. None noticed Van's arrival.

Van didn't know what to do. *Is a monster going to eat the children?* She mentally prepared herself for battle, to protect these children, who, quite frankly, she found creepy.

A boy about six years old appeared in front of Van. "You're creepy."

She hadn't seen him until he spoke, yet he stood directly in front of her.

The boy giggled and rushed back into the pond with the other children.

Van surveyed her surroundings. Solid rock enclosed her, trapping her in another fun house, this time filled with weird children.

"You're a weird adult," said a blonde girl about the age of seven, who suddenly appeared near Van. The girl didn't laugh or run back to the collection pond like the boy had. She stared at Van, unblinking.

The girl unnerved her. *Why won't she leave?*

"Shoo!" Van stomped her foot, hoping to scare the girl away.

The girl lurched forward in exactly the same way as Van, and said, "Shoo!"

Confused, and a bit frightened, Van took a few steps backward.

The girl mimicked Van, also taking a few steps back.

Van gazed at the child quizzically.

The girl raised her fingers to her mouth, coyly covering her giggle, and then darted back to join the other children playing in the pond.

Van noticed all the kids had alabaster skin, blond hair, and blue eyes. Like they were clones of each other, although some were girls, some boys, and they were different ages. But all of them seemed to be made from the same genetic makeup.

How is this a test?

Then Van saw it.

A chalice. Shining gold with intricate motifs, encrusted with gemstones of amethyst, orange, and red. Two entwined winged Elementals, perhaps angels, comprised the stem. Their wings wrapped around the base of the bowl.

The Cup of Life rested on a stone pedestal inside a fissure in the cliff between two of the waterfalls. To get it, Van had to cross the collection pond and the eerie children.

She stepped closer to the pond. The children continued playing, paying her no mind. Every step she took, the Cup moved deeper into the fissure, remaining an equal distance from Van.

How can I reach it if it moves farther away with each step?

A handful of children scuttled out of the pond and dashed over to Van. They extended their hands and asked her to dance with them.

Two children each clasped one of Van's hands. Upbeat flute music filled the cavern, coming from nowhere. The surrounding children began dancing, others continued playing in the water. The two holding her hands tugged as they swung their bodies in time to the music, encouraging Van to do the same.

Van wriggled her hands, trying to free herself. Her eye held steady on the Cup. The children clutched harder and insisted she stay and dance. Van complied, figuring it was the best way to get rid of them. She swayed her hips and smiled, using the moves taught to her by Madame Vang.

"See, I'm dancing," she said to the children. *Now, go away.*

Van danced strategically, moving closer to the edge of the pond across from the fissure. In doing so, she found she was enjoying herself and the smiling, giggling children. The music completely captivated Van. She couldn't help but lose herself in it. She grinned and chuckled along with her dance partners.

Out of ingrained determination to complete her mission, her eyes darted to the Cup. It stayed still.

She picked up the groove and moved to the edge of the pond, surprised her dancing held the Cup stationary.

Out of the corner of her eye, Van glimpsed a girl, about four years old, climbing the rocks near a waterfall. The girl jerked and screeched as her ankle jammed between two rocks.

The other children laughed and pointed at her. Some splashed the girl. Van's dancing children plunged back into the pond and gleefully joined in on the bullying.

Tears streaked down the little girl's cheeks. "C-cut it out!" She choked and coughed on the water the other children splashed on her.

While the children were preoccupied with harassing the little girl, Van noticed the Cup remained stationary. She glanced at the girl being bullied, then at the Cup.

She'll be okay.

Confident the other kids were teasing the girl, not trying to kill her, Van stepped into the pond, boots and all. She waded to the far side toward the fissure and the Cup.

The trapped girl's distress escalated. "S-stop," she sputtered while spitting out mouthfuls of water.

This encouraged the other kids to increase the amount of water they splashed on her. A couple of boys climbed higher on the rocks than the stuck girl and used their bodies to redirect the nearby waterfall to wash directly on top of her. Drowning her.

Van stared at the Cup, only about twenty feet from her grasp. Then looked at the little girl. No doubt the girl needed help.

But, if Van got the Cup, she could use it to heal the girl if the other kids injured her.

Unless they drowned her.

Van already knew the Cup couldn't raise children, or anyone, from the dead. She sighed and waded over to the group of kids.

"Hey! Knock it off." Van physically hurtled one of them aside, sending him splashing into the shallow pond water. She climbed onto the rocks and made her way to the little girl.

The children in the pond stopped splashing and silently watched.

Van raised her eyes to the two boys, redirecting the waterfall. "Knock it off! Don't make me come up there."

The boys stopped.

As Van bent down to look at the girl's ankle, the girl squirmed and clawed at the rocks trying to get away from Van.

Startled, Van pulled back. "I'm here to help."

The girl calmed.

Van wrapped her hands around the girl's dead-cold ankle.

The child said, "I want to help."

The girl's words puzzled Van as she effortlessly released the child's ankle from the wedge. To Van's surprise, it wasn't stuck at all, and there were no signs of injury.

The girl's daunting blue eyes stared at Van, unblinking.

The other kids held still and quiet, their eyes focused on Van.

The girl extended her arm in the same mannerism as Thalassa, showing Van the fissure between the waterfalls.

Van didn't know what was going on, but the Cup remained on the rock pedestal. Except this time, it was closer to the entrance of the fissure.

The children turned and walked away as if the end-of-shift bell had rung and their workday ended. They vanished into the rock walls, leaving Van alone in the cavern.

With the Cup so close, Van didn't waste time trying to figure out what had just happened. She descended the rocks, cautiously made her way across the pond, and climbed the rocky edge to the fissure.

Weirdest test ever.

With every step behind the waterfall, the mist sprayed Van's face and her waterlogged boots grew heavier. She made it to the fissure. The Cup was not more than six feet away.

She slipped into the narrow opening. In a blink, the scenery changed.

Van had entered an enormous circular area, though still enclosed by stone. The fissure behind her rumbled closed, trapping Van in another cavern.

Spread before her were concentric pathways level to the ground, alternating between rivers and grassy land. A circular labyrinth. Not created by nature, but by Thalassa's magic. The Elemental had designed the landscape around a pedestal holding a centerpiece. The Cup.

The annular rivers were too wide for Van to leap over, preventing her from reaching the grassy land pathways by hopping from one piece of land to another. Her unpleasant encounters with sea monsters made her unwilling to swim across the rivers and risk encountering more creatures lurking beneath the water's surface.

The concentric rings weren't continuous. They were broken in certain places like a massive maze. To reach the center, Van had to navigate through a series of land pathways.

She sprinted toward the nearest entrance of the labyrinth and raced down the grassy pathway. When it connected to the inner land ring next to it, she turned and quickly made her way down that strip.

A river blocked Van's path as she reached a crossing. She turned around and headed back, keeping an eye on the Cup in the maze's center.

After many fruitless attempts to reach the Cup, she noticed the maze's center kept changing positions. If she moved to the left, the Cup moved to the right, and vice versa.

She had reached the inner rings, yet had gotten no closer to her goal as more and more rings kept appearing between her and the Cup.

The water in the rivers grew rough as Van became more frustrated. She tried to plot a course but couldn't grasp the complicated overall structure of the maze.

Van dashed away, but had to change course abruptly. She ran again and stopped to change direction. Then again, and again.

Every time she discovered a pathway and reached another inner ring, the Cup moved farther away. She cried out in exasperation.

The river's water became more disturbed. The waves surged up and down, becoming as tall as Van. Water sloshed onto the grassy path, drenching her already soaked boots.

The Cup appeared and disappeared from view as the wave's peaks rolled up and down. Van found herself just as far away as when she first entered the outer ring.

"I'm sick of this!" Van reached into her pocket and pulled out the Coin.

It's not cheating, she said to herself, hoping to shake the nagging feeling the truth was the opposite.

She protected the Coin from the splashing water and asked it to show her the best path to reach the center of the maze.

The Coin pointed. Van dashed away.

Her feet lost their footing as the ground vanished. It happened so fast, Van's legs continued running as she plummeted.

Her stomach churned with unease as she fell endlessly into a dark abyss.

Did the Coin betray me?

Her panicked brain recalled Jacynthia's guidance, urging her not to seek an easy way out of her problems.

"Do not act out of a desire to escape the circumstances or you will fall into an abysmal pit," Jacynthia had said.

More words came rushing back to Van, but they weren't Jacynthia's. *"An abyss cannot be filled to overflowing."* Who said them? She couldn't remember.

No matter. Van had an idea.

To save herself, she needed to get in touch with the base of her power. Her feelings.

She had accepted her right to *have* power last year. Now, she acknowledged her right to *feel* her power. She was born with the ability to reconnect with the force that made her. The Creator's infinite power.

What does the Creator do? Create.

Although she continued to grip the Coin, she focused instead on her blood magic. Not an easy task while descending through bottomless darkness.

I call on my infinite power, passed down to me by my ancestors, given to me by the Creator, to fill this abyss to overflowing.

A massive amount of water rushed upward. Van plummeted into it, slowing her descent.

Van found herself submerged underwater, her oxygen running out.

Jacynthia had told her the Creator detached a piece of Itself and made a place for Van's existence in the worlds. To survive, Van needed to reclaim this space, to be fully present in her body so she could connect the physical and spiritual parts of her Self. She reached deep inside, to her inner light, and felt the power of her Anchoress magic as it coursed through her veins.

In her head, she said her own version of the protective mantra she had learned in school. *This is my space, given to me by the Creator. I have the right to feel my power. Nothing shall enter my space unless it is for my highest good. Nothing can harm me. I will it so, and so it is.*

An invisible protective sphere encircled Van, preventing her from drowning and giving her much needed oxygen.

Van floated upward, safe in her bubble. She tucked the Coin into her pocket.

The sphere broke the surface and disappeared, causing her to flail her arms and kick her legs to keep afloat.

Once she became oriented, Van realized she was in one of the concentric rivers surrounding the Cup. The water in the rings had calmed and now only rippled.

Van continued to feel the connection to her power—to the Creator—and did not fear it. She trusted it.

"You can never manifest anything without feeling." Jacynthia's words filled her head.

With every emotional fiber of her being, and without using the Coin, Van declared her desire for the fastest route to the Cup. "I need a bridge."

A wooden bridge appeared, rolling out plank by plank over the surface of the rivers and the grassy pathways from Van to the center of the maze. Just as she had pictured it in her mind.

She swam to the bridge and hauled herself out of the river. Confident and trusting of her creation, Van rushed across the planks without caution, keeping a steady eye on her goal.

She reached the pedestal. Without waiting to catch her breath, she snatched the Cup.

Overwhelmed by waves of dizziness, Van's vision blurred...

CHAPTER 50

Van lay in Zurial's bed. Sandstone walls and pillars adorned her bedroom in Balefire Palace. Pain throbbed in her pelvic area as blood gushed between her legs onto the bedsheets.

"Queen Zurial, you delivered early." The midwife was the only person in the room with her.

Zurial knew the baby wasn't early. She'd been two months pregnant when she married Manik. The midwife, aware of this, was simply playing along with the official word.

"This is why you are bleeding so much." The midwife's pinched face pulled even tighter.

With dread, Zurial realized one of Goustav's followers had delivered her baby. "Where is Mehal?"

The midwife turned her back to Zurial, fussing with the dirty linens. "Safe."

Zurial tried to sit up, but was too feeble from blood loss. She could barely lift her hand, never mind her body. "Enough with the pretense. Where is my baby?"

"Fine." The midwife twisted around. "We know you are poisoning the water supply. Twisting the minds of every person who takes but a drink in Aduro."

"Not poisoning." Zurial lay helpless on the bed. "Healing."

"You are not healing." The midwife snarled, full of anger. "Forcing unwitting people to drink your spell!" She waved a fist in the air to emphasize the horror of Zurial's action.

"I... I—" Zurial gathered all her energy to speak. "I did it for peace. To placate the opposers. To stop Goustav's rebellion."

"Nothing could stop his rebellion!"

"I did it for the good of our people."

The midwife snorted. "You will never be our people."

"I wanted to spread the love I shared with Manik. He and I made our kingdom better."

"Everyone knows you used magic to put a love spell on King Manik! You are too different. Your beliefs are too strange. Our tribes will never get along."

"Accepting others' differences is a form of healing," Zurial muttered. The room spun.

"The Cup should only be used to combat true evil," the midwife said. "Not for your personal gain."

"If our tribes healed their emotional differences, we could live in peace. Vichors could love terrigens. Balish could love Lodians. We could pray to both the moon and the sun. Some could worship the Balish king, others the Creator. Together we would balance, like everything in nature."

"No good comes from casting spells. Only evil." The midwife bent close to Zurial's ear, making sure the queen heard every word. "I know the folklore. I know what happens when you misuse an Item of Creation. Your soul becomes darkened by its power."

"I should have returned the Cup to the Elementals after the war ended when the truce was in place. But—"

"You were selfish." The midwife curled her lip in disgust at Zurial. "Always wanting more. Pushing your agenda onto those who opposed your very existence. Using your authority, your spells. Taking away our power!" She beat her fist into her chest. "Incorrect use! The healer turns to hurting!"

She saw the midwife's point-of-view. Zurial's overuse of the powers of the Cup had turned into a gluttonous obsession and had corrupted her soul.

The midwife tensed as the queen raised her trembling hand.

Zurial reached for the Cup on her nightstand, hoping to heal herself. Her hand dropped onto the bed, too weak to grasp the Item. The consequences of her misuse of the Cup resulted in the ultimate irony. The healer could not heal herself.

"It will not be long now." The midwife looked relieved.

Zurial knew she meant the rebellion and Zurial's death. Even if the Cup had healed Zurial, the midwife would have made sure the rebels slaughtered her.

Screaming and banging of furniture carried to Zurial's ears. Through the walls of the bedroom, she heard swords clanking, running feet, and slamming doors.

The midwife smirked. She turned and fled from the room.

Zurial's blood continued to stream from the place between her legs, and she grew tranquil.

Her life faded, and yet she did not fear death.

Images of Manik, baby Mehal, Amaryl, Zurial's parents, King Halldor and Queen Cordelia, streamed through Zurial's thoughts, along with the love Zurial felt for them. But she did not connect to this love in physical form. She connected to it in eternal form, through the Creator.

She found comfort in the few remaining seconds of her life, knowing the love she shared with Manik would live on through Mehal. The mother tree where they met would stand long after everyone they knew had died. And her sister, Amaryl, would pass the Anchoress magic onto her first-born girl, continuing the protective bloodline.

"My love for Manik is not wrong," Zurial muttered to herself. "I have a right to feel the way I feel. A right to act on what is in my heart, despite opposition from other people."

And Zurial had a right to be sad her life was slipping away...

ZURIAL RELEASED Van from her vision.

Van regained consciousness. The maze of concentric rivers and grassy pathways had disappeared. She was back in the lagoon, sprawled on the beach near Thalassa's feet.

She assumed it was Thalassa. The Water Elemental stood in front of her grand throne. She wore the same crown, but differed in overall appearance. Her eyes had changed to the color of mist over the sea. Her hair, a blue and white ombre, cascaded down to her waist. A glorious dress made entirely of seashells had replaced her robe.

Van rose, holding the Cup in one hand and brushing the sand off her damp clothes with the other. She faced Thalassa, relieved she had passed the Elemental's test, which seemed pretty easy compared to what she had gone through to get the Coin.

"You completed the Walk of Faith and have retrieved the Cup," Thalassa said with no fanfare.

Van waited, expecting more commentary.

"You arrived here estranged from your own truth," Thalassa continued. "The concentric philter cut through the weeds of falseness and fear. When doubt exists at the heart level, when you are unsure of what you feel, mistakes will be made in the direction you take. Feeling is an important step in fully connecting to your power."

Van thought of herself back in Uxa's office before she went on this mission. She couldn't believe how much she had grown since then. The emotional numbness she felt at the beginning of her journey had blocked her power, cutting off her connection to the Creator.

"You trusted in your Self to create what you needed to pass the test of the concentric philter by tapping into the infinite abundance of the divine force. If one lives in connection with their higher Self through trust and faith, true creativity is effortless."

Van beamed. Proud of Thalassa's confirmation she had manifested the water in the abyss, and the bridge. "And the kids? What kind of test was that?"

"Reclaiming your right to feel is only one part of your empowerment. Emotions must be expressed correctly to aid in the will of the Creator."

"Correctly?" Van didn't have any agenda when she encountered the children, other than to retrieve the Cup.

"True expression of the Self enables you to convey your feelings, but you must have consideration for others. To look at them with love and compassion," Thalassa said. "Those who will tell any lie to avoid hurting others do not walk in accordance with the Creator. Same as those who tell the truth about how they think and feel, blurting their perception without consideration of the pain they might cause to others. To reach a balance, one must be truthful about their feelings while remaining aware of how the recipient will respond. This is an important lesson regarding relationships. What you give is what you get back."

The Elemental's words prompted Van to ask, "Will the Cup cure those infected with the demon illness?"

"All healing is Self healing through our connection to the divine source. By accepting the Creator has already provided for healing even before the illness has taken hold, you can either eliminate the sickness before it manifests or heal the part of the Self that incurred the sickness. Healing the physical illness in the body and healing the inner darkness of the soul are the same. Reach toward the soul, and the body will be healed."

Van had heard something similar from Jacynthia.

"Healing inner darkness?" Van thought of her damaged soul. Then of the last time she saw Paley, crazed and demonic, and hoped her friend was still alive. "So I can use the power of the Cup to heal those who have turned into a demon?"

Thalassa half-nodded, causing Van's stomach to churn with dread thinking maybe this wasn't so.

"Anyone who drinks from the Cup will connect to the divine source, and their physical body can, therefore, heal from the demon illness. However, once a person expels a demon from their body, their soul remains damaged. The essence of its evil lingers. A never-ending compulsion tempts them to worship darkness. Dancing with darkness of any kind leaves a permanent mark. To heal the soul, one must use their own connection to the divine source."

Van gulped. She had personal experience with this dance.

She had glimpsed the mark in Solana. A dark thread wrapped so tightly there was no redemption for the Balish princess. When Van had misused the Coin to kill Solana, she had given rise to the dark part of her Self. The darkness inside Van always struggled to rise. To take her power and consume her soul, same as it had done to Solana.

Van wanted to heal this darkness inside her Self but had feared facing it.

By regaining her ability to feel, Van proved herself worthy of the Elemental's test and demonstrated her belief in her own power to overcome this darkness.

She wondered why Thalassa didn't leave now that her duty of protecting the Cup had ended. Why didn't she float away like Lady Loka did after Van had retrieved the Coin of Creation?

A heavy pause large enough to fill the cavern hung in the balance.

Finally, Thalassa spoke. "I am not satisfied you have learned my lesson."

"What? Why? I got the Cup." Van raised the Item as if Thalassa needed reassurance Van had indeed passed her test and learned her lesson.

"The Coin was also a test. To see if you would choose to use it rather than trust in your own abilities to complete the Walk of Faith."

"That's why you dropped me into the abyss?" Van raised her brow.

Thalassa nodded. "You needed to use your own abilities without the Coin to get out of the abyss and retrieve the Cup, and you did. You trusted in your connection to the Creator." She paused and then said, "However, your questions demonstrate you still do not understand."

Thalassa's reasoning hit a cord within Van. It reconfirmed the nagging truth she couldn't handle her power as Anchoress because of her damaged soul. Which meant Uxa was right. Van wasn't ready to retrieve the Cup.

"You have successfully passed my first test. But you will not leave the lagoon until you have learned the entire lesson."

Thalassa's appearance changed again. Her seashell dress had turned into thousands of transparent beads, collectively giving the stunning impression she shimmered like a waterfall. Her hair turned completely blue and wavered again as if it were underwater. Van realized Thalassa had been changing subtly the whole time they had been talking. The combination of the slight changes had accumulated enough to make the differences obvious now.

"Humans can choose their fate." Thalassa's eyes turned a dark, stormy blue. "Every other creature has been placed in a confined and predetermined circumstance. You can co-create your destiny with the power given to you by fate of your birth. Thus, your responsibility is greater."

Van cast her eyes downward. "I have to give back the Cup?"

"Not quite."

Van heard a snort and scraping claws.

The hair on her arms stood on end.

A snarl rolled out from the darkness in a nearby crevasse. A shadow between the rocks stretched forward and took form. Its eyes glowed red.

Van stood paralyzed by fear. *No... Thalassa wouldn't...*

Her worst nightmare had become a reality.

Van's eyes widened in terror as she gaped at the saliva dripping from fanged teeth.

A low growl rumbled deep from the belly of the Quasher.

CHAPTER 51

"Welcome to your final exam," Thalassa said.

Van wanted to run, scream, and disappear all at the same time. She wished she had never been born rather than face this moment.

"Y-you set the Quasher free? How?" Van was still within her time limit of the Alignment. It should be bound by the magic of the Elementals. *Oh, right. Thalassa's an Elemental. She has the power to release the Quasher.*

"Your salvation comes down to the decision you make right now." Thalassa's voice rang from every angle of the lagoon, yet she was nowhere in sight.

The snarling beast curled its massive paws. It crouched, growling, and lurched forward.

Van leaped aside, so fast her ankle collapsed when she landed, sending her sprawling onto the sand. The Cup flew from her hand and tumbled away.

The monstrous, wolf-like creature raised its paw and swiped at Van with blade-like claws.

She rolled aside, narrowly missing the beast's claws as its paw pounded deep into the sand, inches from her head.

It roared in frustration.

Van scrambled to stand. On shaking legs, she dashed to the rocks that formed the cliff by Thalassa's throne. Pain flared in her ankle as she climbed. The snarling Quasher nipped at her heels.

Thalassa didn't want Van to use the Coin, but this was an emergency and—*yeah*—the Quasher counted as pure evil.

Van tucked herself between two rocks, using them to shield her body from the beast. She frantically searched her pockets for the Coin.

The Quasher's paws and snout reached between the rocks, narrowly missing Van. It snapped and clawed in an attempt to achieve its goal of ripping Van to shreds. Its red eyes never wavered from her, not once.

"Darkness is a dominating state, but it is not a balanced state." Thalassa's voice filled the lagoon. "The Creator gave the Anchoress a magical bloodline to ensure there would always be enough light present in the worlds to balance the darkness."

Rocks crumbled around Van as the shadow beast tore its way to her.

"If the Quasher kills you, the Anchoress light will be extinguished forever," Thalassa said. "There will be no one to save your people when demons rise and bring forth Dishora."

The Coin wasn't in any of her pockets. Van's eyes darted across the beach. She saw it lying by the Cup. She must've lost it when she tumbled to the ground. Or, perhaps, Thalassa had magically taken it away.

Anger surged in Van. Talk about an unfair fight. She pushed down her feelings. She knew Thalassa's first lesson involved connecting to her feelings, but Van had become skilled at squelching them. The Water Elemental was right. Van hadn't learned the lesson.

Van's ire rose. She needed to focus without emotional interference. The more furious and dark her thoughts became, the greater the Quasher's rage and determination.

She didn't want to die. Death terrified her. Now it had come knocking on her door in the form of the Quasher. Van needed to stay alive to help her people, to stop the spread of the demon illness.

The rocks surrounding Van shook from the Quasher's pounding body. She couldn't hide behind them forever. A barrage of emotions burst inside her, none of them good.

The calm water of the lagoon rippled, mimicking the turbulence of Van's inner turmoil. The Quasher grew stronger as her vexation persisted.

She tried to connect to her ancestral line but couldn't concentrate with the shadow beast snarling five feet away. Or perhaps the creature blocked her connection?

Van knew she couldn't fight the shadow-wolf on her own, not without her Items of Creation. She had access to magic but didn't know what spell to conjure. If she leaped out from behind the rocks, tried an incantation and failed, it would result in her body being torn to shreds.

I'm a terrible person. What kind of warrior fears death?

Thalassa's first lesson had taught Van to trust her inner Self. *So what do I do? Leap out and face the Quasher and... what? Die?*

Suddenly a white dot appeared on the rocks a good distance from Van. Her stomach dropped.

Wiglaf! Looking as frail as ever.

"Mrrup. Epp."

His weak voice carried across the lagoon to Van *and* the Quasher's ears.

The beast snapped its wolf-like head toward Wiglaf, who lay draped across a rock.

"No!" Van screamed, still cowering between the protective rocks.

The Quasher stopped snapping and clawing. It took a step in Wiglaf's direction in a blatant attempt to lure Van out from between the rocks.

As the Quasher lumbered across the beach, it gave Van a few precious seconds to think. She cleared her anger by focusing on feelings of love. Her eyes tingled and turned phosphorescent violet. Her blood vibrated, as Van's Anchoress power emanated through her body, connecting her to her ancestral line.

Van wriggled out from between the rocks. Her hands clapped together overhead and then separated. They moved on their own, guided by her spirit ancestors. With her palms facing the lagoon, she chanted words that filled her mind.

"I am my power. I am divine. I am the Anchoress by design. Magic, magic from the sea. Together, we are meant to be. Water rise from the lagoon. Give me help and bring it soon."

The lagoon swirled. Water flooded the beach. The rising tide engulfed the Quasher. But the beast quickly regained its balance and treaded water.

The lagoon inundated the beach and rose higher.

"No!" Van yelled as the tide swept Wiglaf from the rock.

His tiny paws flailed in the rushing water. The bunfy struggled to remain afloat. His floppy ears floated as he strived to keep his head above the rippling waves.

The Quasher used its massive paws to swim closer and closer to Wiglaf.

"No!" Van took several steps forward until she came to the edge of the precipice. "Stop!"

The water stopped rising as it reached Van's feet, where she stood on the rock protrusion.

She bent down and splashed the water with her hands, hoping to get the Quasher's attention. "Over here!"

Wiglaf's eyes widened as the Quasher got close enough to raise its massive claws over him.

The Quasher's paw cut short the bunfy's squeaky cry as it crashed down on its target.

Van screamed. "No-o-o!"

The Quasher turned to Van. It belted an ear-piercing roar. Its plan to lure her out from the crevasse had worked but it was too far away to pounce on her. The Quasher furiously paddled in Van's direction.

A spot of white fluff rose to the surface. As Wiglaf drifted, blood pooled around him. His long ears floated like seaweed. He raised his tiny nose barely above the surface. Van could see his little ribs moving up and down. He was alive!

She heard a faint clink in the water by her feet and looked down. *The Cup!* It had drifted over to her and tapped against the rocks.

Van snapped it up before Thalassa could change her mind, although the Water Elemental was still nowhere to be seen.

I can use the Cup to heal Wiglaf! Thank you, thank you, thank you, Thalassa.

The Cup filled with an orange liquid.

"If Wiglaf drinks the from the Cup, it will save him," Thalassa's voice rang through the lagoon. "But you will die."

The Quasher neared Van, though it struggled against Thalassa's magically made currents designed to work against it.

Wiglaf had drifted to the edge of the rocks, close enough for Van to get to him.

"Whoever drinks it will be protected from the shadow beast," Thalassa said. "The Cup will save one. Either you, or Wiglaf."

The Quasher continued its relentless paddling through the currents. Its red eyes never wavered from Van, even as she plodded across the rocks to reach Wiglaf.

"If you drink the potion, the Quasher cannot harm you and your protection from it will last forever. You will be able to move about the Living World anytime, not only during Luxta. But Wiglaf will die."

Van scooped the unconscious bunfy from the water, carried him up the cliff, and gently laid him on a smooth rock. Open wounds gaped through his once white fur, now stained pink with his blood. His little ribs barely moved up and down. Time was running out.

As the Quasher thrashed its paws in the water, moving closer, thoughts swirled through Van's mind.

Thalassa made it clear Van needed to drink the potion to survive her battle with the Quasher. Last year, Van had been ready to give her life to the shadow beast to save Brux's. But she didn't fully understand the value of her existence to the Lodian tribe then. Now, everything was different. She carried the legacy of her people. Her life was not hers to give away.

Images of Ferox in the moonlight entered her mind. She couldn't stop a feeling of love from flooding her senses.

And Brux. He consistently put his life on the line to protect her. She believed his caring for her extended past the line of duty. Despite his feelings for Van, she had a right to feel romantic love for someone else.

It was okay for her to love them both. Brux as a friend and Ferox as her boyfriend.

Regret struck Van as she remembered the bad choices she had made in the past. And sadness over the people she had cared about and lost. According to Zurial's message and Thalassa's first test, Van had a right to embrace all of her feelings. Which meant she had the right to save someone she loved and still be considered a powerful warrior.

Van bent down, and lifted Wiglaf's head, about to give her bunfy the drink, when Thalassa upped the ante.

"The potion will make you immortal. Drink it and you will be the Anchoress for eternity. You will become a deity, an Elemental. Able to watch over your people forever."

The Quasher had gotten so close to the shoreline, water from the strokes of its enormous paws splashed onto the rocks. Thalassa wouldn't allow her magical currents to hold it off much longer.

Van had to choose. It was her death, or Wiglaf's.

She closed her eyes and cleared everything from her mind. She turned inward, seeking an answer. Her spirit ancestors remained quiet. Their message was clear. This decision was hers alone.

Van opened her eyes.

The Quasher's paws stretched and clasped the rocks at the waterline. The stony surface below its grasp crumbled from the sheer ferocity of the snarling beast as it clawed its way up the cliff toward Van.

A guttural growl rolled from its throat. Its angry red eyes locked onto hers, ready to fulfill its goal, its reason for existence. To kill Van.

Her decision became obvious.

She gently rested Wiglaf's head onto the rocks and said goodbye.

CHAPTER 52

Van placed the Cup on the rock next to Wiglaf.

She lifted his head and upper body so he could drink the healing liquid on his own. She didn't have time to watch him sip the entire Cup. Not with the Quasher seconds away.

Wiglaf's head flopped back to the ground after Van took her hands away. She bent down to lift his head again, but Wiglaf didn't need to drink the liquid. After the first sip, it flowed from the Cup into the bunfy's mouth on its own. The whole cupful disappeared into his tiny mouth in a second.

The Quasher's snarl blew its hot breath on Van's neck.

With a deep breath, she mustered her bravery and faced the shadow beast, trembling.

It raised its paw and swiped at Van.

She ducked and rolled aside, away from Wiglaf.

It sprung and slammed its paw into the rock inches from Van's face, shattering it with enough force to make the cavern's rocky wall quake.

With each swipe, Van dashed and leaped aside, narrowly escaping its sharp sword-like claws.

The Quasher's smashing paws caused the masks decorating the

cavern around the lagoon to fall. They crashed like rain onto the rocks below and shattered to pieces.

Van scuttled higher up the rocks, if for nothing else, to get the beast farther away from Wiglaf.

The Quasher snarled louder and swiped at Van's feet. She screeched in pain as its claw tore into her ankle so deep it shredded her boot.

She wedged herself behind a rock and pulled up her leg. Blood gushed from her throbbing ankle wound. She frantically tried to stop it by pushing her palms against the deep gash. Blood streamed between her fingers.

Her mind whirled, trying to come up with a way to defeat the Quasher. But she had nothing to fight it with. No Coin, no Cup, no spell, no weapon. She was on her own.

Jacynthia's earlier advice broke into her thoughts, putting a stop to Van's fear spiral. She struggled to recall her spirit guide's exact words. Something like, "All fear is a lack of faith in the Self. To overcome this, you must embrace your dark side."

Zurial's memory engram had mentioned something similar. Both were messages for Van to accept and embrace the duality of life *and* the duality within her Self.

Is facing the dark part of my Self worse than facing the Quasher?

Van connected together everything she had learned on this journey and had an epiphany.

The Quasher was Van's balancing force against her light, the essence of her inner darkness.

The Quasher is my duality!

This realization exhilarated her, but she still didn't know what to do.

Accept and embrace the Quasher?

Van couldn't escape its slashing claws much longer. She had no choice but to accept and embrace, not the Quasher, but her deeper fear. Death.

A bigger revelation struck Van. She was never alone, never separate from the Creator. Van learned from Thalassa's initial test that what she gives to the Creator is what she gets back. In Zurial's last memory engram, the ancient warrior sent Van a message about not fearing death.

A fog lifted in Van's mind. She knew the answer to the Elemental's final exam.

Van had made the right choice by not drinking the potion. Thalassa claimed it would've made Van immortal. What the Elemental meant was that Van's physical body would've become immortal. If Van had taken a sip from the Cup, the potion would've trapped her soul in her body forever like a prison.

According to Jacynthia, "The soul cannot be permanently diminished." Van's soul was formed by the Creator, who gave a piece of Itself, and just like the Creator, her soul was eternal.

Secure in this knowledge, Van no longer feared death of the physical body. She accepted death as part of life.

She began to hobble out from behind the protective rock, knowing that despite her magical abilities and strong ancestral ties, she couldn't overpower the Quasher through force.

Three words drifted to the forefront of her thoughts.

Force versus strength.

She remembered Zurial's memory engram, when Manik mentioned harnessing emotions to show strength, not force. Ferox had suggested the same thing.

Van didn't need to use force to fight the Quasher. She possessed inner *strength* through her connection to the Creator.

Her soul had been made from a piece of the Creator, and the Creator was made entirely of light. There was no darkness in the Creator, therefore, no darkness existed inside Van.

But darkness could enter her being if she allowed it into her *space* with incorrect actions or thoughts. Again, Van became aware she had the right to reclaim this space—*her* space—to keep out anything that wasn't part of her essence. Like darkness.

The Quasher, as Van's natural balancing force, was not part of her inner Self. Like night and day, they were two separate but balancing entities allowed by nature to exist in peace, as long as each respected the other's boundaries.

Van emerged completely from the safety of the rocks.

True to the Quasher's nature, the shadow beast rushed at her, to consume her light as darkness does to gain strength.

She didn't flinch or brace for impact.

Instead, she communed with the positive eternal presence within her Self and declared, "This darkness is not me. I refuse to give it my light. I reclaim all the energy it has taken from me. It has no power over me and no right to be in my space, given to me by the Creator. By the will of the Creator, it cannot harm me."

Snarling, the Quasher extended its hooked claws and leapt forward.

It dissipated as it struck Van, going straight through her as if it were a hologram. And just like that, it vanished.

An unnerving silence strained Van's ears.

Her eyes darted up and down the rocky sides of the cavern and across the lagoon, searching for any sign of trouble. But the water had calmed and receded back to its original size. Pieces from the shattered masks lay scattered across the beach and the rocks. Wiglaf silently peered at Van from atop a nearby stone. He stretched his ears straight and tall. His fur, white and fluffy.

Van wasn't sure what had happened. She wasn't even sure if what she had done counted as defeating the Quasher. *Did I pass the Elemental's test?*

Her eyes roamed the shoreline. The Cup's shiny outer rim jutted out from the sand near her. Next to it rested the Coin. She cautiously climbed down the rocks onto the beach, ignoring her aches, bruises, bleeding ankle, and her partially shredded boot.

Still unsure if she had completed her tests, Van didn't make any sudden movements.

"First, I tested your capacity to connect with your emotions, to feel your connection to the Creator," Thalassa said from behind Van.

Van whirled around, arms raised in defensive mode.

"Feeling is the fountainhead of power." Thalassa had reverted to her original appearance. Her dirty-blond, seaweed-like hair and silver robe had returned. She stood on the beach several yards from Van.

At that moment, Van knew the Quasher she had encountered was in actuality Thalassa. The beast, merely another of Thalassa's many changing faces. One of the Elemental's illusions.

Van relaxed her fighter's stance, relieved by the pleased expression on the Water Elemental's face.

"Next, I presented you with a choice," Thalassa continued. "To save your life by drinking from the Cup or use it to heal Wiglaf. To make the correct choice in that moment, you needed to *feel* love for Wiglaf."

At the beginning of her journey, Van had been so sure emotions made her a weak warrior. Now, she knew her feelings were an integral part of making her a stronger one. Zurial's memory engrams, Jacynthia's advice, Paley's illness, Daisy's poisoning, Wiglaf, Hiccup, Brux, Ferox. All of them helped heal Van so she could reclaim her right to feel.

As if on cue, Thalassa said, "Being able to feel compassion and love allowed you to accept the duality of others and of your Self. This led to your understanding that the ultimate form of healing is to accept nature's greatest duality, that of life and death."

The Elemental spoke matter-of-factly. Her eyes never blinked and remained focused on Van. "Knowing death is not the end, that there is a continuity of life through the soul, eliminated your fear of death. By doing so, you transcended your earthbound status and grew closer to your spiritual power as Anchoress."

Thalassa paused.

Van squirmed. The Water Elemental did the same thing after Van's first test. Then decided Van needed additional testing.

Confident she had learned her lessons, Van squared her shoulders. Whatever Thalassa threw at her next, Van would face head-on.

"The choice you made during your last test proved you truly understand the Elemental Law of Healing," Thalassa said. "By healing your emotional Self, you can accept the duality of all things. Including acknowledging the Creator only creates. There is no death, only different life. This led to your ability to counter the second plague of humanity, the Plague of Death."

Thalassa smiled, startling Van.

"Congratulations," she said. "I am satisfied you have passed my tests. The Cup of Life is now your responsibility."

Thalassa changed appearance again. Her dress turned into tiny beads that looked like water droplets.

"My time as a guardian has come to an end."

The Elemental's dress merged with her skin and hair, transforming her whole body into water droplets.

"Remember, the Cup only heals the body, not the soul."

The water droplets defied gravity, rising like reverse rain, and Thalassa vanished as vapor into the sky.

CHAPTER 53

With Thalassa and her illusions gone, a quietness filled the lagoon.

Wiglaf raised his whiskery nose at Van. His round, blue eyes peered up at her. "Mrrwp ilp."

Van crouched down and scooped him into her arms, giving him a big squeeze.

He snuggled in, draping his paws over her shoulder and nuzzling his face by her ear.

Van made her way across the beach, clutching Wiglaf and leaving footprints in the damp sand. She picked up the Cup, shifted Wiglaf, and tucked the Item into her jacket's inner pocket.

"Let's get back to the ship," she said to her bunfy.

After falling into the mouth of Charybdis, Van had entered a magical lagoon deep under the sea. Perhaps even at the bottom of the Bottomless Sea.

Van didn't know where to find the others or if they had even survived the attack by Scylla and Charybdis. She picked up the Coin and wiped off the sand with her thumb, still cradling Wiglaf with her other hand. She held the Coin in her palm and asked for the best direction back to *The Obelus*.

Wiglaf squirmed. "Irp weep!"

"What?" Van turned to see what upset Wiglaf.

The water in the lagoon rose steadily.

Van took several steps backward. "It's flooding the cavern."

Van hastily changed her request and asked the Coin for the best path out of the lagoon. Van hurried away from the rising water in the direction pointed out by the Coin.

She came to a fissure in the rocky side of the cavern. Van placed Wiglaf on the ground, giving him the choice to return to his magical realm or accompany her. She turned sideways to fit into the narrow opening and wedged her way into the fissure.

Van barely had room to breathe. Her steps got damp as the water level rose. She felt a wave of panic as she envisioned herself trapped between the rocks with the sea water rising, eventually drowning her.

I survived the Quasher, only to drown five minutes later?

With her luck? Probably.

Van's anxiety abated. What's the worst that could happen? Death? She no longer feared death.

Van shuffled sideways between the suffocating stone walls. She stumbled forward when the walls opened into a vast tunnel system. The blackness of the tunnels activated Van's magical ability to see in the dark by turning on her "flashlight eyes."

Trusting in the Coin's guidance, she and Wiglaf followed it through tunnel after tunnel until they reached an underground cavern with a wide cenote.

Van's boots sunk into the beach sand, but unlike the lagoon, this sand was dotted with dried seaweed and bunches of scattered seashells. As the sand grew damp, Van scrutinized the peculiar appearance of the beach. A realization struck her—they weren't on a beach. They were standing on the sea floor!

Water rose in the cavern, perhaps returning to its original state now that Thalassa no longer needed the space to guard the Cup.

Van's eyes darted to Wiglaf.

"Wurp?" He peered up at her.

"Go," Van commanded.

In a snap, Wiglaf disappeared back to the safety of his magical realm.

The sea rose high enough to merge with the water from the cenote. It continued to flood the cavern as if someone had cranked an underground faucet to full-throttle. Van consulted the Coin as the sea water reached her knees.

It pointed to the cenote.

But—how am I supposed to breathe underwater?

She was reasonably sure becoming a fish wasn't one of her magical abilities. She thought about her protective bubble, but was uncertain the invisible sphere would surround her as she edged her way back through the fissure and swam to the surface. Van was also afraid of getting trapped on the cavern ceiling in her bubble, forever floating at the bottom of the Bottomless Sea.

She didn't know why the Coin led her there, but she was certain it didn't mean for her to drown.

Wait a minute.

She was at the bottom of the Bottomless Sea.

Duh! The Coin led her to the second seal! It was in the cenote.

The water level reached her hips, yet she could still perceive the cenote beneath, its hue a distinct, paler blend of blue and green compared to the advancing sea.

Her hand grazed the protruding lump inside her jacket pocket. The Cup! Maybe she could fill it with life-saving liquid. She tucked the Coin in her pocket and pulled it out as the seawater reached her neck.

Van stood on her tiptoes to keep her nose and mouth out of the water.

If I need my hands to stay afloat, how can I drink from the Cup?

The sea rose higher, and her toes no longer touched the ground. She quickly glanced up at the stone ceiling, getting closer.

While treading water, Van flailed her arms so much that she smacked herself in the face with the Cup, causing it to move on its own. The Cup's bowl suctioned onto her skin and changed position to cover her nose and mouth.

Terrified of suffocating, Van struggled to yank it off as she sank below the water. The whole time, she gulped down air.

Air!

The Cup acted as a magical scuba mask, providing oxygen to her without a tank.

Van calmed. She glanced around the murky water, completely submerged. Her injured ankle throbbed as she swam over to the cenote and dived deeper into the blue-green water.

The cenote walls surrounded Van, but provided enough room for her to swim to the bottom. She didn't know if the seal would be obvious and wondered if it was worth the risk of consulting the Coin.

Reaching the bottom made the decision unnecessary. Embedded into the side of the cenote were multiple striated bands, each approximately twice as wide as her hand. There was a granite band, a reddish-orange stone strand, and a deep-blue, watery strip. The bands reminded Van of the portal in the House of Lacus.

She had reached the second seal.

Her eyes moved along the wall as she turned full circle, getting a good look at the bands. Silver sparkles twinkled throughout all three layers. There were no cracks, breaks, or ruptures anywhere. She circled again, this time running her hands over the strands. Everything appeared fine. There was no crack in the second seal.

Did this mean the Cup was the actual mission?

The seal and the Cup happened to be in the same geographical location. Van needed to use the Cup to breathe so she could check the seal. Thankfully, her team's change of plans worked out, and she had retrieved it.

Was it a coincidence? Fate? Or did Uxa know the seal was intact?

Did Uxa send me to check the seal because she knew I would need the Cup to complete the mission?

Van's gut churned. Again, her intuition questioned her mentor's motives.

Is Uxa the spy at Lodestar?

Van made triple, quadruple sure the seal was undamaged, then began her ascent out of the cenote.

She reached the cavern and swam back through the tunnels. She wedged her way through the tight-fitting fissure, turning her face upward to fit the "scuba" Cup, and swam into the submerged lagoon.

As she moved through the murky seawater, Van glimpsed Thalassa's throne. It looked eerily abandoned, like a relic from a lost culture reclaimed by the fury of Poseidon.

She swam higher into the darkness, half expecting to hit a stone ceiling. Without stopping, she continued to swim. Suddenly, the water surrounding her filled with tiny, swirling bubbles, sweeping her upward, increasing the speed of her ascent.

Light filtered down, and the bubbles stopped.

Van broke the surface. The Cup detached from her face. She scrambled to catch it and fumbled, almost losing it to the sea. Her heart raced, knowing if the Cup slipped from her grip, it would be lost forever.

Van secured the Cup into the inner pocket of her jacket while treading water, then surveyed the horizon.

In the near distance, she saw a battered ship.

CHAPTER 54

Although exhausted, Van swam toward *The Obelus.*

The man stationed in the crow's nest spotted her before she reached the ship. Within minutes, the crew had lowered a rowboat into the water.

Relieved, Van took a needed a break from swimming. All the muscles in her body ached, and her injured ankle throbbed.

Ferox perched on the bow with a worried look on his face. Brux's powerful arms rowed the boat.

After reaching Van, they gripped her shoulders and hauled her onboard.

Brux embraced her. "We thought you were... dead."

"Same here." Van smiled, hugging him back.

"Good to see you're alive." Ferox hesitated, as if unsure whether he should show a full-on display of his affection. Then, he embraced Van in a hug that was much more intimate than the one Brux had given her.

Ferox volunteered to row back to the ship. "You rowed here," he said to Brux. "I'll row back. It's only fair."

All of them had questions. Van considered hers the most urgent.

"How's Paley? Is-is she... alive?"

"She's..." Brux paused, searching for the right words.

"Alive, yes," Ferox added. "But not well."

"Pernilla? Thyra?" Van asked. "Is it really true? They're... gone?"

The guys nodded sadly.

The thought of how Pernilla's death would affect her parents and Ken made Van's heart ache. She extended her hands toward Brux and Ferox.

Ferox raised the oars and secured them inside the rowboat to prevent them from drifting away.

Van held their hands and said a prayer to the light for the souls of Pernilla, Thyra, and all those they lost on their journey to find solace in the embrace of the Creator.

Once they reached *The Obelus,* Van discovered the crew had been busy making repairs to the ship.

"We kept a constant watch for your return," Ferox said.

"I knew you'd come back to me," Brux said as he attended to her ankle.

"How long was I gone?" Van asked.

"Two days," Brux said.

A troubled look clouded Ferox's face. "We have less than a week until the Alignment ends."

Van grinned. "Oh, I'm not worried."

She filled them in on her encounter with the weird children, the ever-changing maze, meeting with Thalassa, and her confrontation with the Quasher.

"The Quasher?" Brux gasped. "For the love of the light!"

"It was Thalassa," Ferox correctly guessed. "Disguised as the Quasher, as part of your test."

Van didn't mention getting the Cup, and they didn't ask. She thought it wise to find out if Ferox was concerned with her safety or simply interested in her retrieval of the Item.

She also didn't tell them she had found the Coin, or that she had checked the second seal. Van needed to observe the current situation before revealing too much.

Brux, she one hundred percent trusted.

Ferox. Well, the thought of him made her insides tingle with excitement. Her gut told her to trust him. But to protect her people, she had to confirm his genuine interest in her and make sure he had no ulterior motives. He was Balish after all.

They both seemed relieved to see Van alive. Neither pressed her about the bulge in her jacket.

After Brux treated Van's ankle, she asked to see Paley.

"I'll take her," Brux said before Ferox could open his mouth.

"I'll go check on the repairs," Ferox muttered as he walked away.

Brux reached for the doorknob to Paley's cabin and paused. "Prepare yourself. It's not pretty." He slowly opened the door. "Just take a peek, for now."

Light from a single porthole filtered into the cabin. Before Van's eyes had adjusted to the darkness, she heard Paley. Her stomach churned with dread.

Sounds came from Paley like those from a wild animal. Guttural growls. Spittle sprayed into the strip of light filtering through the porthole. Paley strained and writhed against the ropes binding her to the bed.

"We set her off by entering the room." Brux backed out, nudging Van to do the same.

"She's in worse shape than I imagined." Van stared wide-eyed at Brux.

"The illness hasn't killed her yet." Brux rubbed his chin with his forefinger. "I think the colloidal silver helped with that."

"But... she's a demon," Van said, perplexed.

"Not yet. She's possessed by the darkness of the illness."

"What's the difference?"

Brux sighed. The circles under his eyes suddenly looked more prominent. "I don't know."

"I think I do." Van remembered what she had learned during Thalassa's test. "The colloidal silver helped keep the illness from killing her, but Paley allowed the darkness in."

"Are you able to cure her?"

It was Brux's way of asking Van if she had retrieved the Cup.

"Let's go to the galley. You can grab something to eat," he said. "If you feel like it, you can tell me the rest of what happened." He flashed Van a lopsided smile.

Van grinned back. Brux knew her so well he could detect deliberate omissions of important details from her experiences during their time apart. He seemed pleased she she kept part of her encounters to herself in front of Ferox.

They went down to the galley. Brux slopped some goo into a wooden bowl for Van.

"Oatmeal?" Van asked.

"Yeah. Let's go with that."

Van dug into the flavorless grain. She figured they were short on supplies and didn't care what it was. She needed food to regain her strength, especially after discovering she hadn't eaten in two days. Although time in the Water Elemental's lagoon probably didn't flow on the same clock as the Living World.

"Oh, good." Ferox popped into the galley to check on Van. "You're eating something. You need food to regain your strength."

That's exactly what I thought. Van's heart whirled. They were so connected.

Ferox's skin glistened with sweat and grime from helping with the ship's repairs. His stained white t-shirt stretched tightly over his chest, leaving little to the imagination. Van couldn't tear her eyes away from him. She lost interest in eating.

All three sat at the rectangular table fastened to the floor to keep it from smashing around during rough weather.

The unspoken question about the Cup lingered heavily in the air.

Ferox broke the silence. "I'm sorry about Paley."

Van reached into her jacket pocket while Ferox continued talking.

"I'm hoping we'll be able to treat her when we get ashore. Maybe Madame Vang—"

Van placed the Cup of Life on the table, stopping him short.

Brux and Ferox remained speechless while they waited for Van to finish fumbling around with her pockets.

She tossed the Coin of Creation onto the kitchen table next to the Cup.

Brux scowled.

Van knew he was worried about exposing both Items of Creation to Ferox.

Ferox raised his brow. "I saw the Coin slide over the side, along with you. I'm amazed you recovered both Items. How?"

Van told them her story, filling in the blanks, including the young alligator and Zurial's warning about not being gluttonous about using the Cup.

"We treat Paley, then we check the seal," Ferox said.

"No," Brux said. "We use the Cup to save Daisy."

"Mending the seal will help save thousands of people from getting sick," Ferox growled.

"My *sister* needs help." Brux rose from his seat, fists clenched.

Ferox did the same. "The seal is in this area. We can't head back to shore now."

"I don't care what you—"

"Stop!" Van slammed her hands on the table. "Calm down." She motioned for them to sit.

Brux and Ferox took their seats, still red-faced and throwing death glares at each other.

"I've already checked the second seal." Van's eyes darted over their faces. Her words had caused their eyes to widen and jaws to slacken. "The Cup gives the holder the ability to breathe underwater."

"What? How?" Brux asked.

"Well, it is the Cup of *Life*," Ferox said. "You needed oxygen to breathe at that moment."

"Right." Van had made the same connection. She loved how in sync she was with Ferox. "The Coin led me to the seal. Thalassa's lagoon rested at the bottom of the Bottomless Sea. But I went farther down, all the way to the floor of a cenote. I checked the seal. There's no crack."

"Thalassa was the guardian of the seal, too?" Brux asked.

Ferox grimaced at Brux, clearly implying Brux didn't get the meaning of an intact seal.

"I don't think so," Van said. "All I know is I couldn't have checked the seal without using the Cup to breathe. And to get the Cup, I had to go through Thalassa."

"Back to the seal." Ferox turned to Van. "If it's not broken, then how did the demon illness get here?"

Brux asked Van, "Are you sure about the seal?"

"Of course I'm sure," Van snapped. "No cracks, no breaks, no dents, no damage. Positive."

"Van," Brux said. "If you had the Cup the whole time you've been back, why haven't you cured Paley yet?"

"Incorrect use?" Ferox asked.

Van shook her head. "Madam Vang told me to place the Cup under a full moon to make the healing potion. Zurial's vision showed me the same—" Van stopped. The solution struck her. "I've got it."

"Got what?" Brux said.

Van snatched the Cup off the table and dashed out of the galley.

She burst into Paley's room, not worried about upsetting her friend, who went berserk upon setting her black eyes on Van.

As the Anchoress, Van could to connect to the moon to amplify her magical power. Some legends claimed she carried a piece of the moon inside her. Van believed she had a strong enough connection to the moon to make the healing spell work.

Van's idea involved her standing in as the full moon. If she could pull this off, it would give her the power to create the orange healing liquid.

Paley spit and growled like the beast of darkness possessing her.

Van used her intuition to guide her. While holding the Cup, she sensed Brux and Ferox guarding the door, ensuring Van's safety. She loved them for it. Just as she loved her ancestors, Paley, and the light of the moon. She felt herself lock into her power.

The Cup filled with an orange-colored potion.

Van took a step toward Paley.

"Wait," Ferox cried. "We'll hold her down while you pour the liquid into her mouth." Ferox and Brux dashed to Paley's bedside.

Paley struggled against her bindings and whipped her head back and forth.

"Careful she doesn't bite you," Brux said.

"Why? Is that a thing?" Van warily stared at her best friend.

Brux shrugged.

"Probably best not to find out," Ferox said. "I'll hold her arms. Brux, you hold her head."

As Van drizzled the healing liquid into Paley's snapping mouth, she thought back to Thalassa's test with the Quasher. The whole time, Van had the power within herself to create more orange liquid, to save both herself and Wiglaf, but didn't know it. Although Van's potion wouldn't have given her protection from the Quasher or immortality.

Paley stopped struggling as Van finished pouring the liquid down her throat.

Brux and Ferox loosened their hold.

"Does anyone else on board need healing?" Van asked.

The rest of the day, Van healed everyone on board while the crew finished the final repairs.

Van asked Brux if he wanted a sip.

He shook his head. "Zurial warned you about over-using the healing potion." He looked as if he wanted to ask her something else, but held his tongue.

"I haven't taken a sip, if that's what you want to know. Neither has Ferox."

"Good." His shoulders visibly relaxed. "I think you should put the Cup away."

"The Cup only heals the physical body, not the soul," Van said.

"Is that why you didn't drink from it?"

Van shrugged. "The advice might have a deeper meaning, something we don't yet understand."

"Your soul is pure," Brux said. "You proved that when you saved Wiglaf over yourself and then faced your worst nightmare, the Quasher."

She glanced at Wiglaf, sunning himself on a nearby crate.

"Death," Van corrected him. "Turns out, death was my biggest issue. The Quasher exacerbated that fear."

"Your actions proved you've healed your soul," Brux persisted. "It's how you passed the Elemental's test, and why you don't feel the need to drink from the Cup. That's your reward."

Van had received a far greater reward than the Cup. Alleviation from the guilt of Solana's death, and the sadness about her mother and father's deaths. This gift came to Van after she accepted there was no death, only continuity of the soul. Thalassa's lessons also taught her that integrating her feelings made her a stronger warrior.

Van smiled. "This little guy." She scooped up Wiglaf from the crate and hugged him tightly. "He's the best reward."

Wiglaf snuggled against Van's chest.

Brux smiled. "Yeah, him too."

"And the Cup and the Coin." Ferox joined them.

Brux looked annoyed at Ferox for interrupting his moment with Van.

"Hate to be a downer," Ferox said. "But we need to talk about the demon illness. If it's not coming from a crack in the seal like Uxa thought, then where's it coming from?"

"Illness or no illness. Demons can't get into this world on their own," Van said.

"But they're here. The Escalation to Dishora has begun," Brux said.

Van glanced at Ferox. "Or Solmor."

Ferox smiled at her appreciatively.

"Closed seal... demon illness... Dishora," Brux said, thinking out loud. "The only other way for demons to get here is by human intervention. Maybe the illness entered the same way. Someone brought it here."

"My sister's master demon could've released the plague at the same time Solana brought its demons into the Living World," Ferox said. "The demon's negative essence still lingers. Maybe it accumulated and formed the illness."

"Even in death, that girl is still a virus." Van shook her head and then thought of how her harsh words might hurt Ferox. "I'm sorry. I didn't mean—"

"It's okay," Ferox said. "I understand."

"Bringing a sickness here is a brilliant plan," Brux said to Van. "The master demon created the illness to make sure you went for the next Item of Creation, the Cup. And as a bonus, if you failed to get the Cup, once people turned into demons, it would have a demon army."

"Wait," Van said. "If Solana's demons carried the illness here, why is the disease still spreading and getting stronger? The demons are gone. For the illness to stay and thrive in this world, something has to feed its negative vibration."

"Van's right," Ferox said. "Light is self-sustaining, but darkness has to have a source to grow. Someone or something is sustaining the illness. We need to find the origin."

"Another concern," Brux said. "How're we going to treat all the thousands that are infected? Time is running out before we have a demon army on our hands." His eyes met Van's. "You can't go around the world treating each person one by one."

"I got this," Van said. "Zurial gave me an idea during one of her memory engrams."

"What idea?" Brux asked.

"I'll put the cure in the water supply."

CHAPTER 55

Ferox commanded *The Obelus* to set sail for Cortica.

During the trip, Paley recovered. Except for a residual headache.

"Where are my contacts?" Paley asked, chewing on her cuticles.

Van breathed a sigh of relief. Her friend was back to her usual unpossessed self.

Once they docked, Van, Brux, and Paley dashed to the Wharf Lizard with the Cup. Ferox stayed on the dock to take care of everyone on the crew financially, and to leave them with enough money to finish the ship's repairs.

In the suite, Kopius sat in the same spot where they'd left him, watching over Daisy. Although, now he looked sallow and thinner. Wiglaf joined the menagerie of animals who had also sustained their vigil by Daisy's bedside.

Brux dashed over to his sister. "How's she doing?"

Kopius kept his gaze on Daisy. "Same." He had the look of someone not taking care of himself, too worried over the health of someone he loved to be bothered.

Daisy rested on the couch. Her hands remained folded over her stomach, a fresh bouquet in her hands. She looked serene and beautiful, not a hair out of place as if she had been preserved in time. She lay so motionless Van couldn't even see her breathing.

"She's still alive?" Van asked.

Kopius gave a weak nod.

Van pulled out the Cup.

"I'm glad Ferox didn't take that from you," Paley said.

"The day's not over yet," Brux muttered.

Van held the Cup between her palms and connected to her magical powers as Anchoress. The Cup filled with orange liquid.

Van went to Daisy and paused.

Kopius sprang into action and stood over Daisy. He gently used his fingers to open her jaw.

Carefully, Van poured the liquid into Daisy's mouth in small increments to prevent choking.

Brux appeared so taut Van thought he might break into a million pieces. Paley wrapped a comforting arm around him.

With the Cup emptied, Kopius closed Daisy's jaw.

Everyone held their breath as they waited.

Daisy's eyes moved under her eyelids. Then her lips parted, and she let out a sigh.

Brux crumbled. His whole body trembled as tears streaked down his cheeks.

Kopius clasped her hand. "Daisy."

She blinked her eyes and then opened them. "Hi."

The animals hooted, bobbed, howled, squeaked, and twittered in delight.

"Hi," Paley replied.

Daisy's eyes darted to each of them. "Why are all of you standing over me? What's wrong?" She sat up.

"Whoa." Brux placed a supporting hand on his sister's back. "Take it easy."

Kopius continued to grip Daisy's hand as if he might never let go.

"What's the last thing you remember?" Van asked.

"I was here." Daisy's eyes scanned the suite. "I was taking a bath. I used a bar of soap from the basket on the table... what happened?"

Brux told Daisy about the poisoned soap intended for Van. They filled in both Daisy and Kopius about their adventures on the high seas, including Van's retrieval of the Cup of Life, and Pernilla and Thyra's deaths.

To help Kopius and Daisy process the loss, they all bowed their heads, even the animals, and Brux said a prayer to the light for their teammate's souls.

"The second seal?" Daisy asked.

"It's not broken," Van said.

"So where's the demon illness coming from?" Kopius had moved onto the couch and sat with his arm around Daisy.

Paley shuddered. "Solana's demons brought it here."

"But how's it being sustained in our world?" Kopius asked. "The vibration here is too high for negativity to linger, whether it be demons or an illness they carry."

"It makes no sense," Brux said in agreement.

"Looks like we still have work to do." Kopius held a handful of dried fruit that looked like apricot twists and tossed one into his mouth. His skin had already regained color, and his perky attitude had returned. He offered some to Daisy.

She popped an apricot twist into her mouth.

It was the most food Van had ever seen Daisy eat.

She turned to Van. "How much time do we have?"

Van knew Daisy meant the Alignment. "The window is closing in six days."

"Six days!" Daisy leaped from the couch. "We must get you back."

Kopius and Brux practically had a nervous breakdown when Daisy exerted herself by hopping to her feet. They fussed and fretted over her.

Daisy waved them away. "I'm fine." She turned to the animals. "Off you go, friends. Thank you for caring. I love each one of you beautiful creatures."

The little ones scurried up her arm, and she kissed each one. The larger animals, like the one that looked similar to a deer, walked over to her, and Daisy bent to kiss each of them. One by one, they scuttled, hopped, dashed, and flew out of the opened window, except the larger ones who stood with their noses to the suite's door.

Paley rushed to open it and happily escorted the larger animals out of the inn.

"We need to get moving," Van said, eager to get back to Lodestar.

They packed their few remaining items, some clothes, food, wine-skins, and cleaned the room.

Van offered Kopius a sip from the Cup. After the emotional torture he had gone through watching over Daisy, she figured he could use a hit.

He shook his head. "I'm good. Don't need it."

"Good choice." Brux zipped his backpack. "Van, put the Cup away. Stop trying to give everyone you see a drink."

"Most people need some kind of healing, Brux," Van snapped as she tucked the Cup away in her backpack.

"Will Ferox take the Cup?" Daisy had changed out of her dress and into marketeers' scouts clothing. Cargo pants with many pockets, a ribbed tank, and an overshirt.

The same worry had crossed Van's mind. "I'm not sure."

"He won't," Paley said. "He's a good guy."

"We have two Items," Brux said. "The Coin and Cup. There's no way Ferox will let us leave with them."

"Checking the seal was our assignment. Not retrieving the Cup," Kopius said. "We successfully completed our mission."

"Even if he took both Items, Ferox would never use them in a war against us," Van said. "It's an incorrect use."

Brux leaned in close and whispered to Van, "I guess we'll see if his feelings for you are real."

His words drove a jolt of fright through Van's heart. "I guess we will." With her chin raised, she pulled on her backpack.

The team left the inn and headed back to the docks.

Van spotted Ferox right away, standing on the bow, discussing some important matter with a crew member. Her insides swirled. She noticed herself smiling and didn't push away her feelings for him.

Ferox saw them tramping down the docks and met them as they came on deck.

"Daisy." Ferox smiled and held out his arms. "Glad to see you're okay." He wrapped her in a hug.

Van watched their every move. She didn't care for Daisy's firm grip around Ferox. She seemed to like his attention a little too much for Van's taste.

Am I overreacting?

Being allowed to feel all of her emotions was new for Van. Integrating them would be an upcoming challenge. But by the looks on Kopius and Brux's faces, they didn't care for the hug either.

"We're all friends now." Daisy's smile seemed to brighten the world.

Ferox's smile grew bigger.

Van didn't like it one bit. "Are we ready to set sail?"

Her comment brought Ferox back down to earth. "Ready when you are." He clasped Van's hand. "How're you doing?"

His attention, along with Kopius escorting Daisy away from Ferox to a cabin, improved Van's mood.

"We have some things to talk about," Van said, meaning the Items.

"We do."

His intense stare told Van he thought she meant their relationship. She blushed.

Everyone settled in, ready for the ride back to the mainland.

The Obelus set sail.

As soon as they docked at the Skeleton Coast, Ferox reunited with a royal squadron sent by his father, King Nequus, to find and retrieve his son.

Brux and Kopius tensed at the sight, but calmed when Ferox didn't order his troops to chain them together and toss them into the dungeon.

Taking Van's hand, Ferox led her to a discreet area tucked away behind the nearby shanties.

"This is where we part." He stood face to face with Van, holding her hands.

Van struggled to keep her tears at bay, her eyes welling up. A single drop trickled down her cheek.

"I have to get back to Balefire and talk to my father." Ferox tenderly wiped her tear away with his thumb. His glossy eyes reflected the emotions of his heart. He would miss her, too.

"Like when Manik left Zurial," Van said.

Ferox smiled. He reached into his pocket, took out the Coin. He held it up. "One Item for me. One Item for you."

"Just like—"

"Manik and Zurial." He slipped the Coin back into his pocket.

They silently gazed into each other's eyes. She carefully stored every detail of his face in her memory to carry with her and cherish.

"We'll meet again. Soon," Ferox said, his voice husky. "I promise."

Van nodded, yet her jerky eagerness betrayed her broken heart. Leaving Ferox was the worst test she had encountered so far. She couldn't bring herself to look at him. She feared it would create a problem—her clutching onto him and never letting go.

He gently raised her chin with his fingers, compelling her to meet his gaze.

"Hey," he whispered, moving so close to Van she could feel the heat of his body. "I mean it."

His lips grazed hers.

Van leaned into him and wrapped her arms around his neck.

He hungrily returned her embrace.

They kissed.

And kissed…

CHAPTER 56

Brux and Kopius grumbled about Ferox keeping the Coin. Though both admitted being pleased he let them take the Cup, given the amount of Balish soldiers surrounding them when they disembarked *The Obelus*.

Van, Daisy, and Paley thought splitting the Items between their tribes was the right thing to do.

The team's main concern was how Uxa would handle the news.

No one commented or cared about Van's lovesickness. Least of all, Brux. They left Van alone to wallow in her misery as the team made their way back to the nearest TAV.

Accepting her emotions proved a tough challenge, including her near-crippling empathy for Brux. Kopius had taken Brux's place as a protector in Daisy's life. And as Van's assigned protector, Brux had to deal with her romantic relationship with the person she needed protection from.

Everyone appeared to be in good spirits about successfully completing their mission. Other than running into Balish soldiers, few dangers awaited them on their journey back to Lodestar.

"Mrrp meep," Wiglaf said as a goodbye before he disappeared back to his magical realm.

Brux walked next to Van. "We should make it back with a few hours to spare before the Alignment ends."

"As long as nothing comes up." Paley chewed on her cuticles.

"Stay positive," Van said. On the outside, Paley appeared fully recovered from her ordeal with the illness, but her eyes reflected a haunted soul.

As they trudged through the woods, Daisy and Kopius stuck together, talking and laughing, uninterested in anything but each other.

Paley and Brux seemed glad to have survived another journey. Paley made a continuous effort to hold Brux's attention, and they bantered in good cheer. Although, the Twin Gemstones continued to take their toll on both their energy levels.

After some time, Brux called for the team to stop and take a break.

Kopius and Daisy sat next to each other on a rock and chatted as if they were the only two people in the worlds.

"Whew! I need to take a load off." Paley plopped down on a rock.

Without a word, Brux strolled toward the trees.

"Excuse me," Van called to him, hands on her hips.

Brux stopped but didn't turn around. "What?"

"Where're you going?"

Brux twisted to glare at her. "To the bathroom, if you must know."

"Oh." Van's cheeks flared. She didn't expect such a personal response. His bathroom habits were none of her business. "Okay."

"You sure?" Brux said. "It's okay with you I go relieve myself? I have your permission?"

Van snorted. "Sorry for caring." She stomped away. *That's what I get for showing my concern?*

Van flopped down next to Paley, who offered Van some apricot twists.

Before Van could take a bite, they heard a commotion coming from the woods.

"Brux!" Van leaped to her feet and rushed toward the noise, along with Paley, Kopius, and Daisy.

They stopped short at a clearing by the edge of a cliff. All of them gasped.

Brux was engaged in full-on, hand-to-hand combat with… *himself*!

Van stared, flabbergasted.

"What the—?" Paley muttered.

"I want to help but…" Kopius' eyes darted from one Brux to the other.

Brux smashed his fist into the other Brux's face. The two grappled dangerously close to the edge of the cliff. One Brux's foot slipped during the struggle. He stumbled, almost falling over the side.

Van wasn't sure who to root for, or if she was happy or sad about the near-death of one of the Bruxes. She didn't know which was the real one.

"Daisy, can you tell which one is Brux?" Paley asked.

Daisy's eyes darted back and forth. "Um."

"It's me," one of them said. "I'm Brux."

They wrestled. One flipped the other, who crashed to the ground. He sprung to his feet.

Van squinted, trying to find a difference in the Bruxes. Checking to see if one looked more tired than the other, or if one had bruises in the wrong spot. Her eyes strained. They were identical.

"I'm Brux," grunted the one now held in a headlock.

Van had a brilliant idea. "Show us the Twin Gemstone."

The Brux in the headlock awkwardly fumbled in his pocket and pulled out the gemstone.

"Aha!" Kopius cried, ready to swoop in and help.

"Wait," the other Brux cried. He released the other from the headlock and also pulled out a gemstone.

"Dammit," Van said. Whatever the creature, it made an exact duplicate of Brux, down to his clothing.

The fight got more brutal and deadly as the Bruxes battled to the death.

Van couldn't take the stress. "Stop!"

Both Bruxes ignored her.

She reached into her pocket to grab the Coin and realized she didn't have it anymore. Ferox did.

Daisy placed a grip on Van's arm. "You couldn't have used it, anyway. They're humans."

"One of them isn't. It's some kind of creature." Van glanced at Daisy. "I was only going to use the Coin to point to the real Brux, not blast them with it."

The Bruxes grappled dangerously close to the edge of the cliff.

"What do we do?" Paley gripped Van's hand.

One Brux slammed the other to the ground.

They heard a loud creaking sound coming from the cliff. A crack inched its way between them and the Bruxes, forming an unstable section on the ledge where the Bruxes fought.

"I don't know what to do." Van's stomach was in knots.

Daisy's eyes glazed over. She stared into the distance at nothing. "We need help," she said, as if talking to someone unseen.

Within seconds, several white birds flew overhead and swooped down from the sky. They looked like overlarge seagulls, but their beaks were sharper, and their feet were wider than the Earth World birds.

Their loud squawks echoed as they zoomed down and pecked at one of the Brux's heads. He raised himself off the ground and swatted at the birds.

"That's the imposter!" Paley pointed at the Brux being attacked by the birds, as if she had figured it out all by herself.

Kopius took a step forward. Van grabbed his arm to stop him.

"We have to be sure." Sweat beaded Van's forehead. The Twin Gemstones bonded Paley and Brux. "If the real Brux is killed by accident, Paley will die, too."

"I didn't think of that." Paley's finger zipped to her mouth. She gnawed on her cuticles again.

"We can trust the larumbelles." Daisy stared proudly at her bird friends.

"I'm going in." Kopius cautiously stepped forward and walked over the crack in the ground and onto the unstable ledge.

The edge of the cliff dropped several inches. Not at the crack between the team and the Bruxes, but the ground under the Bruxes feet.

Kopius stopped, afraid to walk closer to the edge. He stepped back behind the crack.

The Brux, not being attacked by the birds, struggled to maintain his balance. His feet teetered on the edge. As he regained his footing, the ground beneath him completely gave way. He dropped out of sight.

Daisy gasped. "That's the real Brux!"

"No, it isn't," said the other Brux, still swatting away the pecking larumbelles.

"It is!" Daisy insisted. "Lilla sent the birds to us."

The birds stopped attacking the Brux standing near the edge of the cliff, circled around him a few times, and flew away.

"Daisy, you know it's me." Brux had spots of blood on his face and hands from the pecks and scratches caused by the larumbelles.

"Don't listen to him. I'm Brux," the other one shouted. His voice carried upward from the side of the ravine. Apparently, he had stopped his fall by grabbing a protruding rock or a dangling root.

Brux's hands came into view as struggled to climb back onto the cliff. If he hadn't been so drained from the gemstones, the climb back onto solid ground would've been easy for him.

The Brux standing on the cliff angrily glared at the other. He made a move as if about to walk over and make sure the other Brux didn't make it.

"Stop!" Van dashed forward without a thought to the rift in the cliff.

The ledge shook and dropped from her weight, sending the standing Brux tumbling over the side. The other lost his grip and disappeared. Now both Bruxes had fallen over the edge of the cliff.

Kopius dashed over.

"No." Van held up her palm, stopping him. Her weight had caused the ledge to drop by about a foot. "Your extra weight will cause the ledge to drop more. I'll go alone."

Van cautiously made her way over the dangerously unstable ground before Kopius, or anyone else, could object.

She inched her way to the ledge and peered over the side. Both Bruxes clutched onto roots dangling from the side of the ravine. The thin sprigs, their only lifeline.

The Brux with bloody peck marks on his face and hands raised his eyes to Van. "We have a special bond. Look inside. I know you can feel it. You know it's me."

"We have a special bond," the other Brux said, the one dangling to Van's right. He grunted as he gripped the root. "But it's with me."

"These vines can't support our weight for long. We're both going to die if you don't help us," the Brux hanging to the left said. "Pull up both of us. Then we can sort it out."

The other Brux stopped struggling. "Van," he said in a somber tone. "You can't save either of us. Let us both go."

"What? No!" Van cried. Her eyes darted back and forth from Brux to Brux.

"It's the only way to ensure the team's safety."

"Nice try," said the Brux, hanging to Van's left. "He wants me to drop first, then he'll change his mind. Van, don't fall for it."

"He's right," the other Brux said. "Van, I'm going to let go."

"No!" Daisy screamed. She attempted to run to her brother. Kopius grabbed her, holding her back to keep her safe.

"He's lying," said the Brux to Van's left, the one with the peck marks. "Notice how he hasn't let go yet."

"Van, I'll hand you the gemstone. Use your powers to attune it to Paley. Then promise me you'll let that one drop after I go." He nudged his head at the other Brux. "Promise me." He dangled by one hand as he fumbled in his pocket with the other.

"Don't do it, Brux," Paley cried. "I don't know if we can transfer the gemstone to someone else. I could die, too."

Brux gripped the gemstone and stretched his hand toward Van.

Van reached down.

"No!" screamed Daisy and Paley.

Instead of grabbing the gemstone, Van grabbed Brux by his wrist.

The shift in weight caused the unstable section of the cliff to rumble.

Van groaned as she tugged, helping Brux climb to safety. But he was too heavy.

"Van, take the gemstone and let go." Brux's eyes were wide with fright. "We'll both fall."

"No! Save me! I'm the real Brux," said the other Brux.

Kopius hopped down and dashed across the ledge. He crashed to his knees next to Van and stretched his hand to the dangling Brux.

"What're you doing?" Van strained to hold onto Brux. "The ledge can't support your additional weight."

The ground trembled.

Van screeched as the ledge where she and Kopius knelt dropped several feet. She lost her grip on Brux and crashed to her side to maintain her balance, almost toppling over the cliff.

Van rolled onto her stomach to get up, her head hung over the edge, allowing her to see to the bottom of the ravine.

The weak vines supporting the Bruxes had snapped.

Kopius clasped the Brux on the right, firmly holding his arm.

The other fell.

Van watched the plummeting body of the Brux imposter as it changed into a dark form and broke apart.

A rush of back birds burst upward, flurrying so close, Van could feel her hair rustle and felt several sharp whacks from wings on her face.

Crows.

She twisted onto her back and watched as they swirled above her, cawing.

They hovered over Van in a threatening mass, as if they desired to toss her over the edge. In her peripheral vision, she saw Kopius drag Brux back onto the ledge.

"What the—?" Paley muttered, staring at the murder of crows. They weren't fluttering over her head, yet she still took a step back.

Daisy narrowed her eyes, scrutinizing the black birds. "Those aren't Lilla's."

The crows swirled higher and moved away from Van, over to firm ground, close to where Daisy and Paley stood. Their loud caws blended together to where it sounded like mocking laughter.

The birds melded, creating the silhouette of a person.

The hair on Van's arms stood on end as she hustled to her feet. Before the dark shape took full form, Van already knew who it was.

Solana.

She materialized before them, hands on hips. Her raven hair fell thick and straight down to her waist. Her blood-red lips curled into a hateful grin. "So we meet again, *princess*."

Her jeering tone wasn't lost on Van.

"Solana's *alive*?" Paley's eyes popped; Daisy gasped.

Kopius seemed pained not to be close to Daisy, but stayed put. His shift in weight could cause the unstable ledge to slide down into the ravine.

"You... you've been here the whole time." Van's jaw fell open in astonishment.

Solana's golden eyes locked onto Van.

Brux tucked the gemstone into his pocket and moved closer to Van, as if ready to dart in front of anything Solana threw at her.

"You were the demimondaine who visited me with the poisoned soap," Van said to Solana. "You're the one spreading the illness, keeping it here with the help of your Dark Master."

"For once, you're right." Solana tossed her hand flippantly.

"But..." Brux spoke up, a stunned look on his face. "How did you survive? The Coin blew you to smithereens."

"Humph." Solana wore her signature skintight, black unitard, and looked stronger and healthier than ever. "I'm a not just another pretty face, you know. I'm a highly skilled sorceress. Between the power I gained from my master and with the help of my cousin Merloc, who—*news flash*—is a warlock, I was able to survive. Merloc hid me in Windermere and nursed me until I was completely healed."

Daisy shuddered at the mention of Merloc.

Solana turned to Daisy. "You see. He has a nurturing side."

"You wanted immortality." Van curled her lip. "It looks like you got it."

"You know what they say." Kopius's hand hovered over his concealed dagger. "Be careful what you wish for."

"No one is immune from the power of the Anchoress," Daisy said in defiance of Solana.

This new fury in Daisy seemed to take Solana by surprise. Yet, the Balish princess didn't appear intimidated. She sauntered a few steps closer and gripped Daisy's face. "We'll see about that."

"Take your hands off her," Kopius growled. He rushed forward toward the rift and leaped several feet upward onto stable ground.

His movement caused the unstable ledge to rumble. The ground beneath Van and Brux's feet shook. They grasped each other for balance.

Kopius dashed straight for Solana.

Van and Paley gasped; Brux tensed. Kopius didn't know the deviousness and evil capabilities of the Balish princess, at least not yet.

His insubordination enraged Solana. She released Daisy and swept her hand in the air, magically sending Kopius flying.

He crashed onto the ground about forty feet away. Van heard something in his body crack when he landed.

"No wonder Lilla ratted you out," Brux growled at Solana.

Solana dropped her hand, losing interest in Daisy and Kopius. Her gaze turned to Brux.

"She's angry you harmed one of her children, the bunfy," Brux said. "Probably a lot more of her animal children, too."

With clarity, Van recalled the incident that happened last year. Solana skinned a bunfy alive in front of her and Brux. Paley was present too, but unconscious at the time.

Solana meandered toward Brux, unflustered by his comment. "Imagine the outrage when people find out the Grigori intentionally released the illness for job security. More demons, more work." She stopped at the rift, the one separating her, Paley, Kopius, and Daisy from Van and Brux.

Solana rubbed the pointed toe of her knee-high black boot along the ledge and looked down at Brux.

"Life becomes more precious when mortals dangle on the edge of an abyss, don't you think?" She raised her knee, ready to stomp on the ground. A move that would release the fragile hold of the unstable ledge and send Van and Brux plummeting to their deaths at the bottom of the ravine.

Kopius charged forward, hurtling himself at Solana.

Van tensed, terrified, as a hundred horrific outcomes flashed through her mind.

As Kopius made contact with Solana, and before her foot hit the ground, Van heard a *pop*.

Solana's caustic laughter lingered in the air for a few seconds after the Balish princess disappeared.

Kopius stumbled forward, almost falling over the side of the rift onto where Van and Brux stood, clearly not expecting Solana to vanish.

"Where'd she go?" Kopius swept his arms, clasping and unclasping his hands, grabbing nothing but air.

The ledge supporting Van and Brux quavered.

Van shrieked and fell to her knees as the ground below her and Brux's feet dropped several yards.

Kopius crashed down onto his stomach and extended his hands to them. "Come on, grab hold!"

Van stood on the tips of her toes and reached up. Brux grasped her waist and hoisted her. She clasped Kopius's hands. He pulled her upward onto solid ground with little effort.

Kopius immediately reached for Brux.

Brux stretched to reach Kopius's hands but couldn't. He crouched down and then leaped up.

The movement caused the ledge beneath Brux's feet to drop away, just as Kopius gripped his wrist.

Brux dangled over the edge. Kopius grunted as he pulled Brux to safety.

They both lay sprawled on the ground, catching their breath.

Kopius turned his head toward Brux. "Now can I date your sister?"

They both roared with laughter, glad to be alive. Relief glowed on their faces.

All of them breathed easier, having escaped an encounter with Solana, the most evil sorceress ever to walk among the worlds.

"She's gone for now," Daisy said, looking distant. "But I can feel the disruption she's causing in nature's universal grid."

"Sweetie." Kopius smiled at Daisy, as he and Brux stood. "Let's take the win."

Dirt mixed with blood speckled Brux's face and clothes from his grapple with Solana, and his multiple near-death experiences on the ledge. Despite his battered appearance and his lack of energy from the drain of the gemstones, he oozed vigor and strength. Van didn't want to, but she admired his boyish good looks.

Until he opened his mouth.

He frowned at Van. "Seriously, you couldn't tell me apart from Solana?"

CHAPTER 57

"Lilla wants you to know Wiglaf is with her," Daisy said to Van. "They're sharing some bonding time after his ordeal with the Quasher."

"It wasn't the real Quasher," Van said. "It was Thalassa, disguised as the Quasher."

"Yes. We know," Daisy said, meaning both her and Lilla. "Wiglaf's injuries were not an illusion. Thalassa hurt him. Something Lilla will not forget."

Brux offered Van some apricot twists and his pouch full of water.

She waved her hand, turning down the snacks and drink. "Thanks, but I'm good."

"If we don't get moving, the real Quasher will make an appearance," Brux said. "Something I'd rather not face."

"You and me both," Van said.

The team made their way to the nearest TAV and arrived at Lodestar safely.

As expected, a sentinel stood at the foot of the stairs, along with Tussel Fynn.

"Hey! You're right on time! Van, Paley, Brux." Fynn grinned. "Looks like we picked up some people—Daisy!"

"Hello, Fynn."

It surprised Van when they hugged. *Since when have they been friends?*

Fynn greeted Kopius, then his smile faded. "Pernilla?"

Brux and Van sadly shook their heads, the others cast their eyes downward.

"Right." Fynn nodded in stoic understanding. He escorted them through the lobby, up the main staircase, and into Uxa's office.

"Ah, slightly ahead of the deadline. Wonderful." Uxa rose from behind her desk. "I see we have picked up two more." Uxa greeted Kopius and then extended her arms. "Daisy!"

"Hello Uxa."

Again, Van was taken aback when they hugged. Uxa had never hugged her, or Paley. Or Brux. Since when did Daisy become the goodwill ambassador?

Fynn informed Uxa that Pernilla was the only casualty of their mission.

Uxa hung her head in sorrow. "May her soul endure in the arms of the Creator."

The silence in the room lasted for several seconds, then Uxa raised her head and looked at Fynn. "We will head over to Providence Island after the team's debriefing to let her family know."

Fynn solemnly bobbed his head in agreement.

Uxa gave Kopius a congratulatory pat on the shoulder. "Professor Lake will be proud of you for safely returning his daughter."

Kopius straightened his spine. "Proud to serve."

"The illness?" Daisy asked. "Is it progressing?"

Uxa nodded grimly. "Maren and some others have turned. We have them secured in the Grigori's holding area. Since their bodies died and turned to ash before they became demons, there is nothing we can do for them."

Brux turned to Van with a look urging her to mention the Cup.

Although she wanted to, Van couldn't keep the Cup. It belonged in a safe place. One designed to keep the Items out of the wrong hands.

The Celestial Tower. But Van wouldn't give up the Cup until she cured all the sick children and adults.

"The second seal. Did you mend it?" Uxa asked.

Van shook her head.

Fynn pursed his lips and glared at Van like he had something to say.

"I didn't have to," Van said. "It wasn't broken."

"Hm." Uxa leaned back against her desk and raised her fingers to her lips in deep thought.

Van scrutinized Uxa to see if her surprise was an act.

"Then we have a major problem on our hands. We must stop the spread of the infection. Fynn!" Uxa barked. "Call in President Sterling, Senator—"

"I have a way to stop it." Van peered at Uxa, searching for the slightest telltale sign she knew Van had retrieved the Cup, and getting the Item was the actual mission all along.

Uxa spread her hands. "Go on."

Van reached inside her backpack and pulled out the Cup.

Fynn gasped.

Van placed the Item on the desk next to Uxa, half-expecting Uxa to pounce on it with glee.

Uxa appeared indifferent.

"The Cup saved me from the illness," Paley said.

"Yes, but you are a terrigen. The Twin Gemstones raised your vibration," Uxa said. "You drank colloidal silver. These two things protected you from turning. I am certain the Cup cannot change someone back who has died."

"I never died, but I let in the darkness." Paley shuddered.

"Uxa's right," Van said. "The Cup can't bring people back from the dead. But it can cure those who haven't yet turned."

"There is more at stake here," Uxa said. "The situation is more dire than I thought."

"What do you mean?" All of them asked at once.

Uxa pushed her hips away from her desk, full of energy, as if she suddenly realized she had a lot to do. "All of you need to be checked by medical."

Van narrowed her eyes at Uxa's evasive tactic.

"Medics will tend to you in the medical area of the complex, then we will debrief you. Afterward, you will be reunited with your families." Uxa turned to Fynn. "Please take Kopius to the medical wing here and then escort the rest back to Providence Island. Remember to keep Paley and Brux together, and to return the Twin Gemstones."

Brux, Daisy, Paley, and Kopius followed Fynn.

Van watched as the door closed behind them. Exhaustion set in and she wished she could leave, too.

Uxa turned to Van. "We need to talk."

Van sighed, resigned to this one last task. "Yes, we do. I have more to tell you."

"Where is the Coin?" Uxa asked.

She told Uxa the story of her and Ferox, Thalassa, and Zurial's memory engrams.

"Zurial was warning you not to get involved with a Bale," Uxa said, barely able to control her angry tone.

"No, she warned me not to misuse the Cup." Van crossed her arms. "Zurial and Manik had a great relationship. Other people ruined it. That's what she showed me."

"You let the Balish prince take the Coin of Creation?" Uxa's nostrils flared. "Do you realize what you have done? You put your tribe in danger. You gave the Balish the power to engage in a war with us."

"Ferox isn't like that!"

"Do you hear how naive you sound? Like a lovesick little girl."

"You're wrong about him." Van jutted her chin. "And me."

Uxa took a deep breath. "Well." She visibly relaxed her facial muscles. "We will see, won't we?" She moved back behind her desk as if she needed to put space between herself and Van.

"You retrieved the Cup of Life, although it was not your mission."

"The Cup *happened* to be near the second seal," Van said. "Are you sure it was a coincidence?"

"Sending you to check the seal was set in motion by the illness. Your instinct led you to the Cup for a reason."

"Oh, what reason was that? Because you wanted it?"

Uxa stood so fast, her chair flew behind her and hit the wall.

Van flinched, thinking Uxa was about to leap over her desk and throttle her.

"Take the Cup and follow me."

Uxa led Van out of her office and down a marble hallway.

"We must work together in harmony." Uxa's sky-blue cape fluttered from her brisk pace. "Demons have reached our soil through the illness. The Escalation has begun. It is beyond anyone's control now. Destiny has taken hold."

They walked up the familiar stairway with one thousand one hundred and twenty-two steps that led to the Celestial Tower.

"We weren't able to search any ancient documents," Van said. "We didn't hear any folklore about the master demon."

Uxa climbed the stairs in silence.

"Solana's not dead," Van said, point-blank. "She's back."

Uxa paused. "Excuse me?"

"I never killed her. The Coin, it didn't kill her."

A worried look clouded Uxa's face.

"She's working with her Dark Master, plotting something," Van said.

"Yes, I believe they are." Uxa moved up the stairs again, this time slower as to not distract from her deep thoughts.

About halfway up, Uxa said, "Solana's return has put Prince Ferox's ascension to the throne in jeopardy. He would do well to be worried about his life. Is that why you gave him the Coin?"

Van shook her head as her stomach clenched over Uxa's belief Ferox's life was in danger. "I didn't know Solana was alive at the time. I was only thinking of creating balance between our tribes."

A strong instinct to protect Ferox burned inside her heart, but Van didn't think Solana would show her face around Balefire. "She won't be accepted back into the royal court."

Van refused to believe Ferox's life was in danger against such a formidable enemy. His father had correctly assessed him. Ferox was too compassionate, too kind. Van doubted he would win in a fight against his evil sister.

"Perhaps you are right." Uxa turned to Van as they reached the top of the stairs. "Did you find your mother's necklace?"

Van's internal alarm went off again. *Why is Uxa so interested in my mother's necklace?* When Van found it, she made a mental note to keep it far away from Uxa.

Van shook her head.

They entered the Celestial Tower. The cylindrical room hadn't changed since Van had last seen it. The elongated, elaborately braced windows lined the grand, funnel-like ceiling. Four statues in various poses, two women and two men, dressed in togas and sweeping robes, were arranged facing outward, evenly spaced around a mosaic floor. The small, colored floor tiles depicted two serpents forming a figure eight by swallowing each other's tails.

A moonbeam highlighted the statue of a woman sitting on a throne carved entirely of seashells. She wore a toga with seven flowing skirts wrapped tightly around her legs, giving the illusion of being a mermaid. Scallop shells clasped her breasts. On her head, she wore a starfish crown with an upside-down triangle in its center.

"Who is she?" Van asked.

"Yemaya, the Guardian of All Water."

The woman sat with one hand resting on her lap. In the crook of her elbow, she cradled a peacock. She held her other hand raised with her fingers curled, ready for placement of the Cup.

"I can't give her the Cup, not yet." Van turned to face Uxa. "I need to make the healing potion before more people get sick."

"It is okay for you to give Yemaya the Cup. She will keep it safe. Get some rest. I will work with the consilium to decide the best way to distribute the healing potion to the masses."

"No—what? Only I can make the potion."

"Anyone who possesses the Cup can make the healing liquid," Uxa said. "But they must have royal blood so not to become corrupted.

The ancient scrolls have the spell. If I recall correctly, we cannot make any until the next full moon."

"We don't have to wait," Van said. "I can make it right now. I have the power of the moon in my veins."

"Ah," Uxa said, not as surprised as Van would've figured.

"We can put it in the water supply, as much as we need," Van continued. "It will cure those sick and vaccinate everyone else."

"Two water systems feed the entire Living World." Uxa pondered Van's idea. "One is here at Lodestar, the other at Balefire. I will ask the Lodian Consilium for approval. Then our ambassador will seek approval of the Balish Council. The problem being, we do not want to give them control of the Cup." Uxa flexed her jaw. "Especially since they now have the Coin."

"You can trust Ferox. Maybe I can talk to him. It's more important than ever we work with the Balish."

"We need to get back the Coin." Uxa stared at Van with a curious glint to her eyes. Probably figuring out how to use Van's romantic interest in Ferox to her advantage.

If it meant Van got to see Ferox again, she was all for it.

"For now, you rest," Uxa said.

"The two other statues." Van flicked her head at the circle. "Am I looking at my next two missions? I mean, besides getting back the Coin."

"The next cycle of creation draws ever nearer," Uxa said. "It takes four years to retrieve all four Items due to—"

"Yeah, I know," Van said, cutting her off. "Manik and the Elementals designed it that way. The window to retrieve the Items only opens during the Alignment."

"To give you time to absorb your Elemental lessons and grow your power. Also, you have not yet battled the real Quasher," Uxa warned. "What you encountered was Thalassa."

Uxa placed her hand on Van's shoulder. "You are still too important to our people to return here outside the Alignment. There is no need to be reckless, no matter how strongly you want to see Ferox again... or how badly I want the Coin."

Van furrowed her brow as she eyed the statues. "If there are only four Items, why does the Escalation to Dishora take seven years?"

"It gives you, the Anchoress, time to build your strength and hone your powers. To prepare for the seventh stage, the end stage. The year of destruction." Uxa gave Van a stern look. "During the seventh year, a great war will take place. Demons will rise to take control of the worlds. If humanity loses, all light will be extinguished. Everything good will be lost."

The last bit of Van's carefree childhood crumbled away. She claimed her right to feel sad about the things she used to love. Petty things, like hair ribbons, school dances, and being popular. They were no longer important to her now.

"I need to see Ferox. We need to work together," Van said with urgency. "This can't wait until next year."

"Go back to Providence Island. Continue to sharpen your skills. Embrace your Anchoress powers and prepare for next year's Alignment."

Van nodded, fully embracing her role as the Anchoress and accepting the responsibilities of being a warrior of the light.

If that meant waiting, then she would wait.

CHAPTER 58

Van lay on her back, stretched out on her surfboard.

She hadn't put it in the water, but on top of the sand at Whitecap beach. She'd had enough of the ocean to last a lifetime.

The sun's rays warmed her skin. Instead of gazing at the clear blue sky, she turned her head to watch Wiglaf having a wonderful time digging in the beach sand. Her heart filled with joy at seeing him play.

She glimpsed the others playing alphacrosse nearby. Kopius and Brux on a team against Paley and Daisy. A combat sport taught in their special classes. The objective was to prevent each team from capturing the other's flag at opposing goal posts. They hopped around on one leg, trying to knock each other down. But they had modified the rules to involve less bashing and more wrapping their arms around members of the opposing team, making it an ideal sport for people wanting intimate contact with their opponents. All four laughed and goofed around, enjoying the game and each other's company.

Their lighthearted banter caused Van to think of Ferox. Her aching heart longed for him to be there. The two of them making a third team, playing and laughing along with the others. She wondered where he was and what he was doing.

Is he thinking about me, too?

She relaxed and breathed in the salty sea air. Grateful for her friends, her furry animal companion, for meeting Ferox, and for being allowed to *feel*. Integrating her emotions made her life much more enriching and worthwhile.

The Anchoress wasn't made of stone, like the statues in the park and the one in the House of Lacus. She wasn't a mythical creature, only brought to life in the writings of ancient scrolls, but a living person.

Van had a right to feel heartbroken about her father's and mother's deaths. All her losses. Processing the guilt of being alive while they were gone only served to benefit her. Continuing to block her emotions would've led Van to living a miserable half-life. A disservice to her parents, who would've wanted Van to live her life to the fullest. To feel a full range of emotions, including joy, gratitude, and love.

She sensed her parents' presence around her. She knew their souls still existed and were back in the arms of the Creator. Their memory kept alive in Van's heart and mind.

A desire to find her mother's necklace gnawed inside Van. To her, the necklace represented a piece of her mother in physical form, and offered proof Aelia had not been forgotten. Her father's memory would also endure as Van carried on his quest to break the Anchoress curse.

Van's contentment clouded as Solana entered her thoughts. Van's reward for this journey was being released from thinking she had killed the Balish princess. Still, it bothered Van she'd tried to end Solana's life using the Coin. She believed wielding its power with intent to harm another human counted as an incorrect use. Damaging her soul, but to a lesser degree.

However, it was no secret Solana had answered the dark call. The Balish princess worked with her demon master to begin the war of darkness against humanity before Van gained her full Anchoress powers. The evil duo brought the demon illness to the Living World and Solana used her dark magic to keep it there.

Solana also provoked Van into retrieving two of the Items of

Creation, so she and her Dark Master could destroy them. The Items were weapons powerful enough to defeat the demons during Dishora. Van vowed to die before letting either of them get their grubby hands on any of the Items.

Van was glad she had retrieved the Cup. Uxa had allowed Van to use her powers to make the orange healing liquid. After much debate, and at Van's insistence, the Lodian Consilium authorized distribution of the healing potion in Salus Valde's water supply. But to be safe, they also had the cure poured into ampules for distribution to all areas of the Living World.

King Nequus, influenced by Ferox's encouragement, allowed the healing potion to be put in their water supply. He also permitted Lodian ambassadors out of bounds to help distribute ampules filled with the orange liquid that offered both the cure and the vaccine.

As far as Van knew, the Coin remained with the Balish. She had asked Uxa about it several times. Uxa told Van no word had reached her ears as to its whereabouts.

Van sighed with acceptance. It was her destiny to retrieve all four Items of Creation. Her fate was set in motion the moment her father had stolen Manik's text from Balefire Palace last year. But, she couldn't safely go back into the Living World until the next Alignment.

That was fine with her. She had made the right choice by saving Wiglaf's life rather than drinking Thalassa's potion, although the liquid would have given Van year-round protection from the Quasher along with immortality.

Van thought it ironic that in the end, the littlest thing had reached her. Cracked her emotional shield enough for the light to enter. Not her attraction to Brux or Ferox. Not Daisy and Paley's illness. Or Pernilla and Thyra's deaths. But Wiglaf.

Cute, furry Wiglaf.

Still, her newfound feelings for Ferox weren't something she could ignore.

Their relationship would be different from Manik and Zurial's. Van and Ferox wouldn't experience the same tragedies as the ancients, who endured two wars. The Great War between the Lodians and Balish that morphed into the Dark War, humanity against demons. Van didn't plan on becoming obsessed with any Item of Creation, and Ferox didn't have a brother who would cause a secret rebellion.

Van and Ferox would work together to embrace the differences between their tribes. To find solutions to their problems, ensuring there were no underlying issues so everyone could live in peace.

She simply needed to take care of his sister Solana and the Balish princess's master demon first. Those two were the only things standing in the way of—not only her bright future with Ferox—but the peaceful future of their people.

Solana had returned from the dead, along with her unrelenting desire to kill Van and, most likely, Ferox too. Both of them annoying thorns in the Balish princess's battle to destroy all light.

Unease slowly took hold of Van's heart as she admitted her feelings for Ferox and confronted the prospect of losing him. Vulnerability was a steep price to pay for having emotions.

A darker thought continued to haunt her.

Despite what Solana had done, Ferox's family bonds remained strong. If it came down to it, would Ferox choose romantic love and Van? Or would he yield to family love and Solana, along with her access to great power?

Van pushed the question away. She would face the answer later.

Right now, it was imperative she and Ferox set aside their differences. Both tribes needed to be prepared.

The Escalation had begun.

Dishora was coming.

THANK YOU

Thank you for your support and for being part of this journey. As an indie author, your readership is what inspires and motivates me to continue creating.

READ THE FIRST CHAPTER OF BOOK 3, HELM OF AWE

Vanessa Cross slammed her back against the aged chestnut tree, muttering over her cursed life, angered at the Elementals—no, the Creator—for holding her lineage against her.

She hid among the tree's low-lying branches with their spiky, curved leaves to catch her breath. Her heart, determined to burst from her chest, distracted Van as her eyes scanned the surrounding woods. Sweat beaded across her brow. She couldn't risk wiping it. The movement might catch the eye of her enemy.

Van's heart calmed, and her breathing slowed. She assessed her situation. Her teammates had screwed up and gotten themselves captured. Irritation burned in her gut over them leaving her alone to win the Jaychund games.

Her inept team, including her best friend Paley Ash and her ex-boyfriend Brux Lake, had let her down. Losing the games meant bringing dishonor and shame to her classmates at Canterbury Bells, and would lower Van's graduation status. Failing wasn't an option.

Making the situation worse, everyone on Providence Island, including her classmates and step-mother, watched the final game through the gemstone media feeds placed among the trees. The audience didn't miss a trick. Not a twitch, not a blink. Nothing.

Van remained still, her back pressed against the wart-like bark of the chestnut tree. She breathed softly, careful not to disturb the silence that echoed back at her. She knew from her training classes in the reservation program that by staying in one spot, she'd be found. Be the hunter, not the prey.

She took a step and froze as leaves rustled overhead.

A spiked, round husk, the kind that holds a single chestnut inside, tumbled down from the branches above like a falling star, making soft noises as it hit the branches and leaves. The bur landed in the dirt by her foot with a thud that rippled through the silence.

Van braced.

An explosion came from the branches and leaves above her. A figure dropped and landed directly in front of Van.

The girl stood tall, looking natural, wild. Her brown skin, taut with the toned muscles of an elite athlete, shone from her sleeveless, midriff vest that looked like it was handmade with care from an animal skin. From the girl's exposed navel dangled a silver ring with tiny multi-colored jewels.

Suixsha. Unfairly brought to the island by Uxa Huxatec to challenge Van in the final game.

The girl's fist rammed into Van's solar plexus.

Van doubled over and gasped for breath, smoldering with embarrassment. Her bad luck made good content for the viewers.

Suixsha rummaged through the pockets of Van's uniform like a shrew burrowing for a mealworm.

Van's searing gut pain wasn't enough to block her boiling ire. This... *intruder* was not better than her. She snapped upright with her elbows held in square formation and struck Suixsha under the chin. Seizing the advantage of Suixsha's backward momentum, Van used her leg to shove her nemesis to the ground.

She straddled her rival and used her arm to push down against Suixsha's chest. Her free hand foraged the girl's pockets.

"This is over. Where's your token?" growled Van, all too aware the girl's punch had caused the throbbing in her stomach.

Taking another player's token eliminated that student. Sent them to spend the rest of the game in a holding area called "jail." Van couldn't find Suixsha's token and wondered if the girl had swallowed it. Van doubted it since, according to the rules, it would disqualify the unsportsmanlike player from winning.

Suixsha's necklace rested on her chest, strung with charm holders, each filled with a token taken from one of the other players. The girl obviously brought the necklace with her before entering the final, confident she would fill the holders. The pride—*the audacity*—of Suixsha wearing such a necklace infuriated Van.

In one seamless move, Suixsha shifted her hips and twisted using significant force. Van's grip loosened, and she got knocked to the side.

Suixsha contorted her body like a wild animal freeing itself from a trap and lifted herself off the ground, onto her feet.

She pounced on Van with powerful physical strength and dexterity, like no average teen. She possessed a skill level Van had yet to come across on her missions in the Living World or in her training classes with the Grigori.

Suixsha pinned down Van and methodically searched Van's pockets like a machine designed to do only one thing. Get the token.

Using precious seconds, Van assessed her enemy for weaknesses. Suixsha had made a mistake in not tying back her waist-length, spiral curls. Van grabbed a handful and yanked.

Suixsha's chin jutted toward the sky, causing her silver headpiece to tumble to the ground and exposing her necklace. Paley's token tauntingly dangled in Van's face. Yet, the girl didn't budge.

"You have no right to be here," said Van through gritted teeth as she struggled to get free.

Her rival's prying fingers got close to the pocket where Van hid her token. Van wriggled her hip.

Suixsha's sharp hazel eyes noticed the motion.

Van slammed her fists against Suixsha and kicked her legs so hard the muscles in her body strained to the point of bursting. Her impending loss—in her *senior year,* no less—made Van furious and left her frustrated, desperate to win. She needed power.

And power she had. The magical Anchoress bloodline she inherited from her mother. Using this advantage was, of course, against the rules. Van would be in trouble with Uxa and the other Elders if the onlookers who knew nothing of the island's secrets viewed Van using her substantial, otherworldly power.

Suixsha's frenzied fingers found the pocket hiding Van's token and dug in.

Not about to let this newcomer beat her, Van pushed her hip into the ground harder, trying to block the girl's fingers from reaching her token. The insult of losing to Suixsha reverberated down to Van's soul. She allowed the resulting fury to connect her to her inner magic, fully expecting to feel the tingling of her blue eyes as they turned violet, a mark she had engaged in her powers. Van waited.

Her eyes didn't change.

Van's connection shorted out. The drain of trying to access her magical Anchoress bloodline made every muscle in her body feel weighted, causing her to exert extra energy just to move and breathe.

Why can't I access my power? Suixsha must've cast a spell on me! Van gathered her last shreds of strength and clenched her fists.

Suixsha used her knee to force Van onto her side.

Van pounded her nemesis's arms as Suixsha's fingers dug deeper into Van's pocket.

Suixsha released Van and rose to her feet in victory, eyes locked on the token she raised between two fingers.

Van laid on the ground, fuming so hard she thought steam might come from her ears.

Suixsha peered down at her. "Your anger cause you lose energy," she said, not in pride, but as an undeniable truth.

"Shut up, you loser," spat Van, fully aware it wasn't her finest moment.

"Only one loser here," said Suixsha in the monotone of a cold, hard fact. "You."

AFTERWORD

Enjoyed *Plague of Death*? Let's stay connected!

Be the first to know about updates, releases, and exclusive content! Sign up for my newsletter at:

DLArmillei.com

Follow the *Anchoress* Series @anchoressseries

Dive deeper into the adventure and connect with other fans of *Anchoress*!

Facebook Group:

HTTPS://WWW.FACEBOOK.COM/GROUPS/ANCHORESSSERIES/

Instagram:

HTTPS://WWW.INSTAGRAM.COM/ANCHORESSSERIES/

TikTok:

HTTPS://WWW.TIKTOK.COM/@ANCHORESSSERIES

Connect with D.L. Armillei @DLArmillei

Learn more about her, her writing journey, and upcoming projects:

Facebook page:
https://www.facebook.com/DLArmillei/

Instagram:
https://www.instagram.com/dlarmillei/

X (Twitter):
https://x.com/DLArmillei

BookBub:
https://www.bookbub.com/profile/d-l-armillei

GoodReads:
https://www.goodreads.com/DLArmillei

Amazon:
https://www.amazon.com/D.-L.-Armillei/e/B06XD25WT4/

Thank you for being part of this journey. Your support keeps the magic alive!

ABOUT THE AUTHOR

When Donna (D. L.) was four years old she wrote a "story" in "cursive" and gave it to her mother to read out loud. Instead, her mother tucked the pages into a desk drawer and suggested they read her amazing story together in a few years, after Donna had learned how to read and write.

Today, Donna crafts immersive, imaginative stories with emotional depth. Her flagship *Anchoress* series—a young adult epic fantasy—invites readers into a richly layered world of adventure, spiritual self-discovery, and empowerment.

A Massachusetts native, Donna now splits her time between living in her home state and Florida.

ALSO BY D. L. ARMILLEI

* * *

Shock of Fate: Anchoress Series Book One

Plague of Death: Anchoress Series Book Two

Helm of Awe: Anchoress Series Book Three

Echoes of Fate: Anchoress Series Book Four

Hag's Hut on the Hill - a short story/deleted scene Anchoress Series (newsletter sign up)

www.ingramcontent.com/pod-product-compliance
Lightning Source LLC
Chambersburg PA
CBHW020716310726
48979CB00004B/939

* 9 7 8 0 9 9 8 6 7 2 0 6 9 *